By Anne Perry

FEATURING WILLIAM MONK

<table>
<tr><td>The Face of a Stranger</td><td>A Breach of Promise</td></tr>
<tr><td>A Dangerous Mourning</td><td>The Twisted Root</td></tr>
<tr><td>Defend and Betray</td><td>Slaves of Obsession</td></tr>
<tr><td>A Sudden, Fearful Death</td><td>Funeral in Blue</td></tr>
<tr><td>The Sins of the Wolf</td><td>Death of a Stranger</td></tr>
<tr><td>Cain His Brother</td><td>The Shifting Tide</td></tr>
<tr><td>Weighed in the Balance</td><td>Dark Assassin</td></tr>
<tr><td>The Silent Cry</td><td>Execution Dock</td></tr>
</table>

FEATURING CHARLOTTE AND THOMAS PITT

<table>
<tr><td>The Cater Street Hangman</td><td>Traitors Gate</td></tr>
<tr><td>Callandar Square</td><td>Pentecost Alley</td></tr>
<tr><td>Paragon Walk</td><td>Ashworth Hall</td></tr>
<tr><td>Resurrection Row</td><td>Brunswick Gardens</td></tr>
<tr><td>Bluegate Fields</td><td>Bedford Square</td></tr>
<tr><td>Rutland Place</td><td>Half Moon Street</td></tr>
<tr><td>Death in the Devil's Acre</td><td>The Whitechapel Conspiracy</td></tr>
<tr><td>Cardington Crescent</td><td>Southampton Row</td></tr>
<tr><td>Silence in Hanover Close</td><td>Seven Dials</td></tr>
<tr><td>Bethlehem Road</td><td>Long Spoon Lane</td></tr>
<tr><td>Farriers' Lane</td><td>Buckingham Palace Gardens</td></tr>
<tr><td>The Hyde Park Headsman</td><td></td></tr>
</table>

THE WORLD WAR I NOVELS

No Graves as Yet
Shoulder the Sky
Angels in the Gloom
At Some Disputed Barricade
We Shall Not Sleep

THE CHRISTMAS NOVELS

A Christmas Journey
A Christmas Visitor
A Christmas Guest
A Christmas Secret
A Christmas Beginning
A Christmas Grace

EXECUTION DOCK

EXECUTION DOCK

A Novel

ANNE PERRY

BALLANTINE BOOKS · NEW YORK

Published in the United States by Ballantine Books,
an imprint of The Random House Publishing Group,
a division of Random House, Inc., New York.

BALLANTINE and colophon are registered trademarks of Random House, Inc.

LIBRARY OF CONGRESS CATALOGING-IN-PUBLICATION DATA

Perry, Anne.
Execution dock : a novel / Anne Perry.
p. cm.
ISBN 978-0-345-46933-5 (alk. paper)
e-ISBN 978-0-345-51294-9
1. Monk, William (Fictitious character)—Fiction.
2. Police—England—London—Fiction.   I. Title.
PR6066.E693E94   2009
823'.914—dc22   2009000644

Printed in the United States of America on acid-free paper

www.ballantinebooks.com

2 4 6 8 9 7 5 3 1

FIRST EDITION

Book design by Julie Schroeder

EXECUTION DOCK

ONE

The man balanced on the stern of the flat-bottomed lighter, his wild figure outlined against the glittering water of the Thames, hair whipped in the wind, face sharp, lips drawn back. Then, at the last moment, when the other lighter was almost past him, he crouched and sprang. He only just reached the deck, scrambling to secure his footing. He swayed for a moment, then regained his balance and turned. He waved once in grotesque jubilation, then dropped to his knees out of sight behind the close-packed bales of wool.

Monk smiled grimly as the oarsmen strained to bring the police boat around against the outgoing tide and the wash from barges on their way up to the Pool of London. He would not have given orders to shoot, even were he certain of not hitting anyone else in the teeming river traffic. He wanted Jericho Phillips alive, so he could see him tried and hanged.

In the prow of the boat, Orme swore under his breath. He was a grizzled man in his late fifties, a decade older than the lean and elegant Monk who had been in the Thames River Police Force only half a year. It was very different from the force ashore, where his experience lay, but more difficult for him was taking over the leadership of men to whom he was an outsider. He had a reputation for brilliance in detection, but also for a nature ruthless and hard to know, or to like.

Monk had changed since then. The accident eight years ago in 1856, which had wiped out his memory, had also given him a chance to begin again. He had learned to know himself through the eyes of others, and it had been bitterly enlightening. Not that he could explain that to anyone else.

They were gaining on the lighter, where Phillips was crouching out of sight, ignored by the man at the helm. Another hundred feet and they would draw level. There were five of them in the police boat. That was more than usual, but a man like Phillips might require the extra strength to take him down. He was wanted for the murder of a boy of thirteen or fourteen, Walter Figgis, known as Fig. Phillips was thin and undersized, which might have been what had kept him alive so long. His trade was in boys from the age of four or five up to the time when their voices changed and they began to assume some of the physical characteristics of adults, and they were thus of no use in his particular market of pornography.

The police boat's bow sliced through the choppy water. Fifty yards away a pleasure boat went lazily upstream, perhaps eventually towards Kew Gardens. Colored streamers blew in the wind, and there was the sound of laughter mixed with music. Ahead of them nearly a hundred ships from coal barges to tea clippers were anchored in the Upper Pool. Lighters plied back and forth, and stevedores unloaded cargoes brought in from every corner of the earth.

Monk leaned forward a little, drawing in breath to urge the oarsmen to even greater effort, then changed his mind. It would look as if he did not trust them to do their best anyway. But they could not possibly want to catch Phillips as much as he did. It was Monk, not they, who had involved Durban in the Louvain case that had eventually cost him his life. And it was Monk whom Durban had recommended to take his place when he knew he was dying.

Orme had served with Durban for years, but if he resented Monk's command he had never once shown it. He was loyal, diligent, even helpful, but for the most part, impossible to read. However, the longer Monk watched him, the more he realized Orme's respect was necessary to his success, and more than that, he actually wanted it. The thought jarred inside him. He could not remember ever before having cared what a junior thought of him.

The lighter was only twenty feet ahead of them now and slowing as it made way for another lighter crossing its bow, which was laden with casks of raw sugar from a schooner moored fifty yards away. The ship was riding high now with its load almost gone, its huge canvases furled, spars bare and circling gently as it rocked.

The police boat plunged forward and to port as the other lighter crossed to starboard. The first man leapt aboard, then the second, pistols drawn.

Phillips was the one case Durban had not closed, and it had remained, even in his last notes, a still-bleeding wound in his mind. Monk had read every page since he had inherited them from Durban, along with the job. The facts were there, dates, times, people questioned, answers, conclusions, resolutions as to what to pursue next. But through all the words, the letters, sprawled and jagged, burned the emotion. There was an anger far deeper than the mere frustration of failure, or the injured pride at being outwitted. There was a deep, scalding fury at the suffering of children, and a pity for all the victims of Phillips's trade. And whether Monk wanted it to or not, it scarred him too. He thought about it when the day was ended and he was at home. It invaded the peace of mealtimes. It intruded into his conversations with his wife, Hester. Very little else had ever done that.

He sat rigid in the stern of the boat now, aching to join the men on the lighter. Where were they? Why had they not reappeared with Phillips?

Then he understood—they were on the wrong side. Phillips had judged it exactly. Knowing they would have to pass to port to avoid ramming the other lighter, he had gone to starboard and jumped again. It was risky, but he had nothing to lose. When they caught him he would be tried, and there could be only one verdict. Three Sundays later, he would be hanged.

"Get the men back!" he shouted, half rising from the seat. "He's gone to starboard! On the other lighter!"

They must have realized it too. Orme took the other oar, unshipped it, and began to pull hard to bring the boat astern of the first lighter.

The two men returned, leaping down, sending the boat rocking violently. This was no time to change places with Orme. The other lighter was already twenty yards away and heading towards the dock.

If Phillips made it before they caught him he would disappear among the boxes and bales, the tea chests, rum and sugar casks, the piles of timber, horn, hides, and pottery that crowded the quayside.

Monk's body was rigid, the wind blowing in his face sharp with the smells of salt and fish on the outgoing tide. Catching Phillips was the one thing he could still do for Durban. It would justify the trust Durban had placed in him after knowing him only a few weeks. They had shared nothing of daily life and routine, only one case of a horror almost beyond imagination.

The lighter ahead passed out of sight for a few moments, hidden by the stern of a five-masted schooner. Monk watched intently. It seemed to take far too long to reappear. Was Phillips catching a loose rope, calling out for help from the stevedores, anything to board the ship? If so, Monk would have to go back to the station at Wapping and get more men. Anything could happen in that time.

Orme must have seen the possibility too. He hurled his weight behind his oar, shouting at the other men. The boat leapt forward and the lighter appeared again, still comfortably ahead of them. Monk swiveled to stare at the hull of the schooner, but there was no one on the ropes over its sides. The stevedores on the deck were still bent-backed, hauling casks up out of the hold.

Relief swept over Monk as they closed on the lighter. Another minute or two and they would have Phillips. The long chase would be over. With him in custody it would only be a matter of waiting for the law to take its course.

The police boat came alongside the lighter. Again two armed men boarded, and came back moments later, bleak-faced and shaking their heads. This time Monk swore. Phillips had not gone up the sides onto the schooner, he was certain of that. No matter how agile, a man could not climb the ropes swiftly enough in the few minutes he had been out of sight. No lighter had passed them going to the north bank. It could only have been to the south.

Angry, rowing with tight-knotted shoulders, the men sent the boat straight around the stern of the schooner into the wash of a stream of barges going upriver. They bucked and veered, slapping hard down into the water and sending up spray. Monk clung on to the sides, snarling between his teeth as he saw another lighter going south to Rotherhithe.

Orme saw it at the same moment, and gave the order.

They wove through the traffic. A ferry crossed swiftly in front of them, passengers crouched against the wind; a pleasure boat sent snatches of music into the air. This time the lighter made it to the dockside only twenty yards ahead of them, and they saw Phillips's agile figure, hair and coattails flying, jump from the stern as they passed the East Lane Stairs. He landed on the lowest step, which was slimed over from the tide. He teetered for a moment, arms wheeling, and then fell sideways, hard against the stone wall green with weed. It must have hurt, but he knew the police boat was not far behind him, and fear must have spurred him to scramble to his hands and knees and clamber upwards. It was a maneuver utterly without dignity, and a couple of lightermen jeered at him, but it was extremely rapid. By the time the police boat jarred against the stone, Phillips was at the top on the dry surface. He sprinted towards the Fore and Aft Dock with its crates of pottery from Spain, dumped haphazardly amid dark brown barrels and lighter piles of unfinished timber. The stench of hides was thick in the air, mixed with the sickening sweetness of raw sugar and the heady aroma of spices. Beyond that was the Bermondsey Road, and a whole network of streets and alleys, doss-houses, pawnshops, chandleries, taverns, and brothels.

Monk hesitated only a moment, fearing wrenched ankles, the howls of laughter from the dockers and lightermen if he actually fell into the river, and how idiotic he would feel if Phillips escaped because his own men had had to stop to fish him out. There was no time for such weighing and judging. He stood up, felt the boat pitch sideways, and launched himself towards the steps.

He landed awkwardly. His hands hit stone and weed, but his one goal kept him going. He slipped on to one knee, cracking it hard on the ledge of the next rise. Pain shot through him, but no numbness to prevent him from straightening up and climbing behind Phillips, almost as if he had meant to land as he did.

He reached the top of the steps and saw Phillips thirty feet ahead, running towards a stack of dark, wooden barrels and the winch beyond it. The lumpers unloading more from a lighter below took no notice at all. Some of them were bare-chested in the sun, skin glistening with sweat.

Monk ran across the open space. Then he hesitated when he reached the barrels, knowing Phillips could be just behind them, at best with a length of wood or pipe, at worst a blade. Instead he swung around and went along the length of the stack and around the farther side.

Phillips must have counted on exactly that. He was climbing the long barrier of a pile of bales, going up it as an able seaman might climb a spar, hand over hand, easily. He looked back once, his mouth pulled wide in a sneer, then heaved himself over the top and stopped just for an instant before dropping down the far side.

Monk had no choice but to follow, or lose him. Phillips might leave his wretched boat, find some hovel on the bank for a while, then reappear in half a year, and in the meantime God knew how many more boys would suffer, or even be killed.

Monk shinned awkwardly up the bales, more slowly than Phillips, and reached the top with relief. He crawled over to the far edge and looked down. It was a long drop, perhaps fifteen feet. Phillips was in the distance, making for more mounds of cargo, casks of wine, cases of spice or tobacco.

Monk was not going to risk the jump. A broken ankle would lose him Phillips altogether. Instead he lowered himself, clung for a moment by his hands, then let go and fell the rest of the way. He turned and sprinted, reaching the casks of wine just as Phillips bolted across an open patch of stone towards the shadowed overhang of a cargo ship moored close up to the wharf. Its ropes were trailing, a crane beside her, a load of timber being lowered as they watched.

A horse-drawn wagon moved closer, wheels rumbling on the uneven stone. A gang of lumpers was walking towards the crane. A couple of idlers argued over what looked like a piece of paper. Everywhere there was noise: men shouting, the cry of gulls, the clang of chains, the creak of wood, the constant slap of river water against the stone. There was the incessant movement of the sun reflected on the water, sharp and glittering. The huge moored ships rose and fell.

Men in grays and browns toiled at a score of tasks. Smells filled the air: river mud thick and sour, the harsh cleanness of salt, the sickly sweetness of raw sugar, the stench of hides and fish and ships' bilges, and, a few yards ahead, the bewitching perfume of spices.

Monk took a chance. Phillips wouldn't try for the ship; he would be too exposed as he went up the side, like a black fly on a brown wall. He would head the other way, and disappear into the alleys.

Or would he bluff? Double bluff?

Orme was on Monk's heels.

Monk headed towards the alley entrance between the warehouses. Orme drew in a breath, and then followed him. The third policeman stayed on the quayside. He had done this sort of thing often enough to know men could double back. He would be waiting.

The alley, which was no more than six feet wide, went down steps, then twisted one way, then the other. The stink of urine was sharp in Monk's nose. There was a chandler's shop to the right, its narrow doorway surrounded by coils of rope, ships' lanterns, wooden cleats, and a bucket full of hard-bristle brushes.

It was not far enough into the alley for Phillips to hide. Monk went past it. There was a paint shop next. He could see through the windows that it was empty inside. Orme was on his heels.

"Next alley's blind," Orme said quietly. "He could be up that waiting for us." It was a warning. Phillips had a knife, and would not hesitate to use it. "He's facing the gallows," he went on. "The moment we get the manacles on it's the beginning of the end for him. He knows that."

Monk found himself smiling. They were close now, so very close. "I know," he said almost under his breath. "Believe me, I've never wanted any villain more than I want this one."

Orme did not reply. They walked forward slowly. There was movement ahead of them, the sound of scratching on the stones. Orme's hand went to his pistol.

A brown rat shot out of a side passage and passed within a yard of them. There was a gasp somewhere ahead, then a curse. Phillips?

There was no stirring in the air. It was dark, and the smell was growing worse with the mix of stale beer from a nearby tavern. Monk moved more quickly. Phillips would not be slowed by any of this. Everything he had to fear was behind him.

The alley divided, the left going back towards the quayside, the right into a further warren of byways. There was a doss-house to the right. A man slouched in the doorway, one eye blind, his stomach bulging over his trousers, an old top hat balanced crookedly on his head.

Would Phillips have gone in there? Monk suddenly realized how many friends Phillips might have in these places: profiteers dependent on his business, suppliers, and hangers-on.

"No," Orme said urgently, putting his hand on Monk's arm, holding him with surprising strength. "We go in there, we'll not come out."

Monk was angry. He wanted to argue.

Even in the play of shadows across Orme's face his resolve was unmistakable. "Dockside isn't the only place that's got patches police can't go," he said quietly. "Don't tell me reg'lar police goes into Blue-gate Fields, or the Devil's Acre, 'cause we all know different. It's us against them, and we don't always win."

Monk shook his arm free, but he didn't pull away. "I'm not letting that bastard escape," he said slowly and clearly. "Murdering Fig is only the tip of what he does, like the mast of a sunken wreck above the water."

"There'll be a back way out," Orme added. "Likely more'n one."

It was on the edge of Monk's tongue to snap that he knew that, but he bit it back. Orme deserved to catch Phillips as much as Monk did, maybe more. He had worked with Durban on the original case. The only difference was that Durban's death was nothing to do with him, and it was all to do with Monk.

They continued along the alley away from the dock, moving more swiftly now. There were doorways on either side, and sometimes passages no more than a yard wide, mostly dead ends, perhaps ten or twelve feet along.

"He'll keep going a bit," Orme said grimly. "Instinct. Although he's a fly sod, an' all."

"He'll have friends here," Monk agreed.

"And enemies," Orme said wryly. "He's a nasty piece o' work. He'd shop anyone for sixpence, so he won't expect any favors. Try that one." He pointed to the left, a twisted passageway leading back towards the open dock. As he spoke he increased his pace, like a dog scenting the prey anew.

Monk did not argue but kept up just behind him. There was no room for them to move abreast. Somewhere to the left a man cursed and a woman shouted abuse at him. A dog started to bark, and ahead of them there were footsteps. Orme began to run, Monk on his heels. There was a low arch to the right, and something moved across it. There was a scatter of stones. Orme stopped so abruptly Monk collided with him and bumped into the wall, which was seeping wet from a loose drain in the shadows above.

Orme started forward again, very carefully now. It was always they who had to be on guard. Phillips could wait behind any wall, any arch or doorway, knife in hand. He could and would disembowel a man who was a threat to him. A policeman could kill a man only to save his own life, or that of someone else in mortal danger. And he would still have to prove he had had no other course.

Phillips could be getting away in either direction along the docks, up the ropes into one of the ships, or down the steps to a lighter and back across the river. They could not stand there hiding forever.

"Together!" Monk said harshly. "He can't get both of us. Now!"

Orme obeyed. They charged the opening and burst out into the sudden sunlight. Phillips was nowhere. Monk felt a wave of such bitter defeat pass over him that he struggled for breath, conscious of a physical pain in the pit of his stomach. There was a score of places for Phillips to disappear. It had been stupid to take anything for granted until they actually had him in a cell with the door closed and the bolt shot home. He had grasped at victory too soon. The arrogance of it was like bile in his mouth now.

He wanted to lash out at somebody, and there was no one to blame but himself. He knew he should be stronger than this, more in control. A good leader should be able to swallow his own misery and think of the next step to take, hide the disappointment or the rage, smother the personal pain. Durban would have. Monk needed to measure up to that, more than ever now that he had lost Phillips.

"Go north," he told Orme. "I'll go south. Where's Coulter?" He looked for the man they had left on the quayside. He swiveled as he spoke, searching for a familiar figure among the dockworkers. He saw the dark uniform at the same moment Orme did, and Coulter started waving his arms in the air.

They both ran forward, swerving to avoid a horse and wagon and a lumper with a heavy load on his shoulders.

"Down the steps!" Coulter shouted, gesticulating at the water beyond the ship. "Got a lighterman at knifepoint. Hurry!"

"Where's our boat?" Monk shouted back, jumping over a loose keg and landing hard on the uneven stones. "Where are they?"

"Went after him," Coulter answered, turning instinctively to Orme. Usually he was careful to be correct, but in the heat of the chase old habits of loyalty came back. Monk was still too new. "They'll be closing on him. Lighters are slow, but I've got a ferry waiting down there. Hurry up, sir!" He led the way back to the steps and started down them without turning to see if Monk and Orme were following.

Monk went after him. He must praise Coulter and not spoil it with criticism of his lapse in etiquette. He went down the slime-coated steps as fast as he could and clambered into the ferry, crushing his disappointment that the oarsmen in the boat would be the ones who made the arrest and saw the fury in Phillips's face. He would only get there in time to congratulate them.

But this was a team, he told himself as Orme landed behind him, shouting at the ferryman to pull out. Monk was in charge, but that was all. He did not have to be the one who made the arrest, faced Phillips and saw the fury in his face. As long as it was done, that was all that mattered. It was nothing like his days as a private agent, relying on no one, taking both the credit and the risks. He didn't cooperate—that was what Runcorn, his old superior in the Metropolitan force, had said of him, no idea how to help others, or to rely on their help when he needed it. Selfish.

They were slicing through the water now. The ferryman was skilled.

He did not look very strong—he was wiry rather than powerful—but he steered a course that cut yards off their distance. Monk admired his skill.

"There!" Coulter pointed at a lighter ahead, which was slowing a little to make way for a string of barges going downriver. There was a figure crouching low to the deck. It could be Phillips; it was impossible to tell at this distance.

Cooperation. That was why in the end Runcorn had been promoted rather than Monk. Runcorn knew how to keep silent about his own opinions, even when he was right. He knew how to please the men with power. Monk despised that, and had said so.

But Runcorn had been right: Monk was not easy to work with. He had not allowed himself to be.

The barges had passed and the lighter was picking up speed again, but they were far closer to it now. He could see Phillips clearly. This time they were in the open river and he could not hide. The space between them was narrowing: fifty feet, forty feet, thirty feet.

Suddenly Phillips was on his feet, his left arm clasped around the lighterman, his right hand with a long knife in it across the lighterman's throat. He was smiling.

There were only twenty feet between them now, and the lighter was losing speed rapidly as both men stood frozen. More barges were heading for them, already altering course to avoid ramming them.

With pounding rage Monk realized what Phillips was going to do, and there was no way to prevent it. He felt completely helpless, cold inside.

Ten feet now and still closing. The barges were bearing down on them.

Phillips whipped the knife from the man's throat and drove it hard into the side of his belly. Blood gushed out, and the lighterman collapsed just as Coulter leapt at him. Phillips scrambled beyond his reach, hesitated a moment, then leapt for the lead barge. He fell short and landed in the water, throwing up a huge splash. But after the first shock, he struggled to the surface, mouth open as he gulped frantically at the air, arms and legs thrashing.

Coulter did what any decent man would. He swore a string of

curses at Phillips, and bent to help the wounded lighterman, gathering as much cloth as he could into his fist and holding it on the wound while Orme—who had followed Coulter—took off his jacket, then his shirt, folded the shirt into a pad, and held it, stopping the blood as much as possible.

The bargees had pulled Phillips out of the water, already opening the distance between them and the drifting lighter with the ferry alongside it. Whether they meant to or not, their weight and speed meant that they could not stop easily. Phillips would be around the curve of the river beyond the Isle of Dogs in fifteen or twenty minutes.

Monk looked at the lighterman. His face was ashen, but if he reached medical help he might still be saved. That was what Phillips was counting on. He had never intended to kill him.

The ferryman was stunned, not knowing what to do.

"Take him to the nearest doctor," Monk ordered. "You, get rowing as fast as you can. Coulter, look after him. Orme, put your jacket on and come with me."

"Yes, sir!" Orme snatched up his jacket, and stood ready.

The ferryman took up the oars.

Orme and Coulter very gently and awkwardly picked up the injured man and laid him in the bottom of the ferry, Coulter holding the pad over his wound all the time.

Monk went to the fallen oar of the low, flat-bottomed lighter, and gripped it with both hands, balancing his weight. The moment Orme was on board Monk began to pull away. It came to him more naturally than he had expected. He knew, from flashes of memory and things he had been told, that he had grown up in Northumberland around boats, mostly fishing and in bad weather lifeboats. The way of the sea was ingrained in his experience, some inner sense of discipline. One can rebel against man and laws, but only a fool rebels against the sea, and he does 'it only once.

"We'll not catch up with him!" Orme said desperately. "I'd tie the noose around his neck with my own hands, and pull the trapdoor."

Monk did not answer. He was getting the weight and movement of the long oar right, and learning how to turn it to gain the greatest purchase against the water. At last they were going with the tide now, but then so were the barges, fifty yards ahead of them at least.

There was nothing Orme could do to help; it was a one-man job. He sat a little way over to the other side to balance Monk's weight, staring ahead, his uniform jacket fastened to hide as much as possible the fact that he now had no shirt. Certainly he would never wear that one again.

"They're longer than we are," Monk said with determined optimism. "They can't weave through the anchored shipping, but we can. They'll have to go around."

"If we go in between those ships we'll lose sight of them," Orme warned grimly. "God knows where he could get to!"

"If we don't, we'll lose them anyway," Monk replied. "They're fifty yards ahead now, and gaining." He threw his weight onto the oar, and pulled it the wrong way. He knew the moment he felt the resistance that he had made a mistake. It took him more than a minute to get into the rhythm again.

Orme deliberately looked the other way, as if he had not noticed.

The barges swung wide around an East Indiaman anchored ahead of them, stevedores working on deck with chests of spices, silks, and probably tea.

Monk took the chance, veering to the port to pass between the East Indiaman and a Spanish schooner off-loading pottery and oranges. He concentrated on the regularity of his strokes and keeping his balance exactly right, and trying not to think that the barges were going over to the far shore now that they were out of sight. If they did, he might lose them, but if he did not take the chance to catch up, he certainly would.

He passed as close as he dared to the East Indiaman, almost under the shadow of her hull. He could hear the water slapping against her and the faint hum and rattle of the wind in the shrouds.

The moment he was back in the sun again he looked to starboard. The line of barges was nearer, no more than forty yards ahead. He controlled himself with an effort. Orme was straining forward also, hands clenched, shoulders tight. His lips were moving as he counted the barges, just to make certain they had not cast one adrift when they were out of sight.

The gap was still closing. They could not see Phillips, and Monk searched back and forth along the line of canvas coverings. He could be behind a bale or keg, under the canvas, or even have taken a bargee's coat and cap and at this distance look like one of them. It meant nothing. Still he wanted to see him and be certain that Phillips was there.

He would have to go on to the barges alone. One of them had to stay with the lighter, or they would have no way to take Phillips back. It was a long time since he had fought alone against a man with a knife. In fact, he was not sure if he ever had. He remembered nothing from the years since the accident. Would he find some instinct to fall back on?

Ten yards now. He must get ready to jump. They were passing into the lee of a clipper. The masts seemed to scrape the sky, barely moving, since the hull was too large and heavy to roll in the short, choppy water. The lighter skimmed the surface easily, then bucked the moment it hit the tide again, but now they were closing on the last barge very quickly. Four yards, three, two—Monk leapt. Orme swung over and took the oar.

Monk landed on the barge, swayed for a moment, then regained his balance. The bargee took no notice. It was all a drama playing out in front of him in which he had no part.

Since Monk was on the last barge, if Phillips had moved at all, it had to have been forward. Monk started towards the front. He stood warily on top of the canvas, moving from one shapeless mound to the next, altering his weight all the time, arms wide, footing precarious. His eyes moved from one side to the other, expecting surprise.

He was almost at the prow, ready to jump to the next barge, when he saw a flicker of movement. Then Phillips was on him, knife arcing high and wide. Monk kicked forward, low and moving sideways, almost overbalancing, then righting himself at the last instant.

Phillips missed his mark, expecting to strike flesh and meet resistance, but not meeting it. He teetered on one foot, whirled his arms wildly for an instant, and fell forward onto his knees, ignoring the pain of Monk's boot on his flesh. He lashed out again immediately, catching the very front of Monk's shin and ripping his trousers, drawing blood.

Monk was startled. The pain was searing. He had expected Phillips to be more taken aback, longer in recovering, a mistake he would not make again. He had no weapon but the pistol in his belt. He drew it now, not to shoot but to bludgeon. Then he changed his mind and kicked again, hard and high, aiming more carefully this time. He caught Phillips on the side of the head, sending him sprawling. But Phillips had seen it coming and moved back, and the impact was not so great.

Now Monk had to go forward, over the lumpy canvas, and he had no idea what was underneath it. The barges were all hit by the wake of a coal barge, sails set, passing upriver. They bucked and slewed, throwing the men off balance again. Monk suffered most because he was standing. He should have seen that coming. Phillips, younger and more agile, had. Monk swayed, staggered, and fell almost on top of Phillips, who twisted and squirmed away from him. He landed hard, feeling the kegs under the canvas bruise him, and the next moment Phillips was on top of him, arms and legs like steel.

Monk was pinned. He was alone. Orme might even be able to see what was happening, but he could not help, and the bargees were going to take no part.

For a moment Phillips's face was so close, Monk could smell his skin, his hair, the exhale of his breath. His eyes were glittering, and he smiled as he brought the knife up in his hand.

Monk headbutted him as hard as he could. It hurt—bone against bone—but it was Phillips who yelled, and his grip went suddenly slack. Monk threw him off and slid away, crablike, then spun around instantly, the pistol in his hand.

But he was too late to shoot. Blood smeared over his face and running from his mouth, Phillips had risen to a crouch and turned away, as if he knew Monk would not shoot him in the back. He launched himself from the barge and landed spread-eagle on the canvas of the one ahead.

Without a moment's thought Monk followed.

Phillips staggered to his feet and started along the central ridge of the canvas. Monk went straight after him, this time finding the balance more difficult. Whatever was under the tarpaulin rolled beneath his feet and pitched him forward harder and faster than he intended.

Phillips reached the prow and jumped again. Again Monk went after him. This time it was tight, canvas-lashed bales underfoot, which were easier to balance on. He jumped from one to the other, catching up, tripping Phillips who went down hard. Monk struck him in the chest, crushing the air out of his lungs and hearing the long, grating rasp as he tried to fill them again. Then he felt pain in his forearm and saw blood. But it was only a slice, too shallow to cripple. He hit Phillips again in the chest, and the knife fell from Phillips's hand. Monk heard it slide down the canvas and clatter on the decking.

The blood was making his hand slippery now. Phillips was squirming like an eel, strong and hard, elbows and knees all powerful bone and angles, and Monk could not hold on.

Suddenly Phillips was free, staggering towards the front, ready to leap to the next barge. There was a lighter about to cross ahead of them, just one. His intention was clear. He would jump to it, and there would be no boat in which Monk could follow him.

Monk clambered up and reached the prow, just as Phillips jumped and fell short. He went into the water and along the lighter's side in the white wash of the bow.

Monk hesitated. He could let him drown, easily. He needed to be only a moment late and it would be beyond anyone's skill to fish him out. Injured as he was, he would drown in minutes. It would be an end better than he deserved. But Monk wanted him alive, so he could be tried and hanged. Durban would be proved right, and all the boys Phillips had used and tortured would have a proper answer.

Monk leaned forward with both arms over the side and caught Phillips by the shoulders, felt his hands lock onto his arms, and used all the strength he possessed to haul him out. He was wet, heavy, and almost a dead weight. His lungs were already filling with water, and he made no resistance.

Monk took out the handcuffs and locked them on before he balanced to roll Phillips over and pump his chest to get the water out. "Breathe!" he said between his teeth. "Breathe, you swine!"

Phillips coughed, vomited up river water, and drew in his breath.

"Well done, Mr. Monk, sir," Orme said from the lighter coming alongside. "Mr. Durban'd have been happy to see that."

Monk felt the warmth spread through him like fire and music, and peace after desperate exertion. "It needed tidying up," he said modestly. "Thank you for your assistance, Mr. Orme."

Monk arrived home at Paradise Place in Rotherhithe before six, a time that was relatively early for him. He had walked rapidly up the street from where the ferry had landed at Princes Stairs, and walked all the way up to Church Street, then the dogleg into Paradise Place. All the way he was refusing to think that Hester might not yet be home and he would have to wait to tell her that they had Phillips at last. And yet idiotically he could not get the fear of it out of his mind.

The police surgeon had stitched up the gashes Phillips had made in his arm and leg, but he was bruised, filthy, and covered with blood. He had also bought an excellent bottle of brandy for his men, and shared it with them. It had been for all the station, so no one was the worse for wear, but he knew the flavor of it hung around him. However, he did not even think of such a thing as he skipped a step, ran the last few dozen yards up the short length of Paradise Place, and unlocked his own front door.

"Hester!" he called, even before he closed it behind him. "Hester?" Only now did he fully face the possibility that she was not yet home. "I got him!"

The words fell on silence.

Then there was a clatter at the top of the stairs and she came running down, feet flying. Her hair was half undone, thick and fair and unruly as always. She hugged him with all her strength, which was considerable, in spite of her slender frame and lack of fashionable curves.

He picked her up and swung her around, kissing her with all the joy and victory he felt, and the sudden upsurge of belief in everything good. Most of all his elation was due to the possibility that she was right to have had faith in him, not just in his skill but in his honor, that core of him that was good and could treasure and hold on to love.

And Phillips's capture at last meant that Durban was right to have trusted him too, which he realized now had also mattered.

TWO

On an evening nearly two weeks after the capture of Jericho Phillips, Sir Oliver Rathbone, arguably the best attorney in London, returned a little early from his offices at the Inns of Court to his elegant and extremely comfortable home. It was the middle of August, and the air was hot and still. It was much pleasanter in his own sitting room, with the French windows open onto the lawn and the perfume of the second flush of roses rather than the odor of the streets, the sweat and dung of horses, the dust and the noise.

Like Monk, Rathbone was in his late forties, but very different in appearance. He was slender, fair-haired, with the air of confidence of one who has long proved his worth. Margaret greeted him with the same pleasure she always had since their marriage not so long ago. She came down the stairs with a swirl of pale green and white muslin, looking impossibly cool in the heat. She kissed him gently, smiling perhaps still a trifle self-consciously. He found a pleasure in it that he thought might be tactless to show.

They talked of many things over dinner: a new art exhibition that was proving more controversial than expected; the queen's absence from the London Season due to the recent death of Prince Albert, and quite how much difference that was going to make in the future; and of course the wretchedly miserable matter of the civil war in America.

The conversation was sufficiently interesting to occupy his mind, and yet also supremely comfortable. He could not remember ever having been happier, and when he retired to read a few necessary papers in his study he found himself smiling for no other reason than his inner peace.

Dusk was already gathering, and the air was mercifully cooler when the butler knocked on the door and told him that his father-in-law had called and wished to see him. Naturally Rathbone accepted immediately, although somewhat surprised that Arthur Ballinger would specifically ask to see him, rather than including his daughter as well.

When Ballinger came in, hard on the servant's heels, Rathbone saw at once that the matter was professional rather than personal. Ballinger was an attorney of high standing and very considerable re-pute. From time to time they had had dealings, but so far no clients in common, Rathbone's practice being almost entirely in major cases of criminal law.

Ballinger closed the study door behind him to ensure their privacy, then walked over to the chair opposite Rathbone. Barely acknowledg-ing the greeting, he sat down. He was a large, rather heavy man with thick, brown hair that had only touches of gray. His features were powerful. Margaret had gained all the delicacy of her face and bearing from her mother.

"I am in a difficult position, Oliver," he began without preamble. "A long-standing client has asked a favor of me that I am loath to grant, and yet I feel I cannot refuse him. It is a business that frankly I would prefer to have nothing to do with, but I can see no honorable way of escape." He gave a slight shrug, with one shoulder only. "And I suppose, to be honest, no legal way either. One cannot pick and choose in which matters you will act for people, and in which you will not. That would make a mockery of the entire concept of justice, which must be for all, or it is for no one."

Rathbone was startled by such a speech; it suggested a lack of confidence quite uncharacteristic of Ballinger. Something had clearly disturbed him. "Can I be of help, without breaking your client's priv-ilege of discretion?" he asked hopefully. It would please him to assist Margaret's father in a matter that was important to him. It would make Margaret herself happy, and it would draw him closer into the family, which was not a situation he found naturally easy. He had a deep instinct for privacy. Apart from an intense friendship with his own father, he had found few ties in his adult years. In some ways William Monk, of all people, was the truest friend he had. That excluded Hester, of course, but his feeling for her had been different: stronger, more intimate, and in ways more painful, he was not ready to examine it any more closely.

Ballinger relaxed a fraction more, at least outwardly, although he still concealed his hands in his lap, as if they might have given him away.

"It would break no confidences at all," he said quickly. "I am seeking your professional skills to represent a case I fear you will find repellent, and have very little chance of winning. However you will, of course, be properly paid for your time and your skill, which I regard as unique." He was wise enough not to overpraise.

Rathbone was confused. His profession was to represent clients in court; very occasionally he prosecuted for the crown, but not as a habit. Why was Ballinger nervous about this, as undoubtedly he was? Why come to Rathbone at home, and not in his office, as would be far more usual? What was so different about this case? He had defended people accused of murder, arson, blackmail, theft, almost every crime one could think of, even rape.

"What is your client accused of?" he asked. Could it be something as contentious as treason? Against whom? The queen?

Ballinger gave a slight shrug. "Murder. But he is an unpopular man, unsympathetic to a jury. He will not appear well," he hastened to explain. He must have seen the doubt in Rathbone's face. He leaned forward a little. "But that is not the problem, Oliver. I know you have represented all manner of people, on charges that have had no public sympathy at all. Although I deplore everything about this particular case, it is the issue of justice that is paramount in my client's mind."

Rathbone found a wry irony in the remark. Few accused men phrased their attempts to be defended successfully in such general and rather pompous terms.

Ballinger's eyes flickered and something altered in the set of his features.

"I have not explained myself fully," he went on. "My client wishes to pay your fees to defend another person entirely. He has no relation-ship to the man accused, and no personal stake in the outcome, only the matter of justice, impartial, clear of all gain or loss to himself. He fears that this man will appear so vile to average jurors that without the best defense in the country, he will be found guilty and hanged on emotion, not on the facts."

"Very altruistic," Rathbone remarked, although there was a sud-den lift of excitement inside him, as if he had glimpsed something beautiful, a battle with all the passion and commitment he could give it. But it was only a glimpse, a flash of light gone before he was sure he had seen it at all. "Who is he?" he asked.

Ballinger smiled, a small bleak movement of the mouth. "That I cannot disclose. He wishes to remain anonymous. He has not told me his reasons, but I have to respect his wish." From his expression and the peculiar, hunched angle of his shoulders, it was clear that this was the moment of decision, the trial in which he was afraid he might fail.

Rathbone was taken aback. Why would a man in so noble an en-deavor wish to remain anonymous even from his attorney? From the public was easy enough to understand. They might well assume that he had some sympathy for the accused, and it would be only too clear to see why he would avoid that. "If I am bound to secrecy, I shall ob-serve it," Rathbone said gently. "Surely you told him that?"

"Of course I did," Ballinger said quickly. "However, he is adamant. I cannot move him on the subject. As far as you are concerned, I shall represent the accused man to you, and act on his behalf. All you need to know is that you will be paid in full, by a man of the utmost honor and probity, and that the money is earned by his own skills, which are in every way above suspicion. I will swear to that." He sat motionless, staring earnestly at Rathbone. In a man of less composure it might even have been thought imploringly.

Rathbone felt uncomfortable that his own father-in-law should have to plead for the professional assistance he had always been will-ing to give, even to strangers and men he profoundly disliked, because it was his calling. He was an advocate; his job was to speak on behalf of those who were not equipped to speak for themselves, and who would suffer injustice if there were no one to take their part. The system of the law was adversarial. The sides must be equal in skill and in dedication; otherwise the whole issue was a farce.

"Of course I will act for your client," he said earnestly. "Give me the necessary papers and a retaining fee, and then all we say will be privileged."

Ballinger relaxed fully at last. "Your word is good enough, Oliver. I shall have all that you need sent to your office in the morning. I am extremely grateful. I wish I could tell Margaret what an excellent man you are, but no doubt she is already perfectly aware. I am delighted now that she had enough sense not to allow her mother earlier to push her into a marriage of convenience, although I admit I was exasperated at the time." He smiled ruefully. "If you are going to have a strong-minded woman in the house, it is better to have two, preferably of opposing views. Then you can back one or the other, and achieve the goal you wish." He sighed, and there was a momentary sadness in his face, in spite of the relief. "I cannot say how much I appreciate you, Oliver."

Rathbone did not know how to answer; he was even a trifle embarrassed by Ballinger's regard. He directed the conversation towards the practical. "Who am I to defend? You said the charge was murder?"

"Yes. Yes, regrettably so."

"Who is he, and who was the victim?" He knew better than to warn Ballinger not to tell him of any confession, which would jeopardize his standing as an officer of the court.

"Jericho Phillips," Ballinger replied, almost casually.

Rathbone suddenly became aware that Ballinger was watching him intently, but beneath his lashes, as if he could conceal the fact. "The man charged with killing the boy found down the river at Greenwich?" he asked. He had read a little about it, and already he was unaccountably chilled.

"That's right," Ballinger replied. "He denies it. Says the boy ran away, and he has no idea who killed him."

"Then why is he charged? They must have some evidence. River Police, isn't it? Monk is not a fool."

"Of course not," Ballinger said smoothly. "I know he is a friend of yours, or at least he has been in the past. But even good men can make mistakes, especially when they are new to a job, and a little too eager to succeed."

Rathbone felt more stung on Monk's behalf than he would have expected to. "I haven't seen him lately. I have been busy, and I imagine so has he, but I still regard him as a friend."

Regret and contrition filled Ballinger's face. "I apologize. I did not mean to imply otherwise. I hope I have not placed you in a position where you will have to question the judgment of a man you like and respect."

"Liking Monk has nothing to do with defending someone he has arrested!" Rathbone said hotly, realizing exactly how much it could, if he allowed it to. "Do you imagine that my acquaintance with the police, the prosecution, or the judge, for that matter, will have any effect on my conduct of a case? Any case?"

"No, my dear chap, of course I don't," Ballinger said with profound feeling. "That is exactly why my client chose you, and why I fully concurred with his judgment. Jericho Phillips will receive the fairest trial possible if you speak for him, and even if he is found guilty and hanged, we will all be easy at heart that justice has been done. We will never need to waken in the night with doubt or guilt that perhaps we hanged him because his style of life, his occupation, or his personal repulsiveness moved us more than honest judgment. If we are fair to the likes of him, then we are fair to all." He rose to his feet and offered his hand. "Thank you, Oliver. Margaret is justly proud of you. I see her happiness in her face, and know that it will always be so."

Rathbone had no choice but to take Ballinger's hand and clasp it, still with a faint trace of self-consciousness because he was not accustomed to such frankness in matters of emotion.

But after Ballinger had gone, he was also pleased. This would be a supreme challenge, and he would not like losing, but it was an honorable thing Ballinger had asked him to do—obliquely, dangerously honorable. And it would be intensely precious to have Margaret truly proud of him.

———

It was several more days before Rathbone actually went to Newgate Prison to meet with Jericho Phillips. By this time he had a much greater knowledge of both the specific crime he was charged with and—far more worrying to him—Phillips's general pattern of life.

Even so, he was still unprepared for the acute distaste he felt when they met. It was in a small, stone room with no furniture other than a table and two chairs. The single window was high in the wall and let in daylight, but there was nothing to see beyond it but the sky. The motionless air inside smelled stale, as if it held a century's sweat of fear that all the carbolic in the world could not wash away.

Phillips himself was little above average height, but the leanness of his body and the angular way he stood made him look taller. He possessed no grace at all, and yet there was a suggestion of power in him in even the simple act of rising to his feet as Rathbone came in and the guard closed the door behind him.

"Mornin', Sir Oliver," Phillips said civilly. His voice was rasping, as if his throat were sore. He made no move to offer his hand, for which Rathbone was grateful.

"Good morning, Mr. Phillips," he replied. "Please sit down. Our time is limited, so let us use it to the full." He was slightly uncomfortable already. He felt an unease almost like a brush of physical fear. And yet Phillips was no threat to him at all. As far as he knew, to Phillips he was the one man on his side.

Phillips obeyed, moving stiffly. It was the only thing that betrayed his fear. His hands were perfectly still, and he did not stammer or shake.

"Yes, sir," he said obediently.

Rathbone looked at him. Phillips had sharp features and the pallid skin of one who lives largely away from the sunlight, but there was nothing soft in him, from his spiky hair to his glittering eyes, his strong hands, and his narrow, bony shoulders. He had the physical build of poverty—thin chest, slightly crooked legs—and yet he had learned not to show the usual limp of deformity.

"Your attorney informs me that you wish to plead 'not guilty,' " Rathbone began. "The evidence against you is good, but not conclusive. Our greatest difficulty will be your reputation. Jurors will weigh the facts, but they will also be moved by emotion, whether they are aware of it or not." He watched Phillips's face to judge whether he understood. He saw the instant flash of intelligence, and something that could almost have been mistaken for humor, were the situation not so desperate.

" 'Course they will," Phillips agreed with the faintest smile. "Feeling's where we get 'em, 'cause yer see Mr. Durban weren't anything like the good man they think 'e were. 'E 'ated me for a long time, an' 'e made it 'is life's work ter see me 'ang, whether I done anything for it or not. An' Mr. Monk took over from 'im just like 'e stepped into a dead man's shoes, an' 'is coat and trousers as well. Careless, they were, both of 'em. An' from wot Mr. Ballinger says, yer clever enough an' straight enough ter show it, if it's true, whether they were yer friends or not."

Rathbone became uncomfortably aware that just as he was studying Phillips, so Phillips in turn was studying him equally as closely, and probably with just as acute a judgment. He did everything he could to keep all expression from his face.

"I see. I shall look at the evidence in that light, not only for its validity, but as to how it was obtained. If there were errors it may work to our advantage."

Phillips shivered involuntarily, struggled to conceal it, and failed.

The room was chilly because the damp never seemed to entirely leave it, in spite of the August heat outside.

"Are you cold, Mr. Phillips?" Rathbone forced himself to remember that this man was his client, and innocent of the crime he was charged with until such time as he was proven guilty beyond a reasonable doubt.

Something flared in Phillips's eyes: memory, fear. "No," he lied. Then he changed his mind. "It's just this room." His voice changed and became hoarser. "It's wet. In my cell I can hear . . . dripping." His body went rigid. "I hate dripping."

And yet the man chose to live on the river. He must never be away from the slap of the waves and the shifting of the tide. It was only in here, where the walls sweated and dripped, that he could not control his hatred of it. Rathbone found himself looking at Phillips with a new interest, something almost like respect. Was it possible that he deliberately forced himself to face his phobia, live with it, test himself against it every day? That would be a strength few men possessed, and a discipline most would very definitely avoid. Perhaps he had assumed a great deal about Jericho Phillips that he should not have.

"I will look into your accommodation closely," he promised. "Now let us put our attention to what we have so far."

Two weeks later, when the morning of the trial came, Rathbone was as ready as it was possible to be. The excitement of the eve of battle fluttered inside him, tightening his muscles, making his stomach knot, burning within him like a fire. He was afraid of failure, full of doubts as to whether the wild plan he had in mind could work—and even in darker moments, whether it ought to. And yet the hunger to try was compulsive, consuming. It would be a landmark in history if he succeeded in gaining an acquittal for a man like Phillips, because the procedure was flawed, well-motivated but essentially dishonest, drawn by emotion, not fact. That path, no matter how understandable in the individual instance, would in the end only lead to injustice, and therefore sooner or later to the hanging of an innocent man, which was the ultimate failure of the law.

He looked at himself in the mirror and saw his reflection with its long nose, sensitive mouth, and, as always, humor in the dark eyes. He stepped back and adjusted his wig and gown until they were perfect. There were approximately fifteen minutes to go.

He still wished that he knew who was paying his very considerable fee, but Ballinger had steadily refused to tell him. It was quite true that Rathbone did not need to know. Ballinger's assurance that the man was reputable, and that the money was obtained honestly, was sufficient to put all suspicion to rest. It was curiosity that drove Rathbone, and possibly a desire to know if there were facts to do with someone else's guilt that were being held from him. It was that second possibility that above all compelled him to give Phillips the finest defense he could.

There was a discreet knock on the door. It was the usher to tell him that it was time.

The trial began with all the ceremony the Old Bailey commanded. Lord Justice Sullivan was presiding, a man in his late fifties with a handsome nose and very slightly receding chin. His shock of dark hair was hidden beneath his heavy, full-bottomed wig, but his bristling brows accentuated the somewhat tense expression of his face. He conducted the opening procedures with dispatch. A jury was sworn, the charges were read, and Richard Tremayne, Q.C., began the case for Her Majesty against Jericho Phillips.

Tremayne was a little older than Rathbone, a man with a curious face, full of humor and imagination. He would have appeared much more at home in a poet's loose-sleeved shirt and extravagant cravat. Rathbone in fact had seen him wear exactly that, one evening at a party in his large house whose lawn backed on to the Thames. They had been playing croquet, and losing an inordinate number of balls. The late sun was setting, falling in reds and peaches on the water, bees were buzzing lazily in the lilies, and nobody knew or cared who won.

And yet despite this lack of competition, Rathbone knew that Tremayne both loved and understood the law. Rathbone was not sure at all whether he was a fortunate choice, or an unfortunate one as his opponent.

The first witness he called was Walters of the Thames River Police, a solid man with a mild manner and buttons that had such a high polish they shone in the light. He climbed the steep, curving steps to the witness box and was sworn in.

In the dock, higher up opposite the judge's bench, and sideways to the jury, Jericho Phillips sat between two blank-faced guards. He looked very sober, almost as if he might be frightened. Was that to impress the jury, or did he really believe Rathbone would fail? Rathbone hoped it was the latter, because then Phillips would maintain his appearance without the chance of it slipping and betraying him.

Rathbone listened to see what the river policeman would say. It would be foolish for him to question any of the facts; that was not the tactic he proposed to use. Now all he needed to do was take note.

Tremayne was intelligent, charming, born to privilege, and perhaps a little lazy. He was due for an unpleasant surprise.

"The message came to us at the Wapping Station," Walters was saying. "Lightermen'd found a body, an' they reckoned as we should go and look at it."

"Is that usual, Mr. Walters?" Tremayne asked. "I presume there are tragically many bodies found in the river."

"Yes, sir, there are. But this one weren't an accident. Poor beggar'd 'ad 'is throat cut from ear to ear," Walters replied grimly. He did not look up at Phillips, but it was obvious from the rigidity of his shoulders and the way he stared fixedly at Tremayne that he had been told not to.

Tremayne was very careful. "Could that have happened accidentally?" he asked.

Walters's impatience sounded in his voice. " 'Ardly, sir. Apart from 'is throat cut, an' 'e were only a boy, there were burn marks on 'is arms, like from cigars. They called us because they thought 'e'd been murdered."

"How do you know that, Mr. Walters?"

Rathbone smiled to himself. Tremayne was nervous, even though he believed his case to be unassailable, or he would not be so pedantic. He was expecting Rathbone to attack at every opportunity. It would be pointless to object to this as hearsay. It would make Rathbone look desperate, because the answer was obvious.

Lord Justice Sullivan's lips curved in a very slight smile also. It seemed he read both of them and understood. For the first time since they began, there was a flash of interest in his eyes. He sensed a duel of equals, not the execution he had expected.

"I know it 'cause they said so when they asked us to come," Walters replied stolidly.

"Thank you. Who is the 'us' you refer to? I mean, who from the River Police did go?"

"Mr. Durban an' me, sir."

"Mr. Durban being your commanding officer, the head of the River Police at Wapping?"

"Yes, sir."

Rathbone considered asking why Durban was not testifying, although of course he knew, but most of the jury would not.

Lord Justice Sullivan beat him to it. He leaned forward, his expression mild and curious. "Mr. Tremayne, are we to hear from this Commander Durban?"

"No, my lord," Tremayne said grimly. "I regret to say that Mr. Durban died at the very end of last year, giving his life to save others. That is the reason we have called Mr. Walters."

"I see. Please proceed," Sullivan directed.

"Thank you, my lord. Mr. Walters, will you please tell the court where you went in answer to the summons, and what you found there?"

"Yes, sir." Walters squared his shoulders. "We went down the Limehouse Reach, about level with Cuckold's Point, an' there was a lighterman, a ferryman, and a couple o' barges all anchored an' waiting. One o' the barges'd caught up the body of a boy, maybe twelve or thirteen years old. The lighterman'd seen it and raised the cry. O' course you can't stop a barge, still less a string of 'em, all of a sudden, like. So they'd gone a good 'undred yards or so before they threw out an anchor an' got to look at what they 'ad." His voice sank even lower, and he was unable to keep the emotion out of it. "Poor kid was in an 'ell of a mess. Throat cut right across, from one ear to the other, an' been dragged an' bashed around so it were a wonder 'is 'ead 'adn't come off altogether. 'E were caught in some ropes, otherwise, of course, he'd 'ave gone out with the tide, an' we'd never 'ave found him before the sea an' the fish 'ad 'im down to bone."

On his high seat Sullivan winced and closed his eyes. Rathbone wondered if any of the jurors had seen that small gesture of revulsion or noticed that Sullivan was more than usually pale.

"Yes, I see." Tremayne gave the tragedy of it full importance by waiting to make sure the court had time to dwell on it also. "What did you do as a result of this discovery?"

"We asked 'em to tell us exactly what 'appened, where they were when they reckoned the barge'd run onto the body, 'ow far they'd dragged it without realizing . . ."

Sullivan frowned, looking sharply at Tremayne.

Tremayne saw it. "Mr. Walters, if they did not know the body was there, how could they have estimated how far they had dragged it?"

Rathbone hid a smile not because he was unamused by the irony of the arguments, and Tremayne's exactness, but because if he were seen to display any lack of horror or pity now it would work against him later.

"Because o' the last time someone would 'ave 'ad to 'ave seen it if it were there, sir," Walters said grimly. "If someone passed astern o' you, they'd 'ave seen."

Tremayne nodded. "Precisely so. And how far had that been?"

"Around Horseferry Stairs. Passed a ferry going in, pretty close. Must 'ave run afoul o' the poor little begger some time after that."

"Did you know who he was, this dead child?"

Walters winced, his face suddenly transformed by anger and pity. "No, sir, not then. There's thousands o' children on the river, one way or the other."

"Did you work on the case after that, Mr. Walters?"

"No, sir. It was mostly Mr. Durban hisself, and Mr. Orme."

"Thank you. Please remain there, in case my learned friend, Sir Oliver, wishes to ask you anything." Tremayne walked back across the open space of the floor and gestured an invitation to Rathbone.

Rathbone rose to his feet, thanked him, and walked calmly into the center of the court. Then he looked up at the witness stand to where Walters was waiting, his face heavy and apprehensive.

"Good morning, Mr. Walters," he began. "I shall not detain you long. May I compliment you on the marvelous work the River Police do for us. I believe that in the nearly three quarters of a century that you have existed you have reduced crime on the river by a staggering amount. In fact, you solve more than ninety percent of the crimes you address, do you not?"

Walters straightened himself. "Yes, sir. Thank you, sir."

"You are rightly proud. It is a great service to Her Majesty, and to the people of London. Am I correct in thinking that the murder of this boy stirred a deep anger in you?"

"Yes, sir, you are. 'E'd not only been murdered. From the burns on 'is arms and body, 'e'd been tortured as well." Walters's face was ashen, his voice hoarse as though his throat were dry.

"It is very terrible," Rathbone agreed. This was proceeding exactly as he had intended. Walters was a deeply sympathetic witness. "Was

Mr. Durban similarly affected?" he went on. "Or perhaps I should more correctly ask you, what was Mr. Durban's manner, his reaction, when he saw the boy's corpse with his throat slashed open so his head hung half off, and the marks of deliberate torture on his flesh?"

Walters winced at the brutal words. He closed his eyes as if taking himself back to that fearful scene. " 'E wept, sir," he said quietly. " 'E swore that 'e'd find 'oo done it, an' see 'im 'ang till 'is own 'ead were near off 'is body too. 'E'd never, ever do that to another child."

"I imagine we can all understand how he felt." Rathbone spoke quietly, yet his voice had a timbre that carried to every seat in the silent court. He knew Lord Justice Sullivan was staring at him as if he had taken leave of his senses. He was probably wondering whether to remind Rathbone which side he was on. "And Commander Durban pursued it himself," he continued. "With the assistance of Mr. Orme, you said? Mr. Orme, I believe, was his immediate right-hand man."

"Yes, sir. He's still second in command, sir," Walters agreed.

"Just so. These events you describe happened some year and a half ago. And we are only just come to trial. Did Mr. Durban abandon the case?"

Walters's face flushed with indignation. "No, sir! Mr. Durban worked on it day and night, until 'e 'ad to give over to other things, an' then 'e followed it on 'is own time. 'E never, ever gave up on it."

Rathbone lowered his voice, while making sure that every word still carried to the jury and to the benches where the public sat awed and silent.

"Are you saying that he felt so passionately that he devoted his off-duty time to it, until the tragedy of his own early death cut short his dedication, to finding the person who had tortured and then killed this boy?"

"Yes, sir, I am. An' then when 'e found the notes Mr. Durban left, Mr. Monk took up after 'im," Walters said defiantly.

"Thank you." Rathbone held up his hand to stop any more revelations. "We will get to Mr. Monk in due time. He can testify himself, should that prove necessary. You have made it all very clear, Mr. Walters. That is all I have to ask you."

Tremayne shook his head, his face a little tight, concealing a certain unease.

The judge thanked Walters and excused him.

Tremayne called his next witness: the police surgeon who had examined the body of the boy. He was a thin, tired man with receding sandy hair and a surprisingly good voice, in spite of having to stop and sneeze, then blow his nose from time to time. He was obviously practiced at such court appearances. He had every answer on the tip of his tongue, and told them of the state of the boy's body briefly and precisely. Tremayne did not need to prompt him in anything. He used no scientific language to describe the wasted flesh, which was underdeveloped, barely beginning to show signs of puberty. He spoke simply of the flesh scarring that could have been made only by something like the lit end of a cigar. Finally he told them that the throat was cut so violently that the wound reached to the spine, so the whole head was only just attached. In such unaffected words the description seemed immeasurably more appalling. There was no passion or disgust in his language; it was all in his eyes, and in the rigid angles of his body as he gripped the rail of the witness stand.

Rathbone found it hard to speak to him. Legal tactics melted away. He was face-to-face with the reality of the crime, as if the surgeon had brought the smell of the mortuary with him, the blood and carbolic and running water, but nothing washed away the memory.

Rathbone stood in the middle of the floor with every eye in the room on him, and wondered suddenly if he really knew what he was doing. There was nothing this man could add that would help him. Yet to fail to ask him at least one question would make that obvious. He must never let Tremayne see any weakness. Tremayne might look like a dandy, a poet and dreamer caught by chance in the wrong place, but it was an illusion. His mind was keen as a razor, and he would scent weakness as a shark scents blood in the water.

"You were obviously very moved by this particular case, sir," Rathbone said with great gravity. "Perhaps it was one of the most distressing you had seen?"

"It was," the surgeon agreed.

"Did Mr. Durban seem to you similarly distressed by it?"

"Yes, sir. Any civilized man would be." The surgeon looked at him with distaste, as if Rathbone himself were devoid of decency. "Mr. Monk after him was equally upset, if you were going to ask," he added.

"It had occurred to me," Rathbone acknowledged. "As you've implied, it is an appalling piece of savagery, and against a child who had obviously suffered already. Thank you." He turned away.

"Is that all you have to ask me?" the surgeon called after him, his voice harder, challenging.

"Yes, thank you," Rathbone replied with a slight smile. "Unless my learned friend has anything further, you are free to leave."

Tremayne next called Orme. He was a solemn figure, not overtly nervous. He held his hands at his sides, not gripping the rail except when he went up the steps. Then he stood square in the box and faced Tremayne with as little expression on his face as he could manage.

Rathbone knew he would be a difficult man to break, and if he did so and the jury saw it, they would not forgive him. He glanced at them now, for the first time. Immediately he wished he had kept his resolve not to. They were mostly middle-aged men, old enough to have sons the victim's age. They sat stiffly in their sober best suits, white-faced and unhappy. Society had entrusted them not only with weighing the facts, but also with seeing the horror and dealing with it on behalf of everyone. If they sensed that they were being manipulated they would not pardon the man who did it.

"Mr. Orme." Tremayne began his questions, which were likely to go on until the adjournment for lunch, and long into the afternoon, perhaps until evening. "You worked with Mr. Durban during the rest of his life, from the time the boy's body was pulled out of the river until Mr. Durban's own death at the end of last year?"

"Yes, sir, I did."

"We have already heard that Mr. Durban took a special interest in this case. As far as you know from your own direct observation, will you describe what was done to solve it, either by him, of which you have the evidence, or by yourself?"

"Yes, sir." Orme stood stiffly. "It was plain from the beginning that the boy was murdered, and that he'd been pretty badly used before that," he said distinctly, his voice carrying throughout the room. No one moved or whispered in the jury box or the gallery. "We 'ad to find out who he was, and where he came from. There was nothing on the body that'd give 'is name, but the way 'e'd been treated it seemed likely 'e'd fallen into the 'ands of one o' them who sells children for the use of brothels an' pornographers and the like." He said the words with withering disgust.

"You could tell that from a body?" Tremayne said, affecting some surprise.

All this was exactly what Rathbone had expected, and what he would have done had their roles been reversed—draw it all out in the fashion of a story, and with detail the jury would never forget. The poor devils would probably have nightmares for years to come. They would waken in a sweat with the sound of running water in their ears.

"Yes, sir, pretty likely," Orme replied. "Lots of boys, an' girls too, is 'alf starved. You're poor, you've got no choice. But the burns are different."

"Is it not possible that a poor man, violent, perhaps drunken, in his despair might hurt even his own children?" Tremayne pressed.

"Yes, sir," Orme conceded. " 'Course it is. But poor men don't 'ave cigars to do it with. It isn't a bad temper that makes you light a cigar, smoke it till it's hot, then hold the end of it against a child's body till it burns through the skin into the flesh, and then makes scabs that bleed."

Several people in the gallery cried out, stifling the sound instantly, and one of the jurors looked as if he might be sick. His face was sweaty, and had a faintly greenish hue. The man next to him grasped his arm to steady him.

Tremayne waited a moment before going on.

Rathbone understood. He would have done the same.

"Did that prompt any particular course of action from you?" Tremayne asked, retaining his composure as if with difficulty.

"Yes, sir," Orme answered. "We visited the places we knew of where people kept boys o' that age to use. We'd looked at them pretty hard, sir. 'E wasn't a chimney sweep's boy, nor a laborer of any kind. Easy enough to see by 'is 'ands. No dirt from chimneys, no calluses from oakum picking or any other sort of thing like that. But if you'll pardon me, sir, in public like, there were other parts of his body that'd been 'ard used." His face was red, his voice cracking with emotion.

"The surgeon didn't testify to that," Tremayne pointed out reluctantly. His body was oddly stiff as he stood, his usual grace lost.

"We didn't ask 'im, sir. It isn't medical, it's common sense," Orme told him.

"I see. Did that cause you to look anywhere in particular?"

"We tried lots o' places up and down the river. It's our job to know where they are."

"And did you find out where he came from?"

"No, sir, not for sure."

"Only 'sure' will do here, Mr. Orme."

"I know that!" Orme's temper was suddenly close to the surface, the emotion too raw to govern. "We know that Jericho Phillips kept a lot o' boys, especially young ones, small as five or six years old. Took them in from wherever 'e found them, and gave them a bed and food. Lot of them lived on a boat, but we'd never find anything there. He had lookouts, and they always knew who we were."

Rathbone considered objecting that Orme was stating an opinion rather than presenting evidence, but it was hardly worth making a fuss over. He decided against it.

"So you never saw anything amiss on his boat?" Tremayne concluded.

"No, sir."

"Then why did you raise his name at all?" Tremayne asked gently, as if he were puzzled. "What was it that drew him to your attention, other than a growing desperation to find at least a name for this dead boy?"

Orme let out his breath in a sigh. "An informant came to us and said that Jericho Phillips was keeping a kind o' cross between a brothel and a peep show on his boat. He 'ad young boys there and forced them to perform certain...acts..." He stopped, obviously embarrassed. His eyes flickered to the public gallery, aware that there must be women there. Then he looked away again, angry with himself for his weakness.

Tremayne did not help him. It was clear from the expression on his face, the slight downturn of his mouth, that he found the subject repellent, and touched on it only because he owed it to the dead, and to the truth.

"Unnatural acts, with children," Orme said miserably. "Boys. 'E used cameras to make pictures, so 'e could sell them to people. Get more money than just from those who watched." His face was hot, the color reaching all the way up to his hair.

Tremayne was exquisitely careful. "That is what this man told you, Mr. Orme?"

"Yes, sir."

"I see." Tremayne shifted his balance a little. "And did you request that he take you so you might ascertain for yourself if this were true? After all, he could have invented the entire story, couldn't he?"

"Yes, sir, 'e could. But 'e refused to take us, or to testify. 'E said he was being blackmailed, because 'e'd looked at the pictures. It was my opinion that 'e'd probably bought some as well. 'E was scared stiff."

This time Rathbone did rise to his feet and object. "The witness may be of that opinion, my lord, but that is not evidence."

Tremayne inclined his head in acknowledgment, smiling a little, then turned again to Orme. "Did he say so, Mr. Orme?"

"No, sir, he wouldn't even give us 'is name."

Tremayne shrugged in a very slight, elegant gesture of confusion. "Was there any purpose in his coming forward at all, if he was prepared to say so little, and not to swear to any of it?"

"No, sir, not really," Orme admitted. "Maybe it just helped us narrow the search, so to speak. Mr. Durban was rather good at drawing. He made a sketch of the dead boy's face, and then a picture of how he might 'ave looked standing up and dressed. We took it around for a couple of weeks or so, to see if anyone could give 'im a name, or say anything about 'im."

"And could they?"

"Yes, sir. They said 'e used to be a mudlark. A young lad came and told us they picked coal up off the tideline o' the river when they were six or seven years old. He just knew him as Fig, but he was certain it was 'im, because of the funny way his hair grew at the front. Never knew his 'ole name, or where he come from. Maybe he was a foundling, and nobody knew much more. He disappeared a few years ago, but this mudlark wouldn't say exactly where or when. Couldn't remember, and it wasn't any use pushing 'im. We went and found a few more lads, and they confirmed what 'e said. They all knew 'im as 'Fig.' "

Tremayne turned towards Rathbone, but there was no point contesting the identification. Whether it was the same boy or not was immaterial to the charge. He was somebody's child.

Tremayne led Orme in some detail through the process of the various other people who had confirmed that they knew the boy. One had added that his whole name was Walter Figgis. Others, through a laborious process that Rathbone allowed Tremayne to abbreviate, confirmed that there were boats on the river that gave shelter to children. On some of them the boys were appallingly misused. But of course there was no proof. Tremayne, wisely, barely touched on that. The generality was enough to shake the jury, and the audience in court, to a revulsion so deep that many of them were physically trembling. Some looked nauseated to the point that Rathbone was afraid they might not be able to control themselves.

Rathbone himself was aware of a depth of distress he had seldom felt before, only perhaps in cases of the most depraved rape and torture. He looked up at Phillips and saw nothing in him at all resembling human pity or shame. A wave of fury almost drowned him. The sweat broke out on his body, and the wig on his head was like a helmet. The black silk gown suffocated him as he held his arms to his sides. He was imprisoned in it.

Then he was afraid. Was Phillips beyond human emotions, unreachable? And Rathbone had promised to use all his skills to set him free again to go back to the river. He had no escape from doing it; it was his covenantal duty, which he had already accepted, and he had given his word, not only to the court, but also to Arthur Ballinger, and thus obliquely to Margaret. To refuse now would suggest to the jury that he knew something that condemned the accused beyond doubt. He was trapped by the law that he wanted above all to serve.

He had the ugly sense that Phillips knew that just as well as he did himself. Indeed, that was why he showed no fear.

They adjourned for lunch before Tremayne was finished. Orme was one of his major witnesses, and he intended to gain every word of damnation from him that he could.

They resumed after the shortest adjournment possible, and began the afternoon with Tremayne asking Orme about Durban's death.

"Mr. Durban died last December. Is that correct, Mr. Orme?" Tremayne asked, his manner suitably grave.

"Yes, sir."

"And Mr. Monk succeeded him as commander of the River Police at the main station, which is in Wapping?"

"Yes, sir."

Lord Justice Sullivan was beginning to look a trifle impatient. His frown deepened. "Is there some point to this, Mr. Tremayne? The succession of events seem to be plain enough. Mr. Durban did all he could to solve the case for the police, and did not succeed, so he continued on his own time. Unfortunately, he died, and Mr. Monk took over his position, and presumably his papers, including notes on unsolved cases. Is there more to it than that?"

Tremayne was slightly taken aback. "No, my lord. I believe there is nothing to contest."

"Then I daresay the jury will follow it simply enough. Proceed." There was an edge to Sullivan's voice, and his hands on the great bench in front of him were clenched. He was not enjoying this case. Perhaps to him it was simply a tragedy of the darkest and most squalid sort. Certainly there were no fine points of law, and none of the intellectual rigor Rathbone knew he liked. He wondered quickly whether Tremayne knew him socially. They lived not far from each other, to the south of the river. Were they friends, enemies, or possibly not even acquaintances? Rathbone knew Tremayne and liked him. Sullivan he had never met outside the courtroom.

Tremayne turned back to Orme in the witness box. "Mr. Orme, was the case officially reopened? New evidence, perhaps?"

"No, sir. Mr. Monk was just looking through the papers to see if there was anything . . ."

Rathbone rose to his feet.

"Yes, yes, yes!" Sullivan said quickly. "Mr. Orme, please restrict yourself to what you know, what you saw, and what you did."

Orme flushed. "Yes, my lord." He looked at Tremayne with reproach. "Mr. Monk told me 'e'd found papers about a case we'd never closed, and 'e showed me Mr. Durban's notes on the Figgis case. He said it would be a good thing if we could close it now. I agreed with him. It always bothered me that we 'adn't finished it."

"Will you please tell the court what you yourself did then? Since you worked on it with Mr. Durban, presumably Mr. Monk was keen to avail himself of your knowledge?"

"Yes, sir, very keen."

Tremayne then took Orme through the trail of evidence. He asked about the lightermen, bargees, lumpers, stevedores, ferrymen, chandlers, landlords, pawnbrokers, tobacconists, and quayside news vendors he and Monk had spoken to in the endless pursuit of the connection between the boy, Fig, and the boat in which Jericho Phillips plied his trade. They were always looking for someone who could and would swear to the use of Phillips's boat, and the fact that Fig was there against his will. It was all circumstantial, little threads, second- and thirdhand links.

Rathbone looked at the jury and saw the confusion in their faces, and eventually the boredom. They could not follow it. The disgust was there, the anger and the helplessness, but the certainty of legal proof still eluded them. They were lost in complexity, and because they were still sickeningly aware of the crime, they were frustrated and becoming angry. The day closed with a feeling of hatred in the room, and the police crowded closely around Phillips as he was taken down the stairs to the prison below the court. The mood was ugly with the weight of old, unresolved pain.

Rathbone began cross-examining Orme the next morning. He knew exactly what he needed to draw from him, but he was also aware that he must be extremely careful not to antagonize the jury, whose sympathies were entirely with the victim, and with the police who had tried so very hard to bring him some kind of justice. He stood in the middle of the courtroom floor in the open space between the gallery and the witness stand, deliberately at ease, as if he were a trifle in awe of the occasion, identifying with Orme, not with the machinery of the law.

"I imagine you deal with many harrowing tragedies, Mr. Orme," he said quietly. He wanted to force the jury to strain to hear him, to make their attention total. The emotion must be grave, subdued, even private with each man, as though he were alone with the horror and the burden of it. Then they would understand Durban, and why Monk, in his turn, had taken the same path. He had not expected to dislike doing this so much. Facing the real man was very different from the intellectual theories of justice, no matter how passionately felt. But there was no way to turn back now without betrayal. When he had to question Hester it would be worse.

"Yes, sir," Orme agreed.

Rathbone nodded.

"But it has not blunted your sensibilities, or made you any less dedicated to finding justice for the victims of unspeakable torture and death."

"No, sir." Orme's face was pale, his hands hidden by his sides, but his shoulders were high and tight.

"Did Mr. Durban feel as deeply?"

"Yes, sir. This case was . . . was one of the worst. If you'd seen that boy's body, sir, wasted and burned like it was, then 'is throat cut near through, and dumped in the river as if he were an animal, you'd have felt the same."

"I imagine I would," Rathbone said quietly, his head bent a trifle as if he were in the presence of the dead now.

Lord Justice Sullivan leaned forward, his face pinched, his mouth drawn tight. "Is there some purpose to this, Sir Oliver? I trust it has not slipped your mind which party you represent in this case?" There was a note of warning in his voice, and his eyes were suddenly flat and hard.

"No, my lord," Rathbone said respectfully. "I wish to find the truth. It is far too grave and too terrible a matter to settle for anything less, in the interests of humanity."

Sullivan grunted, and for a moment Rathbone was afraid he had taken his play too far. He glanced sideways at the jury, and knew he was right. Relief washed over him with physical warmth. Then he remembered Phillips shivering in Newgate and his horror of dripping water, and his satisfaction vanished. He turned again to Orme. "You and Mr. Durban worked all your duty hours, and many beyond?"

"Yes, sir." Orme knew not to answer more than he was asked.

"Was this same passionate dedication also true of Mr. Monk?" He had to ask; it was the plan.

"Yes, sir." There was no hesitation in Orme; if anything, he was more positive.

"I see. It is not surprising, and much to be respected."

Tremayne was fidgeting in his seat, growing restive at what seemed to be a purposeless reaffirmation of what he himself had just established. He suspected Rathbone of something, but he could not deduce what, and it troubled him.

The jury was merely puzzled.

Rathbone knew he must make his point now. One by one he touched on the evidence that first Durban and then Monk had pursued, asking Orme for the facts that specifically connected the abuse of the boys to Phillips's boat. Never once did he suggest that it had not happened, only that the horror of the facts had obscured the lack of defining links to Phillips.

The boat existed. Boys from the age of five or six up to about thirteen unquestionably lived on it. There were floating brothels for the use of men with any kind of taste in sexual pleasures, either to participate, or merely to watch. There were pornographic photographs for sale in the dark alleys and byways of the river. What unquestionable proof had Durban, Monk, or Orme himself found that the boys so abused were the ones to whom Phillips gave a home?

There was none. The horror of the cruelty, the greed, and the obscenity of it, had moved all three men so deeply that they had been too desperate to stop it and punish the perpetrators of it than to make certain of their facts. It was only too easy to understand. Any decent man might fall into the same error. But surely any decent man would also be appalled at the idea of convicting the wrong person of such a heinous crime, deserving of the gallows?

The court adjourned for lunch with quite suddenly a complete and awful confusion, a knowledge that all the certainties had been swept away. Only the horror remained, and a sense of helplessness.

Rathbone had accomplished exactly what he had intended. It was brilliant. Even the subtle and clever Tremayne had not seen the trap before he was in it. He had left pale-faced, angry with himself.

Hester was waiting to testify to her part in the investigation when Tremayne came to her during the lunch adjournment. She was sitting in one of the public houses that provided food, but she was too tense to do more than take an occasional bite of her sandwich, and then found it difficult to swallow.

He sat down opposite her, his face grim, his manner apologetic. He too declined to eat more than a sandwich and drink a glass of white wine.

"I'm sorry, Mrs. Monk," he said immediately once they were alone. He spoke quickly, so as not to be overheard by others passing close to them. "It has not gone as well as I had hoped, in fact, rather as I had taken for granted. It is proving harder to make the connections between Phillips and the victims of his depravity than I had expected."

He must have seen the surprise on her face. "Sir Oliver is one of the most brilliant attorneys in England, far too clever to attack us openly," he said. "I knew there was something wrong when he played up the horror of the crime. It should have warned me of what he was doing."

She felt a chill of dismay. "What is he doing?"

Tremayne blushed, and the last shred of irony vanished from his face, replaced by gentleness. "Did you not know he was defending this case, Mrs. Monk?"

"No." Then instantly she saw the understanding in his face and wished she had not admitted it. He must have known or have sensed something of her friendship with Rathbone, and had seen her sense of betrayal.

"I'm sorry," he said quietly. "How clumsy of me. He is suggesting that the police were moved as much by pity and outrage as by logic. They proved the crime was committed, but forgot the finer elements of connecting it unarguably with Jericho Phillips."

He took a sip of his wine, his eyes not leaving hers. "He has made it obvious that so far we have provided no motive for him to have tortured and murdered one of his own boys—assuming we can ever prove Figgis was one of his. And he is quite right that we have not so far done that beyond a reasonable doubt."

"Who could doubt it?" she said hotly. "It all fits together and makes the most excellent sense. In fact, it is the only answer that makes sense at all."

"On balance of probability it does," he agreed. He leaned across the table a little. "The law requires that it be beyond all reasonable doubt, if we are to hang a man for it. You know that, Mrs. Monk. You are not a novice at the law."

Now she was shivering, in spite of the heat inside the stuffy room with its gleaming tankards on the bar, its sawdust floor muffling footsteps, and the smells of ale, food, and too many people crushed together.

"You don't mean he's going to get away with it?" she asked huskily. It was a possibility she had not even considered. Phillips was guilty. He was brutal, sadistic, and profoundly corrupt. He had abused numberless children, and murdered at least one. He had nearly murdered a lighterman, simply to divert the river police so he could escape. Monk and Orme had seen him do it.

"No, of course not," Tremayne assured her. "But I will have to describe some very violent and offensive scenes, and ask you to relive on the witness stand things that I am sure you would rather forget. I apologize for it, because I had hoped to spare you."

"For heaven's sake, Mr. Tremayne," she said sharply. "I don't care in the slightest what you question me about, or whom! If it is unpleasant, or discomfiting, what on earth does that matter? We are talking about the misery and death of children. What kind of person is concerned about such trivialities as comfort at such a cost?"

"Some people will allow others to pay almost anything, in order to avoid embarrassment to themselves, Mrs. Monk," he replied.

She did not consider that worthy of an answer.

She took the stand, climbing up the steep, curving steps carefully so as not to trip over her skirt. She faced the court, seeing Tremayne below her in the open space reserved for the lawyers. Lord Justice Sullivan sat in his high, magnificently carved seat to the right. The twelve somber jurymen were opposite in their double row under the windows. The public gallery was behind the lawyers' tables.

She was not afraid to look ahead to where Jericho Phillips sat in the dock, above the whole proceedings. His face was jagged: the high-boned nose, sharp cheekbones, crooked eyebrows, and hair that even water would not make lie straight. She recognized no emotion whatever in his face. Perhaps it was in locked hands or a shivering body behind the high ledge, out of sight.

She did not look to where Rathbone sat quietly, waiting his turn, nor did she try to see if Margaret was in the public gallery behind him. Just at the moment she did not wish to know.

Tremayne began. His voice sounded confident, but she had come to know him well enough over the last few weeks to notice the slightly awkward way he stood and that his hands were restless. He was not as sure of himself as he had been before the trial began.

"Mrs. Monk, is it correct that you have created and now run a clinic situated in the Portpool Lane, for the treatment, at no charge, of street women who are ill or injured, and unable to obtain help any other way?"

"Yes it is."

"Are you financially rewarded for this?"

"No." The answer sounded very bare. She wanted to add something, but could not find the words. She was saved from the attempt by Rathbone rising to his feet.

"If it may please the court, my lord, the defense will stipulate to the fact that Mrs. Monk was an outstanding nurse under Miss Florence Nightingale during the Crimean War, and that on her return to this country she worked in hospitals, courageously and tirelessly, endeavoring to bring about some very necessary reforms."

There was a murmur of admiration from the gallery.

"She then turned her attention to the plight of street women," Rathbone continued. "Reduced to prostitution by abandonment, or whatever other crime. She created, at her own expense, a clinic where they could come for treatment of injury or disease. It is now a recognized establishment drawing voluntary help from Society in general. Indeed, my own wife gives much of her time in its cause, both to raise charitable contributions, and to work there at cooking, cleaning, and tending the sick. I can think of no finer work a woman may perform."

Several of the jurors gasped and their faces brightened into uncertain smiles. Even Sullivan was moved to an expression of admiration. Only Tremayne looked nervous.

"Do you have anything to add, Mr. Tremayne?" Sullivan asked.

Tremayne was off balance. "No, my lord, thank you." A little more tight-lipped, he looked up at Hester and resumed his questioning. "In the nature of this work, Mrs. Monk, have you had occasion to learn a great deal more than most of us could know about the business of those who sell their bodies for the sexual indulgence of others?"

"Yes, one cannot help learning."

"I imagine so. In order to avail himself of such knowledge, did Mr. Monk ask for your assistance in discovering more about how Walter Figgis might have lived, been abused, and then killed?"

"Yes. It was far easier for me to gain the trust of those who deal in such things. I knew people who could help me, and take me to speak to others who might never speak to the police."

"Precisely. Would you please tell the court, step by step, what you found out with reference to Walter Figgis?" Tremayne directed. "I regret the necessity of such distasteful material, but I require you to be specific. Otherwise the jury cannot decide fairly what is true, and what we have suggested but failed to prove. Do you understand?"

"Yes, of course I do."

Then gently and very clearly he led her through all the long questioning, collecting, deducing, then more questioning, until they had gathered the evidence creating a portion of Fig's life, his disappearance from the riverbank to Phillips's floating brothel, his years there, and finally his death. Every piece of information was gained from someone she could name, although she chose to give only the nicknames by which they were known on the street, and Rathbone did not object.

"If Fig was working as the evidence says," Tremayne continued, "why on earth would Phillips, or any other brothel keeper, wish to harm his property at all, let alone murder it? What use is Fig to him dead?"

Hester knew her face showed her revulsion, but she could not control it. "Men whose taste is in children have no interest in the same person once they begin to show the signs of coming manhood. It has nothing to do with any kind of affection. They are used to relieve a need, as a public lavatory is used."

There was a ripple of disgust around the room, as if someone had opened a door into a cesspit and the smell had drifted in.

Tremayne's own wry, sensitive face reflected it most of all. "Are you suggesting that such men murder all children as they begin to show signs of growing up?" he asked.

"No," she replied as steadily as she could. Reliving her fury and pity in careful words was making her feel a little queasy. It seemed offensively clinical, although the faces of the jury reflected it as anything but. She drew in her breath. "No, I have been informed that usually they are sold to any merchant captain willing to buy them, and they serve as cabin boys, or whatever is needed." She permitted her expression to convey the darker meaning of the phrase. "They leave port on the next ship out, and are maybe years gone. In fact, they may never come back."

"I see." Tremayne looked pale himself. Perhaps he had sons. "Then why would this not happen to Fig?"

"It might have been intended to," she answered, for the first time moving her glance from Tremayne and looking at Rathbone. She saw misery and revulsion in his face, and wondered what could possibly have happened that had compelled him to defend Jericho Phillips. Surely he could not ever have done it willingly? He was a civilized man, offended by vulgarity, an honorable man. She had once thought him too fastidious in his passions for him to love her with the totality that she needed.

"Mrs. Monk?" Tremayne prompted her.

"He might have rebelled," she completed her thought. "If he caused trouble he would be less easy to sell. He might have been a leader of the younger boys, and been murdered as an example of discipline. No quicker way to suppress a rebellion in the ranks than to execute the leader." She sounded cynical, even to her own ears. Did the crowd, the jury, Rathbone himself, realize that she spoke so to hide a pain of understanding that was unbearable?

Was Rathbone being pressured by someone into doing this? Was it possible that he had not realized how repulsive the reality was? Did he even think how the money was earned that he took in payment? If he had, how could he accept it?

"Thank you, Mrs. Monk," Tremayne said softly, his face bleak and lips tight as if the grief of it were clenched inside him. "You have shown us a very terrible picture, but one that is tragically believable. May I commend you for your courage and pity in the work you do."

There was a murmur of approval. Two of the jurors nodded and one blew his nose fiercely.

"The court is obliged to you, madam," Lord Justice Sullivan said quietly. His face was a mask of disgust, and there was high color in his cheeks, as if the blood burned beneath his skin. "You are excused for today. No doubt tomorrow Sir Oliver Rathbone will wish to question you." He glanced at Rathbone.

"May it please the court, my lord," Rathbone affirmed.

The court was duly adjourned and Hester climbed down from the witness stand, grasping the railing. She felt drained, even a little dizzy. One of the ushers offered her his arm, but she declined it, thanking him.

She was in the hall outside the courtroom when she saw Rathbone coming towards her. She had deliberately chosen that way of leaving in hope of meeting him. She wished to ask him, face-to-face, what had made him take such a case. If he were in some kind of trouble, why had he not asked Monk for help? It could hardly be financial. Destitution could hardly be worse than descending to this.

She moved to the center of the hall so he could not avoid encountering her.

He saw her and faltered in his step, but he did not stop. She did, waiting for him to reach her, his eyes on hers.

He moved steadily forward. He was only a few yards from her, and she was about to speak when another man, older, came out of one of the side rooms. His face was familiar, but she could not immediately place him.

"Oliver!" he called.

Rathbone turned, his relief at escape momentarily undisguised. "Arthur! Good to see you. How are you?"

Of course: Arthur Ballinger, Margaret's father. There was nothing Hester could do now. The conversation she wished for could only be held in absolute private, even from Margaret. In fact, perhaps most of all from Margaret. She did not wish her to ever know how close Hester and Rathbone had once been. What she might guess was one thing; knowledge was another.

She lifted her chin a little higher, and kept walking.

THREE

*R*athbone's cross-examination of Hester began as soon as court resumed the next morning. She took her place again in the witness stand. She was wearing a plain, blue-gray dress, not unlike the sort of uniform a nurse would wear, but more flatteringly cut, and she knew it made the most of her fair coloring and steady wide gray eyes. She wanted to appear both competent and feminine, and of course respectable. Tremayne had mentioned this to her, quite unnecessarily. She understood what a jury wanted and what kind of person they would believe. During Monk's many cases there had been times when she had testified, or seen others do so, and watched the faces of the jurors.

"May I add my admiration to that of the court, Mrs. Monk," Rathbone began. "It is a brave and charitable work that you do."

"Thank you." She did not trust him, even though she knew he did admire her, intensely, even with a degree of envy for her passion. Too often thought had robbed him of action. She simply cared enough to take the risk anyway. Now he stood elegantly in the middle of the floor, and complimented her.

"How much of your time do you put to your work in Portpool Lane, Mrs. Monk?" he went on.

Tremayne moved in his seat uneasily. Hester knew it was because he was waiting for Rathbone to attack, and he did not know from which direction it would come.

"It varies," Hester replied, meeting Rathbone's eyes. "At times of crisis we work all the time, taking turns to sleep. At other times when there is relatively little to do, I may not go in every day, perhaps only two or three times a week."

"A crisis?" Rathbone turned the word over as if tasting it. "What would constitute a crisis, Mrs. Monk?"

The question sounded innocent, and yet Hester sensed a trap in it, if not now, then later, after he had led her carefully with other questions. The ease with which he asked it was like a warning. Why was he defending Jericho Phillips? What had happened to him while she had not been paying attention?

He was waiting for her answer. It felt as if everyone in the court was looking at her, waiting with him.

"Several people seriously injured at once, perhaps in a fight," she answered levelly. "Or worse than that, in the winter, seven or eight people with pneumonia, or bronchitis, or perhaps consumption. And then a bad wound, or gangrene on top of it."

He looked impressed. "And how do you cope with all of that?"

Tremayne stared forward, as if he would object, but no one was listening or watching him.

"We don't always succeed," Hester replied. "But we help. Most of the time it isn't nearly as bad as that."

"Don't you get the same people in again and again?" Rathbone asked.

"Yes, of course. Any doctor does." She smiled very slightly. "What has that to do with it? You try to help whom you can, one person, one day at a time."

"Or day, and night, and day," he amended.

"If necessary." She was anxious now as well. He was making a heroine out of her, as if he had temporarily forgotten that she was there to give the evidence that would damn Jericho Phillips.

"You have a marvelous dedication to the poor and the wretched, Mrs. Monk." Rathbone said it with respect, even admiration, but she was waiting for the question beyond, the one that hid an attack.

"Thank you. I don't think of it that way, but simply as an attempt to do what you can," she answered.

"You say that quite casually, Mrs. Monk." Rathbone moved back and then turned and walked the other way. The gesture had a grace that drew the eyes. He looked up at her again. "But surely you are speaking of a passion, a self-sacrifice that is far beyond that which most people experience?"

"I don't see it as such," she answered, not merely in modesty, but because it was true. She loved her work. She would be hypocritical were she to allow it to be painted as a nobility, at cost to herself.

Rathbone smiled. "I expected that you would say that, Mrs. Monk. There are some women, like your mentor, Miss Nightingale, whose life is to give their time and emotion to bettering the lot of others."

There was a murmur of approval around the room.

Tremayne rose to his feet, his expression confused and unhappy. Something was happening that he did not understand, but he knew it was dangerous. "My lord, I am aware that Sir Oliver is long and well acquainted with Mrs. Monk, and that Lady Rathbone also gives her time freely to the Portpool Lane Clinic. Admirable as this is, there is no question in Sir Oliver's observations, and they seem irrelevant to the case against Jericho Phillips."

Sullivan raised his eyebrows. "Sir Oliver, in the unlikelihood that Mrs. Monk is unaware of your regard for her, would it not be better to make such remarks privately?"

Rathbone colored, perhaps at the implication, but he was not disconcerted with his tactic. "The relevance will become clear, my lord," he replied, with an edge to his voice. "If you will permit me?" But without waiting he turned again to Hester.

Reluctantly Tremayne resumed his seat.

"Were you acquainted with the late Commander Durban, Mrs. Monk?" Rathbone asked mildly.

He knew the circumstances of the Louvain case; he had played a major part in it. Of course he already knew that she did not know Durban, except through Monk.

"No," she answered, uncertain why he had asked. He was not challenging her evidence, which was what she had expected, and prepared for. "Only by repute."

"From whom?" he asked.

"To begin with, my husband. Later I also heard Mr. Orme speak very highly of him."

"What opinion did you form of his character?"

She could not understand why he asked. Her answer was bound to be against every point he must establish to raise any doubt as to Phillips's guilt. Surely it was inconceivable that he would deliberately sabotage his own case? It was contrary to everything she had ever known of him that he would take a case, any case whatever, in order to deliberately lose it!

"Mrs. Monk?" he prompted.

"That he was a man of passion, humor, and great integrity," she answered. "He was a good policeman, and an exceptional leader of men. He was honorable and brave, and in the end he gave his life to save others."

Rathbone smiled very slightly, as if that were the answer he had not only foreseen, but also wanted.

"I will not ask you the circumstances. I know what they are; I also was there at the time, and it was exactly as you say. But it was a matter that, for the public good, must be kept discreet." He moved a step or two, as if to mark the change of subject. "There is no purpose in my asking if you are devoted to your husband; how else would you answer but in the affirmative? But I will ask you to describe your circumstances at the time Mr. Monk first met Mr. Durban. For example, were you well off? How was your husband employed? Had he good opportunities for advancement?"

Lord Justice Sullivan moved uncomfortably on his high seat and looked at Rathbone with a flicker of anxiety, then away from him and beyond to somewhere in the body of the court, as if to gauge how the public mood interpreted this extraordinary direction of events.

Tremayne half rose to his feet, then sank back again. By not allowing Hester to answer, he would be implying that she or Monk had something to hide or to be ashamed of. The jury might imagine all kinds of things, all of them discreditable.

"My husband was a private agent of inquiry," Hester replied. "Our circumstances were uncertain from week to week. Occasionally clients did not pay, and some cases were incapable of solution."

"That cannot have been easy for you," Rathbone sympathized. "And obviously no advancement was possible. As the court is aware, Mr. Monk succeeded Mr. Durban as commander of the Wapping Station of the River Police, which is a fine job, with good remuneration, high status, and opportunity for advancement to even higher rank eventually. Even Commissioner of Police would not be impossible for an able and ambitious man. How did it come about that Mr. Monk took this position, and not one of the men already employed there? Mr. Orme, for example."

"Mr. Durban recommended him," Hester replied, now with some idea where Rathbone might be leading. But even if she were correct, and saw every step ahead before she reached it, she could see no way of escape. Her hands felt clammy on the railing, and yet she was cold inside. The air was stale in the crowded room.

"You must be very grateful for such a remarkable and unforeseen improvement in your circumstances," Rathbone went on. "Your husband is now a commander in the River Police, and you have financial security and social respect. And apart from yourself, you must be very pleased for your husband also. Is he happy in the River Police?"

She could not possibly say other than that he was, even if in fact he hated it. Fortunately she did not have to lie, as Rathbone knew.

"Yes, he is. They are a fine body of men with a high reputation for both skill and honor, and he is proud to be among them."

"Let us not be overmodest, Mrs. Monk; to lead them!" Rathbone corrected her. "Are you not proud of him also? It is a great achievement."

"Yes, of course I am proud of him." Again, she could give no other answer.

He did not belabor the point. He had made it sufficiently for the jury. Both she and Monk owed Durban a great deal, personally and professionally. Rathbone had placed her in a position where she had to say so, or appear utterly graceless. Now anything in which she supported Durban would appear as gratitude, and be suspected as founded in emotion rather than fact. How well he knew her. He had forgotten nothing of her from the days when they had been much closer, when he had been in love with her, not with Margaret.

She felt very alone in the stand with everyone in the court staring at her, and with Rathbone's knowledge of her so delicate and intimate. She was horribly vulnerable.

"Mrs. Monk," Rathbone resumed. "You played a large part in helping identify this tragic boy, through your knowledge of the abuse of women and children in the trade of sexual relations." He said it with distaste, reflecting what all the people in the gallery—and more particularly in the jury box—must feel. "It was you who learned that he was once a mudlark." He turned slightly in a peculiarly graceful gesture. "In case there is anyone in the jury who does not understand the term, would you be good enough to explain it to us?"

She had no choice but to do as he asked. He was guiding her as a skilled rider does a horse, and she felt equally controlled. To rebel in the public gaze of the court would make her appear ridiculous. How well he knew her!

"A mudlark is a person who spends their time on the banks of the river, between low and high tide lines," she said obediently. "They salvage anything that may be of value, and then sell it. Most of them are children, but not all. The things they find are largely brass screws and fittings, pieces of china, lumps of coal, that sort of thing."

He looked interested, as if he were not already familiar with every detail of the facts.

"How do you come to know this? It does not seem to lie within the area of your usual assistance. Who did you ask for the information that led to your discovering that the boy, Fig, had once been a mudlark?"

"In a case a short while ago a young mudlark was injured. I looked after him for a couple of weeks." She wondered why he was asking about Scuff. Did he mean to challenge the identification of the body?

"Really? How old was he? What was his name?" he inquired.

Why was he asking? He knew Scuff. He had been in the sewers with them, as desperate to ensure Scuff's safety as any of them.

"He is known as Scuff, and he thinks he is about eleven," she replied, her voice catching with emotion in spite of her efforts to remain detached.

Rathbone raised his eyebrows. "He thinks?"

"Yes. He doesn't know."

"Did he identify Fig?"

So it was the identification! "No. He introduced me to older boys, and vouched for me, so they would tell me the truth."

"This boy Scuff trusts you?"

"I hope so."

"You took him into your home when he was injured, and cared for him, nursed him back to health?"

"Yes."

"And an affection grew between you?"

"Yes."

"Do you have children of your own, Mrs. Monk?"

She felt as if he had slapped her without warning. It was not that she had desperately wanted children; she was happy with Monk and her work. It was the implication that somehow she was lacking, which hurt, that she had taken Scuff in not because she liked him, but to fill an emptiness in herself. By a sort of oblique reference backward, it made it seem as if all she had done in the clinic, and even in the Crimea, had been to compensate for her own lack of family, of purpose, in the more usual sense.

It was not true. She had a husband she loved far more than most women did theirs; she was married of choice, not convenience or ambition or need. She had work to do that stretched her intellect, and used her imagination and courage. Most women got up in the morning to the same endless domestic round, filling their days with words rather than actions, or accomplishing small tasks that had to be begun again in exactly the same fashion the next day, and the day after. Hester had only once in her life been bored, and that was for the brief time spent in the social round before going to the Crimea.

But if she said any of that, she would sound as if she were defensive. He had attacked her so delicately, so obliquely, that people would think she was protesting too much. She would immediately make him seem right.

They were all waiting now for her to reply. She could see the beginning of pity in their faces. Even Tremayne looked uncomfortable.

"No, I don't have children," she answered the question. It was on the tip of her tongue to point out that neither did he, but that would be unbecoming; again, an attack in order to defend, before there was justification for it.

"May I say that it is a very noble thing you are doing, giving of your time and means to fight for those children of others who suffer from the abuse and neglect of the very people who should be caring for them." He spoke sincerely, and yet after what he had said before, it still managed to sound like pity. He moved his hand in the air as if to dismiss the subject. "So you sought the help of other mudlarks to identify the body of this poor boy who was found near Horseferry Stairs. And because of your rescue of Scuff, they were willing to help you, in a manner that they would not help the police. Is that accurate?"

"They helped," she replied. "I did not attribute motive to them." It sounded sharp, as if she were defending herself. It took all the self-control she could muster to keep her voice from shaking and her expression mild. "But if I had, I would think it to protect themselves, and perhaps act in some fairness to the boy who had been one of them."

Rathbone smiled. "You think well of them, Mrs. Monk. Your trust and affection do you credit. I am sure every woman in this court would like to think she might do the same."

In one sentence he had turned it into an issue of being feminine, something charitable but unrealistic. How clever of him, and how very unfair. He knew she was the least sentimental of people. She must attack him back, or be mowed under.

"I am an army nurse, Sir Oliver, as you mentioned earlier." Her voice shook in spite of all her efforts, and the tone was sharper than she meant it to be. "Wounds are real; they do not stop bleeding because of well-meaning idealism or kind judgments of affection. Gangrene, typhoid, and starvation do not respond to woolly-minded good wishes. I have quite often failed, especially in reforms I would like to have brought in, but because I spoke too bluntly, not because I was sentimental. I thought you knew that of me. But perhaps it was you who were too kind in your judgments, and saw what you wished to see, what you thought womanly and becoming, and easy to deal with."

A flare of surprise lit in his eyes, and of admiration. This time it was honest, not assumed for the jury.

"I stand corrected, Mrs. Monk," he apologized. "Of course you are right. You never lacked courage, only tact. You saw what needed to be done, but did not have the knowledge of human nature to persuade people to do it. You did not foresee the arrogance, the short-sightedness, or the selfishness of those with interests vested in things remaining as they are. You are idealistic; you see what could be and strive to bring it about. You fight with passion, courage, and honor for the oppressed, the sick, the forgotten of the world. You are disobedient to the law when it is unjust, and loyal at any cost to what is right. Is that a fairer assessment of your character?"

It was fair, even generous. It was also damning of her as an impartial witness. The court might both like and admire her, but it would always judge whatever she said against the force of her beliefs, and emotion would win. She had turned Rathbone's argument around, but he had still beaten her.

He went on to take apart all the evidence she had gathered through the witnesses learned of in her dealings with Portpool Lane. For every one of them he could show that they had benefited from her care. He worded it so it seemed that their indebtedness would cause them to say whatever she wished them to, not in deliberate deceit but in the desire to please a woman whose help they depended upon. In spite of the praise he had given her, she still appeared worthy but driven more by feelings than by reason, passionately tireless for justice towards those she saw as needy, and furious for vengeance against those who preyed upon them. She was feminine; he had harped on about her womanliness. She was vulnerable; he had subtly reminded them that she was childless. And she had poor judgment; he gave no example of that, but by then he was believed without it.

She stood helpless on the stand, surrounded by strangers who saw her through Rathbone's words, and she wondered if he actually saw her that way. Was this his true opinion, and all the past courtesy was only good manners towards a woman with whom he had once been in love, but had now grown beyond? His arrogance infuriated her.

Then she was touched by the first cold splash of fear that he could be right. Perhaps she *was* led by emotion rather than a fair and equal rationality. Perhaps Monk was led by his sense of debt to Durban, as Rathbone implied, and she simply went along with it in blind loyalty.

Rathbone sat down, knowing he had succeeded superbly. She looked at his face and had no idea what he felt, or if he felt anything at all. Perhaps his intellect would always dominate his heart. That was why she had not accepted his offer of marriage, turning it aside gently, as if it had not really been made, in order not to hurt him.

Poor Margaret.

Tremayne stood up and attempted to redress the balance, but it was impossible, and he realized it quickly enough to do little damage before he sat down again.

Hester remained in the courtroom afterwards as Rathbone called other witnesses who cast doubt on Durban's honesty. It was done so subtly that at first she did not realize the impact of it. A revenue man testified as to Durban's zeal in pursuing Phillips.

"Oh, yes, sir," he said, nodding his head vigorously. " 'E was very keen. Like a terrier with a rat 'e were. Wouldn't let go fer love ner money."

"Wouldn't let go," Rathbone repeated. "For the sake of the jury, Mr. Simmons, would you describe exactly the kind of thing you are referring to? The gentlemen may have had little to do with police procedure and be unfamiliar with what is usual, and what is not. I assume you are speaking of behavior that was out of the ordinary?"

Simmons nodded again. "Yes, sir. I see what yer mean. Folks might think as all policemen are like that, an' they in't. 'E were very different, Mr. Durban were. 'E'd ask one question, and if yer didn't give 'im the answer 'e wanted, 'e'd go round it a different way, an' then another again. I've seen some o' them bull terriers what didn't 'ave a grip like 'e 'ad. If I'd been less than 'onest, I'd 'ave told 'im what 'e wanted, just to get 'im off me back."

"Indeed. Did he tell you why he was so determined to find out who killed the boy, Fig, Mr. Simmons?" Rathbone was very careful not to lead the witness, not to ask him for assumptions or evidence that was hearsay. Tremayne was unhappy with it, but there were no grounds for him to object. Hester could see it as clearly as watching a game of chess. Every move was plain, obvious the moment after it had been made, and yet impossible to forestall.

"No, sir, 'e din't," Simmons answered. "Couldn't say whether 'e 'ated Phillips 'cause 'e killed the boy, or cared about the boy 'cause it was Phillips 'oo killed 'im."

Rathbone responded quickly before Tremayne could object, or Sullivan sustain him.

"You mean his behavior gave you reason to think there was a personal dislike, above the matter of the crime? What behavior was that, Mr. Simmons?"

Tremayne half rose, then changed his mind and sank back again.

Sullivan looked at him inquiringly, a sharp interest in his face, as if he were watching a personal battle beneath the professional one, and it interested him intensely, almost excited him. Was this why he loved the law, for the combat?

Simmons was struggling with his answer, his face furrowed. "It were personal," he said at length. "I can't really say 'ow I know. Look on 'is face, way 'e spoke about 'im, language 'e used. 'E'd sometimes let go of other things, but never Phillips. 'E were real torn up with the way the boy 'ad been used, but 'e were still glad to 'ave a reason ter go after Phillips."

There was an almost indiscernible ripple of appreciation around the room.

Lord Justice Sullivan leaned sideways a little to face the witness, his face earnest, one hand clenched on the beautiful polished surface in front of him.

"Mr. Simmons, you may not state that the accused is guilty of having murdered the boy, unless you know of your own observation that he did so. Is that the case? Did you see him kill Walter Figgis?"

Simmons looked startled. He blinked, then he went white as the full import of what he had been asked dawned on him. "No, me lud, I didn't see it. I weren't there. If I 'ad been, I'd've said so at the time, an' Mr. Durban wouldn't've needed to ride me like 'e did. I don't know for meself 'oo killed the poor little devil, nor any o' them other kids up and down the river what go missing and get beaten, or whatever else 'appens to 'em."

Rathbone raised his eyebrows. "Are you saying that Mr. Durban appeared to you to be more interested in this lost child than in any other, Mr. Simmons?"

"Damn right 'e did," Simmons agreed. "Like a dog with a bone, 'e were. Couldn't 'ardly think o' nothing else."

"Surely he was equally concerned with the theft, fraud, smuggling, and other crimes that happen on the water, and dockside?" Rathbone said innocently.

"Not that I saw, no sir," Simmons replied. "Always on about Phillips, and that boy. 'Ated him, he did. Wanted to see 'im 'anged. 'E said so." He glanced up at Sullivan and then away again. "That I 'eard with me own ears."

Rathbone thanked him, and invited Tremayne to take his turn.

Hester could think of a dozen things to ask in rebuttal. She stared at Tremayne as if by force of will she could prompt him into doing so. She watched him rise, a little of his usual grace lost to tension. What had seemed a certainty was slipping out of his hands. He looked pale.

"Mr. Simmons," he began very politely. "You say that Mr. Durban gave you no reason for his eagerness to catch whoever abused, tortured, and then murdered this boy, and as you yourself suggest, perhaps many others like him?"

Simmons shifted his weight uncomfortably. "No, sir, 'e didn't."

"And you found it hard to understand that he should consider the lives of children much more important than the evasion of customs duty on a cask of brandy, for example?"

Simmons started to speak, then changed his mind.

"Do you have children, Mr. Simmons?" Tremayne inquired gently, as one might of a new acquaintance.

Hester held her breath. Did he? Did it matter? What was Tremayne going to make of it? At least some of the jurors would have children, if not all of them. Her nails dug into the palms of her hands. She found that she was holding her breath.

"No, sir," Simmons answered.

Tremayne smiled very slightly. "Neither does Sir Oliver. Perhaps that might explain a great deal. It is not everyone who has Mrs. Monk's compassion for the injured and the dead who do not belong to their own family, or even their own social class."

There was a distinct rustle in the gallery now. The people on either side of Hester quite blatantly turned to look at her. One even smiled and nodded.

Simmons blushed furiously.

Tremayne wisely hid his victory. He inclined his head towards the judge, as if to thank him, and then returned to his seat.

Rathbone sounded a little less certain as he called his next witness, a dockmaster named Trenton from the Pool of London. He testified to Durban's friendship over several years with the mudlarks, beggars, and petty thieves who spent most of their lives at the river's edge. This time Rathbone was more careful to allow his witness to express his own opinions. Tremayne had scored an emotional victory, but he was going to find it a great deal more difficult to score another.

"Spent time with them," Trenton said with a slight shrug. He was a small, squarely built man with a heavy nose and mild manner, but under the respect for authority there was considerable strength, and more than fifty years of ever-hardening opinion. "Talked to 'em, gave 'em advice, sometimes even shared 'is food, or gave 'em the odd sixpence or the like."

"Was he looking for information?" Rathbone asked.

"If 'e was, 'e was a fool," Trenton answered. "You get a reputation for being a soft touch like that, an' you'll 'ave a line o' folks from Tower Bridge to the Isle o' Dogs, all ready to tell you anything you want to 'ear, for a penny or two."

"I see. Then what could he have been doing? Do you know?"

Trenton was well prepared. Tremayne leaned forward, ready to object to speculation, but he did not have the opportunity.

"Don't know what 'e was doing," he said, pushing his lower lip out in an expression of puzzlement. "Never seen another River Police, nor land neither, who spent time with beggars and drifters like 'e did, not with boys, like. They don't know much an' won't tell you anything that matters even if they do."

"How do you know that, Mr. Trenton?"

"I run a dock, Sir Oliver. I 'ave to know what people are doing on my patch, 'specially if there's a chance it's something as they shouldn't. I kept an eye on 'im, over the years. There aren't that many bent River Police, but it's not impossible. Not that I'm saying 'e was, mind you!" he added hastily. "But I watched. Thought at first 'e might be a kidsman."

"A kidsman?" Rathbone inquired, although of course he knew the word. He asked for the benefit of the jury.

Trenton understood. "A man who gets kids to do 'is stealing for 'im," he replied simply. "Mostly it's silk handkerchiefs, bits o' money, things like that. A good leather purse, maybe. But 'e weren't, of course." He shrugged again. "Just River Police with more interest in kids than anyone else."

"I see. Did he ask you about Jericho Phillips?"

Trenton rolled his eyes. "Over and over, till I was sick of telling 'im that as far as I know 'e's just a petty thief, a chancer. Maybe does a bit of smuggling, although we've never caught 'im at it. Per'aps a bit of informing, but that's all."

"Did Mr. Durban accept that answer?"

Trenton's face darkened. "No, 'e didn't. Obsession 'e 'ad, and got worse towards the time 'e died. Which was a shame," he added quickly.

"Thank you." Rathbone released him.

Tremayne looked indecisive from the moment he stood up. His face and his voice reflected exactly the fears that were beginning to touch Hester. Could they have been mistaken about Durban? Had he been a man who committed one marvelous act of nobility in an effort to redeem a life otherwise deeply flawed? Had they come in at the end, and thought all the rest was the same, when in fact it was not at all?

Tremayne was floundering, and he was acutely aware of it. It had been a decade since he had last been so subtly set off balance. There was nothing in Trenton's evidence to contest, nothing he could grasp firmly enough to turn or twist to any other meaning.

Hester wondered if he was beginning to have doubts as well. Did he wonder if Monk had been naive, driven by loyalty to a man he had known only a short time, a matter of weeks, and whose real character he had only guessed at?

For the first time Hester actually entertained the thought, for an instant, that Rathbone could be right. Yes, Phillips was an evil man, one who preyed on the weaknesses and appetites of others, but he might not be guilty of torture or murder as Durban had believed, or as Monk had accepted from him. She pushed the thought away, refusing to entertain it. It was ugly, and it was disloyal.

Rathbone resumed the presentation of the defense. He called a lighterman who had known Durban well and admired him. He asked questions gently, drawing out pieces of information as if he were aware that the process would sooner or later become painful. He was right. At the start it was easy: merely a pattern of dates and questions asked and answered. Durban had asked the lighterman about comings and goings on the water, mostly of Jericho Phillips and his boat, occasionally of other men who patronized whatever its facilities were. They professed that it offered ale and entertainment, a simple matter of an evening on the river with refreshment and a little music, performed to the taste of whatever audience presented itself.

Lord Justice Sullivan leaned forward, listening intently, his face grave.

Did the lighterman, Hurst, know for certain what that entertainment was? Rathbone continued. No, he had no personal knowledge at all. Durban had asked him that, many times. The answer was always the same. He did not know, or wish to. As far as he was aware, the boys could have been there to serve ale, wait on tables, clear up, anything at all.

It seemed very routine, even tedious, until Hester saw something alter in Rathbone's stance, and a new, suppressed energy enter him. Was Durban's interest in Phillips consistent from the time it began?

Hurst looked puzzled, as if he remembered something odd. No, it wasn't. For several months Durban had shown no interest at all, as if he had forgotten about him. Then equally without explanation, his interest had resumed again, even more fiercely than before. His pursuit had become almost savage, exceeding his duty. He had been seen on the river in all weather, even in the small hours of the night when all sane men were in their beds.

Could Hurst explain any of this? In fact, had Durban offered any reason for his extraordinary obsession and the erratic manner of his occupation with it?

No. Hurst was disillusioned. He had no idea.

Tremayne must have known that in questioning him further he would gain nothing, and might even lose. He declined.

To end the day Rathbone added another member of the River Police who had been serving at the Wapping Station during Durban's latter years. The man made it quite apparent that he was there against his will. His loyalty was to the police in general, and to his immediate colleagues in particular. He was openly hostile to Rathbone, and to anyone else who questioned Durban's integrity, and by implication, that of all the police.

However, he was obliged to admit that he knew beyond any doubt at all that towards the end of his life Durban had spent the little spare time he had, and much of his own money, in his endless, fruitless pursuit of Jericho Phillips. In spite of his careful wording, or perhaps because of it, it made Durban sound obsessed to the point of madness. Suddenly Phillips, as unpleasant as he was, appeared to be the victim.

Hester saw several confused faces in the gallery around her, even glances towards the figure of Phillips as he was escorted from the dock back down to the cells for the night. Now they were curious, and not as certain of his guilt as they had been even a few hours ago.

She left the courtroom feeling betrayed. She moved through the open doors into the hallway beyond, not literally buffeted by the crowd, but it seemed as if they pressed in on her from all sides. They were puffed up with their own convictions, there to see and hear, unaffected by what anyone believed.

She cared passionately. She cared whether Durban was the hero Monk believed him to be, both because he was one of the few men Monk admired, and also because Monk himself had founded his career in the Thames Police on finishing his predecessor's last case. It was his gift of gratitude to a man he could thank in no other way.

She could see now that they had both allowed it to become too important. All the rage they felt towards everyone who had beaten, neglected, or abused a child had centered on Phillips. Perhaps that was unfair, and it was that thought reflected in other people's eyes that humiliated and confused her now.

She came face-to-face with Margaret Rathbone on the steps as she was leaving. She had turned for an instant, uncertainly, and Margaret was only a couple of paces behind her.

Margaret stopped, but she did not lower her eyes. There was an embarrassed silence. Hester had always been the leader. She was the one with the medical experience, the knowledge. She had been to the Crimea; Margaret had never been out of England, except for family holidays to France, carefully chaperoned. Hester had watched Margaret fall in love with Rathbone, and try so hard to win him. They had said little; neither was someone who discussed their deepest fears or dreams, but there had been a wealth of silent understanding between them.

They had nursed the sick and dying together, and faced the truth of violence and crime. Now for the first time they were on different sides, and there was nothing to say that would not make it worse. Rathbone had attacked Hester on the stand personally, and stripped the covering decencies from her beliefs by revealing those she had trusted. Above all, he had exposed Monk to disillusion, and to the appearance of having let down his colleagues who had followed him into the battle.

Margaret's loyalty was committed to Rathbone. She had no room to ask anything or to yield in her position. The lines were set.

Margaret hesitated, as if she would smile, say something, offer commiseration. Then she knew that everything could be misunderstood, and she changed her mind.

Hester made it easier for her by turning away again, and continuing down the steps.

Margaret would catch a cab. Hester took the public bus to the ferry across the river, then walked up to Paradise Place and let herself in through the front door. The house was warm in the summer sun, and quiet. They were close to Southwark Park, and the distant sound of laughter carried through the trees.

She spent a wretched evening alone. There had been a bad incident on the river, on Limehouse Reach, and by the time Monk came home he was too tired to talk about anything. She did not have the opportunity to discuss the day's events with him.

Rathbone also had an acutely uncomfortable evening, in spite of Margaret's unconditional praise of his skill, and surprisingly, of his morality.

"Of course it disturbs you," she said to him gently after dinner. They were sitting opposite each other with the French windows open again onto the quiet garden with its birdsong and the slight rustling of leaves in the late sunset wind. "No one likes to show up the weakness of their friends, especially in public," she continued. "But it was not your choice that they go after Jericho Phillips. It would be totally wrong for you to refuse to defend him, or anyone else, on the grounds that you have friends in the prosecution. If it were right, then anyone could refuse to defend any case they might lose, or that might challenge their opinions, or even their social standing. No man of honor does only what is comfortable to him." Her eyes were bright, and there was warm color in her skin.

It gave Rathbone pleasure that she admired him so genuinely, but it was the guilty pleasure of stolen fruit, or at least of that obtained dishonestly. He struggled for words to explain it to her, but it was too complicated to frame, and he knew from her smile that she was not really listening. He ended up saying nothing, and was ashamed of himself.

Rathbone began the next day's proceedings with what he intended to be his coup de grâce. He had no choice now but to go ahead with it.

It was inconceivable that he would do less than his best, because even in the defense of a man like Jericho Phillips, that would be to betray every principle that he believed in. Above the political battles, the good or bad governments, the judiciary at its most brilliant, corrupt, or incompetent, the impartiality of the law—and its power to deal with all people without fear or favor—was the bedrock upon which every civilized nation depended.

When lawyers made judgments the jury of the common man was betrayed, and in the end would become extinct. The law itself would pass from the people to the few who held power. There would no longer be a check on their prejudices, or in time, on their ability to remain above the tides of corruption, bribery, the threat of loss, or the hope of gain.

He now found himself in a position in which he must call William Monk to the stand, and force him to testify against the man to whom he owed the best opportunity of his life.

They faced each other in a silent court. This might well prove to be the last day of a trial that had begun as a mere formality but was now a very real battle in which it was even possible that Jericho Phillips's fight for his life could end in victory. People in the gallery were straining to look at him. He had assumed a sudden public stature that was both frightening and fascinating.

Monk had already been identified. Both the jury and the spectators had heard of him from earlier witnesses. Now they stared in sharp interest as the questions began.

"I did not call you earlier, Commander Monk," Rathbone began, "because you are familiar with only part of this case, and Mr. Orme was involved from the beginning, when Mr. Durban was first called to the discovery of the boy's body." He walked elegantly across the open space, as if he were very much at ease. Only someone who knew him as well as Monk did would see that his shoulders were stiff, and he did not carry his hands quite naturally. "However," he continued, turning to face the witness stand, "certain facts have come to our attention that suggest unusual elements with which you could help us." He waited, for dramatic effect, not because there was any question in his words.

Tremayne shifted in his seat as though he could not find a comfortable position.

"This case had been dropped, Mr. Monk." Rathbone's voice was suddenly challenging. "Why did you choose to reopen it?"

Monk had expected exactly this question. "Because I came across a record of it in Mr. Durban's papers, and the fact that it was still unsolved bothered me," he replied.

Rathbone's eyebrows rose. "Indeed? Then I assume you pursued all of Mr. Durban's other unsolved cases with equal zeal?"

"I would like to solve them all," Monk replied. "There were not many: a few minor thefts, one to do with the smuggling of half a dozen kegs of brandy; the fencing of stolen china and ornaments; a couple of incidents of public drunkenness that ended in fights; a few broken windows. The murder of children comes before all those." He too paused for effect, and smiled very slightly. "I'll attend to the rest, if I have time."

Rathbone's face changed slightly, acknowledging that he had an adversary not to be trifled with. "Of course that takes priority," he agreed, changing his angle of attack with barely a trace of awkwardness. "It seems from what we have heard that it comes before a great many things in your estimation. You appear to have read Mr. Durban's notes with great attention. Why is that?"

Monk had not foreseen the question phrased quite that way. "I have held Mr. Durban's position since shortly after his death. I thought I had a great deal to learn from his experience, and what he had written about."

"How modest of you," Rathbone observed. "So you admired Mr. Durban a great deal?"

There was only one possible answer. "I did."

"Why?" Rathbone asked innocently.

Monk had opened the way to such a question; now he had to answer it. He had no time to concoct a reply that was careful or measured to safeguard the case. "Because he held command without abuse of his authority," he said. "His men both liked and respected him. For the short time that I knew him, before he gave his life in the call of duty, I found him to have humor, kindness, and integrity." He nearly said something about hating injustice, and stopped himself just in time.

"A fine eulogy for a man who is not here to speak for himself," Rathbone said. "He certainly has a loyal friend in you, Mr. Monk."

"You say that as if loyalty to a friend were an offense," Monk retaliated, just a shade too quickly, betraying his anger.

Rathbone stopped, turned slowly towards Monk up in the witness stand, and smiled. "It is, Mr. Monk, when it places itself before loyalty to truth, and to the law. It is an understandable quality, perhaps even likable—except of course, to the man who is accused of a hideous crime so that one friend may pay a debt to another."

There was a rustle of sharpened interest around the room. One or two of the jurors looked anxious. Lord Justice Sullivan's face was carefully expressionless.

Tremayne rose to his feet, but with anger rather than confidence.

"Profound as Sir Oliver's philosophy may be, my lord, it does not appear to contain a question."

"You are quite correct," Sullivan agreed, but with reluctance. "Such observations more properly belong in your club, Sir Oliver. You called Mr. Monk to the stand; therefore, I assume you have something to ask him. Please proceed with it."

"My lord," Rathbone said, masking only the slightest irritation. He looked back up at Monk. "What was your own occupation when you first met Mr. Durban?"

"I was a private agent of inquiry," Monk answered. He could guess where Rathbone was leading, but he could not avoid going with him.

"Did that fit you for taking over Mr. Durban's position as Commander of the River Police at Wapping?"

"I don't think so. But I had been in the Metropolitan Police before that." Surely Rathbone was not going to bring up his loss of memory? He was seized with a sudden cold uncertainty that he might.

But that was not where Rathbone struck.

"Why did you leave the Metropolitan Police?" he asked.

Sullivan was impassive, but as if he were containing his emotion with difficulty. His color was high, his fist tightly closed on the bench.

"Sir Oliver, are you questioning Mr. Monk's professional ability, his reputation, or his honesty?" he asked.

"None of those, my lord." Irritation marked Rathbone's face now. His hands were closed tight and hard. "I believe Mr. Durban had leadership skills that Mr. Monk intensely admired, because he had failed to exhibit them himself in the past. Mr. Durban, in choosing him as his successor, gave him the opportunity to try a second time, which is a chance few men receive. Mr. Durban also expressed a confidence in him that he did not have in himself. I will show that Mr. Monk's sense of debt to Durban drove him to exceed his authority, and his usual judgment, in pursuit of Jericho Phillips, and that he did so to pay what he perceived as a debt. He also desired profoundly to earn the respect of his men by vindicating Durban's original pursuit of the murderer."

Tremayne shot to his feet, his face filled with consternation, forgetting even to address the judge.

"That is a very large and rather rash assumption, Sir Oliver."

Rathbone turned to Sullivan with an air of innocence.

"My client is accused of a very terrible crime, my lord. If he is found guilty he will be hanged. No lengths within the law are too great to make certain that justice is done, and that we do not also allow our emotions, our pity or our revulsion, to dictate our thoughts and overwhelm our reason. We too wish to see someone pay, but it must be the right someone."

"Of course it must," Sullivan said forcefully. "Proceed, Sir Oliver, but get to the point."

Rathbone bowed very slightly. "Thank you, my lord. Mr. Monk, did you follow Durban's notes to retrace his original detection, or did you accept his observations and deductions as sufficient?"

"I followed them again and questioned the same people again, as far as I could," Monk answered with a tone suggesting that the answer was obvious.

"But in each case you already knew what evidence you were looking for," Rathbone pointed out. "For example, Mr. Durban began with an unidentified corpse and had to do whatever he could to learn who the boy was. You began knowing that Mr. Durban believed it to be Walter Figgis. You had only to prove that he was right. Those are not the same courses of action at all."

Several jurors fidgeted unhappily. They could see the plain difference.

"Are you sure you were not merely confirming what you already wished to believe?" Rathbone hammered the point home.

"Yes, I am sure," Monk said decisively.

Rathbone smiled, his head high, the light gleaming on his fair hair.

"How do you identify the body of a boy who has been in the water for some days, Mr. Monk?" he challenged. "Surely it is . . . severely changed? The flesh . . ." He did not continue.

The mood of the court altered. The reality of death had entered again, and the battle of words seemed faintly irrelevant.

"Of course it is changed," Monk said softly. "What had once been a bruised, burned, and underfed boy, but very much alive, had become so much cold meat, like something the butcher discarded. But that is what we had to work with. It still mattered that we learn who he was." He leaned forward a little over the railings of the stand. "He still had hair, and height, shape of face, possibly some clothes left, and quite a bit of skin, enough to guess his coloring, and of course his teeth. People's teeth are different."

There were gasps of breath drawn in sharply. More than one woman stifled a sob.

Monk did not hesitate to be graphic. "In this case, Durban had written down that the boy had the marks of burns old and new on the inside of his arms and thighs." The full obscenity of it should be known. "No one burns themselves in those places by accident."

Rathbone's face was pale, his body awkward where he stood. "That is vile, Mr. Monk," he said softly. "But it is not proof of identity."

"It is a beginning," Monk contradicted him. "An undernourished child who has been tortured, and has begun to change from a boy into a man, and no one has complained of his disappearance? That narrows down the places to look very much indeed, thank God. Durban made several drawings of what the boy probably looked like. He was good at it. He showed them up and down the riverbank, particularly to people who might have seen a beggar, a petty thief, or a mudlark."

"He assumed he was one of such a group?"

"I don't know, but it was the obvious place to begin, and as it turned out, the right place."

"Ah, yes," Rathbone nodded. "Somebody recognized one of these drawings that Durban did from what was left of the boy. You mentioned hair, skin coloring to some extent, shape of skull, and so on. Correct me if I am mistaken, Mr. Monk, but could not such bare characteristics produce at least a thousand different sets of features?"

Monk kept his temper, knowing that Rathbone was trying to bait him. "Of course. But desperate as the state of many children is, there are not a thousand boys of that age missing at one time along the bank of the river, and unreported."

"So you fitted this tragic corpse to the face of one boy that a mudlark said was missing, and you identified the body as that of Walter Figgis?" Rathbone's eyes were wide, a very slight smile on his lips.

Monk swallowed his sarcasm. He knew he was playing to an audience who was watching the shadows on his face, hearing the slightest inflection of his voice. "No, Sir Oliver, Commander Durban thought it very likely that the corpse was that of Figgis. When we found obscene photographs of Figgis, taken when he was alive, they were identified by those who knew him, and Commander Durban then matched them to the corpse. He had unusual ears, and one of them had not been destroyed by the water, and the creatures in it who feed on the dead."

Rathbone was forced to accept it.

Tremayne smiled, his body relaxing a little in relief.

Sullivan sat forward a little at his high bench, turning first to Rathbone, then to Tremayne, then back again.

Rathbone moved on. "Did you see these—obscene—photographs?"

"Yes. They were in Durban's papers." Monk could not prevent the violence of his disgust from showing. He tried to; he knew he should keep control. This was evidence. Only facts should matter, but still his body was shaking, and he felt sweat break out on his skin. "The faces were perfectly clear, even three of the burns. We found two of them on the same places."

"And the third?" Rathbone asked very gently.

"That part of him had been eaten away." Monk's voice trembled, thick with the horror and misery of Durban's words on the page in jagged writing, creating a picture of disintegration and loss.

"The vision of tragedy, of bestiality, that you call up, is almost beyond bearing," Rathbone acknowledged. "I do not wonder that you find it hard to speak of, or that Mr. Durban put in endless hours of his own time, and indeed also his own money, to bring to justice whoever did this. Would it be true to say that you felt just as deeply as he did?" He shrugged very slightly. "Or perhaps you did not?"

There was only one answer possible. Rathbone had chosen his words with an artist's precision. Every eye in the court was on Monk.

"Of course I felt as deeply," he said.

"Commander Durban had given his life to save others," Rathbone went on with some reverence. "And he had recommended you to take over his position. That is perhaps the highest mark of trust one man can offer another. Would it be true to say that you owe him a debt of both honor and gratitude?"

Again, there was only one possible reply.

"Yes, I do."

There was a sigh and a rustle of agreement around the room.

"And you will do everything you can to honor it, and bring pride to the men of the River Police who are now in your command, and earn their loyalty, as Durban did?" Rathbone asked, although it was barely a question. The answer spoke for itself.

"Of course."

"Especially completing this task of Durban's, in the way he would have wished. Perhaps you would even give him the credit for its solution?"

"Yes," Monk said without hesitation.

Rathbone was satisfied. He thanked Monk and returned to his seat with a gesture of invitation to Tremayne.

Tremayne hesitated, only too clearly seeking any way to regain the balance. Then he declined. Perhaps he thought that anything Monk might add would only raise the emotion still higher, which would make it even worse. Monk was excused.

In the early afternoon Tremayne gave the prosecution's summary. His movements were graceful, his voice smooth and confident, but Monk knew it was a superb piece of acting. The man should have been on the stage. He even had the striking looks for it. But he was laboring against the tide, and he had to know it.

He mentioned Durban's original deductions only in passing, concentrating on Monk's taking up of the trail again. He avoided the horror of it whenever he could, telling instead the detail of Monk's piecing together the proof of Fig's identity, and the links that connected him to Jericho Phillips and the trade in exploitation and pornography. He could not mention the photographs because they had not been produced, only referred to by Monk. As evidence they did not exist, as Rathbone would have instantly pointed out.

He also spoke of Hester's part in connecting Phillips to the trade that satisfies the sexual appetites of those with money to pay for whatever they wanted, using the poor, willing or unwilling, who had no other way to survive. When he finally sat down, the jury was wrung with emotions of anger and pity, and would clearly have been willing themselves to tie a noose around Phillips's neck.

Rathbone stood up. He looked very somber, as if he too were shaken by what he had heard.

"What happened to this boy is appalling," he began. There was absolute silence in the room, and he had no need to raise his voice. "It should shock all of us, and I believe it has." He stood very still, awed by the horror of it. "The fact that he was a child of poverty and ignorance is completely irrelevant. The fact that he may have made his living at first by begging or stealing, then was very probably forced into acts of the utmost degradation by men in the grip of deviant appetites is also irrelevant. Every human being deserves justice, at the very least. If possible, they deserve mercy and honor as well."

There was a low rumble of assent. The jurors' faces were filled with emotion. They sat huddled forward, bodies tight and uncomfortable.

On the bench Sullivan seemed frozen, his cheeks dark with color.

"What we have heard is sufficient to stir the passions, the rage, the pity of every decent person, man or woman," Rathbone continued. "What would you think of a woman like Hester Monk, who spends her time and her means laboring to help the sick, the destitute, the forgotten, and the outcast of our society, if she had no pity for this misused child? If she does not fight for him, then who will? If she is not moved to fury and to weeping on his behalf, what manner of woman is she? I am bold enough to say that she would not be a woman that I wish to know."

There were strong murmurs of agreement.

Rathbone was speaking to them intimately now. Not a soul moved or made the slightest rustle.

"And Commander Durban, who saw the boy's dead body pulled from where it was tangled in the ropes of the lighter, mangled and unrecognizable, who saw the marks of torture on the dead flesh?" He gestured delicately with his hands. "What sort of a guardian of our law would he be, had he not sworn to spend his professional life seeking the creature who brought this about? In his case, he spent his personal time as well, and his own money, to seek justice, and it seems to me, to put an end to such things happening to other boys as well. Do we want policemen who are not moved by such horror?"

Up in the dock, for the first time, Jericho Phillips stirred anxiously. His eyes flickered with panic, and his body was hunched forward as far as his manacles would allow.

"And Mr. Monk is a worthy successor to Durban," Rathbone continued. "He has the same passion, the same dedication, the driving will that compels him to spend night and day searching for clues, answers, proof, anywhere he can. He will not rest, indeed he cannot rest, until he has captured the man responsible, and taken him to the very foot of the gallows."

Several jurors were nodding now.

Lord Justice Sullivan looked concerned, on the brink of going so far as to interrupt him. Could Rathbone conceivably have forgotten which side he was on?

"Let us consider these excellent people, one by one," Rathbone said reasonably. "And Mr. Orme, as well, of course. We too, I believe, wish that justice may be served, completely and irrevocably." That was almost a question, although he smiled very slightly. "Our position is different from theirs, in that they provide evidence to be considered, while we reach a conclusion that is irrevocable. If we find that Jericho Phillips is guilty, within three weeks he will be hanged, and cannot ever be brought back to this world.

"If, on the other hand, we find that he is not guilty, then he cannot be tried for this crime again. Gentlemen, our decision allows no room for passion, no matter how understandable, how human, how worthy of the noblest pity for the victims of poverty, disease, or inequality. We have not the luxury that others will have after us to alter our mistakes or correct our misjudgments. We have in this room only that final judgment at the bar of God, before whom we will all stand in eternity. We must be right!" He held up his hand in a closed fist, not of any kind of threat, but of an unbreakable grasp.

"We are not partisan." He looked at them one after another, and then quailed a little. "We must not be. To allow emotion of liking or disliking, of horror, or pity or self-indulgence, of fear or favor for anyone"—he sliced the air—"or any other human tenderness to sway our decision is to deny justice. And never believe that the drama here is our purpose—it is not! Our purpose is the measured and equal justice for all people, alive or dead, good or evil, strong or weak..." He hesitated. "Beautiful or hideous. The question is not whether Commander Durban was a good man, even a noble one. It is whether he was right in his collection of and deduction from evidence regarding the murder of Walter Figgis. Did he allow his human passions to direct his course? His dream of justice to hasten his judgments? His revulsion at the crime to make him too quick to grasp at the solution?

"You need to weigh in your minds why it was that he stopped his pursuit of Phillips, and then started it again. His notes do not say.

Why do they not? You need to ask that, and not flinch from the answer."

He turned, paced back, and then faced the jury again. "He chose William Monk to succeed him. Why? He is a good detective. No one knows that better than I. But did Durban, who knew him only a few months, choose him because he saw in Monk a man of profound convictions like his own, of pity for the weak, rage against the abusive, and an unstoppable dedication? A man who would seek to close his own unfinished cases, out of honor and to pay a personal debt?"

The jurors' eyes were fixed unwaveringly on Rathbone. He knew it.

"You must judge the power and the compulsion that drove Monk to follow precisely the course that Durban had taken," he told them. "You have listened to Mrs. Monk and must have formed some opinion of her courage and her passion. This is a woman in the same mold as Florence Nightingale, a woman who has walked the fields of battle among the dead and the dying, and has not fainted or wept, or turned away, but has steeled her courage and made her decisions. With knife and needle, bandages and water, she has saved lives. What would she not do to bring to justice the man who abused and murdered children—including a boy so like the very mudlark she has all but adopted as her own?"

He lowered his voice. "Are you prepared to hang Jericho Phillips in the certainty, beyond any reasonable doubt, that those passionate, justifiably enraged people have made no error in their detached and analytical reasoning, and have found the right man, among all the teeming many who make their livings on this busiest river in the world?"

He stood motionless in the center of the floor. "If you are not certain, then for all our sakes, you must find him not guilty. Above all for the sake of the law, which must protect the weakest, the poorest, and the least loved of all of us, as much as it protects the strong, the beautiful, and the good. If you do not, then it becomes no protection at all, simply the instrument of our power and our prejudice. Gentlemen, I leave the judgment to rest not with your pity or your outrage, but with your honor to the sacred principle of justice, by which one day we will all be judged."

He sat down in total silence. Not another person moved even to rustle in their seats.

After a moment, in a hushed voice, Lord Justice Sullivan invited the jury to retire to consider its verdict.

They came back within the hour, looking at no one. They were unhappy, but they were resolute.

Sullivan asked their foreman to speak for them.

"Not guilty," he said in a low, clear voice.

FOUR

Sitting in the courtroom Monk was stunned. Beside him Hester was rigid. He could feel it as if he were touching her, although actually there were several inches between them. Then he heard her move and knew she had turned to look at him. What could he say to her? He had been so certain of the verdict that he had not even suggested that the prosecution charge Phillips with the attempted murder of the ferryman. Now, as if he had dissolved into the air, Phillips had escaped.

They walked out of the courtroom and through the crowds in silence, then instead of looking for a bus, as if by unspoken agreement, they went along Ludgate Hill and left down to Blackfriars Bridge. The river was bright in the low, late-afternoon sun. Pleasure boats had bright flags up and streamers rippling in the wind. The sound of a barrel organ drifted from the bank, somewhere just out of sight.

They were less than a mile upstream from the Southwark Bridge. They walked over slowly, watching the bright wake of boats below them, and caught a bus on the farther bank. They sat still without speaking until they alighted a quarter of a mile from Paradise Place, and walked uphill, a longer way around than they needed, for the pleasure of the air.

The park was quiet, a faint breeze moving the leaves, like someone breathing softly in their sleep.

Half a dozen times, Monk had wanted to speak, but each time the words he had been going to say seemed clumsy, like an attempt at self-justification. What did she think of him? Rathbone had called him as a witness. He must have counted on Monk saying and doing exactly what he had.

"Did he know I was going to do that?" he said at last as they passed under one of the towering trees, the shade deep beneath the boughs. "Am I so predictable, or did he manipulate me into it?"

She thought before she answered. "Both, I think," she said finally. "That's his skill, to ask the question in such a way that you can really give only one answer. He painted a picture of Durban as overemotional, and then asked if you cared just as much. You could hardly say that you didn't." She was frowning. "I understand the principle that the law must be based on evidence, not love or hate. That's hard, but it's true. You can't condemn him because you don't like him. But I don't understand why he chose this case to demonstrate it. I could have sworn that he would find Phillips as repulsive as the rest of us do. It seems . . ." she searched for the right word. "Perverse."

It solidified Monk's thoughts. "Yes, it does. And that is not the man he used to be . . . is it?"

They crossed the road and walked side by side up towards Paradise Place.

"No," she said at last as they reached their own door and he took out the key to let them in. It smelled closed up in the warmth of the day, but the faint aroma of lavender and beeswax was pleasing, as was the cleanness of freshly laundered linen hanging on the airing rail in the kitchen. There was a maid who came twice a week for the heavy work, and she had obviously been there today.

"Do you think he's changed as much as it seems?" Hester stopped and turned to face him.

He did not know how to answer. He realized only now how much he had liked Rathbone, in spite of the difference between them. If Rathbone no longer held the beliefs he used to, then Monk had also lost something. "I don't know," he said honestly.

She nodded, lips closed tightly, eyes suddenly sad. She walked through to the kitchen and he followed, sitting on one of the hard-backed chairs as she picked up the kettle and filled it before setting it on the stove. He knew the change in Rathbone would hurt her also, even more than it would him. People did change when they married, sometimes only a little, but it could be a great deal. He was different since marrying Hester, although he believed that was entirely for the good. He did not like to admit it, but looking back, he had formerly been harder to please, quicker to lose his temper and to see the ugly or the weak in anyone. Happiness had made him kinder. That was something to be grateful for, though not proud of; he should have managed it anyway. Pride might have been justified if he had been gentler, without his own inner peace or safety from the wounds of loneliness.

If this change in Rathbone were to do with Margaret then it would be an even deeper loss to Hester, because Margaret had been her friend also. They had worked hard together, shared pain and fear, and more than a little of each other's dreams.

He watched Hester now as she worked quietly at preparing supper. It was simple, but then in the warmth of summer, cold food was not only easier, it was pleasanter. It was supremely comfortable looking at her as she turned from one bench to another, finding what she wanted, chopping, slicing, carrying. Her hands were slender and quick, and she moved with grace. Some men might not have thought her beautiful; in fact, he had not himself when they first knew each other. She was too thin. Far richer curves were fashionable, and a face with less passion or strength and with more demureness and an inclination to obedience.

But he knew her in all her moods, and the play of laughter and sorrow in her features, the flare of anger or the quick pain of contrition, and the stab of pity were all familiar to him. He knew how powerfully they worked in her. Now the shallower emotions of bland, pretty women seemed empty, leaving him starving for reality.

What did Margaret Rathbone offer, compared with Hester? What did she want that had made Rathbone defend Jericho Phillips so brilliantly? And Monk would be dishonest were he to say that it was less than brilliant. Rathbone had turned an untenable situation into one of dignity, even some kind of honor, at least on the surface.

But what about afterwards? What was underneath the momentary victory in the courtroom, the amazement of the crowd, the admiration for his skills? What about the question why? Who had paid him to do this? If it were a favor, then to whom? Who could ask something, or offer something, that could be wanted by a man such as Rathbone used to be? In the past, Hester, Monk, and he had fought great battles that had taxed every ounce of their courage, imagination, and intelligence, because they believed in the causes.

If Rathbone were honest, what did he believe of this? Phillips was an evil man. Even Rathbone had not said that he was innocent, only that they had failed to prove him guilty beyond a reasonable doubt. The defense was based on a legality, not a weighing of the facts, and certainly not a moral judgment. If Rathbone really loved the law above all else, then Monk had misjudged him the entire time they had known each other, and that was not only an ugly thought, but a sad one.

Surely Rathbone's motivation had to be something better than money. Monk refused to believe it was as simple and as grubby as that.

The food was ready and they sat down to eat it in silence. It was not uncompanionable; they were each lost in their own thoughts, but they concerned the same subject. He looked at her eyes momentarily, and knew that, as she knew it of him. Neither of them was ready yet to find the words.

They had not obtained justice. No matter what Rathbone had claimed, the use of the law had enabled a deeply guilty man to go free, and to repeat his offenses as often as he chose. The message to the people was that skill wins, not honor. And Monk himself was as much to blame as Rathbone for that. If he had done his job more completely, if he had been as clever as Rathbone, then Phillips would be on his way to the gallows. In taking it for granted that because he was right he had some kind of invulnerability against defeat, he had been careless, and he had let down Orme, who had worked so hard, and who had trusted him. And he had let down Durban as well. This was to have been an act of gratitude, the one thing he could give him, even beyond the grave—to do his job honorably.

And by bringing Phillips to face trial, and then be acquitted, he had freed him from ever being charged with that crime again, which was worse than not having caught him. All the River Police were betrayed in that.

The confidence, the inner peace that he had won so hard and treasured so dearly, was slipping out of his grasp like water through his fingers. One day it was there, and then he looked, and it was draining away while he was helpless to stop it. It was the cold truth; he was not the man he had begun to hope and believe he was. He had failed. Jericho Phillips was guilty at the very least of child abuse and pornography, and—Monk had no doubt—also of murder. It was Monk's carelessness, his incompetence to make sure of every single detail, to check and check again, to prove everything, that had allowed Rathbone to paint him as driven more by emotion than reason, so Phillips slipped through the blurring of doubts, and escaped.

He looked up at Hester. "I can't leave it like this," he said aloud. "I can't for myself, I can't for the River Police."

She put her spoon down and looked at him steadily, almost unblinking. "What can you do? You can't try him again."

He drew his breath in sharply to respond, then saw the honesty and gentleness in her eyes. "I know that. And we were so certain of convicting him for Figgis's murder we didn't even charge him with assaulting the ferryman. If we try that now it'll look as if we're only doing it because we failed. He'll say he slipped, it was an accident, he was fighting for his life. It'll make us look even more . . . incompetent."

She bit her lip. "Then this time we need to know what it is we are trying to do—exactly. Seeing the truth is not enough—is it?" That was a challenge, an invitation to face something far beyond the bitterness of the day. How practical she was. But then to nurse she had to be. The treatment of the illnesses of the body was, above all, practical. There was no time, no room for mistakes or excuses. It demanded a very immediate kind of courage, a faith in the value of trying no matter what the result. Fail this time, you must still give everything you have next time, and the time after, and after that.

She had stopped eating her plum pie, waiting for an answer.

"If I learn enough about him I shall prove him guilty of something," he replied. "Even if it doesn't hang him, a good stretch in the Coldbath Fields would save a score of boys from abuse, maybe a hundred. By the time he gets out a lot of things could be different. Maybe he would even die in there. People do."

She smiled. "Then we'll start again, from the beginning." She ate her last mouthful and rose to her feet. "But a cup of tea first. If we're going to sit up all night, we'll need it."

He felt a sudden wave of gratitude choke him too much to answer her. He bent and concentrated on finishing his own pie.

Afterwards he fetched Durban's notes again, and side by side they spread them all over the table, the seats, and the floor of the parlor, and read every one of them again. For the first time Monk realized just how patchy they were. Some were full of description, seemingly no detail omitted. Others were so brief as to be little more than words jotted down as reminders of whole trains of thought never completed. In some the writing was done in such haste that it was barely legible, and from the jagged forms of the letters and the heaviness of the strokes, it had been in the heat of great emotion.

"Do you know what this means?" Hester asked him, holding up a torn piece of paper with the words *Was it money? What else?* written across it with a different pen.

"I don't know," he admitted. He had found other notes, scribbled sentences, unanswered questions that he had assumed referred to Phillips, but perhaps did not. He had reread the notes on all other cases at the time, both of Durban's and those kept in the station by anyone else. He had checked all the prosecutions recorded in the station archives too.

Hester was still watching him. He thought he knew what she was going to say, if not with this piece of paper then with the next, or the one after.

"It could be something to do with his own life," he said to her at last. "Personal. I hadn't realized how little I really know about him." He remembered back to those few, hectic days together searching for the crew of the *Maude Idris*, believing they were ashore somewhere in the teeming docks, and knowing they were infected and dying. He and Durban had worked until they were so exhausted they slept where they collapsed. They woke again after an hour or two, and staggered on. He had never had a more desperate or terrible case, and yet there had been a feeling of companionship whose memory still made him smile. Durban had liked him, and he did not know anyone else who had done so with instant and unquestioning honesty.

If he had had any other friend like that, it had been in that huge part of the past he could no longer remember. He had sudden moments of light on the shadow, so brief as to give him only an image, never a story. Judging from what he had heard and deduced of who he was, the intelligence and the ruthlessness, the relentless energy that drove him, even Durban would not have liked him then. Certainly Runcorn had not, and neither Hester nor Oliver Rathbone had known him. Hester might have tamed him, but without that searing vulnerability of his confusion and the fear of his own guilt in Joscelyn Gray's death, why would she have bothered? He had little humanity to offer until he was forced to look within himself and examine the worst.

He was glad Durban had known only the man he had become, and not the original.

What lay in the spaces around his mental construction of Durban that Monk did not know? Was the compulsion to catch Jericho Phillips going to force him to intrude into the areas of Durban's life that Durban had chosen to keep private, perhaps because there was pain there, failure, old wounds he needed to forget?

"I can remember his voice," he said aloud, meeting her steady eyes. "His face, the way he walked, what made him laugh, what he liked to eat. He loved to see dawn on the river and watch the early ferries start out across the water. He used to walk alone and watch the play of light and shadow, the mist evaporating like silk gauze. He liked to see the forest of spars when we had a lot of tall ships in the Pool. He liked the sound and smells of the wharves, especially when the spice ships were unloading. He liked to listen to the cry of gulls, and men talking all the different foreign languages, as if the whole earth with its wealth and variety had come here to London. He never said so, but I think he was proud to be a Londoner."

He stopped, his emotion too strong for the moment. Then he drew in a deep breath.

"I didn't want to talk about my past, and I didn't care about his. For any of us, it's who you are today that matters."

Hester smiled, looked away, then back again at him. "Durban was a real person, William," she said gently. "Good and bad, wise and stupid. Picking out bits to like isn't really liking at all. It isn't friendship, it's comfort for you. You're better than that, whether he was or not. Are your dreams, or Durban's memory, worth more than the lives of other boys like Fig?" She bit her lip. "Or Scuff?"

He winced. He had been lulled into forgetting how honest she could be, even if her words were harsh.

"I know it's intrusive to examine the whole man," she said. "Even indecent, when he's dead and cannot defend himself, or explain, or even repent. But the alternative is to let it go, and isn't that worse?"

It was a bitter choice, but if Durban had been careless, or even dishonest, that had to be faced. "Yes," he conceded. "Pass me the papers. We'll sort them into those we understand, those we don't, and those I expect we never will. I'll get that bastard Phillips, however long or hard the trail. I made the mistake, and I'll undo it."

"We did," she corrected him, her face pinched a little. "I let Oliver paint me as an overemotional woman whose childlessness led her to hysterical and ill-thought-out judgments."

He saw the pain in her face, the self-mockery, and for that he would not forgive Rathbone until he had paid the last ounce, and maybe not even then. That was something else she had lost, the real and precious friendship with Rathbone. Like Monk, she had no close, loving family left. She had lost a brother in the Crimea, her father to suicide, and her mother to a broken heart. Her one surviving brother was a stiff and distant man, not really a friend. One day, when he had time, Monk must go and visit the sister he barely remembered. He did not think they had been close, even when his memory had been whole, and that was probably his fault.

He put the papers down and leaned over, touching Hester gently, then drawing her closer to him and kissing her, then closer again. "There's tomorrow," he whispered. "Let it be—for now."

Monk rose early and went to buy the newspapers. He considered not taking them home so Hester would not see how bad they were, and then discarded the idea. She did not need his protection, and probably would not wish for it. It would not mean tenderness to her as much as exclusion. And after both the honesty and the passion of the previous night, she deserved better from him. He thought, with a smile, that perhaps he was beginning to understand women, or at least one woman.

There was nothing else to smile at. When he sat at the breakfast table opposite her, each with their newspapers propped open in front of them, the full ugliness of the situation was extremely clear. Durban was drawn as incompetent, a man whose death saved him from the indignity of having been removed from office for at best a personal vengeance against a particularly grubby criminal on the river, at worst a seriously questionable professional ethic.

Monk himself was painted as little better, an amateur drafted in over the heads of more experienced men. He was out of his depth and beyond his skill. He had been trying too hard to pay a debt that he imagined he owed a friend, but whom in truth he barely knew.

Hester came off more lightly, at first glance. She was portrayed as overemotional, driven by loyalty to her husband and a foolish attachment to a class of child her thwarted maternal instincts had fastened on, and caused her to reach out and cherish, quite inappropriately. But from a woman denied her natural role in society by a misguided devotion to charitable causes, and a certain belligerence that made her unattractive to decent men of her own station, what else could one expect? It should be a lesson to all young ladies of good breeding to remain in the paths that nature and society had set for them. Only then might they expect fulfillment in life. It was immeasurably condescending.

When Hester read it she used some language about the writer and his antecedents that she had learned in her Army days. After several minutes she looked nervously at Monk, and apologized, concerned in case she had shocked him.

He grinned at her, possibly a little bleakly, because the remarks about her had stung him perhaps even more than they had hurt her.

"You'll have to tell me what that means," he responded. "I think I may have use for some of those expressions myself."

She colored deeply, and looked away, but the tension eased out of her body, and her hands unknotted in her lap.

The worst thing in the papers actually was a single line suggesting, almost as an afterthought, that possibly the River Police had outlived their usefulness. Perhaps the time had come for them to relinquish any separate identity, and simply come under the command of whatever local force was nearest. They had so badly mishandled the case that Jericho Phillips, were he guilty, had escaped the noose forever, at least for the murder of Walter Figgis. He was now free to continue his trade unmolested. It made a mockery of the law, and that could not be permitted, no matter which well-intentioned but incompetent officer had to be dismissed.

A hot, tight resolution settled in Hester to prove them wrong, but immeasurably more important than that was to prove Monk right. But she was realistic enough to know that that was not necessarily possible. She had no doubt at all that Phillips was capable of murder, or even that he had committed it, if not of Fig, then of others. But the truth was that, in their outrage and their certainty, they had been careless, and they had forgotten the precision of the law, when used by someone like Oliver Rathbone.

And that was another, different kind of pain. It was less urgent: a wide, blind ache that intruded into all sorts of other areas of life, darkening and hurting. The only way to begin again was with her own investigation, which meant at the clinic. And of course that also meant seeing Margaret. Hester had liked Margaret from the first time they had met, when Margaret had been shy and wounded from the repeated humiliation of her mother constantly trying to marry her off to someone suitable—according to her own assessment, not Margaret's, of course. To Margaret's mortification, when they had encountered Rathbone, at some ball or other, Mrs. Ballinger had praised Margaret's virtue to him, in front of Margaret herself, with the all-too-obvious intent of engaging Rathbone's matrimonial interest.

Hester understood with sharp compassion. She would never forget her own family's similar attempts on her behalf. It had made her feel like jetsam, to be cast overboard at the first opportunity. Her acute understanding of Margaret's situation had forged a bond between them. Margaret had found purpose and freedom working in the clinic, and even a sense of her own worth, which no one else had given her, or could now take away.

Then Rathbone had realized that he really did love her. Kindness had nothing to do with it. He was not rescuing her at all. It was his privilege to earn her love in return.

Now, with the acquittal of Jericho Phillips, Hester's closeness with the Rathbones was gone too, tarnished and made uncomfortable.

The long bus ride came to an end and Hester walked the short distance along Portpool Lane, under the huge shadow of the brewery. She went through the door of the rambling tenement houses that were now connected inside to form one large clinic where the sick and injured would be treated, lodged, and nursed if necessary. They were even operated on there if emergency required it and the procedure was comparatively slight, such as the amputation of a finger or toe, the setting of bones, or the stitching of knife wounds. Once or twice there had been the removal of bullets, and once the amputation of a gangrenous foot. The extraction of splinters of various kinds, the repair of dislocations, the occasional difficult birth, and the nursing of bronchitis, fever, pneumonia, and consumption were usual in their daily work. More than one woman had died of a bungled abortion, beyond repair even after their most exhaustive and desperate efforts to save her. There was too much shared triumph and loss to let go of friendship easily.

But as Hester went in through the front door and Bessie greeted her, she felt none of her usual anticipation of warmth. She responded, and then asked Bessie about the previous two days' happenings, when she had been occupied in court, and could not be there. Of course Bessie knew why she had been absent, as they all did; and telling them the outcome was not something she was looking forward to. Like drinking castor oil, it was better done swiftly.

"We lost," she said, before Bessie could ask. "Phillips got away with it."

Bessie was a large woman who wore her hair screwed back fiercely and gripped by pins so tightly Hester had wondered how she could bear it. Bessie looked even angrier than usual, but her eyes were oddly gentle. "I know that," she said tartly. "That lawyer twisted everything to make it look like yer fault. I 'eard already."

That was a complication Hester had not even thought of, divided loyalties in the clinic. More bitter medicine to take. Her chest hurt with the tightness of her breath. "That was Sir Oliver's job, Bessie. We should have got our evidence tight enough so that he couldn't. We weren't sufficiently careful."

"Yer just gonna let it go, then?" Bessie challenged her, disbelief, pity, and hurt crowding her face all at once.

Hester swallowed. "No. I'm going to go back to the beginning and start again."

Bessie flashed a brilliant smile, then it disappeared so rapidly it could have been an illusion. "Good. Then yer'll be needin' me an' the rest of us ter keep comin' 'ere."

"Yes, please. I would appreciate that very much."

Bessie grunted. "Lady Rathbone is in the kitchen, givin' orders, I 'spect," she added. "An' Squeaky's in the office countin' money." She was watching Hester carefully, judging her reaction.

"Thank you," Hester replied with a face as devoid of expression as she could manage, and went to get the encounter done with as soon as possible. Besides, she needed to speak to Squeaky Robinson privately, and at some length.

She swallowed hard and walked along the uneven passage with its twists and its steps up and down until she reached the kitchen. It was a large room, originally intended to serve a family, and it had been added to when the two houses had been turned into one.

She smiled with bitter humor when she remembered how Rathbone had exercised legal skill and some considerable guile in maneuvering Squeaky into yielding his ownership of the brothels, and then taking on the bookkeeping of his own premises as a shelter for the very people he had once owned. Rathbone had left Squeaky no acceptable choice. It had been wildly daring, and from Rathbone's point of view, totally against the spirit of the establishment he had spent his adult life serving. It had also brought him acute moral and emotional pleasure.

But then Hester had also allowed Squeaky little choice in his decision, or as little as she could manage.

Now she was at the kitchen door. Her quick, light step on the wooden boards had alerted Margaret to her coming. Margaret turned with a vegetable knife in her hand. At home she had servants for everything; here she could put her hand to any task that required attention. There was no one else in the room. Hester was not sure if it would have been easier or harder had there been.

"Good morning," Margaret said quietly. She stood motionless, her shoulders square, chin a little high, eyes direct. In that one look Hester knew that she was not going to apologize or offer even the suggestion, however tacit, that the verdict of the trial had been unjust. She was prepared to defend Rathbone to the hilt. Had she any idea why he had chosen to champion Jericho Phillips? From the angle of her head, the unwavering stare, and the slight rigidity of her smile, Hester guessed that she did not.

"Good morning," she replied politely. "How are our stores? Do we need flour, or oatmeal?"

"Not for three or four days," Margaret said. "If the woman with the knife wound in her arm goes home tomorrow, we might last longer. Unless, of course, we get anyone else in. Bessie brought some ham bones this morning, and Claudine brought a string of onions and the bones from a saddle of mutton. We are doing well. I think we should use what money we have for lye, carbolic, vinegar, and a few more bandages. But see what you think yourself."

There was no need for Hester to check; that would have made the most delicate of implications that she did not believe Margaret capable. Before the Phillips affair neither of them would have thought such conspicuous courtesy necessary.

They discussed the medical supplies, simple as they were: alcohol for cleaning wounds and instruments, cotton pads, thread, bandages, salve, laudanum, quinine for fevers, fortified wines to strengthen and warm. The cautious politeness was in the air like a bereavement.

Hester was relieved to escape to the room where Squeaky Robinson, the short-tempered, much-aggrieved ex-brothel-keeper was doing the accounts and guarding every farthing from frivolous and unnecessary expenditure. One would have thought he had labored for it personally rather than received it, through Margaret, from the charitable of the city.

He looked up from his table as she closed the door behind her. His sharp, slightly lopsided face under its long, moth-eaten-looking hair was full of sympathy.

"Made a mess of it," he observed, without specifying whom he meant. "Pity that. Bastard should've 'ad 'is neck stretched, an' no mistake. The fact we got a lot o' money in't much comfort, is it! Not today, any'ow. Mebbe termorrer it'll feel good. Yer can 'ave five pounds ter get more sheets, if yer like." That was an extraordinarily generous offer from a man who begrudged a penny, and regarded sheets for street women as being about as necessary as pearl necklaces in the farmyard. It was his oblique way of trying to comfort her.

She smiled at him, and he looked away, embarrassed. He was slightly ashamed of himself for being generous; he was letting his standards slip.

She sat down in the chair opposite him. "I shall do that. Then we can launder them more often, and keep infection down."

"That'll cost more soap, and more water!" he protested, horrified at the extravagance he had apparently let himself in for. "An' more time to dry 'em."

"And fewer people infected so they'll leave quicker," she elaborated. "But what I really want is your help. That's why I came."

He looked at her carefully. "You seen Mrs . . . Lady Rathbone?" His face was carefully expressionless.

"Yes I have, and dealt with the kitchen accounts," she replied, wondering how much all of them knew about the trial and the verdict. It seemed to be quite a lot.

"Wot can I do? The swine is free!" He said the words with a sudden savagery, and she realized with new pain how much she and Monk had let them all down. They had used every avenue they knew and given Hester the information, and she had failed to get Phillips hanged.

"I'm sorry," she said quietly. "We were so sure he was guilty we weren't careful enough."

Squeaky shrugged. He had no compunction about hitting a man when he was down. Indeed, it was the safest time to do it! But he could not hit Hester; she was different. He did not want to think how fond he was of her; it was a decidedly serious weakness.

"Oo'd've thought Sir Rathbone'd 'ave done that?" he demanded. "We could see if we got enough money to 'ave someone stick a shiv in 'is gizzard. It'd cost, mind. Get bedsheets for 'alf the 'ores in England."

"Oliver?" She was horrified.

He rolled his eyes. "Gawd, woman! I mean Jericho Phillips! Wouldn't cost nothin' ter do Sir Rathbone. Except yer'd 'ave every cop in London after yer, so I s'pose yer'd dance on a rope in the end. An' that's kind o' costly. But Phillips'd be another thing. Like as not 'e'd get yer first. Right nasty piece o' work, 'e is."

"I know that, Squeaky. I'd rather get him legitimately."

"Yer tried that," he pointed out. He pushed a pile of papers across the desk, further out of his way. "Don't want ter rub it in like, but yer didn't exactly get 'im justice, did yer? 'E's better off now than if yer 'adn't bothered. Free, 'e is, the piece o' turd. Now even if yer could prove it an 'e confessed, yer can't touch the sod."

"I know."

"But mebbe wot you in't thought of, Miss 'Ester," he said very seriously, "is that 'e knows yer after 'im, an' 'e knows 'oo can tell yer wot, an' they're gonna 'ave ter tread very careful from now on. 'E's a nasty piece o' work, is Jericho Phillips. 'E in't gonna forgive them wot spoke out o' turn."

She shivered, chilled in the pit of her stomach. Perhaps that was the most serious failure of all: the danger to others, lives now shadowed with fear of Phillips's revenge, when they had been promised safety. She did not want to meet his eyes, but it was cowardly to look down. "Yes, I know that too. It is going to be even harder to do it again."

"In't no point in doin' it again, Miss 'Ester!" he pointed out. "We can't 'ang the bastard anymore! We know 'e should be 'ung, drawn, and quartered an' 'is guts fed ter the birds! But the law says 'e's as innocent as them kids wot 'e sells! Thanks ter Sir bloody Rathbone! Now none o' them wot spoke agin' 'im in't safe, poor sods."

"I know, Squeaky," she agreed. "And I know we let them down. Not you, Mr. Monk and I. We took too much for granted. We let our anger and pity guide us, instead of our brains. But Phillips still needs dealing with, and we owe it to everybody to do it. We'll have to put him away for something else, that's all."

Squeaky shut his eyes and sighed in exasperation, but for all the alarm, there was a very faint smile on his face as well. "Yer don't learn, do yer! Gawd in 'eaven! Wot der yer want now?"

She took it as if it were agreement, or at least acquiescence. She leaned forward on the table. "He is only acquitted of murdering Fig, specifically. He can still be charged with anything else . . ."

"Not 'anged," he said grimly. "An' 'e needs 'angin'."

"Twenty years in Coldbath Fields would do for a start," she countered. "Wouldn't it? It would be a much longer, slower death than on the end of a rope."

He gave it several moments' thought. "I grant yer that," he said finally. "But I like certain. The rope is certain. Once it's done, it's done ferever."

"We don't have that choice anymore," she said glumly.

He looked at her, blinking. "Yer wonderin' 'oo paid 'im, or d'yer know?" he asked.

She was startled. "Paid?"

"Sir Rathbone," he replied. " 'E din't do it fer nothin'. Wot did 'e do it fer, anyway? Does she know?" He jerked his hand in the general direction of the kitchen.

"I've no idea," Hester replied, but her mind was busy with the question of who had paid Rathbone, and why he had accepted the money. She had never considered the possibility of his owing favors before, not of the sort for which such a payment could be asked. How did one incur such a debt? For what? And who would want such payment? Surely anyone Rathbone would consider a friend would want Phillips convicted as much as Monk did.

Squeaky screwed up his face as if he had bitten into a lemon. "If yer believe 'e done it fer free, there in't much 'ope for yer," he said with disgust. "Phillips's got friends in some very 'igh places. Never reckoned Rathbone was one of 'em. Still don't. But some of 'em 'ave a lot o' power, one way an' another." He curled his lip. "Never know where their fingers stretch ter. Lot o' money in dirty pictures, the dirtier, the more money. Got 'em o' little boys, an yer can ask yer own price. First for the pictures, then fer yer silence, like." He tapped the side of his nose and looked at her sourly out of one eye.

She started to say that Rathbone would not have yielded to pressure of any sort, then changed her mind and bit the words off. Who knew what one would do for a friend in deep enough trouble? Someone had paid Rathbone, and he had chosen not to ask why.

Squeaky pursed his lips into an expression of loathing. "Lookin' at the kind o' pictures Phillips sells people can affect yer mind," he said, watching her closely to make sure she understood. "Even people who you wouldn't think. Take 'em out o' them smart trousers an' fancy shirts, an' they think no different from yer beggar or yer thief, when it comes ter queer tastes. Exceptin' some folk 'ave got more ter lose than others, so it leaves 'em open ter a little pressure now an' then."

She stared at him. "Are you saying Jericho Phillips has friends in places high enough to help him before the law, Squeaky?"

He rolled his eyes as if her naiveté had injured some secret part of him. " 'Course I am. Yer don't think 'e's been safe all these years 'cause nobody knows what 'e's doin', do yer?"

"Because of a taste for obscene photographs?" she went on, disbelief thick in her voice. "I know many men keep mistresses, or conduct affairs haphazardly, and in some unlikely places. But photographs? What pleasure can there be in seeing them that is so powerful that you would compromise your honor, reputation, everything to deal with a man like Phillips?"

He shrugged his bony shoulders. "Don' ask me ter explain 'uman nature, Miss. I in't responsible fer it. But there's some things you can make children do that no adult'd do without lookin' at yer like yer'd crawled up out o' the garbage. It in't about love, or even decent appetite, it's about makin' other people do wot you want 'em to, an' tastin' the power over an' over like yer can't get enough of it. Sometimes it's about the thrill o' doin' something that'd ruin yer if yer was caught, an' the danger of it makes yer kind o' drunk. An' neither of them in't always no respecters o' persons, if you get my meanin'. Some people need ter be colder an' 'ungrier ter think on wot matters."

She said nothing.

"Goin' with 'ores is one thing," he continued. "Let's face it, it in't all that serious, as Society looks at it. Most married ladies turn the other way an' gets on wi' their own lives. Keep the bedroom door locked, likely, 'cause they don't want ter wake up wi' no nasty disease, but don't make no scandal about it. Pictures o' little girls is indecent, an' it makes a right-thinkin' person disgusted."

He shook his head.

"But little boys is summink else altogether. It in't only indecent, it's illegal. An' that's entirely another thing. If nobody knows about it, most in't goin' ter go lookin'. We all know that things go on we'd sooner not think about, an' most folk mind their own affairs. But if yer forced ter know, then yer forced ter do summink. Friend or no friend, yer out o' yer clubs and yer job, an' society won't never 'ave yer back. So yer pays 'igh, wide, and 'andsome ter keep it good an' quiet, see?"

"Yes, I do see," Hester said a trifle shakily. A whole new world of misery had yawned open in front of her. Not that she had been unaware of homosexuality. She had been an army nurse. But the use of children to exert a power no adult relationship would tolerate, even one purchased with money, or to gratify a hunger for the thrills of danger, was a new thought, and extremely ugly. The idea of children kept and hired out for such a purpose was sickening.

"I need to destroy Mr. Phillips, Squeaky," she said very softly. "I don't think I can do it without your help. We have to find out who else we can ask to assist us. I imagine Mr. Sutton will be one, and possibly Scuff. Who else can you think of?"

A succession of emotions crossed Squeaky's face: first incredulity, then horror and an intense desire to escape, lastly a kind of amazement at flattery, and the beginning of a daring impulse.

She waited him out.

He cleared his throat, giving himself time. "Well." He coughed slightly. "There's a couple I know of, I s'pose. But they in't very..."

He fished for the right word, and failed to find it. "...nice," he finished lamely.

"Good." She did not hesitate. "Nice people aren't going to be any help at all. Nice people don't even believe in creatures like Jericho Phillips, let alone have the slightest idea how to catch them. He probably eats nice people for breakfast, skewered on a fork."

He smiled mirthlessly, but not without a certain surprised satisfaction.

There was a knock on the door, and without waiting for an answer, Claudine Burroughs came in with a tray of tea. She set it down on the tabletop, a fraction closer to Hester than to Squeaky. The pot was steaming gently, the fragrance of it inviting.

Claudine was a tall woman, roughly the same height as Squeaky, so he always stood a trifle more stiffly when beside her, to add the extra half-inch. She was narrow-shouldered and broad-hipped, handsome enough in her youth, but years of loneliness in an unsatisfying marriage had drawn many of the lines downward in her face. Only since coming to Portpool Lane, searching for some charitable work to do, had she found a genuine and vital purpose.

"Thank you," Hester said with the sudden realization of how welcome the tea was. She wondered if Claudine had any idea of yesterday's desperate disappointment, or if she was simply aware that Hester was tired, even at this hour of the morning. She was weary inside, confused and beaten, which was an even deeper thing.

Claudine was still standing motionlessly, waiting for something.

Squeaky moved in his chair, impatiently, implying that Claudine had interrupted. Hester turned to look at her, and realized that she was uncomfortably aware of his annoyance. Perhaps she did know about yesterday's conclusion.

"I'd like to help," Claudine said awkwardly, her face pink, her eyes unable to look at them. And yet she would not leave. She waited there in acute embarrassment, determined to be part of whatever they were doing, to give her own contribution, regardless of the cost.

"Yer can't," Squeaky said flatly. "Ye're a lady, ye're not part o' the folks wot we need ter be talking ter. Very kind o' yer, but yer wouldn't be no use. Thank yer fer the tea." He probably meant it kindly, but to drop from being part of the plan to fetching the tea was like a slap across her face.

Claudine stood her ground, but she struggled for words. Her face was so pink Hester felt as if her cheeks must be burning.

"We haven't any plans yet," Hester said quickly. "We don't even know where to start. We need to go over everything again, but with more care. And part of the trouble is that the people who testified before are now going to be very afraid. Phillips isn't in prison any longer, and he'll be dangerous."

"Then we will have to be very careful, too," Claudine replied, staring at Hester and ignoring Squeaky. "We will have to question them so they do not realize the importance of what they are saying until they have said it, and cannot retreat. The man Phillips is very terrible, and he must be put away." At last she looked at Squeaky. "I am glad you are going to help. I respect you for it, Mr. Robinson." She turned abruptly and walked to the door, then she looked back at Hester, doubt in her eyes. "I shall be available to do anything I can to help. Please do not forget that." Before either of them could reply, she went out, shutting the latch firmly behind her.

"Yer in't goin' ter use 'er!" Squeaky protested, leaning forward across the desk, his eyes wide. "What can she do? She couldn't find 'er way from one end o' the street ter the other. An' she in't got no right ter respect me. I didn't tell 'er I was goin' ter do anything at all with wot 'e . . ." He stopped, suddenly uncomfortable.

"Are you saying you won't do anything, Squeaky?" Hester asked with a very faint smile.

"Well . . . well, I in't exactly . . . no, I in't. All the same . . ."

"All the same, she led you into saying it and then cut off your retreat," she explained for him.

"Yeah!" He was aggrieved. Then he gave a slow smile, wily and half-amused, perhaps even appreciative. "She did, din't she!" He sniffed. "But I still say she wouldn't be safe in the street."

"She doesn't want to be safe." Hester lost all trace of the smile. "She wants to help, to belong, and you can't belong if you don't take the rough with the smooth. She knows that, Squeaky. We aren't going to shut her out."

He shook his head. "Yer in't got no idea," he said sadly. "That Rathbone's got yer ter rights: all 'eart an' no brains, you are, Gawd 'elp us! 'Ow the 'ell am I goin' ter look after you an' 'er both—daft old thing she is, an' all?"

Hester considered telling him very thoroughly to speak with more respect, and decided against it. This was almost a form of affection, and that was beyond price. She poured the tea carefully, his first. "It will be hard," she agreed. "But you'll manage it. Now let us get started."

The choice of whom to see first was not difficult, nor was it hard to find him and know what to say. Hester was happy to do it alone. Squeaky would be more usefully employed in seeking out his dubious friends.

Sutton was a rat catcher by trade, and proud of being called upon for his services by some of the best households in London. He numbered duchesses among his clients. He was also not too proud to attend to the needs of more humble establishments, and had rid the Portpool Lane clinic of rats at one of the most desperate times in Hester's life. They had been friends in terrible adversity, and indeed Sutton and his terrier, Snoot, had almost perished in the sewers with Monk only a matter of months ago.

Hester always dressed very plainly to go to the clinic, so she did not have any difficulty passing almost unnoticed along the narrow streets to Sutton's house, where she learned from his housekeeper the address where he had gone for the day's business. She found him at his frequent lunchtime haunt, a public house by the name of "The Grinning Rat." It was much like any other, except for the sign that creaked slightly in the wind as it swung outside. The rat in the picture had a look of devilish glee on its painted face. It was dressed in green, and it stood upright on its hind legs, smiling with all its teeth bared.

Hester could not help smiling back before she went inside, trying to look as if she belonged there. She was immediately enveloped in sound. Men were laughing and chattering, there was a clink of glass and pewter, and the scuffle of feet on the sawdust-covered floor, and somewhere in the cellars, barrels being rolled. A dog barked excitedly. There was no point in asking for Sutton; she must simply look.

It took her several minutes to push her way through unyielding bodies of men intent on slaking thirst and enjoying the latest piece of news. She forced her way between two very corpulent bakers, flour still on their sleeves and aprons, and nearly fell into the lap of a neat, slender man sitting by himself eating a cheese and pickle sandwich. There was a tankard of cider in front of him, and a small brown-and-white dog at his feet.

"Mr. Sutton," she said breathlessly, straightening herself and attempting to look respectable. Her hair had fallen out of its pins, as it frequently did, and she had simply poked it behind her ears. "I'm very relieved to have found you."

He stood up politely, partly because there was no second chair for her to be seated. She could see immediately from his expression that he knew Phillips had been acquitted. It made it easier that she did not have to tell him, but she would have preferred that the news not be so very widespread. Perhaps everyone in London knew by now.

"Can I get something fer yer, Miss Hester?" he said dubiously.

"No, thank you, I have already eaten," she answered. It was not strictly true, but she knew he had no time to waste in the middle of his working day. She had enough favors to ask without using them up unnecessarily now.

He remained standing, sandwich in his hand. Snoot stared at it hopefully, but was ignored.

"Please continue," Hester invited him. "I would be most uncomfortable if I spoiled your lunch. All the same, I need to ask your help . . . please?"

He nodded grimly, as if a foreseen disaster were about to break over him, and continued standing. "You're goin' to go after that slimy bastard Phillips again, aren't you." It was a conclusion, not a question. "Don't, Miss Hester," he pleaded anxiously. "He's a bad one, an' he's got friends all over the place, people yer or me wouldn't even think of knowing the likes of 'im. Wait. 'E'll make a mistake one day, an' somebody'll have 'im. 'E was born for the gallows, that one."

"I don't mind if they hang him, or simply lock him up in the

Coldbath Fields and throw away the key," she replied. "What I care about is that they do it soon, in fact, very soon. Before he has the chance to kill any more children, or anyone else, for that matter."

He looked at her carefully for several moments before speaking. She began to feel uncomfortable. His eyes were blue and very clear, as if nothing whatever could impede his vision. It gave her a peculiarly vulnerable feeling. She had to force herself not to try to explain to him even further.

"You want ter go over all the evidence again?" he asked slowly, his expression tense and troubled. "You're sure o' that?"

She felt a chill, even in this hot, close room. What was he trying to warn her from?

"Can you think of a better way?" she countered. "We made a mistake, several in fact, but they were errors in connecting people, not in the basic fact that Jericho Phillips is a child pornographer and murderer."

"You made a mistake in 'ow long 'is arm is," Sutton corrected her, biting into the sandwich at last. "You'll 'ave to be a lot more careful to catch a canny sod like 'im. An' 'e'll be watching for you this time." His eyes creased in concern.

She felt a shiver of fear. "You think he'll come after me? Wouldn't that just prove we're right? Wouldn't he be safer to let us wear ourselves out, and prove nothing?"

"Safer, yes," Sutton agreed. "But he might get annoyed and come after you anyway, if you get close enough to 'im to scare off some of 'is custom. And that in't all. There's the other thing to think about, an' I can't protect you from that, 'cause no one can."

"What thing?" she asked immediately. She trusted Sutton; he had proved both his friendship and his courage. If he feared something, then it was dangerous.

"The way I heard it, it wasn't just you and Mr. Monk who proved a bit sloppy," he said reluctantly. "It was Mr. Durban as well. You trusted in what 'e'd done, so you didn't take care to prove everything so not even a clever beggar like Mr. Rathbone could undo it. But what about Mr. Durban, eh? Why'd he slip up?"

"Because . . ." She had been about to say that he could not have realized how clever Rathbone would be, but that wouldn't do. He should have been prepared for anyone. "He was emotional about it too," she said instead.

Sutton shook his head. "That in't good enough, Miss Hester, an' you know that. He stopped an' started all over the place, way I heard it. You sure you want to know why?" His voice was gentle. "What do you know about him, for sure?"

She did not answer. There was no point in being defensive and saying that she knew he was good. She did not know it, she believed it, and she did that only because Monk did.

Sutton sighed. "Sure you want to?" This time he was not arguing, just waiting to allow her space to retreat, if she needed to.

But there was no point; Monk would go ahead regardless of whether she went with him or not. He could not leave it alone now. Something of his belief in himself, in his value as a friend, depended upon Durban being essentially the man he supposed him to be. And if he were to be disillusioned, he would need Hester's strength all the more. Standing apart would leave him bitterly alone.

"Better to know," she replied.

Sutton sighed and finished the last of his sandwich, still standing, then drained his glass. "Then we'd better go," he said with resignation. "C'mon, Snoot."

"What about your rats?" she asked.

"There's rats . . . an' rats," he replied enigmatically. "I'll take you to see Nellie. What she don't know in't worth the bother. Just follow me, and keep your ears open an' your mouth shut. It in't nice places we're goin'. By rights I'd rather not even take you, but I know you'll insist, and I 'aven't got time for an argument I in't goin' to win."

She smiled bleakly and followed after him along the narrow street, the dog between them. She did not ask what Nellie's occupation might be, and he did not offer any further information.

They took a bus eastwards into Limehouse. After walking with him another further half mile on foot through tangled lanes and cobbles, with awkward roofs almost meeting above them, she had lost her sense of direction entirely. She could not even smell the incoming tide of the river above the other odors of dense, swarming city life: the drains, the stale smoke, the horse manure, the sickly sweetness of a nearby brewery.

They found Nellie in a dim back room behind a public house. She was a small, tidy woman dressed in black that had long ago faded to a variety of grays. She wore a widow's lace cap on hair that sat in absurd little-girl ringlets down the sides of her creased face. Her eyes were small, narrow against the light, and—when Hester met them almost accidentally—as sharp as gimlets. She could probably see a pin on the floor at twenty paces.

Sutton did not introduce them, he merely told Nellie that Hester was all right, that she knew when to speak and when not to.

Nellie grunted. "That's as may be," she said curtly. "What d'yer want?" The last was addressed to Sutton; Hester was already dismissed.

"Like to know a bit more about some o' the river police," Sutton replied.

"Wot for?" Nellie regarded him suspiciously. "They in't never gonna cross your path."

"For a friend of mine," Sutton said.

"If your 'friend' is in trouble, better ter deal wi' the reg'lar cops," she told him unequivocally. "River Police is right bastards. Not many of 'em, an' not much way 'round 'em."

"Straight?" He raised his eyebrows.

"Mostly," she conceded.

"Monk?"

"Used ter be reg'lar p'lice, so I 'eard. Mean bastard, an' clever. 'Ang on ter a case like a bleedin' bulldog." She glanced at Snoot sitting at Sutton's feet. "Bulldog," she repeated.

"But straight?" Sutter insisted.

"Yeah. Leave 'im alone. Best 'e never 'eard of yer."

"Orme?"

"Straight as a stair rod," she replied with a sniff.

"Durban?"

"Don't matter. 'E's dead. Blew 'isself up on a ship."

"But was he straight?"

She tilted her head to one side and twisted her mouth until it looked like she had tasted a bad egg. "If yer after Jericho Phillips again, ye're a fool. 'E 'ad summink on Durban, same as Durban 'ad on 'im. Dunno wot it were, an' reckon I'm best ter keep it that way. Although I like ter know things. Never say when it might come in useful. But someone 'ad the bite on Durban. Dunno if it were Phillips 'isself or just that 'e knew about it. But I do know that Mr. Durban weren't nothin' like wot 'is precious river police thought 'e were. Got secrets, that one, an' I never found out wot they were, so it in't no use askin' me, Mr. Sutton, no matter wot yer thinks I owe yer."

Sutton had to be content with that, at least from her.

Even when they were outside again, he said nothing to Hester, except to ask her if she wished to continue.

"Certainly," she replied, although the misery was knotting up inside her. The word of one woman who might be a fence of stolen goods, a brothel keeper, or worse, should not tarnish the reputation of a good man. It was not Nellie's word that disturbed her, it was her own fear as to why Durban had pursued Phillips so relentlessly, then suddenly stopped. Then why had he taken it up again, when nothing they knew of had changed? Rathbone, with his skill, had revealed weaknesses in her reasoning, questions and doubts that she needed to have answered. She was ashamed of it, but that did not still the voices in her mind.

And she was afraid for Monk, because she knew how much of the peace within him that he had finally gained had come because a man like Durban, honest, wise, and possessed of his own inner strength, had bequeathed him the task he himself could no longer perform. Durban had trusted Monk to lead his men, and leading men was something Monk had never done successfully. He was brave, intelligent, imaginative, sometimes ruthless, but never before likable. He had never before inspired loyalty or the ultimate trust of others.

Over the years since the accident, flashes of memory had lit up individual scenes for him, and deduction had filled in many of the surrounding blanks. The picture that emerged was of a man he did not always like. It was too vividly easy to see why others had not.

He had tried hard to change. Durban was the one man who had seen the best in him and placed his trust in it. Now that Oliver Rathbone had suddenly become a stranger, a man they no longer under-stood, Durban was even more a key to trust.

Hester was afraid of what Monk was going to learn about him, and how deeply it would hurt. Therefore she needed to be the first to know, so she could protect him—or, if that were not possible, at least walk beside him through whatever lay ahead.

She followed Sutton along the dark alley towards the next person he would question on her behalf.

FIVE

onk left home and walked down towards the ferry landing. He was also weighed down with anxiety, and even more with guilt. The view across the river was bright and busy. Heavily laden barges passed in both directions, dark against the sun on the water. All he could think of was that Phillips was free, not only from prison and execution, but from ever being charged again with the murder of Fig. No matter what proof Monk might find now, it could not be used against him. How could failure be more complete?

He crossed Rotherhithe Street and went down the narrow alley to Princes Stairs. The smells of salt and mud were heavy in the air. It was not yet nine in the morning, but at this time of the year the sun had been up for hours, and it was already hot. There was barely any wind to lift the heaviness, and he could hear the shouts of lightermen and stevedores from two hundred yards away. It was high tide; the water was slack and oily-looking. There was not enough current to move the ships at anchor, and the tangles of masts and rigging were motionless against the sky.

He had had the chance to kill Phillips, and it was his own arrogance that had made him so certain he had already won that he had let it go in order to vindicate Durban. And how badly he had wanted to be the one to do this so that all his men would know, and respect him for it. They would see that he had paid his debt to Durban, and earned some kind of right to take his place, instead of merely being given it.

Except, of course, that he had not. Instead he had guaranteed that

Phillips was free from paying the price, not just now but forever. Free to go back to his boat with its children, who would be more than ever imprisoned in their wretched lives.

A ferry bumped against the steps and the ferryman called up, breaking Monk's train of thought.

Monk brought himself to attention and went down. He did not need to give directions; he made this journey every day, and most of the men knew him. A nod good morning was all he needed to give. Probably half the river knew the result of the trial. They might pity him for it, but they would despise him too. Phillips had made a fool of him. Or Rathbone had. Or more honestly, he had made a fool of himself. If he had been lucky, he would have gotten away with it, but it would not have altered the fact that he had taken too much on trust, allowed his emotions to cloud his intellect, and as a result made careless mistakes. There was nothing for him to say to the ferryman. There was not really anything to say to anyone, until he could rescue at least something from the ashes.

He paid his fare, got out at the other side at Wapping New Stairs, and climbed up the short way to the top.

There was a boy standing waiting. He was thin and wiry, his face keen. He had a cap jammed on his head, hiding most of his hair. His shirt was ragged and missing several buttons, and his trouser legs were uneven, which complemented his boots, one brown and one black. He appeared to be about ten or eleven. He was the mudlark Scuff, one of the boys who salvaged small items of value from the river to sell. He had helped Monk before, and chose to continue to help him with his knowledge of the dockside and its ways.

"Sorry sight you are," he said to Monk disparagingly. "Got a face like a burst boot. S'pose you got a right. Made a pig's ear of it, an' all." The boy fell into step behind him as Monk turned to walk along the dockside towards the police station. The boy sniffed. "But yer gonna do summink, in't yer?" There was a note of anxiety in his voice that was close to real fear.

Monk stopped. The ferryman was not worth the effort of pretense, but Scuff deserved both honesty and the courage not to disappoint him. He looked at the boy and saw the vulnerability bright in his eyes.

"Yes, of course I'm going to do something," he said firmly. "I just need to think very hard before I do it, so that I get it right—this time."

Scuff shook his head, drawing his breath in through his teeth, but some of the fear in him eased. "Yer gotta be careful, Mr. Monk. Yer may 'ave been the cat's whiskers wi' villains on shore, but yer in't much use wi' river folk. Though come ter think on it, that lawyer's sharp, all right. Pretty as new paint, 'e is, all striped trousers and shiny shoes." For a moment his face was full of sympathy. "For all that 'e's bent as a dog's 'ind leg." He kept pace with Monk across the stones.

"He's not bent," Monk corrected him. "It's his job to get people off a charge, if he can. It's my fault that I made it possible for him."

Scuff was skeptical. "Someone twistin' 'is arm ter do it, then?"

"Possibly. It might just be that he felt that the principle of the law required that even the worst of us deserve a fair hearing."

Scuff pulled his face into an expression of deep disgust. "The worst of us deserves ter dance on the end of a rope, an' if yer don't know that, then yer in't fit ter be out o' the 'ouse by yerself."

"It doesn't make any difference, Scuff," Monk told him miserably. "Phillips is free, and it's up to me to clear up the mess and nail him for something else."

"I'll 'elp yer," Scuff said immediately. "Yer need me."

"I'd like your help, but I don't need it," Monk said as gently as he could. "I have no very clear idea yet where to begin, except by going over what I already know and seeing where the holes are, then pursuing it until I can at least nail him on pornography or extortion. It's dangerous, and I don't want to risk you getting hurt."

Scuff thought about it for a moment or two. He was trying to keep up with Monk, but his legs were not long enough, and every third or fourth stride he had to put in an extra little skip.

"I in't afraid," he said at length. "Leastways not enough ter stop me."

Monk halted and Scuff halted half a step later.

"I don't doubt your courage," Monk said clearly, meeting Scuff's eyes. "In fact, if you had a trifle less you might be safer."

"Yer want me ter be scaredy-cat?" Scuff asked incredulously.

Monk made a quick decision. "If it will keep you out of the hands of men like Phillips, yes I do."

Scuff stood still on the spot, the stubbornness in his face slowly revealing the hurt. "Yer think I in't no use, don't yer?" he asked, sniffing very slightly.

Monk was furious with himself for having put them both into such a position. Now he was caught between denying the fact that he cared about the boy, which would be a wounding lie whose damage he might never undo, or admitting that his decision was based on emotion rather than reason. Or the alternative, perhaps crueler still, was to suggest that he really did think Scuff was no use. That one he could not even consider.

He started to walk again.

"I think you're a lot of use," he said quietly, falling back a bit to keep step with the boy, rather than letting him skip to keep up. "For knowledge and brains, not for fighting, and this could become very unpleasant. If I have to get out very quickly, I don't want to have to stop to make sure you are all right. Have you ever heard the expression, 'hostage to fortune'?"

"No, I in't," Scuff said dubiously, but there was a spark of hope in his eyes.

"It means caring enough about something that you can't afford to lose it, so people can make you do what they want," Monk explained. "Because you think it's worth a lot, or it's bad that it should be destroyed," he added, in case Scuff should be embarrassed.

Scuff turned the idea over in his mind, examining it. "Oh," he said at last. "So you wouldn't want Phillips ter drown me, take a fr'instance, or cut me throat, like? So you might leave 'im alone. But if it don't bother yer, yer'd tell 'im ter get on with it, an' yer'd nab 'im?"

"Something like that," Monk agreed, thinking that he had made his point rather well.

"I see." Scuff nodded very slightly. "Well, if we get someone as is daft enough ter get caught, we'll 'ave ter make sure it's someone we don't care about . . . not too much. I s'pose Mrs. Monk is one o' them 'ostages, in't she? Yer'd let pretty well the devil 'isself go ter save 'er, wouldn't yer?"

There was no way out of the conclusion. "Yes," he admitted. "That's why she's staying away from Phillips, and the bad places on the river. I'm going there, and—before you argue anymore—you aren't."

"Yer can mebbe tell 'er wot ter do, 'cause she's a woman," Scuff observed, stopping, and standing very stiffly, feet slightly apart. "I in't." He took a deep breath. "An' you in't me pa. But I'll look after yer, anyway. Where are yer gonna start? I know—wi' fishin Fig's body out o' the river. We better get on wi' it. Don' just stand there like yer growin' out o' the ground." And without waiting for a reply, he started to walk nonchalantly towards the edge of the embankment and the nearest steps where they might catch a ferry. He did not look back over his shoulder to see if Monk was following him.

Monk was irritated at being outmaneuvered, and yet underneath the surface, aware that Scuff was also trying to stay with him, without sacrificing his own dignity. He wanted desperately to belong, and he thought his only way was to be of use. What was the risk, really, compared with those he ran every day living on the river edge, cadging his food and shelter by picking up bits of coal or dropped brass screws from the mud when the tide went down?

He caught up with Scuff. "All right," he said, mock grudgingly. "You might help me find the lighterman. You're right; that's where I was going to start."

" 'Course," Scuff said casually, as if he did not really care, but he shrugged his shoulders and then walked a little taller, avoiding Monk's eyes. He did not wish to be read, at this particular moment; he was too vulnerable. "We can get a ferry down a bit," he added. "Find the lightermen 'avin' a cup o' tea, like as not, at this hour."

Monk was uncertain whether to thank him. He decided against it; it might sound a little patronizing. "Hope so," he said instead. "I could do with one too."

Scuff grimaced. Monk knew he had great hopes of being given one himself, if he were lucky; possibly even a sandwich. It was unlikely that he had eaten today.

They took the ferry downstream, as suggested, and asked specifically after the lighterman they wanted. It took them more than an hour to find him, because he was already at work, first loading and then getting his lighter out into the traffic. They made some of their inquiries of a group of men standing around a brazier with boiling water, and Monk purchased a mug of tea and a thick slice of bread. He offered the same to Scuff, who thought about it as long as he dared, then said with practiced indifference that he didn't mind if he did. All the while he watched Monk out of the corner of his eye to make sure he did not miss his chance.

Monk affected not to notice.

"I already told yer," the lighterman said wearily. "Yer let the bastard orff! There in't no more I can say!"

They were sitting on the canvas bales as the flat-bottomed craft made its slow, heavy way downstream towards Greenwich.

"I know what you said," Monk assured him. "And all the evidence bears it out. But we didn't ask you what Mr. Durban said, or if he asked you anything that you didn't mention before."

The lighterman screwed up his face in thought, moving his eyes as if looking at the hard, glittering reflections off the water. " 'E were upset," he replied slowly. "All bent over 'isself like someone'd 'it 'im in the belly. Tell yer the truth, I liked 'im better fer it."

So did Monk, but it was not the answer he needed. He had already asked Orme these questions, but Orme was so defensive of Durban that his answers were no longer useful; they had become simply a repetition that Durban had done the right thing. Monk was hoping the lighterman would remember some other information that Durban had let slip, some word, or even omission, that might lead in a new direction. He was fumbling, and he knew it. The lighterman's face showed his disappointment. He had expected more, and he had not received it. He had endangered himself to testify, and Monk had let him down.

"Are you afraid of Phillips?" Monk asked suddenly.

The lighterman was caught off guard. "No!" he said indignantly. "Why should I be? I never said he done nothin'. In't got no cause ter come after me."

"And if he had cause, would he?" Monk asked, trying to keep all expression out of his voice.

The lighterman stared at him. "Wot's the matter with yer? Yer simple, or summink? 'E'd bloody carve out me guts an' 'ang 'em on Execution Dock ter dry in the wind!"

Monk continued to look skeptical.

Scuff looked from Monk to the lighterman and back again, waiting, his eyes wide.

"An' yer won't catch 'im fer it neither," the lighterman added. "Not that you bleedin' lot could catch a cold soppin' wet in winter. Mr. Durban knew wot 'e were about. Reckon if 'e'd 'a lived, 'e'd a swung the bastard by 'is neck, all right."

Monk felt the words land like a blow, the harder because it was the one case Durban had not solved, and he did not want to admit it. But there was a thread in what the lighterman had said that was worth following. "So he was still working on it?" he asked.

The lighterman looked at him witheringly.

" 'Course 'e were. I reckon 'e'd never 'ave given up." He squinted a little in the hard light, and leaned very slightly on his long oar to steer a few degrees to port.

"What is there to follow?" Monk found the words hard to say, placing himself so vulnerably, as if he were asking a bargee how to do his own job.

The lighterman shrugged. " 'Ow the 'ell do I know? 'E said summink about money, an' making them fat bastards pay for their pleasures twice over. But I dunno wot 'e meant."

"Extortion," Monk replied.

"Yeah? Well, you in't gonna get any o' them exactly ter complain, now are yer?" the lighterman sneered.

Monk kept his voice level and his face as expressionless as he could. "Unlikely," he agreed. "At least not to me."

The lighterman turned slowly from his position holding the oar. He was a lean, angular man, but the movement was unconsciously graceful. For a moment surprise caught him off guard. "Yer not so daft, are yer! Gawd 'elp yer if 'e catches yer is all I can say."

Monk could wrest no more out of him, and twenty minutes later he and Scuff were back on the dockside.

"Yer gonna set 'is customers agin' 'im?" Scuff said in awe. " 'Ow yer gonna do that?" He looked worried.

"I'm not sure what I'm going to do," Monk answered, starting to walk along the dockside. They were on the north bank, back near the Wapping Police Station. "For now I'll settle for learning a great deal more about him."

"If yer can prove for sure that 'e killed Fig, will they 'ang 'im?" Scuff asked hopefully.

"No." Monk kept his pace even, though he was not yet certain where he was going. He did not want Scuff to realize that, although he was beginning to appreciate that Scuff was a far sharper judge of character than he had previously given him credit for. It was disconcerting to be read so well by an eleven-year-old. "No," he said again. "He's been found not guilty. We can't try him again, no matter what we find. In fact, even if he confessed, there'd still be nothing we could do."

Scuff was silent. He turned towards Monk, looking him up and down, his lips tight.

Monk was unpleasantly aware that Scuff was being tactful. He was touched by it, and at the same time he was hurt. Scuff was sorry for him, because he had made a mistake he did not know how to mend. This was a far cry from the brilliant, angry man he had been in the main Metropolitan Police onshore, where criminals and slipshod police alike were frightened of him.

"So we gotta get 'im for summink else, then," Scuff deduced. "Wot like? Thievin'? Forgin'? 'E don't do that, far as I know. Sellin' stuff wot was nicked? 'E don't do that neither. An' 'e don't smuggle nothin' so 'e don't pay the revenue men be'ind 'is back, like." He screwed up his face in an unspoken question.

"I don't know," Monk said frankly. "That's what I need to find out. He does lots of things. Maybe Fig isn't the only boy he's killed, but I need something I can prove."

Scuff grunted in sympathy and walked beside Monk, trying very hard to keep in step with him. Monk wondered whether to shorten his stride. He decided not to; he did not want Scuff to know that he had noticed.

The police surgeon was busy and short-tempered. He met them in one of the stone-floored and utilitarian outer rooms of the mortuary. He had just finished an autopsy and his rolled-up sleeves were still splashed with blood.

"Made a mess of it, didn't you," he said bitterly. It was an accusation, not a question. He glanced at Scuff once, then disregarded him. "If you expect me to rescue you, or excuse you, for that matter, then you're wasting your time."

Scuff let out a wail of fury, and stifled it immediately, terrified Monk would make him go away, and then he would be no use at all. He stood shifting his weight from one foot to the other in his odd boots, and glaring at the surgeon.

Monk controlled his own temper with difficulty, only because his need to find some new charge against Phillips was greater than his impulse for self-defense. "You deal with most of the bodies taken out of this stretch of the river," he replied, his voice tight. "Figgis can't have been the only boy of that age and general type. I'd like to hear about the others."

"You wouldn't," the surgeon contradicted him. "Especially not in front of this one." He indicated Scuff briefly. "Won't give you anything useful, anyway. If we could've tied any of them to Jericho Phillips, don't you think we would have?" His dark face was creased with an inner pain that perhaps he did not realize showed so clearly.

Monk's anger vanished. Suddenly they had everything that mattered in common. The retort that apparently the surgeon had been no cleverer than anyone else died on his tongue.

"I want to get him for anything I can," he said quietly. "Loitering with intent or being a public nuisance, if it would put him away long enough to start on the rest."

"I want to see him hang for what he does to these boys," the surgeon replied. His voice shook very slightly.

"So do I, but I'll settle for what I can get," Monk replied.

The surgeon looked up at him, his eyes hard, then very slowly the disgust seeped out of him and he relaxed.

Scuff stopped fidgeting.

"I've had a few boys I think were his," the surgeon said. "And if I could have proved it I would have. One he acknowledged. Police asked him, and he came in here, brass-faced as the Lord Mayor, and said he knew the boy. Said he'd taken him in, but he'd run away. He knew I couldn't prove anything different. I'd have happily dissected him alive, and he knew it. He enjoyed looking at me and seeing me know that I couldn't." He winced. "But I'd have taken *you* apart when that verdict came in. You so bloody nearly had him! I've no right. I didn't get him myself."

"How sure are you that he's done it before?" Monk asked. "I mean sure, not just instinct."

"Absolutely, but I can't prove a damn thing. If you can get him, I'll be in your debt for life, and I'll pay it. I don't care whether he's on the end of a rope or knifed to death by one of his rivals. Just take him off our river." For a moment it was a plea, the urgency in him undisguised. Then he hid it again, rolling up his sleeves even higher and turning away. "All I can tell you is that he's fond of torturing them with burning cigars, but you probably know that. And when he finishes them it's with a knife." His body was rigid and he kept his back to them. "Now get out of here and do something bloody useful!" He stalked away, leaving them alone in the damp room with its smells of carbolic and death.

Outside, Monk breathed in the air deeply. Scuff said nothing, looking away from him. Perhaps he was frightened at last, not just aware of dangers that he must live with every day, but of something so large and so dark it stripped away all bravado and pretense. His fear was out of his control, and he did not want Monk to see it.

They walked side by side near the edge of the water, both lost in their own thoughts on the reality of death, and its pedestrian, physical immediacy. They were barely aware of the slap of the tide on the wall of the steps, and the shouts of the lightermen and stevedores a hundred yards away unloading a schooner from the Indies.

"This is worse than I thought," Monk said after a while. He stopped walking and looked out over the water. He must be careful how he phrased it or Scuff would know he was being protected, and would resent it. "I don't like to involve you, because it's dangerous," he went on. "But I don't think Orme and I can do it without your help. There are boys who will trust you who won't even speak to us, unless you're there to persuade them."

Scuff's narrow shoulders were tight, as if he were waiting to be struck; it was his only outward sign of fear. Now he stopped, hands in his pockets, and turned slowly to face Monk. His eyes were dark, hollow, and embarrassed by what he saw as his own weakness. "Yeah?" He wanted desperately to meet expectations.

"I think we'll need you all the time, to help with the questioning, until we get him," Monk said casually, starting to walk again. "It would be a sacrifice, I know. But we'd find you a proper place to sleep, where you could shut the door and be alone. And there'd be food, of course."

Scuff was too startled to move. He stood rooted to the spot. "Food?" he repeated.

Monk stopped and turned back. "Well, I can't come looking for you every day. I haven't time."

Suddenly Scuff understood. Joy filled his face, then very quickly he sobered up to a proper dignity. "I reckon I could," he said generously. "Just until yer get 'im, like."

"Thank you," Monk replied, almost certain that Hester would see the necessity of keeping Scuff safe as long as Jericho Phillips was free, however long that might be. "Well, come on then! The first boy we need to find is the one who identified Fig from Durban's drawings. He might know something else, if we ask him the right questions."

"Yeah," Scuff said, as if he thoroughly agreed. " 'E might, an' all."

However, it took them the rest of the day to find the boy, and he was clearly very unhappy about speaking with Monk about anything. They stood where the narrow entrance of an alley opened into the Shadwell Dock. The tide was ebbing and slapping over the stairs a few yards away, leaving the higher steps slimy as it retreated. There was a large ship in the New Basin behind them, its spars and yards black against the fading sky.

"I dunno nothin' more," the boy said urgently. "I told yer 'oo 'e were, same like I told Mr. Durban. I dunno 'oo done 'im, an' I can't 'elp yer."

" 'E won't leave yer alone 'til yer tell 'im." Scuff gestured towards Monk. "So yer might as well get on wif it. It don't do ter be seen talkin' ter the cops, if yer can 'elp it." He gave a philosophical shrug. "It's a bit late for me, but you could save yerself."

The boy gave him a filthy look.

Scuff was impervious. "Wot else did Mr. Durban ask yer?" He looked at Monk, then back at the boy. "Yer don't want 'im as an enemy, believe me. If yer like, 'e'll pretend 'e never 'eard of yer."

The boy knew when to give up. " 'E were askin' fer a woman called Mary Webster, Walker . . . Webber! Summink like that," he said. "Like a dog wif a bone, 'e were. Where was she? 'Ad I seen 'er? 'Ad anybody said anything, even 'er name? I told 'im I'd never 'eard of 'er, but 'e wouldn't leave it. I told 'im I'd ask me sister, just ter shut 'im up, like. 'E said as 'e'd be back. This Mary whatever were 'bout 'is age, 'e said, but 'e din't know much more about 'er 'n that."

Scuff looked across at Monk.

There was a pleasure boat passing down the river, hurdy-gurdy music playing. The sound drifted on the air, loud and then soft, loud and then soft, as the wind carried it.

"So did you ask your sister?" Monk said, curious to know what Durban was looking for. There had been no mention of a middle-aged woman before.

"Not the first time," the boy answered, sucking in his breath. "But Mr. Durban come back an' 'e wouldn't let it go. I seen pit bull terriers as couldn't 'ang on to a thing and worry it like 'e did. So I told 'im ter ask Biddie 'isself, an' told 'im where ter find 'er."

"Where can we find Biddie?"

The boy rolled his eyes, but he told him.

Monk had no desire to take Scuff with him to a brothel, but the alternative was to leave him alone. He could have told him to go to Paradise Place, but it would be bitterly unfair to oblige him to explain to Hester that he had come to stay. And anyway, she might not even be there if they had had some crisis at Portpool Lane. There was nothing to do but allow him to come.

It was completely dark, even on this clear summer night, by the time they found Biddie. She had apparently been plying her trade earlier in the evening, but was now cheerfully available to take a glass of ale and merely talk, for a couple of shillings. She was a plain girl, but buxomly built and relatively clean in a blue dress disturbingly low cut, which did not bother Scuff as much as Monk thought it should have.

"Yeah, Mary Webber," Biddie said, nodding, keeping both hands around her glass as if she feared having it taken from her. "Lookin' fer 'er summink fierce, 'e were. I kep' tellin' 'im I din't know no Mary Webber, which I din't! I never 'eard of 'er." She managed to look aggrieved, even while wiping the foam off her upper lip. " 'E got a temper on 'im, that one. Right paddy 'e were in. Clocked Mr. 'Opkins summink awful. 'It 'im on the side o' the 'ead an' near sent 'im inter the middle o' next week. An 'e's a nasty sod, too, but 'e never 'eard o' Mary Webber no more'n I 'ad."

Monk felt an acute sense of dismay. It sounded nothing like the man he had known. "What did he look like?" he asked. Perhaps this was a case of mistaken identity.

Biddie had a good eye for faces. Perhaps it was part of her trade. It might be the way to remember certain people it would be advisable to avoid. " 'Bout your 'eight, bit less, but more solid. Nice-lookin', 'specially fer a cop. Nice eyes, dark they were. Grayish 'air, wi' sort o' little waves in it. Walked easy, but a bit like mebbe 'e'd once been a sailor."

That was Durban. Monk swallowed. "Did he say why he wanted to find Mary Webber?"

A couple wove their way past them, talking loudly and bumping into people.

"No, an' I din't ask," Biddie said vehemently. "I 'eard 'e went ter old Jetsam, the pawnbroker, an' gave 'im an 'ell of a time. Duffed 'im up summink rotten. Still got the scars, 'e 'as. Not that 'e were ever much ter look at, but 'is own ma wouldn't take ter 'im now." She finished her ale with relish. "Wouldn't mind if yer got me another," she remarked.

Monk dispatched Scuff with the empty glass and threepence. He took a breath. There was no escaping now, whatever the truth was.

"Do you mean that Durban beat the pawnbroker?" She must be lying. Why would he believe her, rather than everything he knew of Durban? And yet he could not leave it alone. In his own past people had been frightened of him. Was he violent too? It was so easy. "Who told you that?" he asked.

"I saw 'im," she said simply. "Told yer. 'Orrible 'e looked."

"But how do you know it was Durban who struck him, or that it was deliberate? Perhaps Jetsam hit him first?"

She gave him a look of incredulity. "Ol' Jetsam? Get on wi' yer. Jetsam's as big a coward as ever were born. 'E wouldn't go 'ittin' a cop even if 'e were soused as an 'erring. Lie 'is way out of a paper bag, cheat 'is own mother out o' sixpence, but 'e wouldn't never 'it nobody face-ter-face."

Monk's stomach clenched and he felt a coldness through him. "Why would Durban hit him?"

"Probably lost 'is temper 'cause Jetsam lied ter 'im," she answered reasonably.

"If Jetsam is that kind of a liar, how do you know it wasn't some customer he cheated who hit him?"

Scuff came back with the ale and gave it to Biddie, and the change to Monk, who thanked him.

"Look," Biddie said patiently. "Yer been fair ter me. I in't gonna lie to yer. The local cop on the beat 'ad ter pull 'em apart, an' 'e were gonna charge Durban, 'cause ol' Jetsam got more'n the worst of it. 'E were near 'avin' 'is 'ead stove in. I reckon Durban'd 'ave been charged if 'e 'adn't bin a cop 'isself, an' put the twist on."

"That shouldn't make any difference," Monk said, then immediately knew it was a mistake. He saw the contempt in her eyes. He knew what she was going to say before she started, and yet the words still hurt like a fresh cut.

She rolled her eyes. "Yeah? Well, the cop wot caught 'im were just the local constable, and Durban were a commander in the River Police. Yer can't be daft enough not ter work that out fer yerself. Constable might 'a grumbled, but 'e din't do nothing, nor Jetsam neither. If any of us 'ad known 'oo Mary Webber were, we'd 'a told 'im."

Monk did not pursue it any further. It was too late today to see if he could substantiate any of it. He walked in silence with Scuff to the nearest steps where there was a light and he could hire a ferry to take them back across the river to Rotherhithe. It was slack tide now and the long stretch of mud and stones gleamed in the yellow glare from the lamps. In its own way it was both sinister and beautiful. The slick surface of the river barely moved. Even the ships at anchor lay still, their spars lumpy with furled sails. The blur of smoke hung above some still-burning factory chimney where industry never slept.

Did he believe Biddie? Who was Mary Webber? Nothing he had learned about Durban had made any mention of a woman. Why such passion? Who was she that Durban would so lose control of himself, and of all the beliefs he had so clearly lived by, that he would attack a man to beat information out of him? And perhaps even worse, he had apparently then coerced a junior officer into ignoring his duty and overlooking the whole episode!

Monk could not imagine Durban doing either of these things. But then, how much had he really known him? He had liked him. They had shared food, warmth, and exhaustion of body and mind in the relentless search to find men who could unknowingly destroy half the world. They had found them. He still relived the horror of it in dreams.

But in the end it had caught up with Durban himself. He had gone nobly, willingly, to death by fire in order to save others, and take the threat with him. And he had gone alone, refusing to allow Monk to share his fate. He had physically thrown him off the stern of the ship into the boiling wake rather than let him also perish, and had not had time to save himself before the magazines exploded.

What kind of friendship or loyalty can you give to someone who is so supremely brave, and yet also desperately flawed? What do you owe to promises made, or understood? What if the other person is gone, and no more explanations can be asked for or given, and still you have to act, and believe something?

Scuff was watching him, waiting to see what he did because of this latest revelation, and Monk was intensely aware of it.

"Mebbe she could 'ave put Phillips away." Scuff said hopefully.

"D'yer think that were why 'e were after 'er? Or mebbe Phillips did 'er in too, d'yer think? An' that's why nobody found 'er?"

Monk had to answer him. "No, not really."

"She might 'ave." Scuff raised his voice to sound more positive, even trying to be cheerful. Monk knew it was for his sake. "She's 'iding 'cause she's scared stiff o' Phillips. She could 'ave seen wot 'appened. Mebbe she's somebody's ma wot Phillips done."

"Perhaps," Monk conceded, although he did not believe it. "Durban never mentioned her in his notes, and surely he would have, if that's who she was."

Scuff thought about that for quite a long time. They had hailed a ferry and were more than halfway across the river, weaving in and out of the great ships at anchor, before he found a solution.

"Mebbe that were to keep 'er safe. If she saw summink Phillips'd kill 'er fer. An' 'e would," he suggested.

Hank could not see Scuff's face in the darkness of the river, but he could see the hunch of his narrow shoulders and the way he held himself when he was hurt.

The oars splashed in and out. The ferryman had a good rhythm, probably from years of practice.

"An' like you said," Scuff replied unhappily, "there's gentlemen in it up ter their necks. Gentlemen wot got enough money ter pay yer friend the lawyer wot spoke up fer Phillips. And yer don't know 'oo they are, 'cause they don't exactly go round tellin' people they go in fer wot 'e does."

"You're right, Scuff," Monk said decisively. "I should have thought of that for myself. Of course you are."

He could see Scuff's grin, even in the dark.

When a bed had been made up for Scuff and he was sound asleep in it, Hester and Monk sat in the kitchen over a very late supper—really no more than two large pieces of fruitcake and two cups of tea.

"I can't let him go back until Phillips is arrested and locked up," he said anxiously, watching her face.

"It's as much my responsibility as yours," she answered. Then she smiled. "Of course we can't. And that might be quite a while, so you had better get him some clean clothes. I'm much too busy to wash these every night, even supposing I could dry them. You might even get a pair of boots that fit him—and really are a pair."

She wanted to talk about something that was worrying her. He could see it in her eyes, in a kind of hesitation, as though she were still looking for a way to avoid saying it at all.

He told her about hearing of Mary Webber, but not of Durban's violence towards the pawnbroker, or his use of rank to prevent the constable from charging him. He realized with surprise that it was not Hester he was protecting—it was Durban. Because he himself cared so intensely what Hester thought of him, he was imagining that Durban would too.

"Why are you smiling?" she asked him, puzzled and a little off balance.

"I don't know," he admitted. "At Scuff's help, I suppose."

Suddenly she was profoundly serious.

"Be careful, William," she warned. "Please? I know he's looked after himself for years, but he's only a child. Lots of people die on the river . . ." She left the rest unsaid. There were more like Fig than like Scuff, and they both knew that.

He looked down at her hands on the table. They were very slender, like a girl's, but strong. Their beauty lay not in soft, white skin or delicate nails, but in grace; they were quick and gentle, and their touch was light. They would be broken before they would let a drowning man go, but they would allow a butterfly to leave as simply as it had come. He loved her hands. He wanted to reach out and touch them, but he felt self-conscious when there was so much more urgent business at hand.

"Durban was being blackmailed," she said quietly, not meeting his eyes. "I don't yet know what for. Could that be to do with this Mary Webber, whoever she is?"

"I don't know," he confessed. He wished he did not have to know. He was overburdened with knowledge already, and the more there was of it, the more it hurt. What was it that drove people on and on to seek the truth, to unravel every knot, even when it was the ignorance and the peace of heart that made it all endurable? Was truth going to heal anything? How much of it could any one person grasp?

She stood up. "That's enough for today. Let's go to bed." She said it gently, but she was not going to accept an argument, and he had no wish to offer any.

Hester was concerned for Durban's reputation too, not so much for himself as for what the discoveries could do to Monk. Her husband had had few friends, at least that he could remember. At one time he and Runcorn had been more than allies. They had shared the involvement and the tragedy of police work, and the dangers.

But Monk's abrasive tongue and his ambition had driven Runcorn to a bitter jealousy. He was a narrower man in both his vision and his ability. The rivalry had brought out the meanest spirit in him. Friendship had eventually become enmity.

Of course she did not explain any of this to Sutton when she met him to take up the search again. He would think their purpose was to find some evidence to prove Phillips guilty of something for which they could try him. He must know that the death of Fig was closed to them now, even if he had been tactful enough to refrain from saying so.

They rode the bus in companionable silence, Snoot by Sutton's feet as always.

Hester sat in the top of the bus watching the narrow, closely crammed houses with the stained walls and sagging roofs as they moved closer to Limehouse and the printer Sutton had told her they were going to. He had helped in many things, and she knew he would do all he could now. He would call in favors, incur more, spend all day away from his own work to help her find what she was seeking.

But Sutton could not tell her what it was that she wanted to find, or what she hoped it would prove. They could not undo the failure of Phillips's trial, nor the fact that Rathbone had defended him. They might find out the reason for that choice—if indeed it had been choice, and not some kind of necessity. But it might be confidential and something they could never learn. Did it matter? Could they not trust Rathbone, after all the battles they had fought together?

In framing the question, she realized with a jolt of cold surprise that the answer must be that she did not, or she would not have asked. She would not have said the same a year ago. Had his marriage to Margaret really changed him so much? Or was it simply that it had brought to the fore a different, weaker part of his character?

Or was it a different part of hers? She had never been in love with him; it had always been Monk, even if she had doubted at times that he would ever love her, or make her happy. In fact, she had considered it impossible that he would even wish to try. But she had liked Rathbone deeply, and she had trusted a decency in him. If this were a lapse, for whatever reason, could she not forgive him? Was her loyalty so shallow that one mistake ended it? Loyalty had to be worth more than that or it was little more than convenience.

The bus stopped again and more people climbed on, standing packed together in the aisle.

And Monk's loyalty to Durban, she thought. That also had to be strong enough to handle the truth. She wanted desperately to protect him from the disillusion she feared was coming. There were moments when she did not want to know why Rathbone had defended Phillips. But they passed. Her better self despised the weakness that preferred ignorance, or worse, lies. She would not want anyone she cared for to love a false reflection of her. After all, could there be a greater loneliness than that?

They reached the terminus and alighted. It was a walk of about half a mile along the busy street, and she had to go behind Sutton and Snoot because the way was so narrow they could not pass together without bumping into the traffic going the other way. Every few moments Sutton would look back to make sure she was still on his heels.

Sutton stopped at a small door next to an alley no more than ten feet long, and ending in a blind wall. Snoot instantly sat at his heels. Sutton knocked, and several moments passed before it was opened by a small hunchbacked man with an extraordinarily sweet expression on his face. He nodded when he recognized Sutton and his dog, then he glanced at Hester, more questioning whether she were with them than for her name or business. Satisfied by Sutton's nod, he led them inside to a room so cluttered with books and papers he had to clear two chairs for them to sit down. There were reams of blank paper stacked against the wall; the smell of ink was sharp in the air. The little man hitched himself back with some difficulty into what was obviously his own chair.

"I din't print it," he said without any preamble. His voice was deep and chesty, and his diction remarkably clear.

Sutton nodded. "I know that. It was Pinky Jones, but he's dead, and he'd lie about the time of day. Just tell Mrs. Monk what it said, if you please, Mr. Palk."

"It's not nice," Palk warned.

"Is it true?" Hester asked, although she had not yet been included in the conversation.

"Oh, yes, it's true. Lots of folks around here know that."

"Then please tell me."

He looked at her, for the first time, curiosity sharp in his face.

"You have to understand, Durban was a man of strong passions," he began. "Nice on the surface, funny when he wanted to be. I've seen him set the whole room laughing. And generous, he could be. But he felt some things hard, and it seems this Mary Webber was one o' them. Never heard why. Never heard who or what she was that made him care."

"He never found her?"

"Don't know, Miss, but if he didn't, it wasn't for want of trying. This all started when he went to Ma Wardlop's house. Brothel it is—mebbe a dozen girls or so. Asking her if she'd seen Mary Webber." He shook his head. "Wouldn't let it drop, no matter what. Finally Ma Wardlop told him one of the girls knew something, and took him to her room. He questioned her in there for more than an hour, until she was screaming at him. That point Ma went an' fetched a revenue man who lived a couple o' doors away. Big man, he was." He pulled his lips into a thin line, an expression of great sadness. "Punched the door in and said he found Durban in a position no policeman should be with a whore, but didn't say what it was, exactly. She claimed he'd forced himself on her. He said he never touched her."

Hester did not reply. Her mind raced from one ugly scene to another, trying to find an answer that would not disgust Monk.

Palk's face was screwed up in revulsion, but it was impossible to say whether it was for Durban, or the lie the prostitute might have told. "Ma Wardlop said she'd keep her mouth shut about it all if Durban would be wise enough to do the same. Only she meant about anything he might see in the future, and he knew that."

"Blackmail," Hester said succinctly.

He nodded again. "He told her to go to hell, and take the revenue man with her." Palk said it with some satisfaction, curling back his lips in a smile that showed surprisingly strong white teeth. "They said they'd not just spread it around the streets, they'd put it in the papers too. He told them he agreed with the Duke of Wellington—'publish and be damned.' He wasn't going to keep his mouth shut about anything he didn't want to."

"And what happened?" she asked, fear and admiration tightening inside her, her stomach knotted, her breath slow, as if the noise of it might stop her hearing what he would say next. It was stupid. Durban was dead and could not be hurt anymore. And yet she cared painfully that he had had the courage and the honor to defy them.

"Nothing, until the next time he caught them robbing a customer," the little man answered. "And put the girl in prison for it. Then they published it all right." His eyes did not move from hers. "Very embarrassing it was for Durban, but he weathered it. Lost a good few he'd thought were friends. Hard way to find out they weren't. Got laughed at in places where they used to call him 'sir.' It hurt him, but I only seen him show it once, and then just for a moment. He took it like a man, never complained, and never, far as I know, looked the other way on anything they did."

"What happened to the girl?" She felt a flood of warmth inside her, an easing of the ache of tension, then the chill again, and fear of the next answer.

"Nothing," Palk told her, his eyes reading her emotions like print on the page. "That wasn't Durban's way. He knew she was only doing what she had to, to get by. He had a hot temper, but he never took it out on women or kids. Soft, he was, in his own fashion, as if he knew what it was like to be poor, or hungry, or alone." He smiled at the memory. "Beat the hell out of Willy Lyme for knocking his wife around, but gentle as a woman with old Bert when 'e got daft and didn't even know who he was anymore. Went into the canal after the poor old sod drowned himself, and cried when he couldn't save him. Poor old Bert. Came to his funeral, Durban did. Never knew for sure, but I reckoned he paid for most of it. Bert hadn't sixpence to his name."

He looked narrowly at Hester. "I don't know why yer want to know, Miss. You can't hurt Durban now, but there's a lot of folk won't take it kindly if you speak ill of him. Wouldn't be a good thing."

"I'm trying to stop those who would," she replied.

He looked puzzled, searching her face.

She smiled at him. "My husband took his place in the River Police, because Durban suggested him. We tried to solve Durban's last case, and we failed so badly we can't go back and do it again. I want to show that the court was wrong and we were right, Durban and my husband and I."

"Won't do any good," Palk told her.

"Yes, it will. We'll know it, and that matters."

"Is Monk the new fellow at Wapping?"

"Yes."

"Won't be easy to follow Durban."

"Depends where he was going."

He looked at her without blinking. "Right and wrong," he said. "No man's right all the time, but he was more than most."

She stood up. "I hope so. But I need the truth, whatever it is."

"And then you'll tell everybody?"

"Depends. I don't know what it is yet."

He nodded. "That'll do. But be careful. There's plenty that'd kill to make sure you don't."

"I know that."

He hitched himself down off his chair, awkward, one shoulder almost half a foot higher than the other, and made his way to the door to show them out.

Unaware of Hester's mission, Monk started out again in the morning, with Scuff beside him, dressed as yesterday in the old boots. Very soon Monk would get him something better, but now he was compelled to go back to tracing Durban's search for Mary Webber. He would rather have been alone. The effort of concealing his emotions and keeping up a civil conversation was more than the value of any help Scuff could give. But he had left himself no choice. Apart from wounding him by rejection, he dare not allow Scuff to wander around by himself now. He had endangered him, and he must do what he could to protect him from the consequences.

By midmorning, after several failed attempts, he was almost robbed by the very scuffle-hunter he was actually looking for. They were at the Black Eagle Wharf, between a cargo of timber and lighter-men unloading tobacco, raw sugar, and rum. There was no breeze off the river to move the smell of it in the air. The tide was low again, and the water slurped over the weed on the steps and the lighters bumped against the stones.

An argument between a lighterman and a docker spread until it involved half a dozen men shouting and pushing. It was a form of robbery Monk had seen many times. Bystanders watched, a crowd gradually gathered, and while their attention was on the fighting, pickpockets did their silent job.

Monk felt the jolt, swung around, and came face-to-face with an old woman who grinned at him toothlessly, and at the same moment there was a touch behind him so light, the thief was a couple of yards away before Monk lunged after him and missed. It was Scuff who brought him down with a swift kick to the shins, which left him sprawling on the ground, yelling indignantly and hugging his left leg.

Monk yanked him to his feet without sympathy. Ten minutes later they were sitting on the top of the steps, the scuffle-hunter between them, looking uncomfortable, but willing to talk.

"I didn't tell 'im nowt 'cause I don't know nuffin'," he said aggrievedly. "I never 'eard o' Mary Webber. I said I'd ask around, an' I did, I swear."

"Why did he want her?" Monk answered. "What kind of woman was she supposed to be? When did he first ask? He must have told you something more than her name. How old was she? What did she look like? What did he want her for? Why ask you? Was she a pawnbroker, a money lender, a receiver, a brothel keeper, an abortionist, a whore, a procuress? What was she?"

The man squirmed. "Gawd! I don't know! 'E said she were about fifty, or summink like that, so she weren't no 'ore. Not any longer, anyway. She could 'a been any o' them other things. All 'e said were 'er name an' that she 'ad goldy-brown eyes an' curly 'air, little fine curls."

"Why did he want her? When did he first ask you?"

"I dunno!" The man shivered and moved an inch or two away from Monk, shrinking into himself. "D'yer think I wouldn't 'a told 'im if I'd 'a known?"

Monk felt the fear eat inside him also, for an utterly different reason. "When?" he insisted. "When did he first ask you about Mary Webber? What else did he ask?"

"Nuffin'! Were about two year ago, mebbe less. Winter. I mind because 'e stood out in the cold an' I were near freezin'. Me 'ands were blue."

"Did he ever find her?"

"I dunno! Nobody 'round 'ere never 'eard of 'er. An' I know all the fences and receivers, all the 'ock shops an' moneylenders from Wappin' ter Blackwall, an' back."

Monk swiveled to face him and the man flinched again.

"Stop it!" Monk snapped. "I'm not going to hit you!" He heard the anger in his voice, almost out of control. The names of Durban and Mary Webber were enough to cause fear.

But the man either could not or would not tell him any more.

He tried other contacts along the water that he had made in the six months since he had been in the River Police, and names that had been in Durban's notes, people Orme or any of the other men had mentioned.

" 'E were lookin' for fat Tilda's boy," an old woman told him with a shake of her head that set her battered straw hat swiveling on her head. They were on the corner of an alley a hundred feet from the dockside. It was noisy, dusty, and hot. She had a basket of shoelaces on her arm, and so far did not seem to have sold many. "Gorn missin', 'e 'ad. Told 'er 'e'd possibly gone thievin' an' been caught, but she were 'fraid that Phillips'd got 'im. Could 'ave. Daft as a brush 'e is, an' all."

"What happened?" Monk asked patiently.

"Stupid little sod fell in the water an' got fished out by a lighterman who took 'im all the way down ter Gravesend. Come back three days later, right as rain." She grinned at the memory as if she found acute satisfaction in it.

"But Mr. Durban looked for the boy?"

"Yeah, I said so. It were 'im as found 'im at Gravesend an' brought 'im back. Otherwise 'e could 'a been took ter sea an' ended up dinner for some cannibal in the South Seas. That's wot I told my boys; do as I tell yer, or yer'll get run off an' be boiled an' ate up."

Monk cringed inwardly at the thought.

"Reckon 'e thought Phillips could 'a got 'im right enough," the old woman said dourly, her smile vanished. "It's a bad shame Mr. Durban is dead. 'E were the one as mebbe could 'a done for Phillips. Didn't take no nonsense from no one, 'e din't, but 'e were fair, an' nothin' weren't too much trouble if yer was down."

Scuff stood suddenly upright.

Monk swallowed. "Durban?"

" 'Course, Durban," she snapped, glaring at him. " 'Oo d'yer think I was talkin' about, the Lord Mayor o' London? 'Ard man if yer was bad, but soft as muck if yer was sick or poor, or old, like me. 'E wouldn't 'ave stood 'ere in the sun leavin' me on me feet, an' me mouth dry as a wooden boot. 'E'd 'a gave me a cup o' tea, an' bought a couple o' pairs o' shoelaces an' all."

"Why was he looking for Tilda's son?" Monk had to examine the moment of kindness, so it would not later fade and slip out of his grasp.

" 'Cause 'e were afraid Phillips might 'ave got 'im, yer fool!" she said in disgust.

"Was that likely?"

" 'E knew. Tried 'is 'ardest ter get the bastard, then 'e got killed 'isself. Now them stupid sods o' the river police in't good for nothin' 'cept smugglers, pickpockets, an' a few 'eavy 'orsemen." She was referring to the thieves who stole goods from the ships and brought them ashore in specially designed pockets inside their coats. The reproof stung less than Monk would have expected, and he shot a glance at Scuff to prevent him from leaping to his defense.

"Then he was going to catch Phillips?" he asked mildly.

She looked him up and down. "Yer want a pair o' laces?" she asked.

He fished tuppence out of his pocket and passed it to her.

She gave him the laces. "Yer in't man enough to do it," she responded. "Yer gotter ask an old woman like me the way?"

Scuff could take it no more. "You mind yer gob, yer ol' mare!" he said furiously. "Mr. Monk's strung up more murderers than yer've 'ad 'ot dinners or like ter 'ave! Mr. Durban never got Phillips neither, an' you in't no 'elp. Where's 'is boat, eh? 'Oo goes on an' off it? 'Oo puts burns on them boys when they get out o' line? 'Oo kills 'em, an' why, eh? D'yer even know wot yer talkin' about, yer ol' bag o' bones?"

She darted her hand out and gave him a swift, hard slap around the ear. Monk winced as he heard the crack of skin on skin.

Scuff let out a howl.

"Wot'd I tell you lot fer?" the old woman demanded furiously. "Yer wouldn't do nothin'. Yer wouldn't take no risks ter keep the little bastards safe, not like 'e did."

"Risks?" Monk asked, gulping down hope and trying to keep his voice steady. He must not let her know it mattered. She would play every advantage. He even tried to invest his tone with some skepticism.

She was still angry. Her contempt was bitter in the deep lines around her eyes and mouth. " 'E got Melcher, din't 'e?" She gave a toothless sneer. "Real clever sod 'e were, when 'e wanted. And 'e conned Melcher every time, if 'e din't keep an eye on other boys, an' Phillips knew it. Pearly Boy too. Weren't till after Durban were dead that Reilly went. But wot'd yer know? Bloody useless." She spat on the dusty ground. "Yer don't make me laugh like 'e did. An' don't give me nothin' ter eat."

He walked away with Scuff, thinking deeply. The insults did not bother him, it was the information whirling in his head that he needed to order. Melcher he knew was a heavy horseman, one of the roughest. According to the old woman, Durban had held something over him. Pearly Boy was an opulent receiver, a fence of the more elegant and expensive goods stolen and resold along the river, a man whose reputation for ruthlessness and greed was well enough known to keep him insulated from the usual dangers and irritations of rivalry in his particular trade. It seemed Durban had somehow manipulated him too. Phillips would not have liked that.

But who was Reilly? Or if the old woman was right, who had he been, and what had happened to him?

Scuff was worried. He glanced at Monk now and again, then away quickly.

"What is it?" Monk asked eventually as they crossed the narrow bridge on the Wapping Basin and moved west.

"She din't ought ter 'ave talked to yer like that," Scuff replied. "Yer shouldn't 'a let 'er get by wi' it. Takes 'erself liberties, she does."

Scuff was right. Monk had been too relieved to hear someone speak so well of Durban that he had ignored the fact that he had allowed her to disparage him, and done nothing to assert his authority. It was an error that would have to be corrected, or he would pay the price later. He conceded the point to Scuff, who was satisfied, but took no pleasure in his victory. In his own way, he was worrying about Monk, afraid he was not fit to do the job, or to look after himself in the dangerous alleys and docksides of his new beat. There was a very strict hierarchy, and Monk was letting his place in it slip.

"I'll deal with her," Monk repeated firmly.

"You watch Pearly Boy." Scuff looked up at him. "I in't never met 'im meself, careful not ter. But I 'eard 'e's real nice to yer face, an' tear yer gizzard open the moment yer in't lookin'."

Monk smiled. "You haven't heard what they used to say about me when I was in the regular shore police."

"Yeah?" But the anxiety in his manner did not diminish at all. Was he being tactful? Afraid for him, a little pitying? It hurt. Monk was allowing his concern for Durban to erode his skill at his own job. It was past time he amended that.

"I will be very careful of Pearly Boy," he assured Scuff. "But I need to find information about him, and at the same time let him know that I am no easier to deal with than Durban was, and no pleasanter."

Scuff's shoulders straightened a little, and his step became a trifle cockier, but he did not answer.

SIX

*M*onk could put it off no longer. He was at Rathbone's office when the clerk opened the door before nine in the morning.

"Good morning, Mr. Monk," he said with some surprise and a certain degree of discomfort. No doubt he knew more about many things than he ever disclosed, even to Rathbone himself. "I am afraid Sir Oliver is not in yet."

"I'll wait," Monk replied. "It is of some importance."

"Yes, sir. May I get you a cup of tea?"

Monk accepted and thanked him for his thought. As soon as he was seated he wondered if the clerk were also concerned that his master, whom he had served for eight years that Monk knew of, was in some kind of moral morass, and his life had taken a darker turn. Or was that whole idea fanciful?

They were all in a morass; Monk too. He could hardly blame Rathbone if pride, a professional arrogance, had made him take a case, even as ugly as Phillips's, to prove that he could win it. He was testing the law to its boundaries, holding it of value above the decency that was the ultimate safeguard of everyone. On the other hand, if Monk had not also been so arrogantly sure of his skill, he could have let Phillips die on the river, and none of the rest of it would have happened.

Rathbone came in half an hour later, dressed immaculately in pale gray and looking as effortlessly elegant as he always did.

"Good morning, Monk." Rathbone made it something of a question. He seemed undecided exactly what manner to assume. "A new case?"

Monk stood up and followed Rathbone into his office. It was tidy and casually elegant, like its inhabitant. There was a cut-glass decanter with an ornate silver stopper on the narrow side table. Two very beautiful paintings of oceangoing ships decorated the one wall on which there were no bookshelves. They were small, and heavily framed. Monk knew at a glance that they were very good indeed. There was at once a simplicity and a power to them that marked them as different from the usual.

Rathbone saw his glance and smiled, but he offered no comment. "What can I do for you, Monk?"

Monk had rehearsed in his mind what he was going to say, and how to begin, but now the words seemed contrived, revealing the vulnerability of his position and his recent total defeat. But he could not stand there saying nothing, and there was no point trying to trick Rathbone, of all people. Candor, at least on the surface, was the only possibility.

"I'm not sure," he replied. "I failed to prove beyond reasonable doubt that Phillips killed Figgis, and the crown didn't charge him with blackmail, pornography, or extortion. Obviously I can't reopen the first, no matter what proof I might find, but the others are still available."

Rathbone smiled bleakly. "I hope you are not looking for me to assist you in that."

Monk opened his eyes wide. "Would that be against the law?"

"It would be against the spirit of it," Rathbone replied. "If not illegal, then certainly unethical."

Monk smiled, aware that it was a bleak, even sarcastic expression.

"Towards whom? Jericho Phillips, or the man who paid you to defend him?"

Rathbone paled very slightly. "Phillips is despicable," he said. "And if you can prosecute him successfully then you must do so. It would be a service to society. But my part in the due legal process is to prosecute or defend, as I am employed to do, but never to judge—

Jericho Phillips or anyone else. We are equal before the law, Monk; that is the essence of any kind of justice."

He stood near the mantel shelf, leaning his weight rather more on one foot than the other. "If we are not, then justice is destroyed. If we charge a man, usually we are right, but not always. The defense is there to safeguard us all against those times when we are wrong. Sometimes mistakes have been made, lies told where we do not expect them, evidence tampered with or misused. Personal hatred or prejudice can be exercised, fears, favors, or self-interest can govern the testimony. Every case must be tested; if it breaks under the pressure, then it is unsafe to convict, and unforgivable to punish."

Monk did not interrupt him.

"You loathe Phillips," Rathbone continued, a little more at ease now. "So do I. I imagine every decent man and woman in the courtroom did. Then there is all the more necessity that we must be fair. If we, of all people, allow our revulsion to control our dealing with justice, what hope is there for anyone else?"

"An excellent speech." Monk applauded. "And absolutely true in every regard. But incomplete. The trial is over. I have already conceded that we were slipshod. We were so certain Phillips was guilty that we left loopholes for you to use, which you did. We can now never try him again for Fig's murder. Any new case would be separate. Are you warning me that you would defend him again, either by choice, or from some kind of necessity, because you owe him, or someone else who has his interests at heart?" Monk changed his position deliberately.

"Or possibly you, or your principal," he continued, "are bribed, coerced, or threatened by Phillips, and feel you have no choice but to defend him in any issue whatever?" It was a bold, even brutal question, and the moment he had said it, he doubted himself.

Rathbone was now very pale. There was no trace of friendship in his eyes. "Did you say 'bribed'?" he asked.

"I included it as a possibility," Monk replied, keeping his eyes and his voice steady. "I don't know the man, or woman, who paid you to defend Phillips. You do. Are you certain you know why?"

Something in Rathbone's stance changed. It was so slight Monk could not identify it, but he knew that a new idea had suddenly occurred to Rathbone, and it was one that troubled him, possibly only very little, but he was uncomfortable nevertheless.

"You may speculate as you please," Rathbone answered him, his voice almost as level as before, almost as assured. "But you must be aware that I cannot comment. My advice to other people is as confidential as is my advice to you."

"Of course," Monk said drily. "And what is your advice to me? I am commander of the River Police at Wapping. I need to prevent the crimes of violence, abuse, and extortion, of pornography and child murder that happen on my beat. I made a mess of Phillips murdering Figgis. How do I prevent the next one, and the one after?"

Rathbone did not answer, but he made no attempt to hide the fact that he gave the matter consideration.

He walked over to his desk.

"Our loyalties are different, Monk," he said at last. "Mine is to the law, and therefore is larger than yours. And I do not mean by that that it is better, simply that the law moves slowly, and its changes can stand for generations. Your loyalty is to your job, to the people on the river today, to their immediate danger or suffering. The simple answer is that I cannot advise you."

"Your loyalty is not larger," Monk replied. "You care for the interests of one man. I care for everyone in that community. Are you certain you want to tie your name and your commitment to that man, and therefore to whomever he in turn is bound, for whatever reason? We all have fears, debts, hostages to fortune. Do you know his well enough to pay the price?" He bit his lip. "Or are they really your own?"

"Ask me that again, Monk, and I shall take offense. I dance to nobody else's tune except the law's." Rathbone's eyes were steady, his face utterly without humor or gentleness. He drew in his breath. "And I might equally ask you if you are as certain of Durban's loyalties as you would like to be. You have tied your reputation and your honor to his. Is that wise? Perhaps if I had any advice to give you, it would be to think far harder before you continue to pursue that. He may have had flaws of which you are unaware."

The blow cut deep, but Monk tried not to show it. He knew he must leave before the interview became a battle in which too much was said for either of them to retreat afterwards. It was on the brink of that point now.

"I didn't expect you to tell me his name, or what you know of him," he said aloud. "I came to advise you that in looking more closely into Phillips's business, I am also learning more of everyone he associated with, what he owed them and what they owed him. I cannot prosecute him for murdering Figgis, but I may be able to for pornography and extortion. That will obviously lead me much closer to those who patronize his business. There is much to suggest that they come from all walks of life."

"Even police," Rathbone said tartly.

"Of course," Monk agreed. "No one is excluded. Even women can have much to lose, or to fear, in those they love." And he turned and walked out the door, wondering if he had said far more than he wanted to.

Rathbone looked at the closed door with far greater disquiet than he had allowed Monk to see. Monk's questions had struck a nerve, and far from fading away, the unease they had caused was increasing. Arthur Ballinger was Margaret's father, a highly respected attorney with whom it was natural—indeed expected—that he would do business. Those facts had dulled his natural edge of inquiry as to why Ballinger had handled the subject of Phillips's defense for whoever it was who was financing it. Was it possibly even Phillips himself? Ballinger had said that it was not, but as Monk had pointed out, did Ballinger really know?

Rathbone admitted to himself that some of the evidence had shaken him more than he had expected. He could no longer dismiss it from his mind or pretend that it was an issue that could be forgotten.

He knew at least the first step he would take, and once that was made, he was able to address the rest of the day's business.

Seven o'clock in the evening found him in a cab on the way up Primrose Hill on the outskirts of London. The evening was bright and warm, and the sun was still high enough that there was no gold in the air yet, no lengthening haze to the light. There was a faint wind in the trees so that the shadows flickered. A man was walking his dog, and the animal raced around, busy with scents and movements, in a whole exciting world of its own.

The cab stopped; Rathbone alighted, paid the driver, and walked up the path to his father's door. He always came here when he had issues that troubled him and he needed to explain them, clarify the questions so that the answers emerged unclouded. He realized now, standing on the step, aware of the heavy perfume of honeysuckle, that since his marriage he had been here a lot less often than before. Was that because Henry Rathbone had been so fond of Hester, and Oliver had not wanted him to make the comparison with Margaret? The fact that he had raised the question was at least in part an answer.

The door opened and the manservant welcomed him in, his face expressionless except for the civility a good butler should always show. If anything were needed to confirm that he had been here too seldom lately, that was it.

In the sitting room French doors were open on to a lawn sloping down towards an orchard in full leaf, the blossom long finished. Henry Rathbone himself was walking up the grass towards the house. He was a tall, lean man, very slightly stooped. He had a mild, pointy face and blue eyes that combined both a burning intelligence and a kind of innocence, as if he would never really understand the pettier, grubbier things of life.

"Oliver!" he said with evident pleasure, increasing his pace. "How very nice to see you! What interesting problem brings you here?"

Oliver felt a sharp jolt of guilt. It was not always comfortable to be known so very well. He drew breath to deny that it was a problem that brought him, and then realized just in time how foolish that would be.

Henry smiled and came in through the doors. "Have you had supper?"

"No, not yet."

"Good. Then let us dine together. Toast, Brussels sprouts, pâté, and I have a rather good Medoc. Then apple pie and clotted cream,"

Henry suggested. "And perhaps a spot of decent cheese, if you feel like it?"

"It sounds perfect." Oliver felt some of the tension slip away. This was probably the best companionship he had ever known: gentle, without manipulation, and also totally honest. There were no lies, either intellectual or emotional. Over the meal he would be able to explain, primarily to himself, the exact nature of his unease.

Henry spoke with his manservant, then he and Oliver walked the length of the garden to the orchard at the end, and watched the light deepen in color as the sky began to burn and fade in the west. The perfume of the honeysuckle became stronger. There was no sound but the humming of insects and in the distance a child calling out to a dog.

They ate in the sitting room with the food on a small table between them, the French doors still open to the evening air.

"So what is it that disturbs you—the case?" Henry prompted, reaching for a second slice of crisp, brown toast.

Oliver had avoided mentioning it. In fact, he could even have let it slide altogether and simply absorbed the peace of the evening. But that was cowardly, and a solution that would evaporate in a few hours. Eventually he would have to go home again, and, in the morning, back to the law.

It was difficult to explain, and as always, it must be done as if it were all merely hypothetical. As he tried to frame it in his mind, he became aware that much of the pain he felt was due to the fact that Monk and Hester were involved, and it was their opinion of him, their friendship and the damage to it, that hurt.

"It concerns a case," he began. "An attorney, to whom I owe certain duties and obligations, told me that a client of his wished to pay for the defense of a man accused of a particularly appalling crime. He said that he feared that the nature of the offense, and the man's occupation and reputed character, might make it impossible for him to receive a fair trial. He would need the best possible representation if justice were to be served. He asked me, as a favor to him, to defend this man."

Henry looked at him steadily. Oliver found the innocence of his gaze unnerving, but he was too experienced an interrogator himself to be maneuvered into speaking before he was ready to.

Henry smiled. "If you would prefer not to discuss it, please don't feel pressured to do so."

Oliver started to protest, then changed his mind. He had been wrong-footed so easily, and it was because he did feel somehow guilty, although he did not know of what.

"I accepted," he said aloud. "Obviously, or I would have no problem."

"Wouldn't you?" Henry asked. "Surely you would then have denied a friend, to whom you owed something. Or at least you felt as if you did. What had this accused man been charged with doing?"

"Killing a child."

"Deliberately?"

"Very. He tortured him first."

"Allegedly?"

"I am almost certain that he did. In my own mind I have no doubt."

"At the time you took the case?" There was no judgment in Henry's voice.

Oliver stopped for a moment, trying to remember how he had felt when Ballinger had first asked him and he had reviewed the facts.

Henry waited in silence.

"My reasoning was sophistry," Oliver admitted unhappily. "I thought he was very probably guilty, but that the law, to be perfect, must convict him only if it was proven. And I sensed an emotional vendetta against him as the driving force behind the case. I took the opposing side in order to give it some . . . balance."

"And perhaps out of a little hubris, because you have the skill to do it?" Henry asked gently. "And to show off a little, to the man who had asked you? You wished to impress him, or someone else who will come to know of it?"

"You know the case?" Oliver felt foolish, as if he had been play-acting and been caught at it half-clothed.

Henry smiled. "Not at all, but I know you. I know your strengths and your weaknesses. If you did not feel guilty about it you would not be troubled. I assume you won? You would always try your best; you are incapable of anything else. Losing justly would not disturb you, if the man were guilty. Winning unjustly is another matter."

"It wasn't unjust," Oliver said immediately, and just as immediately knew that he had spoken too quickly. "It was not by dishonest means," he corrected. "The prosecution was sloppy, too governed by emotion to make certain of all its facts."

"Which weakness you knew, and used," Henry extrapolated. "Why does that trouble you?"

Oliver looked down at the long-familiar carpet, its reds and blues like stained-glass windows in the last of the sunlight slanting low in through the open doors. The evening scent of the honeysuckle was now stronger than the wine.

Again Henry waited.

The silence grew deeper. Homing birds fluttered up across the darkening color of the sky.

"I knew some of the chief witnesses well enough to use my understanding of them to their disadvantage," Oliver admitted at last.

"And lost their friendship?" Henry asked very gently. "Did they not understand the necessity that you defend the man to the best of your ability? You are his advocate, not his judge."

Oliver looked up, surprised. The question cut closer to the truth than he wished, because now he must answer honestly, or deliberately choose to lie. Lying to his father had never been an option. It would unalterably destroy the foundation of his own identity, his belief in the goodness of what mattered. "Yes, they both understood that. What they didn't and still don't understand is why I chose to take that case when I didn't have to, knowing that the man now cannot be tried again, although he will certainly go back to the river, and continue with his filthy trade. If I am honest, I know he will almost certainly kill again. I could have left his defense to someone else who would not have had the privileged knowledge I had, and would have given him a defense adequate before the law, and gained a verdict of guilty, which I believe would have been the right one. I think that is what an equal contest would have produced."

Henry smiled. "You credit the man's escape to your superior ability?"

"Superior knowledge of the emotional involvement of the chief witnesses for the prosecution," Oliver corrected him.

"Are they not, by definition, always involved?"

Oliver hesitated.

"Police?" Henry asked. "Monk?"

"And Hester," Oliver said quietly, staring down at the carpet. "They cared about the boy's murder too much to be thorough. It was Durban's one unfinished case, before he died. Too many debts of love and honor involved." He looked up and met his father's eyes.

"And you used them," Henry concluded.

"Yes."

"And your own debt of honor that caused you to take the case? Does Monk know of that? I imagine he will find out. Perhaps you had better find out first yourself? Have you perhaps caused Monk to pay your debt to someone?"

"No. No, I paid more than I owed, because I wanted to be comfortable," Oliver said with sudden lacerating honesty. "It was to Margaret's father, because I wanted to please her."

"At Hester's expense?"

Oliver knew why his father had asked that, and exactly why the hurt was there in his voice. Henry had always liked Hester better. He tried to hide it. He was fond of Margaret, and would have been kind to any woman Oliver had married. But Margaret could never make him laugh as Hester had, nor would he feel comfortable enough with her to argue for fun, or tell long, rambling tales of gentle adventure and dry humor. Margaret had dignity and grace, morality and honor, but she had not Hester's intelligence, nor her passion. Was she less, or more vulnerable?

Henry was watching his son closely. He saw the change in his eyes. "Hester will survive anything you can do to her, Oliver," he said. "That is not to say that she may not be hurt."

Oliver remembered Hester's face as she had stood in the witness box, the pain and surprise on it. She had not expected him to do such a thing, either to her or to Monk.

"Guilt?" Henry asked him. "Or fear that you have forfeited her good opinion of you?"

That was the crux of it. He was startled at how sharply it cut. He had frayed a tie that had been part of his happiness for a long time. He was not sure if it would eventually break altogether.

"She asked me if I knew where the money to pay me had come from," he said aloud. "And how it had been earned."

"Do you?"

"I know who paid it to me, of course, but I don't know who his client is, or why he should wish the accused man to be defended. And since I don't know who Ballinger's client is, naturally I don't know where the money came from." He looked at the floor. "I suppose I'm afraid it could be the accused man's own money, and I certainly know how that was made, by extortion and pornography."

"I see," Henry said quietly. "What is the decision you have to make?"

Oliver looked up. "I beg your pardon?"

Henry repeated the question.

Oliver thought for several moments. "Actually, I'm not sure. Perhaps there is no decision, except how I am going to come to terms with myself. I defended the man, and I took the money for it. I can't give it back. I could donate it to some charitable cause, but that doesn't undo anything. And if I am remotely honest, it wouldn't salve my conscience either. It smacks of hypocrisy." He smiled very slightly, a small, self-mocking gesture. "Perhaps I simply wanted to confess. I wanted to not feel alone in my sense of having done something vaguely questionable, something I think I may well be increasingly unhappy about."

"I believe so," Henry agreed. "To admit that you are unsatisfied is a step forward. It takes far less energy to confess an error than it does to keep trying to hide it. Would you like another glass of Medoc? We might as well finish the bottle. And the pie too, if you care to. I think there is a spot more cream."

Rathbone arrived home quite late and was startled to find Margaret still up. He was even more surprised, unpleasantly so, to realize that he had counted on her being asleep, so that any explanation of his absence could be put off until the following morning. By that time he would be in a hurry to leave for his office, and could avoid the subject again.

She looked tired and anxious, yet she was trying to conceal it. She was worried because she did not know what to say to him.

He knew it, and wanted to touch her, tell her that such worries were superficial and of no lasting importance, but it seemed an unnatural thing to do. He realized with a jarring loneliness that they did not know each other well enough, intimately enough, to overcome such reservations of the mind.

"You must be tired," she said a little stiffly. "Have you had supper?"

"Yes, thank you. I dined with my father." Now he would have to find an explanation as to why he had gone to Primrose Hill without taking her. He could not tell her the truth, and he resented having put himself in the position where he needed to lie. This was undignified and ridiculous.

He was also suddenly and painfully aware that he would have told Hester the truth. They might have quarreled over it, even shouted at each other. In the end they would have gone to bed at opposite ends of the house, desperately miserable. Then at some point he would have gotten up and gone to her and resumed the quarrel, because he could not bear to live with it as it was. Emotion would have overridden sense, and pride. Need of her would have been stronger than the need for dignity, or the fear of making a fool of himself. Her ability to be hurt would have been more important than his own.

Margaret was more self-controlled. She would ache quietly, within, and he would never be certain of it. It would not show on her calmer, prettier, more traditional face. That was what made her safer for him, a far more comfortable and suitable wife than Hester would ever have been. He had never needed to worry that Margaret would say or do anything that would embarrass him.

Now he owed her an explanation, something resembling the truth, and yet not exposing her to the knowledge that her father had put him in the position of defending Phillips as a favor. She did not ever need to know that; in fact, unless Ballinger told her, she must not. It was a professional confidence.

"I needed to discuss a case," he said aloud. "Hypothetically, of course."

"I see," she said coolly. She felt excluded, and the feeling was too raw for her to hide it.

He must say more. "If I had explained it to you, you would have known who it was, which would have broken a confidence," he added. That at least was true. "I could not do that."

She wanted to believe him. Her eyes widened, hope stirring. "Did it help?"

"Perhaps. At least I understand my problem a little more clearly. The process of thought required to explain sometimes clarifies the mind."

She decided to leave it while she had some form of comfort, rather than press for more. "I'm glad. Would you like a cup of tea?" It was a politeness, something to say. She did not want him to accept; he could hear that in her tone.

"No, thank you. It is quite late. I think I shall simply go to bed."

She smiled very slightly. "I too. Good night."

While Monk was busy, with Scuff's help, searching for further evidence of the darker side of Phillips's trade, Hester set out to learn more about Durban's past, including such family as he might have had.

She needed to know because she was afraid of what Monk might find out that would hurt him, and by extension, eventually, the River Police, and that would hurt him even more.

She understood loyalty within a service, and how in dangerous circumstances where men's lives were often in jeopardy, loyalty must be absolute. Commanding officers were seldom afforded the luxury of time in which to ask or answer questions, and they did not explain themselves. They expected obedience. The army could not function without it. An officer who did not inspire loyalty in his men was ultimately a failure, whether or not that loyalty was warranted by either his ability or his character.

She walked down Gray's Inn Road towards High Holborn. It was hot and dusty, and her skirt was already grimed at the hem. She was passed by traffic, its wheels rattling over the cobbles, the sun glinting on polished harnesses and brass. Four huge shire horses passed, slowly pulling a brewers' dray. Cabs clattered by in the opposite direction, their horses' hooves loud, long whips curling in the air above the horses' ears. An open landau offered a glimpse of summer fashion, pale parasols to keep skin fair, the sound of laughter, the bright silk of a puffed sleeve and satin ribbons in the breeze.

Hester thought of blind loyalty in the army, the unquestioning obedience. Perhaps the alternative was chaos, but she had seen the death and it had stunned her, bruised her heart and mind forever.

She had been on the heights of Sebastopol during the Crimean War, and watched the slaughter at the charge of the Light Brigade into the Russian guns. She had tried afterwards to rescue some of the few mangled but still alive. The senselessness of it still overwhelmed her. She was very uncertain that she would give blind loyalty to anyone. She had tasted its cost.

At the bottom of Gray's Inn Road she turned into High Holborn and walked to the left. When there was a lull in the traffic she crossed over, kept walking, and then turned right into Castle Street. She knew exactly where she was going and for whom she was looking.

Still it took her another half hour to find him, but she was delighted when she learned the reason. She was told at his lodgings that he had obtained a job as a clerk at a trading house, a skill he had acquired since losing a leg in the Crimea nine years ago. At that time even writing his name had been a challenge to his literacy.

When she arrived at the trading house she controlled her urgency as well as she could, but the head clerk still looked at her dubiously, chewing his lip as he considered whether he would give permission for one of his employees to stop work and speak with her.

She smiled. "Please?" she said with as much charm as she could muster. "I was the nurse who looked after him when he lost his leg at Sebastopol. I'm trying to find another man, or at least learn where to look, and I think Mr. Fenneman could help me."

"Well . . . yes, of course," the head clerk said nervously. "I . . . I suppose a few moments wouldn't hurt. Sebastopol? Really? He never said, you know."

"People don't like talking about it," she explained. "It was pretty dreadful."

"I've heard others talk," he argued.

"So have I," she agreed. "Usually they were not there, they only heard about it from tales. The ones who saw it say nothing. I don't actually like talking about it myself, and I only experienced the aftermath, searching among the dead for those still alive that we might be able to help."

The head clerk shuddered, his face a little paler. "I'll fetch Mr. Fenneman for you."

Fenneman appeared a few moments later. He was thinner than the last time she had seen him, and of course no longer in army uniform. He had a wooden peg fitted to the stump of his lost leg, a little above the knee, and he moved with one crutch, balancing quite efficiently. She still felt a little sick when she remembered the agile young man he had been, and the desperate struggle she had had to save him. It had been she who had actually sawn through the bone in the shattered remnants of his leg, unable even to render him unconscious during the agony of it. But she had stopped the bleeding, and with help, gotten him from the battlefield to the hospital.

Now his face lit with pleasure at seeing her. "Miss Latterly! Fancy finding you here in London! Mr. Potts said as I could help you. I'd be happy to, in any way I can." He stood in front of her, smiling, leaning sideways a little to level his weight on his crutch.

She wondered whether to ask if there was somewhere he could sit, and decided against it. He sat at his work, and it might insult him, obliquely, if she took such notice of his disability as to instantly suggest that he could not stand.

"It's good to see you looking so well," she said instead. "And with a good job."

He blushed, but it was with self-conscious pleasure.

"I'm looking for information about a man who died about the turn of the year," she hurried on, aware that the head clerk would be watching the seconds tick by. "His name was Durban. He was commander of the River Police at Wapping, and I believe you grew up in Shadwell. He never spoke about himself, so I hardly know where to begin to look for his family. Can you suggest anyone who might help me?"

"Durban?" he said thoughtfully. "Can't say I know anything about his family, or where he came from, but I heard he was a good man. But Corporal Miller, d'you remember him? Little man, with red hair, and we called him Dusty, but then we call all Millers 'Dusty.' " He smiled at the recollection. In spite of his lost leg, his memories of the companionship in army life were still good. "I can give you the names of two or three others, if you like?"

"Yes, please," she accepted quickly. "And where I can find them, if you know that."

He swung around on his crutch and moved rapidly back to the bench where he worked. He wrote on a sheet of paper, dipping his quill in the inkwell and concentrating on his penmanship. He returned several moments later and handed her the sheet covered with beautiful script letters. He was watching her, pride in his face, anxious to see if she observed his achievement.

She said the names and addresses, and looked up at him. "Thank you," she said sincerely. "I know now if I ever want a job as a clerk not to come here. This standard is something I couldn't achieve. Seeing you has lightened a dark day for me. I'll go and look for these men. Thank you."

He blinked a little, uncertain what to say, and ended by simply smiling back.

It took her the rest of the day and half the next one, but she gained bits and pieces from all the men whose names Fenneman had given her, and gathered a picture of Durban's own account of his youth. Apparently he had been born in Essex. His father, John Durban, had been headmaster of a boys' school there, and his mother a happy and contented woman about the home and the schoolhouse. It had been a large family: several sisters and at least one brother, who had been a captain in the merchant navy, travelling the South Seas, and the coast of Africa. There was no hint of darkness at all, and Durban's own official police record was exemplary.

The village of his birth was only a few miles away along the Thames Estuary. It was still barely past noon. She could be there by two o'clock, find the schoolhouse and the parish church, look at the records, and be home before dark. She felt a twinge of guilt at the whisper of caution that drove her to do it. This was Durban's own account. She would never have doubted him before the trial, and the questions Rathbone had awoken in her.

But the lean, intelligent face of Oliver Rathbone kept coming back into her mind, and the necessity to check, to prove, to be able to answer every question with absolute certainty.

She spent the money and traveled in a crowded carriage out to the stop nearest the village, and then walked the last couple of miles in the wind and sun, the water of the Estuary glinting bright to the south. She went to the schoolhouse, and to the church. There was no record whatsoever of anyone named Durban—no births, no deaths, no marriages. The schoolhouse had every headmaster's name on its board, from 1823 to the present date. There was no Durban.

She felt sick, confused, and very afraid for Monk. As she walked back towards the railway station and the journey home, the road was suddenly hard, her feet hot and sore. The light on the water was no longer beautiful, and she did not notice the sails of the barges coming and going. The ache inside herself for the lies and the disillusion ahead outweighed such peripheral, physical things. And the question beat in her mind, over and over—Why? What did the lies conceal?

In the morning, feet still aching, she was at the clinic on Portpool Lane, intensely relieved that Margaret was not present, who perhaps just now found their meetings as unhappy as Hester did.

She had visited all the patients they currently had, and attended to a little stitching of wounds and the repair of a dislocated shoulder, when Claudine came into the room and closed the door behind her. Her eyes were bright, and she was slightly flushed. She did not wait for Hester to speak.

"I've got a woman in one of the bedrooms," she said urgently. "She came in last night. She has a knife wound and bled rather badly . . ."

Hester was alarmed. "You didn't tell me! Why didn't you have me see her?" She rose to her feet. "Is she . . . ?"

"She's all right," Claudine said quickly, motioning for Hester to sit down again. "She's not nearly as bad as I let her think she is. I spread the blood on to a lot of clothes so it would look dreadful, and she would be afraid to leave."

"Claudine! What on earth . . . ?" Now Hester was frightened not only for the woman, but for Claudine's sanity.

Claudine interrupted her, her face even more flushed. "I needed to speak to you privately before you go to her. She might be able to tell you something important, if you go about it the right way." She barely paused for breath. "She knows Jericho Phillips—has for a long time, since he was a child. Knew Durban a bit also."

"Really?" Now she had Hester's entire attention. "Where is she?" She had started towards the door by the time Claudine replied, and had her hand on the knob before she turned back to thank her, her own voice now also filled with urgency.

Claudine smiled. It was a start, but she knew it could still prove fruitless. She needed to help.

Hester walked quickly along the corridor, up a flight of stairs, and along another, even narrower hall until she came to the last, quite good-sized room at the end. It was out of the way of the normal traffic within the clinic. Sometimes they used it for people who had infectious illnesses, or for those they feared were terminally ill. It was large enough for a second cot where a nurse could catch short naps, so as not to leave anyone alone in their last hours.

The woman inside was far from dying. Claudine had indeed made it look dramatic. There were still bloodstained clothes and bandages lying in a basin and padding sitting on the small table, needles and silk for stitching wounds, and a carafe of water.

The woman looked frightened, lying in the bed with her head propped on pillows and her injured arm lying swathed in bandages beside her, although she had good color in her cheeks, and none of the hollow-eyed stare of the desperately injured.

"Hello," Hester said softly, closing the door behind her. "My name is Mrs. Monk. I've come to look at your wound, and see what I can do for you. What's your name?"

"Mina," the woman said hoarsely, fear choking her voice.

Hester felt a strong twinge of guilt, but did not allow it to alter her intent. She pulled up the hard-backed chair until she was close enough to the bed to work comfortably, then began as gently as she could to unwind the bandages and examine the wound, without taking off the final gauze, which would certainly start it bleeding again. Claudine had done a very good job of cleaning it and stitching the raw edges together. The jagged knife slash was not as deep or as dangerous as Mina had been allowed to believe.

Hester began to talk casually, as if merely to take Mina's mind from what she was doing. It was a rule of the clinic never to ask patients for details they were unwilling to give, unless it was necessary for the treatment of whatever was wrong with them. Sometimes the conditions of where they lived mattered very much, especially if it was mainly on the streets with no bed, no shelter, no water, and only such food as they could beg. Then they would keep them in until they were considerably better. One or two had even remained here as permanent help, paid with lodging and food. Often the sudden new and respectable occupation was a benefit beyond price.

After the usual account of her circumstances, in answer to a question from Hester, Mina went on to describe certain aspects of her daily life, including some dangerous clients past and present.

"And you really know Jericho Phillips?" Hester said in awe.

"Yeah, I know 'im," Mina replied with a smile. It was oddly attractive, in spite of a chipped front tooth, no doubt also sustained in a fight. " 'E weren't that bad, at least for business."

"Your business, or his?" Hester asked with a smile.

"Mine!" Mina said indignantly. "I in't got nothin' ter do wif 'is."

Hester refused to allow her imagination to picture it. She concentrated on examining the wound. Most of the bleeding had stopped; it only seeped through the stitches, but it looked raw and painful. She kept talking, both to probe for information, and to keep Mina's mind off the pain as she cleaned away the dried blood and closed the edges of the flesh a little more, cutting away bloodied gauze. "I suppose you've seen a side of him nobody else has," she remarked.

"Oh, I in't the only one." Mina found that amusing. "I just mebbe know'd 'im longer. But I got more sense'n ter say so. Don't like bein' reminded o' the past, 'e don't. Rotten poor, 'e were. Always cold an' 'ungry, an' knocked about summink wicked. 'Is ma were a bad one. Temper like one o' them rats wot comes out o' the sewers sometimes. Fight anyone."

"What about his father?" Hester asked.

Mina laughed. "Came off some ship, an' then got right back on it," she answered drily, keeping her eyes tightly closed in case she accidentally caught sight of the wound. "Lived down by the river, almost in the water, 'e did. Always cold, poor little sod. Now 'e goes barmy if 'e 'ears anythin' drippin'.'"

"But he lives in a boat!" Hester protested.

"Yeah. Daft, in't it?" Mina agreed. "I knew a feller once 'oo were scared stiff o' rats. Dreamed about 'em, 'e did. Woke up sweatin' like a pig. 'Ear 'im screamin' sometimes. Send yer blood cold, it would. Made 'isself keep a rat in a cage, right there in 'is room. Could 'ear the bleedin' thing scrapin' its silly little feet an' squeakin'.'" She shivered convulsively without realizing it, moving her arm so that Hester momentarily held the scissors away.

"Do you think that's what Jericho Phillips does, with the water?" she asked curiously. She imagined a man forcing himself to live with his haunting fears until he had inured himself to them and no longer panicked. It was the ultimate control. In some ways that might be the most frightening thing about him.

She started to rebandage the wound as gently as she could, while thinking of the bullied child, afraid of the cold, afraid of dripping water, who had grown into a cruel man steeled against every weakness, above all his own. She was not sure if she could pity him or not.

"Are you frightened of him?" she asked Mina when she was nearly finished.

Mina kept her eyes closed. "Nah! Keep me mouf shut, do wot 'e wants, an' 'e pays good. In't me 'e 'ates."

Hester put a few stitches in to keep the bandage from unraveling. "Who does he hate?" she asked.

"Durban," Mina replied.

"He was only doing his job, like all the River Police," Hester pointed out. "You can open your eyes now. I've finished."

Mina looked at it with admiration. "Yer make shirts an' all?" she asked.

"No. I only stitch skin, and bandages. I'm not very good at anything more than mending."

"Yer talk like yer 'ad servants ter do it for yer," Mina remarked.

"I used to."

"On 'ard times, are yer?" There was sympathy in Mina's voice. "Yer want money fer that?" She indicated her arm. "I in't got none. But I'll pay yer when I 'ave."

"No, I don't want money, thank you. You're welcome to a little help," Hester replied. "Did Phillips hate Durban in particular? I think Durban hunted him pretty hard."

"'Course 'e did," Mina agreed. " 'Ated each other, din't they?"

Hester felt the chill back inside her.

"Why?"

"Natural, I s'pose." Mina gave a slight shrug on her uninjured side. "Grew up together, din't they? Durban done good, an' Phillips done bad. Gotter 'ate each other, don't they?"

Hester said nothing. Her mind was whirling, crowded with lies and truths, dishonor and light, fear, and gaping, unanswered questions.

Gently she finished the rebandaging, putting the old gauze and linen aside to be washed.

SEVEN

*M*onk sat quietly in the parlor and went through all Durban's notes yet again, and found nothing in them that he had not seen before. So many pages held just a word or two, reminders in a train of thought that was gone forever now. The only man who might be able to make sense of it was Orme, and so far his loyalty had kept him silent about all except the most obvious.

Hesitantly and with deep unhappiness, Hester had told Monk what the prostitute, Mina, had said about Jericho Phillips, and finally, white-faced, she had added that Durban had grown up in the same area. The whole story of the schoolmaster and the happy family living in a village on the Estuary was a dream, something he created out of his own hungers for things he had never known. Hester had knotted her hands and blinked back sudden tears as she had told him.

Monk had wanted to disbelieve it. What was a blank school registry, a parish record, the word of an injured prostitute, compared with his own knowledge of a man like Durban, who had served the River Police for a quarter of a century? He had earned the love and loyalty of his men, the respect of his superiors, and the healthy fear of criminals great and small the length of the river.

And yet Monk did believe it. He felt guilty, as if it were a kind of betrayal. He was turning his back on a friend when there was no one else to defend him. What did that say of Monk? That he was weak in faith and loyalty, placing himself first? Or a realist who knew that even the best of men have their flaws, their times of temptation and vulnerability?

He could argue with himself forever and resolve nothing. It was time to look harder for the truth, to stop using loyalty to justify evading it. He put the papers away and found Orme.

But it was late in the morning before they were alone where there would be no interruption. They had very satisfactorily solved a warehouse robbery, and the thieves had been arrested. Orme stood on the dock near the King Edward Stairs as Monk finished congratulating him on the arrest.

"Thank you, sir," Orme acknowledged. "The men did a good job."

"Your men," Monk pointed out.

Orme stood a trifle straighter. "Our men, sir."

Monk smiled, feeling worse about what he had to do. There was no time to delay it. He liked Orme and he needed his loyalty. More than that, he admitted, he wanted his respect, but leadership was not about what you wanted. There would not be a better time to ask; maybe not another time at all today.

"How well did Durban know Phillips, Mr. Orme?"

Orme drew in his breath, then studied Monk's face, and hesitated.

"I have a good idea already," Monk told him. "I want your view of it. Was Fig's death the beginning?"

"No, sir." Orme stood more stiffly. The gesture was not one of insolence—there was nothing defiant in his face—just a stiffening against an awaited pain.

"When was the beginning?"

"I don't know, sir. That's the truth." Orme's eyes were clear.

"So far back, then?"

Orme flushed. He had given himself away without meaning to. It was obvious in his tightened lips and squared shoulders that he also saw that Monk knew, and that evasions were no longer possible. It would have to be the truth, or a deliberate, planned lie. But Orme was not a man who could lie, unless it were to save life, and even then it would not come lightly.

Monk hated everything that had put him in the position of having to do this. He still did not wish to give away Durban's own lies about his youth. Orme might guess; that was different from knowing.

"When was the first time you knew it was personal?" Monk asked. He phrased it carefully.

Orme took a deep breath. The sounds and movement of the river were all around them: the ships, swaying in the fast-running tide; the water lapping on the stones; light in ever-shifting patterns, reflected again and again; birds wheeling and crying overhead; the clank of chains; the grind of winches; men shouting in the distance.

"About four years ago, sir," Orme replied. "Or maybe five."

"What happened? How was it different from what you'd seen before?"

Orme shifted his balance. He was very clearly uncomfortable.

Monk waited him out.

"One minute it was just Mr. Durban asking questions, the next minute the whole air of it changed an' they were shouting at each other," Orme replied. "Then before you could do anything about it, Phillips had a knife out—great long thing it was, with a curved blade. He was swinging it wide . . ." He gestured with his own arm. "Like he meant to kill Mr. Durban. But Mr. Durban saw it coming an' moved aside." He swerved with his body, mimicking the action. There was both strength and grace in it. What he was describing became more real.

"Go on," Monk urged.

Orme was unhappy.

"Go on!" Monk ordered. "Obviously he didn't kill Durban. What happened? Why did he want to? Was Durban accusing him of something? Another boy killed? Who stopped Phillips? You?"

"No, sir. Mr. Durban stopped him himself."

"Right. How? How did Durban stop a man like Phillips coming at him with a knife? Did he apologize? Back off?"

"No!" Orme was offended at the thought.

"Did he fight back?"

"Yes."

"With a knife?"

"Yes, sir."

"He was carrying a knife, and he was good enough with it to hold off a man like Jericho Phillips?" Monk's surprise showed in his voice. He could not have done that himself. At least he thought he could not have. Possibly in the closed-up past, further back than his memory, he had learned such things. "Orme!"

"Yes, sir! Yes, he was. Phillips was good, but Mr. Durban was better. He fought him right back to the edge of the water, sir, then he drove him into it. Half drowned, Phillips was, and in a rage fit to kill us all, if he could have."

Monk remembered what Hester had told him about Phillips and the water, and about being cold. Had Durban known that? Had Orme? He looked across at Orme's face and tried to read it. He was startled to see not only reluctance, but also a certain kind of stubbornness he knew he could not break, and he realized he did not want to. Something innate in the man would be damaged. He also saw a kind of pity, and knew without any doubt that he was not only protecting Durban's memory, he was protecting Monk as well. He knew Monk's vulnerability, his need to believe in Durban. Orme was trying to keep a truth from him because he would be hurt by it.

They stood facing each other in the sun and the wind, the smell of the tide and the swirl and slap of the water.

"Why did that make you think they knew each other?" Monk asked. It was only part of the question, allowing Orme to avoid the answer if he wanted to.

Orme cleared his throat. He relaxed so very slightly it was almost invisible. "What they said, sir. Don't remember the words exactly. Something about what they knew, and remembered, that sort of thing."

Monk thought about asking if they had known each other long, since youth, maybe, and then he decided against it. Orme would only say that he did not hear anything like that. Monk understood. The water was the answer, the cold, and Phillips's hatred. Hester's prostitute was not lying.

"Thank you, Mr. Orme," he said quietly. "I appreciate your honesty."

"Yes, sir." Orme totally relaxed at last.

Together they turned and walked back towards Wapping.

For the next two days Monk called into the station only to keep track of the regular work of the police. Reluctantly he took Scuff with him. Scuff himself was delighted. He was quite aware that some of the earlier errands had been to keep him safe rather than because they needed doing. Monk had imagined himself tactful, and was somewhat taken aback to find that Scuff had read him so easily. He certainly could not apologize, at least not openly, but he would be less clumsy in the future, at least in part because Scuff was so determined to prove his value, and his ability to take care not only of himself but of Monk also.

Their paths crossed Durban's several times. He had learned the names of almost a dozen boys of various ages who had ended up in Phillips's care. Surely among them there must have been at least two or three willing to testify against him.

They followed one trail after another, up and down both banks of the river, questioning people, searching for others.

At one point Monk found himself in a fine old building at the Legal Quay. He stood with Scuff in a wooden-paneled room with polished tables and floorboards worn uneven with the tread of feet over a century and a half. It smelled of tobacco and rum, and he almost felt as if he could hear age-old arguments from the history of the river echoing in the tight, closed air.

Scuff stared around him, eyes wide. "I in't never been in 'ere before," he said softly. "Wot der they do 'ere, then?"

"Argue the law," Monk answered.

"In 'ere? I thought they did that in courts."

"Maritime law," Monk explained. "To do with who can ship things, laws of import and export, weights and measures, salvage at sea, that sort of thing. Who unloads, and what duty is owed to the revenue."

Scuff pulled a face of disgust, dragging his mouth down at the corners. "Lot o' thieves," he replied. "Shouldn't believe a thing they tell yer."

"We're looking for a man whose daughter died and whose grandson disappeared. He's a clerk here."

They found the clerk, a sad, pinch-faced man in his fifties.

"How would I know?" he said miserably when Monk began his questions. "Mr. Durban asked me the same things, an' I gave 'im the same answers. Moll's 'usband got killed on the docks when Billy were about two year old. She married again to a great brute wot treated 'er real 'ard. Beat Billy till 'e broke 'is bones, poor little beggar." His face was white, and his eyes were wretched at the memory, and his own helplessness to alter it. "Weren't nothin' I could do. Broke my arm when I tried. Off work for two months, I were. Damn near starved. Billy ran off when 'e were about five. I 'eard Phillips took 'im in an' fed 'im reg'lar, kept 'im warm, gave 'im a bed, an' far as I know, 'e never beat 'im. I let it be. Like I told Mr. Durban, it were better than 'e'd 'ad before. Better than nothin'."

"What happened to Moll?" Monk asked, then instantly wished he had not.

"Took ter the streets, o' course," the clerk answered. "Wot else could she do? Kept movin', so 'e wouldn't find 'er. But 'e did. Killed 'er wi' a knife. Mr. Durban got 'im for that. 'Anged, 'e were." He blinked away tears. "I went an' watched. Gave the 'angman sixpence to 'ave a drink on me. But I never found Billy."

Monk did not reply. There hardly seemed anything to say that was not trite, and in the end, meaningless. There must be many boys like Billy, and Phillips used them. But would their lives without him have been any better, or longer?

Monk and Scuff ate hot meat pies, sitting by the dockside in the noise of unloading, watching the lightermen coming and going across the water. There was a long apprenticeship to the craft of steering them, and Monk watched them with a certain admiration. There was not only skill but also a peculiar grace in the way they balanced, leaned, pushed, realigned their weight, and did it again.

There was steady noise around them as they ate their pies and drank from tin mugs of tea. Winches ground up and down with the clang of chains, dockers shouted at one another, lumpers carried kegs and boxes and bales. There was the occasional jingle of harness and clatter of hooves as horses backed up with heavily loaded drays, and then the rattle of wheels on the stone. The rich, exotic aroma of spices and the gagging smell of raw sugar drifted across from another wharf, mixed with the stinging salt and fish and weed of the tide, and now and then the stench of hides.

Once or twice Scuff looked at Monk as if he were going to say something, then changed his mind. Monk wondered if he were trying to find a way to tell him that boys like Billy were better off with Phillips than frozen or starved to death in some warehouse yard.

"I know," he said abruptly.

"Eh?" Scuff was caught by surprise.

"It isn't all one way. We aren't going to get boys like Billy to tell us anything."

Scuff sighed, and took another huge bite of his pie.

"Would you like another one?" Monk asked him.

Scuff hesitated, unused to generosity and not willing to chance his luck.

Monk was not hungry, but he lied. "I do. If you fetch one for me, you might as well get one for yourself."

"Oh. Well." Scuff considered for about a second, then stood up. "Don't mind if I do." He held out his hand for the money. "D'yer want another cup o' tea, an' all?"

"Thank you," Monk replied. "I don't mind if I do."

It took them quite a while to find a boy willing to speak to them, and it was Orme who finally succeeded. It was in one of the alleys close to the water. The passageway was so narrow a tall man could stretch his arms and touch both sides at the same time, and the buildings almost met at the roof edges, creating the claustrophobic feeling of a series of tunnels. It was crowded with shops: bakers, chandlers, ships' outfitters, ropemakers, tobacconists, pawnbrokers, brothels, cheap lodging houses, and taverns. There were openings into workshops and yards for the making, mending, or fitting of every piece of wood, metal, canvas, rope, or fabric that had to do with the sea and its cargo or its trade.

The wood creaked and settled, water dripped, footsteps sounded uneasily, and the shadows on the walls were always moving. Sometimes it was caused by light from the shifting tide in a dock inlet, water slapping against stone walls, or the thump of timber against the sides. More often it was someone running or creeping, or carrying a load. The stench of river mud and human waste was overpowering.

The boy refused to be named. He was thin and sallow. It was hard to tell his age, but it was probably somewhere between fifteen and twenty. He had a chipped front tooth, and one finger missing on his right hand. He stood with his back to the wall, staring at them as if expecting an attack.

"I in't swearing ter nothin'," he said defensively. "If 'e finds me, 'e'll kill me." His voice wobbled. " 'Ow d'yer find me, anyway?" He looked first at Monk, then at Orme, ignoring Scuff.

"From Mr. Durban's notes," Orme answered. "It's worth two shillings to you to answer truthfully, then we'll forget we ever saw you."

"Answer wot? I dunno nothin'!"

"You know why so few boys ever run away," Monk told him. "Young ones we can understand. They've nowhere to go, and are too small to look after themselves. What about older ones, fourteen or fifteen? If you don't want to go to sea, why not simply leave? Customers are coming and going from the ship, aren't they? Couldn't you go out with one of them? He can't keep you locked up all the time."

The boy gave him a look of withering contempt. "There's twenty of us or more. We can't all go! Some are scared, some are sick, some are just babes. Where can we go? 'Oo'd feed us, get us clothes, give us a place ter sleep? 'Oo'd 'ide us from Phillips, or 'is like? There's just as bad on shore."

"You're on shore now and safe from him. And I'm not talking about the young ones. I asked about boys your age," Monk pressed him. "Why don't they go, one by one, before he sells them to a ship?"

The boy's face was bitter. "You mean why'd 'e kill Fig, an' Reilly, an' them like that? 'Cause they stood up agin' 'im. It's a lesson, see? Do as yer told an' yer'll be all right. Fed, somewhere ter sleep, shoes and a jacket. Mebbe a new one every year. Make trouble an' yer'll get yer throat cut."

"Escape?" Monk reminded him.

The boy gulped, his thin face twisting painfully. "Escape, an' 'e'll 'unt yer down an' kill yer. But before that, 'e'll 'urt the little kids left be'ind, burn their arms an' legs, maybe worse. I wake up in the night 'earin' 'em scream . . . an' find it's just rats. But I still 'ear 'em in me 'ead. That's why I wish I 'adn't left, but I can't go back now. But I in't swearin' ter nothin'. I told Mr. Durban that, an' I'm tellin' you. Yer can't make me."

"I never thought to try," Monk said gently. "I couldn't live with it either. I have enough already, without adding that. I just wanted to know." He fished in his pocket and pulled out the two shillings Orme had promised the boy. He held them out.

The boy hesitated, then snatched them. Monk stood aside so he could pass.

The boy hesitated.

Monk backed further away.

The boy dived past him as if terrified he would be seized, then he ran with surprising speed, almost silent on the cobbles. Only then did Monk realize his feet were bound in rags, not boots. Within seconds he had disappeared into one of the many alleys like a tunnel mouth, and he could have been no more than the voice of a nightmare.

As they walked back towards the open air of the dockside, they kept in step with each other, walking single file because there was no room to do anything else. Monk went first, glad of the enforced silence between them. What the boy had said was hideous, but he never questioned the truth of it. It explained not only why no one had testified against Phillips, but also why Durban had been fired by an uncontrollable anger. Helplessness and a sense of the terror and pain, the sheer despair of others, had drowned the outside world and its balance, its values of caution and judgment.

Monk felt closer to Durban as he made his way along the tortuous alleys, following memory and the sound of water yard by yard towards the open river. He understood not only his actions but also the emotions that must have crowded his mind and made his muscles clench and his stomach churn. He shared the anger, the need to hurt someone in return for all the wrong.

But was Monk remembering him as he had really been? Or was grief painting it in warmer colors of companionship than reality? He did not believe that. It was not only dishonest, it was also cowardly to pretend now that the sense of friendship had been artificial. He could still hear Durban's voice and his laughter, taste the bread and beer, and feel the companionable silence as dawn came up over the river. They watched the light spread across the water, catching the ripples and brightening on the drifting mist that hid some of the harsher outlines, lending beauty to the crooked spars of a wreck and blurring the jagged line of utilitarian buildings.

Scuff was immediately behind him now, padding along, looking warily to either side. Narrowness frightened him. He did not want to think about what hid in the passages. He had heard what the boy said about the others that Phillips had taken. He knew it could happen to him also. Without Monk, it could happen very easily. He wanted to reach out and take hold of Monk's coat, but that would be a very undignified thing to do, and it would tell everybody that he was afraid. He would not like Orme to think that of him, and he could not bear it if Monk did. He might even tell Hester, and that would be worse still.

They worked for several more days questioning lightermen, ferrymen, dockers, and mudlarks. They found thieves and beggars, heavy horsemen, and opulent receivers, asking each about Durban and his pursuit of Phillips. It took them upstream and down both sides of the river, on docksides, and into warehouses, alleys, shops, taverns, doss-houses, and brothels.

On one occasion the search for information took Monk and Scuff into the Strangers' Home in Limehouse. It was a handsome and commodious building on the West India Dock Road.

"Cor!" Scuff said, deeply impressed by the entrance. He stared up and 'round at the sheer size of it, so utterly different from the narrow and squalid houses they had been in earlier where men slept a dozen to a room.

They were passed by an African seaman, his smooth, dark skin like a polished nut against his white shirt. Almost on his heels came a Malay in striped trousers and an old pea jacket, walking with a slight roll, as if still aboard ship.

Scuff stood transfixed. He heard a score of languages and dialects around him in the main room crowded with men of every shade of skin and cast of feature.

Monk yanked him by the hand to waken him from his daydream, and half-dragged him towards the man he was seeking, a seaman from Madras who had apparently given Durban information several times.

"Oh, yes, sir, yes," the seaman agreed when Monk put the question to him. "Certainly I spoke to Mr. Durban on several occasions. He was seeking to apprehend a very bad man, which is uncommonly difficult when the man is protected by the fact that he is using children who are too frightened of him to speak out."

"Why did he ask you?" Monk said without preamble.

The man raised his eyebrows. "There are certain men that I know, you see? Not from any choice, of course, but in a way of business. Mr. Durban thought I might be aware of earlier . . . how shall I express it? Weaknesses? Do you understand me, sir?"

Monk had neither time nor patience for obliqueness. "Patrons of Phillips's boat, and its entertainment?"

The man winced at Monk's bluntness.

"Exactly so. It seemed to me that he had the belief that certain of these men had great influence when it came to bringing the law into such matters, and quite naturally a strong desire that it remain a private affair."

"Among Phillips, these gentlemen, and the children they abused?" Monk said brutally.

"Quite so. I see that you understand entirely."

"And were you able to help him?"

The man shrugged. "I gave him names and instances, but I have no proof."

"What names?" Monk said urgently.

"Certain harbormasters, revenue men, the owner of a brothel, a merchant who is also a receiver, although very few know it. Another name he looked for was the master of a ship who came ashore and set up his own importing business. Friend of a revenue man, so Mr. Durban said."

"That sounds more like corruption of the revenue than anything to do with Phillips," Monk answered.

"Oh, it was about Phillips," the seaman insisted. "Mr. Durban almost had 'im, two or three times. Then the evidence just vanished away like mist when the sun comes up. You can see it happen, but you can never put your hand on it, do you see?" He shook his head. "Mr. Phillips's goods are not cheap to buy, at least not the ones he sells on his dirty little boat. The men who buy them have money, and power comes from money. That's why Mr. Phillips is very difficult to catch in the hangman's noose."

Monk asked more questions, and the man answered him, but when Monk rose to leave, closely followed by Scuff, he was not certain how much more he knew. All kinds of men were involved, and at least some of them had the power to protect Phillips from the River Police.

"Yer better be careful," Scuff said, his voice tight and a little high with anxiety. He had abandoned even trying to look as if he were not frightened. He kept pace with Monk now, putting in an extra little step every so often to make up for his shorter stride. "Them revenue men is summink wicked. Get them on yer tail an' yer might never get out o' trouble. Mebbe that's why Mr. Durban backed off, like?"

"Maybe," Monk agreed.

The day after that Scuff accompanied Orme, and Monk went alone to pursue the few friends or informants he had gained in the short time he had been on the river. He began with Smiler Hobbs, a dour north countryman whose lugubrious face had earned him his nickname.

"Wot are yer after now?" Smiler asked when Monk walked into his pawnshop and closed the door behind him. "I got nothin' stolen, an' don't yer stand there like the judgment o' the Almighty. Yer put off me customers. Worse than buildin' next to a garbage dump, yer are."

"Good morning to you also, Smiler," Monk replied, making his way through the piles of pots and pans, musical instruments, flat irons, several chairs, and an endless variety of odd china. "I'll go as soon as I learn what I want to know."

"Then yer in fer a long wait, 'cause I in't got nowt stolen an' I don't know nowt about owt." Smiler glared at him.

"Of course you don't. And as to what you haven't got, I don't care," Monk responded.

Smiler looked surprised, then his eyes narrowed.

Monk remained exactly where he was. "But I could always become interested," he observed. "Nice sextant you have there. Pity it isn't at sea, doing some good."

Smiler's expression became even more dismal, as if he were staring at the ultimate disaster.

"When Mr. Durban was trying to prove that Jericho Phillips was responsible for the boy's death, did he speak to you about it?" Monk asked.

"Which boy's death?" Smiler retorted.

Monk was about to snap back with Fig's name, then he saw the wider opportunity and seized it. "Reilly," he replied. "Or any of the others?"

"'E asked everyone," Smiler told him. "Like I said, I know nowt about it, or anythin' else. I buy things as people need ter sell, an' I sell things they need ter buy. Public service, it is."

"I know you do. I need to buy information."

"I don't give away nowt."

"Neither do I," Monk agreed. "At least not often. You tell me what I want to know, and I'll pay you by not coming back here to keep on asking."

Smiler pulled down the corners of his mouth until his face was a mask of tragedy. "No better than Durban, yer aren't. Pick on the easy ones an' twist them, an' all the while creatures like Phillips, Pearly Boy, an' the Fat Man cut people's throats like they was rats, an' wot do yer lot do about it? Nowt! Absolutely, bloody nowt!"

"The Fat Man's dead," Monk told him.

"Yeah? Maybe." Smiler was skeptical.

"For certain," Monk responded truthfully. "I saw him go down, and I know for sure he never came up. I was there."

Smiler gave a long sigh. "Then yer done summink right fer once. But yer made an almighty mess o' gettin' Phillips. I s'pose someone got ter yer too, just like they did ter Durban. Yer can't beat the devil. Yer'll learn, if yer live long enough." He sighed again. "Which I doubt."

Monk swallowed. "Who got to Durban?"

" 'Ow do I know?" Smiler asked sadly. " 'Arbormaster, magistrates, men with money and their heads in politics. Lumpers, fer all I know, judges too. Yer cut off one arm, an' while yer lookin' for the second one, it'll grow the first one back again. Yer'll not win. Yer'll just end up dead, like Durban. No one'll care. They'll say yer were a fool, and they'll be right."

"They won't say I didn't try!"

Smiler pulled an exaggerated expression, curling his lips downwards. "An' what good'll that do yer, in yer grave?"

"I'm going to see Phillips hang, I promise you," Monk said rashly. He could feel the rage boil up inside him and see in his mind Phillips's sneering face in the dock as the verdict came in.

"Yer'd best slit 'is throat, if yer can catch 'im," Smiler advised. "Yer'll not catch him fair, any more than Durban did. After 'im like a terrier with a rat one minute, an' the next he backed off like 'e'd been bit 'isself. Then six months later, back after 'im again. Then out of the blue sky, 'ands off an' leave 'im alone as if 'e were the Lord Mayor o' the river. Durban din't call the tune, I can promise you that. An' neither will yer, for all yer swank coat an' yer quality boots. Yer'll end up just like 'im, bitin' yer own tail. I'll give yer ten shillings fer them boots, if yer don't ruin 'em first?"

"So someone's protecting him," Monk said acidly. "I'll get them too. And I'll keep my boots."

Smiler gave a sharp bark that with him passed for laughter. "Yer don't even know 'oo they are. An' before yer start threatening me, like Durban did, I take bloody good care not ter know either. Offer's open on the boots."

"Who is Mary Webber?"

"Gawd! Not yer too?" Smiler rolled his eyes. "I got no idea. I never 'eard of 'er till Durban came threatenin' everyone with Gawd knows what if we didn't tell 'im. I dunno!" His voice rose sharply, aggrieved. "Get it? I dunno!" Now get out of 'ere an' leave me to do me business, before I set the dog on yer . . . by accident, like. I keep 'im on a chain, but sometimes I think it in't too strong. Not my fault. Not that that'll 'elp yer much."

Monk retreated, his mind crowded with thoughts. He was quite sure Smiler would lie if it suited him, but what he had said fit in too well with the facts so far.

Durban was not the simple man that Monk had thought, and that he had wanted him to be.

He crossed the road and turned back towards Shadwell High Street.

Yet Monk could remember the man he had known vividly: his patience, his candor, the way he unquestioningly shared food and warmth, his optimism, his compassion for even the most wretched. Could it all have been a lie, even his laughter?

He shivered even though the sun was bright off the water and the air was warm. There was a sound of music in the distance from a hurdy-gurdy somewhere out of sight.

What a living hell this world was. But for boys like Fig, and perhaps Reilly, and any number of others whose names he would never know, there had been no choice, and no escape, except death.

No wonder Durban had done everything he could to catch Phillips and have him hanged, even at the cost of bending a few rules. Or that the men who had already paid so much paid even more to protect their provider and tormentor. It gave new layers to the concept of corruption.

Who had paid Oliver Rathbone to defend this man in court? And why?

Monk was on the open dock now, not far from Wapping. The tide was rising, and the water lapped over the stone steps, creeping higher and higher. The smell of it was harsh, and yet he had become accustomed to it, welcomed it. This was the greatest maritime highway in the world, beautiful and terrible in all its moods. At night its poverty and dirt were hidden. Lights of ships from Africa and the Pole, China and Barbados, danced on the tides. The city, domed and towered, was black against the stars.

At dawn it would be misted, softened by silver, fast-running waters glittering. There were moments in the flare of sunset when it could have been Venice, the dome of St. Paul's above the shadows a marble palace floating on the lagoon towards the silk roads of the east.

The sea lanes of the world met here: the glory, the squalor, the heroism, and the vice of all humanity, mixed with the riches of every nation known to man.

He faced the question deliberately.

What would Monk have done were it someone he loved who faced exposure and ruin from Phillips? Would he have protected them? Belief in your ideals was one thing, but when it was a living human being who trusted you, or perhaps deepest of all, who loved and protected you in your need, that was different. Could you turn away? Was your own conscience more precious than their lives?

Did you owe loyalty to the dead? Yes, of course you did! You did not forget someone the moment the last breath left their lips.

He looked around the skyline to the north and south, and across the teeming water. This was a city of memories, built of the great men and women of the past.

Around midafternoon of the next day, Monk faced the opulent receiver known as Pearly Boy. He had been known that way for so long nobody could remember what his original name had been, but it was only since the death of the Fat Man the previous winter that he had taken over a far larger slice of business along the river, and prospered to the degree of wealth that he now possessed.

He was slender and soft-faced, and he wore his hair rather long. He always spoke quietly, with a very slight lisp, and no one had seen him, winter or summer, without his waistcoat, which was stitched with hundreds of pearl buttons that gleamed in the light. He was the last man one would expect to have a reputation for ruthlessness not only for a hard bargain, but if necessary, with a knife—pearl-handled, of course.

They were sitting in the small room behind Pearly Boy's shop in Limehouse. The shop was ostensibly to sell ships' instruments: compasses, sextants, quadrants, chronometers, barometers, astrolabes. Set out in order on a table was a variety of dividers and parallel rules. But Pearly's main business took place in the back room, largely concerning stolen jewelry, objets d'art, paintings, carvings, and jewel-encrusted ornaments. He had already taken over most of the Fat Man's territory.

He looked at Monk blandly, but his eyes were as cold as a polar sea. "Always 'appy to 'elp the police," he said. "What are you looking for, Mr. Monk? It is 'Monk,' isn't it? 'Eard word, you know. Reputation."

Monk did not take the bait.

"Yes, indeed," he said with a nod. "Something we have in common."

Pearly Boy was startled. "What's that then?"

"Reputation." Monk was unsmiling. "I understand you're a hard man too."

Pearly Boy thought that was funny. He started to giggle, and it grew and swelled into rich chortling laughter. Finally he stopped abruptly, wiping his cheeks with a large handkerchief. "I'm going to like you," he said, his face beaming, his eyes like wet stones.

"I'm delighted," Monk replied, sounding as though he had smelled spoiling milk. "We might be of use to each other."

That was language Pearly Boy definitely understood, even if he was dubious about believing it. "Oh, yeah, an' how's that then?"

"Friends and enemies in common," Monk explained.

Pearly Boy was interested. He tried to hide it, and failed. "Friends?" he said curiously. " 'Oo's friends o' yours, then?"

"Let's start with enemies," Monk answered with a smile. "One of yours was the Fat Man." He saw the flash of hatred and triumph in Pearly Boy's eyes. "One of mine too," Monk added. "You have me to thank that he's dead."

Pearly Boy licked his lips. "I know that. I 'eard. Drowned in the mud off Jacob's Island, they say."

"That's right. Nasty way to go." Monk shook his head. "Would have fished the body up, but it was hardly worth it. Got the statue, which is what mattered. He'll keep down there nicely."

Pearly Boy shuddered. "You're a hard bastard, all right," he agreed, and Monk was not sure whether he meant it as a compliment or not.

"I am," Monk conceded. "I'm after several people, and I don't forget either a good turn or a bad one. Who is Mary Webber?"

"No idea. Never 'eard of 'er. Which means she's not in my business. She in't a thief nor a receiver nor a customer," Pearly Boy said flatly.

Monk was not surprised; he had not expected her to be. "And I'm after a boy named Reilly, and even more than that, I'm after whoever was forced into looking after him, seeing to it that he didn't get hurt."

Pearly Boy opened his eyes wide. "Forced? 'Ow could anyone be forced? 'Oo would do that, an' why, Mr. Monk?"

"Mr. Durban would have done it," Monk replied steadily. "Because he didn't like having boys murdered."

"Well, I never." Pearly Boy affected amazement, but his curiosity overcame his judgment, as Monk had hoped it would. Pearly Boy dealt not only in stolen goods but in rare or precious information as well— that too at times stolen. " 'Oo could stop that 'appening, then?"

"Someone with power." Monk said it as though he were thinking out loud. "And yet someone who had a lot to lose as well, a lot in danger, if you understand me?"

Pearly Boy was still two steps behind. " 'Oo'd be killin' boys, then?"

"Jericho Phillips, if they get out of line, rebel against . . ." He stopped, seeing Pearly Boy's face go suddenly pallid and his body in its decorated waistcoat stiffen until his arms were rigid. Suddenly Monk was as certain Pearly Boy was one of Durban's informants against Phillips as if he had written it in his notes. He smiled and saw in Pearly Boy's eyes that he had read the understanding, and it knotted his stomach with terror.

"One of Phillips's clients," Monk went on, his voice quite casual now. He leaned elegantly against the mantel, watching Pearly Boy's discomfort. "I can imagine it happening, can't you? Durban would have followed the man until he could confront him, maybe somewhere near Phillips's boat. Perhaps it would be just after this man, whoever he is, had left a night's entertainment, and the excitement and guilt were still hot inside him."

Pearly Boy was motionless, eyes on Monk's face.

"No lie would come to him easily then," Monk continued. "No matter how often he had prepared for such a moment. Durban would have chosen a place where there was enough light to be sure the man recognized his marks of office, his uniform, his cudgel. Yes, he'd definitely take a cudgel, just in case the man was desperate enough to fight. After all, he would have a lot to lose—public disgust, ridicule, loss of position, friends, money, power, perhaps even his family."

Pearly Boy licked his lips nervously.

"Then Durban would make the offer," Monk said. " 'Use your power to protect Reilly, the boy most in danger because of his age and his courage, and I'll protect you. Let Reilly die, and I'll expose you to the whole of London.' "

Pearly Boy licked his lips again. "So 'oo was it then?"

"That is what I want from you, Pearly Boy," Monk answered.

Pearly Boy cleared his throat. "An' if I don't? It could 'ave been lots o' people. I dunno 'oo's got that kind o' weakness. It could be a revenue man, a magistrate, a rich merchant, an 'arbormaster. They got all kinds o' tastes. Or it could 'ave been another policeman! Ever thought o' that?"

"Of course I have. Who could have protected Reilly? That's the key to it. Who had the power? Above all, who was important enough to Phillips that he would listen to him?"

Understanding flashed in Pearly Boy's soft, clever face, and the excitement of knowledge. "You mean 'oo's got an appetite 'e can't control, an' needs Phillips ter feed it, an' yet 'e's got some kind o' power to 'elp Phillips that's so good Phillips 'as got to keep 'im sweet too? That's a nice one, Mr. Monk, a very nice one indeed."

"Yes, it is. And I want a nice answer," Monk agreed.

Pearly Boy's eyebrows rose. "Or what?" He was shivering very slightly. Monk could smell the sweat of fear in the closed air of the room. "What if I can't find out?" He tried a bit of bravado. "Or if I decide not to?"

"I shall see that Phillips knows that you told Mr. Durban about this very interesting client, and are on the point of telling me, when we can agree on a price."

Pearly Boy was white, the sweat beading on his face. "And what price would that be?" he asked hoarsely.

Monk smiled, showing his teeth. "Future silence, and a certain shortsightedness now and then, where the revenue men are concerned."

"Dead men are silent," Pearly Boy said through thin lips.

"Not those who can write, and leave clear instructions behind them. Mr. Durban might have been very nice to you. I won't be."

"I could 'ave you killed. Dark night, narrow alley?"

"The Fat Man's dead. I'm not," Monk reminded him. "Take the easy way, Pearly Boy. You're a receiver, not a murderer. You kill a River Policeman, you'll be tracked down. Do you want to be buried feetfirst in the Thames mud, never come back up again?"

Pearly Boy went even paler still. "You'll owe me!" he challenged, his eyes flickering a little.

Monk smiled. "I told you, I'll forget about you . . . to a point. I'll put you last on my list to close down, rather than first."

Pearly Boy said something obscene under his breath.

"I beg your pardon!" Monk snapped.

"I'll find 'im," Pearly replied.

Suddenly Monk was gracious. "Thank you. It will be to your advantage."

But as he left his emotions were tangled. He walked warily along the narrow street, keeping to the middle, away from the alley entrances and the sunken doorways.

What was the difference between one blackmail and another? Was it of kind, or only of degree? Did the purpose justify it?

He did not even have to think about that. If he could save any child from Phillips, he would, without a thought for the morality of his actions. But did that make him a good policeman or not? He felt uncomfortable, unhappy, uncertain in his judgment, and closer to Durban than ever before. But it was a closeness of emotion, rage and vulnerability.

And of course when Durban had died at the turn of the year, the protection of Reilly had disappeared. He had been left naked to whatever Phillips had wanted to do. That thought made him feel sick, even as he came out of the alley into the wind and the sun of the open dock.

EIGHT

Rathbone sat at his own dinner table and felt curiously without appetite. The room was beautiful, greatly improved from its original, rather sparse elegance, since Margaret's advent into the house. He was not quite sure what it was specifically that was changed, but it was somehow warmer than it had been before. The table had the same clean lines of Adam mahogany, the ceiling still had the heavy plaster borders of acanthus leaves. The blue-and-white curtains were different, far less heavy than before. There were touches of gold here and there, and a bowl of pink roses on the table. They gave both warmth and a sense of ease to the room, as if it were lived in.

He drew in his breath to thank Margaret, because of course it was she who had caused the changes, then he let the moment slip, and ate some more fish instead. It would sound artificial, as if he were searching for something polite to say. They should be talking about real things, not trivia like the curtains and flowers.

She was concentrating on her food, looking down at her plate. Should he compliment her on it? It was she who had engaged the cook. What was she thinking about, with that slight frown between her brows? Had she any idea what was turning over and over in his mind? She had been proud of him for winning the Phillips case. He could remember the brightness in her face, the way she had walked, head high, back even a little straighter than usual. Because it was clever? Did skill matter so much, ahead of wisdom? Was it because she was on the winning side, and Hester had lost?

Or had she not been proud at all, but concealed it very well with that small show of defiance? And loyalty? Was that towards him, or her father? Did she even know that it was her father who had represented Phillips, indirectly? Had she any idea what Phillips was really like? Rathbone was only just beginning to appreciate that himself. How could she know more? And if she could be loyal, could he not at least do as much?

He finished the fish. "I don't know exactly what the changes to this room are," he said aloud, "but it is much pleasanter to eat in. I like it."

She looked up quickly, her eyes questioning. "Do you? I'm glad. It wasn't anything very big."

"Sometimes it is small things that make the difference between beauty and ordinariness," he answered.

"Or good and evil?" she asked. "Small to begin with."

This was becoming a conversation he did not wish to enter.

"That is too philosophical." He looked down at his plate. "A little heavy for the fish course." He smiled very slightly.

"Would you prefer it with the meat?" she asked, her voice perfectly steady. The thought flickered into his mind that Hester would have told him not to be pompous, and charged ahead with the conversation anyway. That was one of the reasons he had hesitated to ask her to marry him, and been so much more comfortable with Margaret.

"I am not sure that I know enough about the origins of good or evil to discuss them at all," he said frankly. "But if you wish to, I suppose I could try." It was meant to dissuade her. She would defer to him; he had been married long enough to know that of her. It was how her mother had taught her to keep her husband's regard.

Hester would have given him an answer that would have scorched his emotions and left him stinging . . . and fiercely alive. Perhaps he would not always have trusted her to be the lady that was Mrs. Ballinger's ideal. But . . . he left the thought there. It must not be pursued, not now. Not ever.

He forced himself to look at Margaret. She had her head bent, but she caught his movement and looked up at him.

"I have compared good and evil enough today, my dear," he said quietly. "I can see too much of both sides, and the cost of each. I should very much prefer to be able to speak with you of something pleasanter, or at least less full of pitfalls and failures, and mistakes that we see too late to help."

Her face filled with concern. "I'm sorry. I should prefer something more agreeable as well. I have spent the day trying to raise money for the clinic, mostly from people who have far more than they need, and are still desperate for something further. So many women of high fashion dress not to please the man they love, but to spite the women they fear."

He had not intended to, but he found himself smiling. Some of the knots inside him eased. They were moving onto surer ground. "I wonder if they have any idea that you have observed them so accurately," he remarked.

She looked alarmed, although not entirely without a flash of humor.

"My goodness, I hope not! They avoid me rapidly enough as it is, because they know I shall ask them for money, if I can manage it—at times and in places where it will be hard for them to refuse."

His eyes widened. "I hadn't realized you were so ruthless."

"You weren't meant to," she retorted.

A flicker of genuine admiration touched him, bringing with it a pleasure he clung to. "I shall immediately forget," he promised. "Let us speak of other things. I am sure there must be some current event that is worthy of debate."

The following day was Saturday; no courts were in session. Normally Rathbone would have spent at least the morning looking through documents for the following week. Finally he made up his mind to face the issue that had been troubling him for several days. He was at last honest enough to admit that ignoring it was an evasion. There would be no right time, no appropriate words.

He excused himself to Margaret without explanation. This was not out of the ordinary; he had deliberately developed the habit of not telling her, often because it was confidential. He said simply that he would return before lunch.

It was a short cab ride to Arthur Ballinger's house. He would have preferred to have this conversation in offices, where there was no possibility of domestic interruption, and no need whatever for Margaret's mother to know that he had called. But he felt he could no longer put it off, or risk professional obligations delaying it yet further.

The maid welcomed him, and he hoped for one breathless moment that he might escape without having to explain himself to his mother-in-law. But she must have heard the door because she came down the stairs with a broad smile, greeting him warmly.

"How delightful to see you, Oliver. You look very well. I hope you are?" She meant "very formal," because he was in his business clothes. He wished Arthur Ballinger would appreciate the gravity of what he was going to ask. Neither friendship nor ties of marriage altered the moral issues involved.

"In excellent health, thank you, Mama-in-law," he replied. "And so is Margaret. I am sure she would have sent you her best wishes had she known I was coming; however, the matter is confidential. It is Mr. Ballinger I need to see. I believe he can advise me in a matter of some importance. Is he at home?" He knew it was Ballinger's habit, as it was his own, to prepare for the following week on a Saturday morning. For one thing, it enabled him to avoid the various domestic or social requirements his wife might ask of him.

"Why, yes, certainly he is at home," she answered, a little crestfallen. She had been hoping it was a personal visit, to lighten the tedium of the morning. "Does he expect you?"

"No. I am afraid I have only just resolved to consult him. I apologize for the inconvenience."

"It is no inconvenience at all." She brushed it aside. "You are always welcome." And with a swish of her abundant skirt she led him across the hall to the study door, where she knocked. At the sound of Ballinger's voice, she opened it and announced Rathbone's presence.

Ballinger had no possible choice but to invite Rathbone in, as if he were delighted to see him. However, as soon as the door was closed, the tension was palpable in the air, in spite of the pretense. They both remained standing.

Ballinger hesitated for a moment, obviously debating how frank to be, and decided on the least possible frankness. "I can't imagine what you could wish my advice for, but of course if I can help then I shall be happy to. Please make yourself comfortable." He waved to the other large armchair opposite his own. "Would you care for tea? Or perhaps something cold?"

Rathbone could afford no time for niceties, and he knew acceptance would mean at least two interruptions, one to request the tea and a second to accept it. "No, thank you," he declined. "I don't wish to disturb you longer than necessary." He sat down, mostly to establish his intention to remain until the business was concluded.

Ballinger sat also, so as not to give the impression that he was urging Rathbone to leave.

Rathbone plunged in. It was not going to get easier with delay. "The Phillips case still troubles me," he admitted. He saw Ballinger's face tighten, so slightly that it could have been a trick of the light, except that he had not moved. "The questioning of police motives was fair, in principle. In fact, it is a tactic one has to consider in any case."

"You conducted the case brilliantly," Ballinger said. "And there is nothing even remotely questionable about it. I don't understand what it is that could disturb you now." The moment he spoke, he realized his mistake. It allowed Rathbone the opening he would otherwise have had to create.

Rathbone smiled very slightly. "I was naturally very careful not to ask Phillips directly if he was guilty. I behaved as if he were not, as I was obliged to, but I find myself more and more convinced that in fact he did murder that child . . ." He saw Ballinger wince, and ignored it. "And probably others as well. I know that the River Police are still investigating him, in the hope of building a different case, and I have no doubt at all that they will be a great deal more careful the second time."

Ballinger shifted very slightly in his chair.

"If they do bring another case," Rathbone continued, "is your client going to wish you to deal with it again? Or, if I may put it more plainly, is this debt of honor now satisfied, or does it stretch to defending Jericho Phillips indefinitely, whatever the charge?"

Ballinger flushed a painful color, and Rathbone felt guilty for having placed him in such a situation. It was going to make friendship between them impossible. He had already crossed a boundary that could not be forgotten. This man was his wife's father; the price was high.

"If you cannot answer for him, which would be perfectly under-standable, perhaps proper," he continued, "then may I speak to him myself?" It was what he had wanted from the outset. The anonymity of the man who would pay to defend Phillips had always troubled him. Now, with so much darker a picture emerging of Phillips's trade, it disturbed him even more. "Who is he?"

"I am afraid I cannot tell you," Ballinger replied. There was no wa-vering in him, not an instant of uncertainty. "The matter is one of complete confidentiality, and, to be professional, I cannot tell you. Cer-tainly I shall convey to him your concern. However, I think it may be premature. The River Police have not arrested Phillips or laid any new charge. Naturally they are distressed at the failure of their case, and at the ensuing suggestion that the late Commander Durban was of ques-tionable competence, even of conduct not always becoming to his of-fice." He moved his hands in a slight gesture of regret. "It is most unfortunate for their reputation that their new man, Monk, seems to be cut from the same cloth. But we cannot alter the law to suit the weaknesses of those who administer it. I am sure you would be among the first to agree."

He smiled very slightly; the warmth was on his lips but not in his eyes. "Your own words in defense of the law still ring in my mind. It must be for all, or it is eventually for no one. If we build either reward or punishment on our own likes, loyalties, or even sense of outrage, then justice is immediately eroded." He shook his head, his gaze di-rect, candid. "The time will come when we ourselves are disliked or misunderstood, or strangers, different from our judges in race or class or creed, and if their sense of justice depends upon their passion rather than their morality, who is to speak for us then, or defend our right to the truth?" He leaned forward. "That is more or less what you said to me, Oliver, here in this room, when we spoke of this very sub-ject earlier. I have never admired any man's honor more than I did yours, and still do."

Rathbone had no answer. His emotions were intensely troubled, and his mind was utterly wrong-footed, off balance as a runner who is tripped, and suddenly finds his own speed his enemy. It flashed into his mind to wonder if the person who had paid to have Phillips defended not only wanted it, but far more than that, needed it. Was he one of Phillips's clients, who could not afford to have him found guilty? Who, exactly, did Phillips cater to? Considering Rathbone's fee for his services, a man of very considerable means indeed. He felt a sharp stab of guilt for that. It was a sizable amount of money, and now it felt dirty in his hands. He could buy nothing with it that would bring him pleasure.

Ballinger was waiting, watching and judging his reactions.

Rathbone was angry, first with Ballinger for knowing so well how to use him, then with himself for being used. Then another thought occurred to him, which was painful, halting his emotions with an icy hand. Was the man a friend of Ballinger's? A man he had possibly known in his youth, before this desperate twist of hunger had imprisoned him in loneliness, shame, deceit, and then terror? Does one ever quite forget the innocence one has known in the past, the times of greater hope, unforced kindness, among boys before they became men? Or the debts incurred then?

Perhaps it was even worse than that? It would be a double pressure, a debt compounded, if it were his other son-in-law, Margaret's sister's husband. It could be. All ages and types of men were subject to hungers that tortured and in the end destroyed both the victim and the oppressor in their grip.

Or was it Mrs. Ballinger's brother, or one of her sisters' husbands? The possibilities were many, all of them harsh and full of entangled obligations and pities, loyalties too complex to untangle, and where words did nothing whatever to ease shame or despair.

Without warning, Rathbone's anger was overtaken by pity. He searched for something to say, and before he found it, there was a tap on the door, but it did not open. It had to be the maid.

Ballinger rose to his feet and went to the door. A low voice spoke with the deferential tones of a servant. Ballinger thanked him and turned back to Rathbone.

"I'm sorry, but I have an unexpected visitor. A client who needs urgent help, and I cannot put him off. Anyway, I think I have explained my position, and there is nothing further I can add. I apologize." He stood as if waiting to usher Rathbone out, and the invitation to leave was implicit.

Rathbone stood up. He had no idea who this new client was, and the fact that Ballinger did not introduce him was not remarkable. Business with one's attorney could be sensitive. In fact, if one called personally on a Saturday morning, then it was at the very least extraordinary and unexpected.

"Thank you for your courtesy in receiving me, without notice," he said with as much grace as he could muster.

"Not at all," Ballinger replied. "Were there not an emergency, it would have been a pleasure to offer you tea, and to speak longer."

They shook hands, and Rathbone went out into an empty hall. Whoever had called to see Ballinger had been shown into another room, at least until Rathbone had left. It flashed into his mind to wonder, with some discomfort, if it was someone he would have recognized. It was not a pleasant thought.

As he was riding home in a cab, a certain degree of anxiety would not leave his mind. If Phillips had among his clientele men with the money to pay Rathbone's fee, and to call on Ballinger uninvited on a Saturday morning, what else could they do, if pressured with sufficient threat of exposure?

Not that he knew that Ballinger's guest this morning had anything to do with Phillips, but the possibility would not leave his mind. Ballinger had made clear that the client was someone to whom he owed loyalty, whatever the nature of his client's problem.

Rathbone was troubled as he rode through the bustling Saturday streets with their tall, elegant facades, their carriages with matched pairs, the horses' coats gleaming, footmen in perfect livery, fashionable ladies. Who else could Jericho Phillips call upon, if he felt threatened by Monk's continuing investigation? And what power might such men have, and be willing to use, to save their reputations?

And, colder and closer to him than that, whose side would Margaret be on, if any of it came into the open, or at the very least, into family hostility? Her father of a lifetime, or her husband of a year? He did not wish to know the answer to that. Either would be painful, and he hoped profoundly that she would never be put to that test. And yet if she were not, wouldn't he still wonder?

Monk took a brief respite over the weekend. He and Hester walked in the park, climbing the slow rise and standing close to each other on the top in the sun. They stared down at the brilliant light on the river below them, watching the boats ply up and down, like long-legged flies, oars dipping and rising. Monk knew exactly the sound the water would make off the blades, if he were close enough to hear it. From this distance, the music drifted in snatches and the breeze was cool, rustling the leaves, mellowing the sharp smell of the tide with the sweetness of grass.

But Monday was different. He was met by Orme on Princes Stairs, on his own side of the river, even before he got on the ferry to take him over to the Wapping Police Station. His uniform was immaculate, but his face was weary, as if even at seven in the morning he had already worked long and exhaustingly.

"Morning, sir," he said, standing to attention. "I've a ferry here for you, if you like?"

Monk met his eyes and felt a tightening in his stomach, a slow clench into a knot. "Thank you," he acknowledged. "Have you learned something since I was in?" He followed Orme to the edge of the dockside and down the steps to where the ferry was rocking gently in the wash of a passing lighter. They stepped in, and the ferryman set out for the farther bank.

"Yes, sir," Orme said quietly, dropping his voice so they would not be overheard above the creak of the oars and the hiss of the water. "I'm afraid charges've been laid against Mr. Durban, though he's dead an' not here to face them or tell them the truth. And if you ask me, that's a coward's way of getting at a man you didn't 'ave the courage to face in life." His voice shook with indignation, and far more powerful than that, a deep, unconcealable pain.

"Then we'll have to answer for him," Monk responded instantly, and realized as the words were on his lips just how rash they were. But he was prepared to follow through. The cowardice of it was despica-ble. "What are they charging? And for that matter, who is saying it?"

Orme's face was stiff. He was a quiet man, gentle, but perhaps lacking in breadth of thought. Once or twice he had hinted at a reli-gious upbringing. Certainly he could be suspicious of laughter, except of the most good-natured sort. He was offended to have to say the words that Monk had asked of him.

They were pulling out into the mainstream of the river now, buck-ing a little against the strength of the tide. The slap of the water was louder, and Orme had to raise his voice against it. "Government offi-cer, sir, a couple of magistrates. They're saying that he got hold o' boys for Phillips in his trade. They're using the same evidence we found as to how Mr. Durban helped some o' the mudlarks and pickpockets and lookouts and sweeps' boys turn to honest work. They're saying that he sent them Phillips's way, into use for prostitution, an' playacting, and photographs." He swallowed with difficulty.

Monk could see he was having trouble even framing the thoughts that followed. "Yes?" he prompted, finding his own throat tight.

"An' that Mr. Durban fell foul o' Phillips an' wanted to put him away so's he could take the business an' run it for himself," Orme fin-ished wretchedly. He looked at Monk, his eyes imploring a denial, and the will and strength to fight.

Monk felt sick. The evidence he had uncovered about Durban could very easily be used to support such allegations. It was all capa-ble of being interpreted against him as well as for him. Why had he pursued Phillips so erratically, harrying him one month, and then ig-noring him the next? Was it to protect Reilly, or another boy like him? Or was it to further his own interests in the business, or worse, to elicit money from Phillips? Was it a personal war? Yes, of course it was! Everything pointed to that, and Orme knew it even better than he did, even if he did not know why. Durban had loathed Phillips with a driving passion. At times it had consumed him. His temper had exploded. He had gone far beyond the limits of the law. But he had also used his power of office to coerce people into what he wanted them to do. Some would say he had abused it.

And who was Mary Webber? No one seemed to know. No one else had connected her name to the case anywhere.

Why had Durban lied about his own origins? Was it the ordinary human weakness that tempts everyone to make themselves more important than they are, more interesting, more talented, more successful? What was his past really that he denied its entirety?

Orme was still watching him, waiting for a word of encouragement. He must feel dreadfully alone, abandoned to a fight for which he had been given no weapons.

"We have to learn the truth," Monk said firmly. "Nothing else is going to help us in this. And we need to be careful whom we trust. There seems to be someone working against us."

"More than one," Orme said unhappily, but his eyes were steady. "I'm sorry, sir, but there's something else. There's talk of the Metropolitan Police taking us over completely, so we don't even have our own commander anymore, just come under the nearest local station. We wouldn't have the river anymore, just our bit at the bank. The newspapers are saying we're corrupt, an' we need sorting out, most of us got rid of. They even said something in the House of Commons! As if we hadn't looked after them near a hundred years! No loyalty. One bad patch, an' they're on us like wolves."

Doubt lurched up inside Monk, like nausea. They were almost at the far bank by the Wapping Stairs. They would reach it and have to go ashore in minutes, then there would be no more time to speak without the risk of being overheard. It would take only minutes to cross the open dockside and reach the station.

Orme was waiting for him to make the decision whether to go forward, fight all the way, or retreat now before even more was exposed, and perhaps all reputation was lost.

They were at the steps. The ferry bumped at the landing, wood against stone. There was no more time. Monk paid the ferryman and climbed out a step behind Orme.

He could not ask anyone else to make the decision. He was the leader; he must lead. Durban would have; that was one thing of which he was certain. And evasion, willing blindness, was no way out. Whatever was discovered, at least it was a way to move forward. Discretion was sometimes an answer, cowardice never. Which was this?

He followed Orme across the quayside to the station, then inside, still without answering.

They had to spend the rest of the morning dealing with the usual River Police business of thefts, smuggling, and the occasional violence. By the middle of the day Monk was back near Wapping again, knowing that with luck he would have most of the afternoon to think about Durban.

Since the charge was that Durban had procured boys, first for Phillips, then later with the intention of using them in the same trade himself, he knew he should go back and retrace every connection Durban had had with boys, seek the proof his enemies would use, pursue it as ruthlessly as they would, and then hopefully not find it. For that he would need Scuff's help.

"South bank, please," he said to the ferryman. "Rotherhithe."

"Thought you said Wapping!" the man responded tartly.

"I did. I've changed my mind. Princes Stairs, and wait for me. I'm going up to Paradise Place, and I'll be back."

The man nodded agreement.

Monk settled back in the stern as they swung around and headed across the river. He knew from the man's manner that word had already spread that the River Police were in trouble. Even in these few hours their influence was beginning to erode.

Monk had a sudden moment of helplessness, a sickening doubt that he would never stop the destruction. How could he find the skill to prevent the rising confidence of the thieves and chancers up and down the river, the thousands of men who were kept reasonably honest only by the certainty of the River Police's authority, the knowledge that crime was punished immediately and effectively? To some extent it was a matter of bravado, of who kept their nerve the longest. Since the days of Harriott and Colquhoun, the River Police had had the upper hand. But now the greedy on the river were gathering, strengthening, circling to attack.

When they reached the far side he went immediately to Paradise Place. He opened the door and shouted for Scuff as loudly as he could. He tried to think of a suitable punishment if the boy had gone, and knew there was none. He had no right to give commands, except those pertaining to conduct in the house. And yet Scuff was roughly eleven, a child in years if not in experience. He might have strong and subtle knowledge of the street, but his emotions were still appallingly easy to hurt, as vulnerable as any other child's.

Scuff appeared at the top of the stairs, his hair damp and a clean shirt on, which was a little too large for his narrow shoulders, and hanging over the top of his trousers.

"Ah!" Monk said with relief. "I need your help. Are you busy?"

"No!" Scuff said eagerly, starting down. Then he remembered his dignity and slowed. "Not very. What're we gonna do?"

Monk had already decided to tell him the truth. "People are saying some very ugly things about Mr. Durban. In fact, they are actually going to charge that he was guilty of getting boys for Phillips to use on his boat, knowing what it was for."

"That's stupid!" Scuff said disgustedly. " 'E'd 'a never done that! Anyway, 'e's dead." Then instantly he was sorry, but now it was too late to take it back. "I din't mean ter say that," he apologized, looking ruefully at Monk to see how hurt he was. "But wot fer? They can't do nothin' to 'im now, even if it was true."

"It's a cowardly thing to blame a dead man who can't answer you back," Monk said with as much composure as he could. He did not want Scuff to think he had been clumsy. "And it's a good way to get out of it yourself. It turns us away from what we should really be looking at, but all the same, I'm going to find out."

Scuff looked doubtful. "It won't 'ang Phillips."

Monk had a sudden flash of understanding. Scuff was afraid it might be true, and he was imagining how Monk would be disillusioned by it.

"Not directly," Monk agreed casually, keeping the emotion out of his voice with difficulty. "But just at the moment I'm even more concerned with saving Mr. Durban's good name . . ." He stopped, catching the anxiety in Scuff's eyes. "Because he was commander of the River Police, and now people are beginning to say we're all rotten, and they're taking liberties," he explained. "I have to put a stop to that."

Scuff drew in a deep breath, understanding flooding his face, and then anger. "Yer gotter, Mr. Monk," he agreed seriously. "Let 'em get at it once, an' yer'll 'ave twice the trouble gettin' 'em back ter straight."

"Well, come on then!" Monk turned and went back to the front door. He heard Scuff's feet clattering down the stairs and running after him to the step. The door slammed, and then Scuff was beside him.

Monk smiled.

They worked for the rest of the afternoon and into the early evening, tracking down the name and fate of every boy, and what he said of Durban. The next day they started far earlier. By midafternoon, Scuff had been off by himself for several hours, and was late returning to the place they had agreed to meet. Monk was pacing from crate to embankment edge and back again, wishing he had not allowed the boy to go off alone. When Scuff finally showed up, his face was dirty, his shirt torn, and he looked apprehensive.

Monk was too pleased to see him to care about the torn new shirt. Scuff was also unconcerned, and that worried him far more. Scuff was very aware that the clothes were a present, and he was half afraid he would have to give them back one day. If they were torn or stained he could be in a lot of trouble. Worse than that, Hester might think he was not grateful.

Now he stood uncertainly, as if to deliver bad news.

"What did you find out?" Monk asked him. No doubt Scuff was tired and hungry, but relief would have to wait.

Scuff hesitated. He looked as if he had already been considering for some time how to tell Monk whatever it was. He drew in his breath, and then let it out again.

"What did you find out?" Monk repeated, his voice sharper than he meant it to be.

Scuff sniffed. "Mr. Durban. Sometimes 'e caught boys thievin'— just little stuff, 'andkerchiefs, sixpence, or a bob 'ere an' there—an' 'e'd let 'em off. Give 'em a clip 'round the ear, but also mebbe a cup o' tea an' a sandwich, or even a piece o' cake. Other cops'd 'ave 'ad 'em, locked 'em up. Some folks thought 'e were good for that, others said 'e were doin' it for 'is own reasons. Some of 'em boys weren't around anymore after that." He frowned, searching Monk's face to watch how he took the news.

"I see," Monk said levelly. "How old were these boys, and how often did that happen? Were they talking about once or twice, or lots of times?"

Scuff chewed his lip. "Lots o' times. An' one fat ol' scuffle-'unter told me some o' their crimes was worse than light fingers. 'E said one boy Mr. Durban caught weren't five or six at all, 'e were more like ten, an' 'e were a right thief, 'alfway ter bein' a fine wirer. That's someone as can pick a lady's pocket an' she'll never even feel it."

"I know what a fine wirer is. Why did Durban not arrest him, if he stole valuable property? Was there some doubt about it?"

Scuff's eyes lowered till he was staring at the ground. " 'E were a fine-lookin' boy, wi' fair 'air. Some said Mr. Durban 'ad another place fer 'im." He looked up again quickly. "Not that they got any proof, o' course, seein' as it in't true."

"Who said that sort of thing?" Monk asked him.

"I dunno," Scuff said too quickly.

"Yes, you do. You know better than to come with stories out of nowhere. Who said it?"

Scuff hesitated again.

Monk was on the verge of shouting at him, then saw his misery and knew that it was not on his own behalf, but came from a powerful awareness of Monk's own vulnerability. He knew what it was to admire someone, to rely on them as your teacher and friend, and in some ways both your protector and your responsibility. That was how Scuff regarded Monk. Was he imagining that Monk regarded Durban the same way?

"Scuff," he said gently. "Whatever it is, I need to know. We'll find out if it's true or not, but we can't do that if I don't know what it is, and who said it."

Scuff sniffed again, and pulled his face into an expression of reluctant concentration. "Mudlarks I know," he replied. "Taffy—I dunno 'is last name 'cause 'e don't know it neither. Potter, an' Jimmy Mac—summink. An' Mucker James. They all said they knew o' Mr.

Durban seein' boys steal, sometimes something that'd 'ave fetched 'em two or three years in the Coldbath Fields, an' tellin' 'em off. Mostly little kids."

"Little?" Monk asked, feeling the chill inside him, and his skin hot and then cold.

"Five or six, mebbe." Scuff looked miserable. "Most o' them took 'cause they was 'ungry or scared o' 'oever it were put 'em up to it."

"Are they still around, the little boys?"

"I dunno. I din't find any." Scuff looked defiant. "That don't mean they in't there. They could be keepin' out o' the way. They're just the kind Phillips'd take."

"Yes. I know that. Thank you for telling me."

Scuff said nothing.

But that evening, when Hester was in the kitchen, Scuff steeled his courage, stomach knotted, fingers digging into his palms, and went in to see her, hoping intensely that he would find the words before Monk should come, either to speak to Hester himself, or to see what he was doing there.

Hester was bending over the sink, washing the supper dishes. He took a deep, shivering breath and plunged in. "Miss 'Ester. Can I say summink?"

She straightened her back slowly, hands dripping soapy water, but she did not turn to face him. He knew she was listening by the way she stood so still. He liked the smell in this room: warm food and cleanness. There were times when he did not want to ever leave it.

"Yes, of course," she answered. "What is it?"

He pushed his hands into his pockets so that if she turned she would not see his white knuckles. "I did summink today that . . . that 'urt Mr. Monk, but I din't mean ter."

Now she did look at him. "What did you do?"

There was no help but to tell her the truth. "I asked some boys I knew about Mr. Durban, an' I 'eard some things that was pretty bad." He stopped, afraid to tell her the rest. Would she know anyway? She often seemed to know what he was thinking, even when he did not say it. Sometimes that was very comfortable, and sometimes it wasn't.

"I see. Did you tell him the truth as to what you heard?"

"Yeah." He gulped. She was going to say he shouldn't have. He knew it.

She smiled, but her eyes were dark with worry, he could see that. He knew fear and recognized it with instant familiarity. He felt sick.

"That was the right thing," she told him. She moved her hand to touch him, then changed her mind. He wished she hadn't; it would be nice to be touched. But why should she? He did not really belong here.

"They said Mr. Durban let kids off wot should 'a gone ter prison fer stealin'," he said quickly. "Little kids, like Phillips takes. They said Mr. Durban weren't no better. They're wrong, in't they?"

Now she hesitated, then seemed to make her mind up. "I don't know. I hope so. But if they're right, we've got to face that. Mr. Monk will be all right, because we'll be here."

He stared at her, searching her face to know if she meant it, or if she was just being nice to him, thinking he was a child, and could not take anything worse. Gradually he became sure that she did mean it. She did not have children, and she was not treating him like one. He smiled at her.

She smiled back, and, reaching out, touched him quickly and very gently on the cheek. He felt the warmth of it run right through him. He turned away and went back upstairs, before Monk could catch him and somehow take the moment away. It was private, just between him and Hester.

He reached the top of the stairs and touched his cheek experimentally, to see if it was still warm.

In the morning Hester went to see Oliver Rathbone at his office. She did not go to Portpool Lane first; she did not want to have to speak to Margaret. She felt guilty about that. They had been close friends, perhaps the closest woman friend Hester had known—at least in normal circumstances, away from the horrors of war. To avoid her now, because of Rathbone's part in the trial, and the fear and confusion she felt, added to her unhappiness.

Yet she could no longer put off facing Rathbone. She rode the bus along as far as London Bridge, then alighted and took a cab across the river to Rathbone's office near the Inns of Court. His clerk recognized her immediately and invited her in with a mixture of pleasure and embarrassment. She wondered what his own opinion was of the Phillips case, and Rathbone's part in it. Of course, it would be completely improper to ask him, and he could not possibly answer her.

"I'm sorry, Mrs. Monk, but Sir Oliver has a gentleman in to see him," the clerk apologized. "I can't say how long it will be before he is free." He remained standing where he was. It was intended as a polite discouragement.

"If I may, I will wait," she replied, meeting his eyes squarely and not moving a step.

"Of course, ma'am," he conceded, reading her correctly that she intended to wait whatever he said, in the office, or even outside in the street, if that were forced upon her. "May I bring you a cup of tea, and perhaps a biscuit or two?"

She beamed at him. "Thank you. That would be most kind of you."

He retreated, knowing well when he was beaten, and in this case not minding at all. She did wonder fleetingly if she might be about to fight this battle for him, as well as for herself.

She had rather more than three-quarters of an hour to wait, because as soon as the first client left another arrived, and she had to wait for his departure also before being shown into Rathbone's office.

"Good morning, Hester," he said somewhat warily.

"Good morning, Oliver," she replied as the clerk closed the door behind her. She accepted the seat opposite his desk. "I am sure you are busy—in fact, I have already seen two clients come and go—so I shall not waste your time with polite conversation. You may take it for granted that I am interested in your health and happiness, and that I have assumed all the usual polite inquiries from you about mine."

He sighed very slightly and sat down behind his desk.

"And that I have already had tea," she added. "Most graciously served."

"Naturally." There was the very faintest smile on his lips. "Should I apologize for keeping you waiting, or is that to be taken for granted as well?"

"You did not keep me waiting," she replied. "I have no appointment with you."

"Oh, dear. I see we are to be honest to the point of . . . I am not sure. What are we being honest about? Or am I going to regret asking such a question?"

"I seem to remember you telling me, a long time ago, that a good lawyer—and you are extremely good—does not ask a question unless he already knows the answer," she replied.

He winced so slightly, she was not sure if she had seen it or imagined it. "You are not going to prompt me into assuming the answer, Hester," he replied. "You are very good yourself, but I have had rather more practice."

She gave a very slight shrug. "A great deal more. The people you deal with are captive in quite a different way from those that I do. And though they do not always realize it, I also have their interests at heart."

"That is easy to do," he rejoined. "Their interests do not conflict with each other."

"You are naive, Oliver. I have only so much money, so much medicine, so many beds. Of course they conflict with each other!"

He was caught off guard.

"I know that you were employed to defend Phillips," she said, leaning forward in her chair. "And that bound you to his interests, just as the prosecution was bound against them. Once you had accepted the case, unless he admitted his guilt, you had no choice but to defend him. Was that why you did not call him to the stand to deny that he killed Fig? You were certain in your own mind that he had?"

"No, I was not!" he said with sudden vehemence. "He did deny it. I simply did not think that the jury would believe him. He is not an attractive character, and if he had spoken that would very definitely have shown. The jury should weigh only the evidence, but they are people—passionate, vulnerable, full of pity and outrage for the crime, and intensely afraid both of doing the wrong thing and of one day being victims of crime themselves." He spoke so quickly he scarcely had time for breath. "They would have been led by dislike into believing him guilty. They could very easily have crossed the line from being convinced that he had committed other crimes, which I have no doubt he has, to believing that he had committed this one also. They do not have to give reasons for their verdict. I cannot argue with them and point out that their logic is flawed. Once they have spoken, I have to accept, unless there is a point of law on which I can argue. Illogic is not such a point."

"I know," she said drily. "Tremayne could have used emotion to sway them against Phillips, and you would have had no recourse because they would not have realized what he had done. They would have imagined that the feelings were entirely their own, not manipulated by counsel."

He smiled very slightly. "Exactly. I am pleased you see it with such a fair mind."

It was her turn to smile with the same chilly humor. "Of course I do, now," she replied. "Unfortunately, I didn't see it so plainly when you were manipulating me. Nor, I'm afraid, did Mr. Tremayne. You are better at it than either of us. But then I dare say you are right in that you are more practiced."

The color washed deep red up his face. "I had no choice, Hester. Should I have done less than my best for him, because you were the witness? If I had when defending someone you liked, you would have been the first to call me dishonorable. You can't have justice dealt one way for those you like and another for those you don't."

"Of course not," she agreed, her voice tighter than she had meant it to be. It gave her away, and she knew he would hear it. "I followed the case because I believed passionately that Phillips was an evil man who tortured and murdered a child who had the courage to stand up against him. I still believe it. But I know that I let my emotions rule me instead of my intelligence. I was not impartial in my judgment, and it let me down. You took advantage of my weakness because you knew me well enough to do so."

She ignored the flare of anger, and perhaps shame in his eyes. "I am not sure whether I know you well enough or not, Oliver. I used to think I did, but people change, and those closest to them do not always see it. Was it love of justice, or emotion that caused you to take up the defense of Jericho Phillips?"

He was startled.

She did not stop to allow him the chance to interrupt her. "Did you defend him because you thought no one else would do it adequately, or even at all? Perhaps you are right if you think no one else would have done it as well. Or did you do it to pay a debt to some friend to whom you owe a loyalty, a pity, or a matter of honor, past or future?" She swallowed. "Or to show off, because it seemed impossible, and yet you accomplished it?"

He was very pale now. "Is that what you think of me, Hester?"

She did not flinch.

"It is not what I wish to think. Before the trial I would have stood in that witness box and sworn that you would not." She thought of mentioning money, and decided against that ultimate insult. "Do you even know who actually paid you?" she said instead. "Are you certain it was not Phillips himself? Isn't he clever enough to have done it through so many other avenues you could not trace it back to him? Then the question is, if he had come to you directly, not through a client, and a friend, would you still have taken the case?"

"I don't know. That is not how it happened," he replied. "I cannot explain it to you because it is in confidence, as are all legal consultations. You know that, and you knew it when you came here. You are not usually impractical enough to waste time and energy railing against the past. What is it you want?" It was blunt. His eyes were hard and hurt. He was also surprised that she had outmaneuvered him.

"I would like to know who paid you . . ." she began.

"Don't be foolish," he said sharply. "You know I cannot possibly tell you that!"

"I didn't ask you that!" she answered equally sharply. "I know you cannot. If either you or they were willing to own up to it you would have done so already." She allowed her fear to show through, brittle and bright. "I wanted you to know that because of the doubt cast on Commander Durban's honor, now the whole of the Thames River Police is under suspicion to the degree that they may even be taken over completely, as a separate arm of the Metropolitan Police. All their specialist experience will be lost. And don't bother to tell me that that is as much my fault as yours. I know it is. I am not concerned with blame. As you said, it is a waste of time to cry over the past, which cannot be changed. I am concerned for the future."

She leaned towards him. "Oliver, between us we have come close to destroying something that is good. You can help us save Durban's reputation without damaging your own."

"And Monk's, of course," he said cruelly.

Again she did not flinch. "Of course. And mine too, for that matter. Is helping us a reason for not doing it?"

"Hester, for . . . no, of course it isn't!" he protested. "I didn't expose any of you because I wanted to. You left yourselves wide open. I did what I had to do, to uphold the law."

"So now do what you can to uphold justice," she returned. "Jericho Phillips killed Fig, although it is pointless to prove that now, even if we could. He killed others too, and we'll be a lot more careful about our evidence next time. But in order to do that, the River Police have to survive with their own command, not broken up into a dozen different entities, each just part of their local station."

She stood up slowly, careful to straighten her skirt—something with which she did not usually bother. "We have all done something ugly, all three of us. I am asking you to help us mend it, as much as it can be mended. We may never catch Phillips, but we can do all that is possible to prove to London that the River Police need and deserve to remain a separate department, with their own command."

He looked at her with what for him was an extraordinary sense of confusion. Emotions conflicted with intellect: loneliness, dismay, perhaps guilt, breaking apart his usual sanctuary of reason.

"I'll do what I can," he said quietly. "I have no idea if it will be of use."

She did not argue. "Thank you," she said simply. Then she smiled at him. "I thought you would."

He blushed, and looked down at the papers on his desk, overwhelmed with relief when the clerk knocked on the door.

She considered returning home to change from her most flattering dress, which naturally she had worn to see Rathbone, before going to Portpool Lane, but decided that it was a waste of the fare. She always kept clean working clothes at the clinic in case of accidents, which happened quite often.

She found the clinic busy with its regular affairs, tending to the few who were sick enough to require days in bed, and the walking patients with knife or razor wounds who needed stitching, bandaging, general comfort, and a little respite from the streets, perhaps a decent meal. The regular chores of cleaning, laundry, and cooking never stopped.

She offered words of approval and encouragement, a minor criticism here and there, then went to find Squeaky Robinson in his office. He had taken his bookkeeping duties very seriously this last year or so. She had not recently heard him complain about having been cheated out of the building, which, when it was his, had been the most successful brothel in the area. His new vision of himself, more or less on the right side of the law, seemed to please him.

"Good morning, Squeaky," she said as she closed the door, giving them privacy in the cluttered room with its shelves of ledgers. The desk was scattered with sheets of paper, pencils, two inkwells, one red, one blue, and a tray of sand for blotting. This last was seldom used; he just liked the look of it.

"Mornin', Miss 'Ester," he replied, searching her face with concern. He did not ask her how she was; he would make the judgment himself.

She sat down in the chair opposite him. "This whole business is becoming extremely ugly," she said frankly. "There are whispers of accusation that Mr. Durban was procuring boys for Jericho Phillips, and the River Police in general are being dirtied with that accusation. There seem to be several incidents where he found boys stealing and deliberately did not charge them. There may be other explanations as to why that happened, but the worst is being assumed."

He nodded. "Looks bad," he agreed, sucking air in through his teeth. "In't nobody 'oo in't tempted by summink, whether it's money or power or pleasure, or just 'avin' people owe 'em. I've seen some where it's just feelin' superior as does it. Specially women. Seen some awful superior women. Beggin' yer pardon."

She smiled. "So have I, and I wanted to slap them, until I realized that's probably all they had. A friend of mine used to say that there are none as virtuous as those who have never been asked."

"I like that," he said with profound appreciation. He mulled it over, like a good wine. "Yeah, I do."

"Squeaky, I need to know how Phillips gets his boys."

There was a tap on the door, and as soon as Hester answered, Claudine came in. "Good morning," she said cheerfully. "Would you like a cup of tea?"

Both Hester and Squeaky knew that she had come because she could not bear to be left out of the detection. She desperately wanted to help, but she had not yet let down her barriers of dignity enough to say so outright.

"Thank you," Hester declined quickly. "But I need to go out, and I think I need Squeaky with me. He knows people that I don't."

Claudine looked crestfallen. She tried to hide it, but the feeling was too deep to conceal it from her eyes.

"In't summink you would know about," Squeaky said brusquely. "Don't s'pose you even know why girls take ter sellin' theirselves on the streets, let alone kids."

"Of course I know," she snapped. "Do you think I can't hear what they're saying? Or that I don't listen to them?"

Squeaky relented a fraction. "Boys," he explained. "We don't get no little boys in 'ere. If they get beat no one knows, 'ceptin' 'ooever's keepin' 'em, like Jericho Phillips."

Claudine snorted. "And what is going to be so different about why they take to the streets?" she asked. "Cold, hunger, fear, nowhere else to go. Lonely, someone offers to take them in, easy money, at first."

"You're right," Hester agreed, surprised that Claudine had apparently listened so closely to what was voiced, including the words themselves, which were often shallow and repetitive, sometimes full of excuses or self-pity, more often with a bitter humor and an endless variety of bad jokes. "But I need to prove that it wasn't Commander Durban procuring them, so it has to be specific."

"Commander Durban?" Claudine was clearly horrified. "I never heard anything so wicked. Don't worry, I'll look after everything here. You find out all you can, but be careful!" She glared at Squeaky. "You look after her, or I shall hold you accountable. Believe me, you will be sorry you were born." And with that she turned around, whisking her very plain gray skirt as if it had been crimson silk, and marched out.

Squeaky smiled. Then he saw Hester and assumed instant gravity. "We'll be goin', then," he said flatly. "I'll put on me oldest boots."

"Thank you," she accepted. "I will wait for you by the door."

They spent a miserable afternoon well into the early evening moving from one to another of Squeaky's contacts in his previous life as a brothel owner.

They continued the next day, going deeper into the network of alleys in Limehouse, Shadwell, and the Isle of Dogs on the north bank of the river, and Rotherhithe and Deptford on the south. Hester felt as if she had walked as far as from London to York circling the same narrow byways crowded with doss-houses, taverns, pawnshops, brothels, and all the multitudinous traders associated with the river.

Squeaky was very careful, even secretive about their search, but his whole manner changed when it was time to bargain. The casual, rather inconspicuous air vanished, and he became subtly menacing. There was a stillness about him, a gentleness to his voice that contrasted with the noise and bustle around him.

"I think yer know better than that, Mr. Kelp," he said in almost a whisper. They were standing in what was ostensibly a tobacconist's shop, darkly wood paneled, one small window, its glass ringed like the base of a bottle. The lamps were lit or they would not have been able to see the wares laid out, although the pungent aroma was powerful enough to drift out into the alley and tempt people, even above the stench of rotting wood and human waste.

Kelp opened his mouth to deny it, and reconsidered. There was something about Squeaky's motionless figure in its faded, striped trousers and ancient frock coat, his stringy hair and lantern face that frightened him. It was as if Squeaky somehow knew himself to be invulnerable, in spite of not apparently having any weapon, and no one with him but one rather slightly built woman. It was inexplicable, and anything he could not understand alarmed Mr. Kelp.

He swallowed. "Well . . ." he prevaricated. "I heard things, o' course, if that's wot you want, like?"

Squeaky nodded slowly. "That's wot I want, Mr. Kelp, things you've 'eard, accurate things, things you believe yerself. An' yer would be very wise indeed not ter tell anybody else that I 'ave asked, an' that yer 'ave been good enough ter 'elp me. There are those with long an' careful ears who would not be pleased. Let us leave them in their ignorance, shall we?"

Kelp shuddered. "Oh, yes, Mr. Robinson, sir. Very definitely." He did not even glance at Hester standing a little behind Squeaky. She was watching with growing surprise. This was a side of Squeaky she had not imagined, and her own blindness to its possibility was disturbing. She had grown accustomed to his compliance in the clinic, and forgotten the man he used to be. In fact, she had never really known more than the superficial fact that he had owned the brothel that had occupied the Portpool Lane houses.

Squeaky was approximately in his fifties, but she had thought of him as old, because he sat in a bent, hunched position, and his hair was long and gray, hanging thinly down to his collar. He had complained vociferously about being cheated and abused, as if he were a man of peaceful habits wrongfully treated. The man she saw here in the tobacconists' was nothing like that. Kelp was afraid of him. She could see it in his face, even smell it in the air. She felt a shiver of doubt at her own foolhardiness, and forced it from her mind with some difficulty.

Kelp swallowed what appeared to be a lump in his throat, and proceeded to tell Squeaky everything he knew about the procuring of boys for men like Jericho Phillips. It was sad and very ugly, full of human failure and the opportunism of the greedy who preyed on the weak.

It also included Durban catching boys, some no more than five or six years old, stealing food and small articles to sell. He had seldom charged them, and the assumption was that he had bought them from their parents in order to sell them to Phillips, or others like him. There was no proof, one way or the other, but too many of them had not been seen again in the usual places, nor was anyone saying where they had gone, or with whom.

"I'm sorry," Squeaky said as towards evening they walked along the path close to the river on the Isle of Dogs. They were making for All Saints Stairs to catch a ferry across to the pier on the south side, and then a bus to Rotherhithe Street, from which it was a short walk to Paradise Place. Squeaky had insisted on seeing her home, even though she frequently rode the bus or a cab by herself. "Looks as if yer Durban could 'a been bent as a pig's tail," he added.

She found it difficult to speak. What was she going to tell Monk? She needed to know before he did, so that she could do something to soften the blow. But what? If this were true, it was worse than she had imagined. "I know," she said huskily.

"D'yer want ter keep on?" he asked.

"Yes, of course I do!"

"That's wot I thought, but I gotter ask." He glanced at her, then away again. "It could get worse."

"I know that too."

"Even good men 'ave got their weaknesses," he said. "An' women too, I s'pose. I reckon yers is believin' people. It's not a bad one ter 'ave, mind."

"Am I supposed to be grateful for that?"

"No. I reckon it 'urts yer. But if yer knew everythin' yer'd be too cocky ter be nice."

"Not much chance of that," she replied, but she did smile, faintly, even though he could not see it in the fitful street lighting.

They made their way down towards the top of the All Saints Stairs. Just before they reached them, a figure stepped out of the shadows of a crane, and the light from the street lamp showed his face like a yellow mask, wide, thin mouth leering. Jericho Phillips. He looked at Hester, ignoring Squeaky.

"I know you've been looking for Reilly, Miss. Yer don't want ter do that."

Squeaky was taken aback, but he hid it quickly. "You threatenin' 'er, Mr. Phillips?" he asked with exaggerated politeness.

"Spot of advice," Phillips replied. "Friendly, as it were. Reckon I owe 'er a lot." He smiled, showing his teeth. "Might be swingin' on a gibbet by me neck, if it weren't for 'er evidence at me trial." He laughed softly, his eyes dead as stones. "Yer would find out a lot o' things yer'd be 'appier not knowin', seein' as you admired Mr. Durban so much. Yer find Reilly, poor boy, an' you'll like as not find out what 'appened to 'im. An' believe me, Miss, yer won't like that at all."

There was a ferry making its way across the oily black surface of the water, oars dipping in and out rhythmically.

"Brave boy, Reilly," Phillips added. "Foolish, mind. Trusted those 'e shouldn't 'ave, like River Police. Found out more'n it's good fer a boy like 'im ter know."

"So you killed him, just as you killed Fig," Hester said bitterly.

"No reason to, Miss," Phillips told her. "It weren't me Reilly were goin' ter tell on. I treat my boys very well. Stupid not to. Ask 'em! You won't find one as'll speak against me. I don't beat 'em, don't forget me-self an' 'oller and scream at 'em. I know me business, an' I look after it proper."

She looked at him with total loathing, but she could find no answer with which to retaliate.

"Think about it, Miss," Phillips went on. "Yer been askin' a lot o' questions about Durban. Wot did yer find out, eh? Liar, weren't 'e? Lied about everythin', even where 'e came from. Lost 'is temper something rotten, beat the tar out o' some folks. Covered up crime in some, lied about it in others. Now me, I might do that, but then yer'd expect it o' me." He smiled utterly without humor. "Durban's different. Nobody trusts me, but they trusted 'im. That makes it somethin' else, a kind o' betrayal, right? Fer 'im ter break the law is bad, very bad. Believe me, Miss, yer don't want ter know all about Mr. Durban, yer really don't. Neither does your good man. Saved my life twice over, 'e did. Once in the river . . . oh?" He raised his eyebrows. "Din't 'e tell you that?"

She stared at him with hatred.

His smile widened. "Yeah, could 'a let me drown, but 'e saved me. An' then o'course all that evidence of 'is in court. Reckon without that I would've 'anged, fer sure. Not a pretty way ter go, Miss, the rope dance.

Not at all. You don't want ter know what 'appened ter poor Reilly, Miss, nor all about Mary Webber neither. Now here's a ferryboat come ter take yer 'ome. Yer sleep well, an' in the mornin' go tend to yer clinic, an' all them poor 'ores wot yer bent on savin'." He turned and stalked away, consumed almost immediately by the shadows.

Hester stood on the steps shivering with rage, but also fear. She could not refute a single thing Phillips had said. She felt helpless, and so cold in the summer night that she might as well have fallen in the dark, swift-moving water.

The ferry was now bumping on the steps, the oarsman waiting.

"Yer want ter leave it, Miss 'Ester?" Squeaky asked.

She could not see his face; they had their backs to the light now. How could she read his emotions from his voice? "Can it get any worse?" she asked. "Hasn't anything got to be better than accepting this?"

" 'Course it can!" he said instantly. "It can get a lot worse. Yer could find out that Durban killed Reilly, an' Phillips can prove it."

"No, he can't," she said with a sudden burst of logic. "If he could prove that, he would have done so already, and destroyed Durban's evidence without having to hope Rathbone could discredit us. It would have been much safer."

"Then if yer want, I'm 'appy ter go on. Nailin' that bastard'd be better than a bottle o' Napoleon Brandy."

"Do you like Napoleon Brandy?" she said in surprise.

"No idea," he admitted. "But I'd like ter find out!"

NINE

*H*ester slept late the next morning, and was far less disturbed than usual to find that Monk had already left. There was a note from him on the kitchen table. Scuff was nowhere to be seen, so she assumed that he had gone with Monk.

However, she was halfway through her breakfast of tea and toast when the boy appeared in the doorway looking anxious. He was already dressed and had obviously been out. He was holding a newspaper in his hands. He seemed uncertain whether to offer it to her or not. She knew he could not read, but she did not want to embarrass him by referring to the fact.

"Good morning," she said casually. "Would you like some breakfast?"

"I 'ad some," he replied, coming a couple of steps into the kitchen.

"There is no reason not to have some more, if you would like it," she offered. "It's only toast and jam, but the jam is very good. And tea, of course."

"Oh," he said, eyes following her hand with the toast in it. "Well, I don't mind if I do."

"Then come and sit down, and I will make it for you." She finished her own toast and raspberry jam, holding it in one hand while she cut and toasted more bread with the other.

They sat at opposite sides of the table and ate in silence for some time. He took apricot jam, twice.

"May I look at your newspaper please?" she asked at length.

" 'Course." He pushed it over towards her. "I got it fer yer. Yer in't gonna like it." He looked worried. "I 'eard 'em talkin' around the newsboy, that's why I got it. They're sayin' bad things."

She reached for the paper and looked at the headlines, then opened it and read inside. Scuff was right, she did not like it at all. The suggestions were veiled, but they were not so very far from the sort of thing that Phillips had said on the dockside the previous evening. There were questions about the River Police, their record of success suspiciously high. But were the figures honest? How had they come to recruit a man as obsessed with personal vengeance as Durban had been—and apparently not just once, but twice? Was the new man, William Monk, any better? What was known about him? For that matter, what was known about any of them, including Durban?

It was a dangerous state of affairs for the nation when a body of men such as the River Police had the kind of power they did, and there was no check upon the way they used it, or abused it. If the members of Parliament who represented the constituencies along the river were doing their duty, there would be questions asked in the House.

She looked up at Scuff. He was watching her, trying to judge what the paper said from her expression.

"Yes, they are saying bad things," she told him. "But so far it is just talk. I need to know whether they are true or not, because we can't deal with it until we know."

"Wot'll 'appen to us if it's true?" he asked.

She heard the fear in his voice, and the inclusion of himself in their fate. She wondered if he had meant her to notice that or not. She would be very careful to reply in the same tones, equally casually.

"We'll have to face it," she answered. "If we can, we'll prove that we're not like that, but if we aren't given the chance, then we'll have to find some other job. We will, don't worry. There are lots of things we can do. I could go back to nursing. I used to earn my own living before I married Mr. Monk, you know."

"Did yer? Like lookin' after the sick? They pay yer fer that?" His eyes were wide, his toast and jam halfway to his mouth.

"Definitely," she assured him. "If you do it well enough, and I was very good. I did it in the army, for soldiers injured in battle."

"When they come 'ome again?"

"Certainly not! I went to the battlefield and tended them there, where they fell."

He blushed, then he grinned, sure that she was making a joke, even if he didn't understand it.

She thought of teasing him back, then decided he was too genuinely frightened to absorb it right now. He had just found some kind of safety, perhaps for the first time in his life, people not only to love but also to trust, and it was slipping out of his hands.

"Really in the battlefield," she answered. "That's where soldiers need doctors and nurses. I went to the Crimea with the army. So did quite a few other ladies. The fighting was pretty close to us. People used to go out in carriages to the heights above the valley and watch the fighting. It's not dangerous, or of course they wouldn't do it. But we nurses sometimes saw it too, and then went to find those who were still alive, and who we could help."

"Weren't it 'orrible?" he asked in a whisper, toast still ignored.

"Yes, it was. More horrible than I ever want to think of again. But looking away doesn't solve anything, does it." That was a statement more than a question.

"Wot can yer do fer soldiers as are 'urt real awful?" he asked. "Don't they 'ave ter 'ave doctors, an' such?"

"There aren't enough doctors to attend to everybody at once," she told him, remembering in spite of herself the sounds of men in agony, the chaos of the wounded and dying, and the smell of blood. She had not felt overwhelmed then, she had been too busy being practical, trying to pack wounds, amputate shattered limbs, and save men from dying of shock. "I learned how to do some things myself, because it was so bad I couldn't make it worse. When it's desperate, you try, even if you don't know what to do to begin with. You can be a lot of help with a knife, a saw, a bottle of brandy, and a needle and thread, and of course as much water and bandages as you can carry with you."

"Wot's a saw for?" he asked quietly.

She hesitated, then decided that lies would be worse than the truth. "To saw through jagged bones so you can make a clean cut, and sew it up," she told him. "And sometimes you have to take somebody's arm or leg off, if it's gone bad with gangrene, which is sort of like rotten meat. If you don't, it will go all through them, and they'll die."

He stared at her. He felt as if he were seeing her for the first time, with all the lights on. Before it had been almost as if they were in the half dark. She was not as pretty as some of the women he had seen, certainly not as fancy as some of the ladies; in fact, the clothes she wore were downright ordinary. He'd seen just as good on women near the docks when they went out on Sundays. But there was something extra in her face, especially in her eyes, and when she smiled, as if she could see things other people didn't even think of.

He always used to think that women were nice, and certainly useful in the house, the best of them. But most of them had to be told what to do, and they were weak, and scared, when it came to fighting. Looking after important things was men's work; protecting, fighting, seeing that nobody stepped out of line had to be done by a man. And for clever things, it was always men, of course. That went without anybody needing to say it.

Hester was smiling at him, but there were tears in her eyes, and she blinked quickly when she talked about the soldiers dying, the ones she couldn't help. He knew what that felt like, the ache in your throat so big you couldn't swallow, the way you kept gulping breath, but it didn't get any better, nor did the tightness go out of your chest.

But she didn't cry. He hoped to goodness Mr. Monk looked after her properly. She was a bit thin. Usually real ladies had a bit more ... softness ... about them. Somebody should take care of her.

"Yer gonna 'ave another piece o' toast?" he asked.

"Would you like one?" She misunderstood him. He was not asking for himself.

"Will yer 'ave one?" he changed his approach. "I'll make it fer yer. I know 'ow ter make toast."

"Thank you," she accepted. "That would be very nice. Perhaps I should boil the kettle again?" She began to rise.

"I'll do it!" He stepped in her way so she had to sit down. "All I gotta do is move it over on ter the 'eat."

"Thank you," she said again, slightly puzzled, but willing to accept.

Very carefully indeed he cut two more slices of bread, a little thick, a trifle crooked, but good enough. He put them on the toasting fork and held them to the open door of the stove. This was not going to be easy, but he could look after her. It needed doing, and it was his new job. He would see to it from now on.

The toast started to smoke. He turned it 'round just before it burnt. He had better concentrate.

Hester had debated whether to take Scuff with her or not when she went back to look further into Durban's history and whether the charges against him were in any part true. The matter was taken out of her hands by Scuff himself. He simply came.

"I'm not sure . . ." she began.

He smiled at her, continuing to look oddly important. "You need me," he said simply, then fell in step beside her as if that settled the matter.

She drew in her breath to argue, and found that she had no idea how to tell him that she did not really need him. The silence grew until it became impossible, and by default she had accepted that she did.

As it transpired, he helped her find most of the people she eventually wished to speak to. It was long and tiring walking from one narrow, crowded street to another, arguing, asking, pleading for information and then trying to sort out the lies and the mistakes and find the elements of truth. Scuff was better at that than she was. He had a sharp instinct for evasion and manipulation. He was also more prepared than she to threaten or call a bluff.

"Don't let 'em get away with nothin'!" he said to her urgently as they left one smooth-tongued man with a wispy black mustache. "That's a load o' . . ." He bit his tongue to avoid the word he had been going to use. "I reckon as it were Mr. Durban 'as pulled 'im out o' the muck, an' 'e's too . . . mean ter say it. That's wot that is." He stood in the middle of the narrow pavement looking up at her seriously.

A costermonger wheeled his barrow past them, knowing at a glance that she would not buy.

"Yer din't ought ter b'lieve every stupid sod as tells yer," Scuff continued. "Well, yer din't," he granted generously. "I'll tell yer if it's true or not. We better go and find this Willie the Dip, if 'e's real."

Two washerwomen barged past them, sheets tied around dirty laundry bouncing on their ample hips.

"You don't think he is?" Hester asked.

Scuff gave her a skeptical look. "Dip means 'e picks pockets. 'Oo don't, round 'ere? I reckon 'e's all guff."

And so it turned out. But by the end of the day they had heard many stories of Durban from a variety of people up and down the dockside. They had been discreet, and Hester believed with some pride that they had also been inventive enough not to betray the reason for their interest.

It was well after dusk with the last of the light faded even from the flat surface of the water when they finally made their way up Elephant Stairs just a few yards along from Princes Street. The tide was running hard, slapping against the stone, and the sharp river smell was almost pleasant in the air after the closed-in alleys they had walked all day, and the heavy, throat-filling odors of the docks, where men were unpacking all manner of cargoes, pungent, clinging, some so sweet as to be rancid. The quiet movement of water was a relief after the shouting, clatter of hooves, and clank of chains and winches and thus of heavy loads.

They were tired and thirsty. Scuff did not say that his feet were sore, but possibly he regarded it as a condition of life. Hester ached all the way up to her knees, and beyond, but in the face of his stoicism, she felt that it would be self-indulgent to let it be known.

"Thank you," she said as they started to walk up in the direction of Paradise Place. "You are quite right. I do need you."

"S'all right," he said casually, giving a little lift of his shoulder visible as he passed under the street lamp.

He took a deep breath. " 'E weren't a bad man," he said, then looked sideways at her quickly.

"I know, Scuff."

"Does it matter if 'e told a few lies about 'oo 'e were or where 'e come from?"

"I don't know. I suppose it depends what the truth is."

"Yer think it's bad, then?"

They came to the end of Elephant Lane and turned right into Church Street. It was completely dark now and the lamps were like yellow moons reflected over and over again right to the end. There was a faint mist drifting up in patches from the water, like castaway silk scarves.

"I think it might be. Otherwise why would he lie about it?" she asked. "We don't usually lie about good things."

He was quiet.

"Scuff?"

"Yes, Miss."

"You can't go on calling me 'miss'! Would you like to call me 'Hester'?"

He stopped and tried to look at her. "Hester?" he said carefully, sounding the *H*. "Don't you think Mr. Monk might say I'm bein' cheeky?"

"I shall tell him I suggested it."

"Hester," he said again, experimentally, then he grinned.

Hester lay awake and thought hard about what steps she should take next. Durban had tried for a long time, well over a year, to find Mary Webber. He was a skilled policeman with a lifetime of experience in learning, questioning, and finding, and he had apparently failed. How was she to succeed? She had no advantages over him, as far as she knew.

Beside her, Monk was asleep, she thought. She lay still, not wanting to disturb him, above all not wanting him to know that she was thinking, puzzling.

Durban must have searched for all the families named Webber who lived in the area and gone to them. He would even have traced any who had lived there and moved, if it were possible. If he had not found Mary that way, then Hester would not either.

Then just as she was finally drifting off towards sleep, another thought occurred to her. Had Durban gone backwards? Had he found out where they had come from before that?

The idea did not seem nearly as clever in the morning, but she could think of nothing better. She would try it, at least until another avenue occurred to her. It would be better than doing nothing.

It was not particularly difficult to find the local families by the name of Webber who had a Mary of roughly the right age. It was simply tedious looking through parish registers, asking questions, and walking around. People were willing to help, because she embroidered the truth a little. She really was looking for someone on behalf of a friend who had died tragically before finding them, but whether Mary Webber was a friend or witness, help or a fugitive, she had no idea. If it had not been for Monk's sake, she might have given up.

After some time, she found what appeared to be the right family, only to discover that Mary had been adopted from the local foundling hospital. Her mother had died giving birth to her brother, and the adoptive family had no ability to care for a baby, the wife being handicapped herself. There was only one such hospital in the area, and it was no more than half an hour's bus ride to its doors. It was a further half hour before Hester, now with Scuff determinedly on her heels, was shown into the office of Donna Myers, the brisk and rather starched matron who ran it from day to day.

"Now, what can I do for you?" she asked pleasantly, looking Hester up and down, and then regarding Scuff with a measuring eye.

Scuff drew in his breath to protest that he needed nobody to look after him, then realized that that was not what Miss Myers had in mind, and let it out in a sigh of relief.

"We've got plenty of work," Mrs. Myers told Hester. "Wages are poor, but we'll feed you and the boy, three square meals a day, porridge and bread mostly, but meat when we have it. No drink allowed, and no men, but the place is clean and we don't treat anyone unkindly. I'm sure the boy could find something too, errands or the like."

Hester smiled at her, appreciating from her own experience in running the clinic just how strict one had to be, no matter how deep or how genuine your pity. To indulge one was to rob another.

"Thank you, Mrs. Myers. I appreciate your offer, but it is only information I'm looking for. I already have work, running a clinic of my own." She saw Miss Myers's eyes open wider and a sudden respect flickered alive in them.

"Really?" Mrs. Myers said guardedly. "And what is it that I can do for you, then?"

Hester wondered whether to mention that Monk was in the River Police, and decided that in view of the present highly unfavorable publicity, it would not be a good idea.

"I am seeking information about a woman who came here as a girl of about six, with her mother," she answered. "Perhaps about forty-five years ago. The mother died in childbirth, and the girl was adopted. I believe the baby remained here. I would like to know as much about them as your records show, and if there is anyone who knows what happened to them I would be most grateful."

"And why is it you wish to know?" Mrs. Myers looked at her more closely. "Are they related to you in any way? What was the mother's name?"

Hester had known that the question would be asked, but she still felt foolish that she could not answer. "I don't know her name." There was no choice but the truth; anything else would make her look dishonest. So much of what she was saying was no more than an enlightened guess, but it made the only decent sense.

"It is the baby who concerns me," she went on. "He would be in his fifties now, but he died over six months ago, and I want to trace the sister and tell her. Perhaps she would like to know what a fine man he was. He was doing all he could to find her, but he failed. I am sure you understand why I wish to complete that for him." She was leaping far to such a conclusion. If Durban had really been born in a foundling hospital, was that why he had invented for himself a gentler, more respectable background, and a family that loved him? Poverty was not a sin, but many people were ashamed of it. No child should grow up with nobody to whom he was important and precious.

Mrs. Myers's face was touched with pity. For a moment she looked younger, wearier, and more vulnerable. Hester felt a sudden warmth towards her, a momentary understanding of what her task must be to keep such a hospital functioning and not be overwhelmed by the enormity of her task. The individual tragedies were intensely real, the fear of hunger and loneliness; too many bewildered women were exhausted and at their wits' end to find the next place to rest, the next mouthful to give their children. The searing loneliness of giving birth in such a place stunned her, and ridiculously she found herself gulping and tears stinging her eyes. She imagined passing over your newborn child, perhaps holding it only once, and then bleeding to death alone, buried by strangers. No wonder Mrs. Myers was careful, and tired, or that she kept a shell around her to close out some of that tide of grief.

"I'll ask my daughter," Mrs. Myers said quietly. "I doubt she'll know, but it is the best place to try.

"Thank you," Hester accepted immediately. "I would be very grateful indeed."

"What year would that be?" Mrs. Myers inquired, turning to lead them through bare, clean corridors, sharp with the smell of lye and carbolic.

"About 1810, the best calculation I can make," Hester answered. "But I am going on memory of neighbors of the family."

"I will do what I can," Mrs. Myers replied dubiously, her heels clicking sharply on the hard wooden floors. Maids with mops and buckets redoubled their efforts to look busy. A pale-faced woman hobbled out of sight around a corner. Two children with straggling hair and tearstained faces peeped around a doorway, staring as Mrs. Myers, followed by Hester and Scuff, striding past without looking to either side.

They found Stella in a warm room facing the sun, sharing a large, enamel pot of tea with three other young women, all dressed in what looked like a simple uniform of gray blouse and skirt, and short black boots. All of their boots were dirty and worn lopsidedly at the heels. It was one of the younger women who stood up to lift the heavy pot and refill all the cups, while Stella remained seated.

Hester assumed that was the privilege of being the matron's daughter until they were level with the table and she saw that Stella was blind. She turned at the sound of unfamiliar footsteps, but she did not speak or rise.

Mrs. Myers introduced Hester without mentioning Scuff, and explained what she had come for.

Stella considered for several moments, her head raised as if she were staring at the ceiling.

"I don't know," she said at last. "I can't think of anyone who would remember that far back."

"We have our people the right age," her mother prompted.

"Do we? I can't think who," Stella said very quickly.

Mrs. Myers smiled but Hester saw a sadness in it that for a moment was almost overwhelming.

"Mr. Woods might recall . . ."

"Mina, he barely remembers his name," Stella cut in, her voice gentle but very definite. "He gets terribly confused."

Mrs. Myers stood quite still. "Mrs. Cordwainer?" she suggested.

There seemed to be a complete silence in the room. No one moved.

"I don't know her well enough to ask her such things," Stella replied huskily. "She's very . . . old. She might . . ." She did not finish the sentence.

"Perhaps," Mrs. Myers conceded. She appeared to hesitate, then came to a decision. "I will leave Mrs. Monk to talk with you. You may be able to think of something else. Excuse me." And she walked away, gathering speed, and they could hear her footsteps fading away.

Hester looked at Stella, wondering if the blind girl were aware of her scrutiny. Did she read voices as other people read expressions on a face?

"Miss Myers," Hester began. "It really is of very great importance to several other people, as well as to me. I did not tell your mother the full extent of how much this matters. If I can find her, she may be able to clear away certain suspicions I believe to be urgent, but without her help I cannot prove it. If there is anyone at all you can think of to ask, I have no other source left to try."

Stella turned towards her, her brow puckered. She was clearly struggling with some decision she found intensely difficult. There was pity in her expression as sharp as if she had not just seen Hester's face but also read the emotions behind her eyes. It was strange to be looked at so perceptively by someone who had no sight.

"Mrs. Monk, if . . . if I take you to see Mrs. Cordwainer, will you be discreet about anything you may see or hear in her house? Will you give me your word?"

Hester was startled. It was the last sort of request she had expected. What on earth could Mrs. Cordwainer be doing that required such a promise? Was Hester going to be asked to do something that would trouble her conscience? Was the old woman being cheated or abused in some way? Looking at Stella, she did not think that likely.

"If I give you such a promise, am I going to regret it?" she asked.

Stella's lip trembled. "Possibly," she whispered. "But I cannot take you if you don't promise."

"Is Mrs. Cordwainer suffering in some way? Because if she is, I should find it very hard indeed not to do what I could to help."

Stella almost laughed, but she choked on the sound. "She is not, that I can say absolutely."

Hester was even more puzzled, but the only alternative to accepting the conditions was to give up altogether. "Then I give you my word," she replied.

Stella smiled and stood up. "Then I shall take you to see Mrs. Cordwainer. She lives in a small house on the hospital grounds. She'll be asleep at this time of day, but she won't mind being woken up if it's to ask questions about the past. She likes to tell tales of times back then."

"Can . . . can I 'elp yer?" Scuff offered hesitantly.

It was her turn to consider her answer. She decided to accept, although Hester realized she must know her way around the hospital more easily than Scuff. She followed as side by side they made their way out of the room and down the corridor, Stella pretending she did not know where she was going, and Scuff pretending that he did.

They left the main building of the hospital and made their way along a well-worn path, up a short flight of steps, and to a row of cottages. Stella knew her way by the exact number of paces. Never once did she hesitate or miss her footing. She could have done it in the pitch-dark. Then Hester realized with a jolt that in fact that was what she was doing, always, and she felt almost guilty for the bright sunlight and the color she could see.

Stella knocked on the door of one of the cottages and it was immediately opened by a man in his middle forties, shy and plain, but with an acute intelligence in his eyes, and his whole countenance lit with pleasure when he saw Stella. It was a moment before he even realized that there was anyone else with her.

Stella introduced them, and explained their purpose. The man was Mrs. Cordwainer's son. If she were as old as Mrs. Myers had suggested, then he must have been born to her late in life.

"Of course," he said, smiling at Hester and Scuff. "I'm sure Mama will be pleased to tell you whatever she can." He led them through into a small, sunlit room where an ancient woman sat in an armchair, wrapped around with a light shawl, quite obviously asleep. Mr. Cordwainer's book, a translation of the plays of Sophocles, was lying faceup where he had left it to answer the door.

It was only as Stella sat down in one of the other chairs that Hester realized with amazement, and then a wave of understanding, that Cordwainer had not guided her in here, nor had he indicated to her where the chair was. She must be sufficiently familiar with the room not to need such assistance, and he knew that. Perhaps for her, they were careful never to move anything even a few inches from its accustomed place.

Was that the secret that she must not tell? Cordwainer was perhaps twenty years older than she, and quite clearly he loved her.

There was no time to think of such things. Mrs. Cordwainer had woken up and was full of interest. With very little prompting, she recalled Mary and her mother, and the birth of the baby.

" 'Ard thing it were," she said sadly, blinking sharp gray eyes. "She weren't the last I seen die, but she were the first, an' I din't never forget 'er, poor soul. Just young, she were, for all that the little girl were about five, near as we could tell." She sighed. "Got 'er adopted out in a year or so. Nice family as were keen to 'ave 'er. Webb, they was called, or something like that. But they couldn't take the babe, couldn't manage a babe. Woman were crippled. We don't like ter split 'em up, but we got too many mouths ter feed as it were, an' they really wanted 'er."

"What happened to the little boy?" Hester asked softly. She could imagine him, growing up motherless, one of many, cared for but not special to anyone; fed, clothed, possibly even taught, but not loved. It was so desperately easy to see why he had invented a happiness that had never existed.

"Nice little lad, 'e were," Mrs. Cordwainer said dreamily. "Curly 'air, 'andsome enough, even if 'e were a bit of a scrapper now an' then. But that in't something I mind in a boy. Bit o' spirit. Used ter make me laugh, 'e did. I were young—then. Got away wi' all sorts, 'cause 'e made me laugh. An' 'e knew it."

"What happened to him?" Hester said again.

"I dunno. 'E stayed 'ere till 'e were eight, then we let 'im go."

"Where to? Who took him?"

"Took 'im? Bless you, nobody took 'im. 'E were old enough to work for 'isself. I dunno where 'e went."

Hester glanced at Scuff, who seemed to understand perfectly. He shrugged and put his hands in his pockets. She realized he had almost certainly been more or less alone since he was that age. Perhaps Durban had been a mudlark as well.

"Was Durban his mother's name?" she asked aloud.

"We never knew 'is mother's name," the old lady replied. "Can't recall as we ever asked 'er. We called 'im Durban after a man from Africa 'oo gave us money one time. Seemed like a good enough name, an' 'e din't mind."

"Did he ever come back?"

"Went ter Africa again, far as I know."

"Not the man, the boy?"

"Oh. Not as I can think of. Went to look fer 'is sister, little Mary, but she'd gone. 'E did tell us that. Don't know nothin' else. Sorry. Were all a long time ago."

"Thank you so much. You've been very helpful," Hester said sincerely.

Mrs. Cordwainer looked at her, her face puckered. "Wot 'appened to 'im then? D'you know?"

"He grew into a fine man," Hester replied. "Joined the River Police, and died about six months ago, giving his life to save others. I'm looking for Mary Webber, to tell her, and give her his things, if she's his sister. But she's hard to find. He was looking for her before he died, but he never found her."

Mrs. Cordwainer shook her head, but she said nothing.

They declined a cup of tea, not wishing to put them to trouble, and Mr. Cordwainer escorted them to the door. When they reached it and Scuff and Stella were already outside, he put his hand on Hester's arm and held her back.

"You'll not find Mary," he said very softly. He looked acutely unhappy. "It's a long story. Carelessness a bit, lonely, wanting to please, and maybe a bit too trusting, but not fault, not really."

Hester was lost again. "What are you talking about?" She found that she was whispering in turn.

"Mary," he replied. "She's in prison. My mother kept up with her, for the boy's sake. Then when she got old, I kind of took her place."

"Which prison is she in?" Hester felt the knot of pain tighten inside her. No wonder Durban had not found her. Or had he? And the end of his search was tragedy? How that must have hurt him. Was that how she was connected to Jericho Phillips? Suddenly she wished with a passion that she had not asked Mrs. Myers, or old Mrs. Cordwainer. It was too late now.

"Holloway," he replied. He was watching her, seeing the hurt and the disillusion in her face. "She's not a bad woman," he said gently. "She married a chandler named Fishburn. He was killed when a dray came loose and crushed him. Left her the house, but not much else. She sold it and bought another one miles away, in Deptford. Turned it into a lodging house. Called herself Myers, to get away from Fishburn's debts. Seems he'd been a bit of a gambler." He sighed. "One of her lodgers was a thief. She didn't know it, but when he slipped, she got caught with the things he'd taken. She'd kept them against his rent, but the police wouldn't believe that. She got six months for it, and lost the house, of course."

"I'm sorry." She meant it. "What'll happen to her when she gets out?"

The sadness in his expression answered her.

"Maybe I can find a job for her," she said before thinking what it would involve. She might not like her. She had only Cordwainer's word that she was not really a thief or a receiver.

He smiled, and nodded slowly.

Stella and Scuff were waiting. She thanked Cordwainer again, and followed after them.

Back in the hospital she thanked Stella, who looked at her anxiously, and reminded her of her promise. Hester assured her that she had not forgotten, and took her leave.

But as she approached the main door out she encountered Mrs. Myers again. She hoped profoundly that she was not going to have to lie to her, but she was perfectly prepared to if necessary. She had given Stella her word not to disclose anything of her romance. However, she had been gone so long she could not pretend not to have seen old Mrs. Cordwainer. She was also acutely aware of Scuff at her elbow, and his opinion of her honesty, which she found mattered to her even more than she had expected it would.

Mrs. Myers smiled. "Did Stella take you to see old Mrs. Cordwainer after all?" she asked.

"I prevailed upon her," Hester replied, thinking how she could word her reply so that it would sound as if the old lady had given her all the information, and not even suggest that Mr. Cordwainer had been present at all. Nothing clever came to her. She was left with simply lying. It would have been so much easier had Scuff not been there.

Mrs. Myers nodded. "I don't imagine it was difficult."

Hester said nothing. It was more uncomfortable than she had expected.

"Was she able to help?" Mrs. Myers asked.

Another lie. But it was either that, or admit that he had been there. The lie was the better of the two evils. "Yes, thank you. I now have a better idea at last where to look."

"I don't mind, you know," Mrs. Myers said gently.

"I beg your pardon?" Now Hester was at a loss and knew she must look foolish.

"I think John Cordwainer is a very decent man, and exactly right for Stella," Mrs. Myers said frankly. "I just wish she would stop assuming I disapprove, and accept him. She is quite old enough not to mind what I think. She owes me no more than to make the very best of her life."

Hester felt a great weight slip from her, and found herself smiling idiotically. "Really?" she said with feigned innocence, as if she had no idea what they were talking about.

"Your smile gives you away," Mrs. Myers said drily. "But I am glad you kept your word. Although if you hadn't, it would make it easier for me to broach the subject. How on earth do I say something, without letting her know I have intruded on her privacy?"

Hester thanked her again for her help, and went down the steps, smiling even more widely.

Of course it was not so easy to gain admittance to Holloway Prison, or permission to see any particular person held there. Her first instinct was to ask Monk to obtain it for her, then she bit the words back and grasped for something else to say. Her whole purpose was to protect him.

She asked instead what he expected to do the following day, and when he told her, she chose a time when he would be alone, away from the Wapping Station, in which to go there and see if she could speak with Orme. She could explain to him exactly what she wanted, and he would understand why.

Orme chose to go with her and ask permission on the spot. It might have been out of kindness to her, but she felt that his own curiosity was also urgent. And perhaps he wanted to meet the only sister of a man he had known, respected, and cared for for a great deal of his adult life.

It was this last that troubled Hester. She did not know how to say to him that she preferred to see Mary alone, and his presence might inhibit her from being open. Also, as deeply felt, if not as important to the case, she was afraid that it would be an emotionally distressing experience for him. She had seen his face when they had uncovered facts about Durban that were ugly, that threw doubt on his honesty, his morality, even the kindness that had long been part of his character. Orme had tried desperately to hide such unpleasantness, to drown it out with loyalty, but it was there, growing slowly.

She turned to face him in the bleak stone corridor.

"Thank you, Mr. Orme. I could not have done this without you, but I need now, at least the first time, to speak with her alone. You knew Mr. Durban for years. Far better than she ever did. Think how she will feel. She may care too much what you think of her to be frank. We need the truth." She said that firmly, emphasizing the last word, holding his gaze. "If we lose this chance, there will not be another. Please let me speak to her alone the first time."

He gave a funny, lopsided little smile. "Are you protecting me too, ma'am?"

She realized that perhaps she had been. Would he be pleased, or offended? She had no idea. The truth had at least the advantage of easing her conscience. "I'm sorry," she admitted. "I suppose I was."

He blinked very faintly; she could barely see it in the flat light, but she knew he was not displeased.

She was shown into a plain cell with a wooden table and two chairs, and a moment later the wardress brought in a woman in her middle fifties. She was of average height and a little gaunt in the face, causing Hester to look a second time before realizing that she was handsome beneath the pallor and the fear, and her eyes were golden brown, just as Durban's had been.

She sat down when Hester invited her to, but slowly, stiff with anxiety.

Hester sat also, as the wardress said she would be immediately outside the door, if she were needed, and they had thirty minutes. Then she left.

Hester smiled, wishing she knew of a way to ease the woman's fear without at the same time jeopardizing her mission.

"My name is Hester Monk," she began. "My husband is now head of the Thames River Police at Wapping, the position your brother held." Then suddenly she wondered if Mary knew of his death. Had she been incredibly clumsy? How long was it since she and Durban had met? What were the emotions between them?

Mary moved her head minutely, less than a nod.

It was time to stop prevaricating. She lowered her voice. "Did anyone tell you that he died, heroically, at the turn of last year? He gave his life to save the lives of many others." She waited, watching.

Mary Webber nodded, and her eyes filled with tears, running unchecked down her thin cheeks.

Hester took her handkerchief out of her small purse and placed it on the table where Mary could take it. "I'm sorry. I wish I did not have to bring this up. He was looking for you, frantically, but as far as I know he didn't find you. Did he?"

Mary shook her head. She reached out to the white cotton handkerchief, then hesitated. It was dazzlingly clean compared with her gray prison sleeve.

"Please . . ." Hester urged.

Mary picked it up and pressed it to her cheek. It was faintly perfumed, but such a thing may have been far from her mind now.

Hester continued, mindful of the minutes ticking into oblivion. "Mr. Durban was a hero to his men, but there are other people now who are trying to destroy the River Police, and they are blackening his name to do it. I already know where he was born and spent the first eight years of his life. I spoke to Mrs. Myers . . ." She saw a smile touch Mary's lips, but dim, struggling against grief. "I know that you saved money and sent him all you could. Do you know what happened to him after he left the hospital?"

Mary blinked and wiped the tears off her cheeks. "Yes. We kept in touch for a long time." She gulped. "Until I realized what kind of man Fishburn was." She looked down. "After that, I was ashamed, and I kept out of my brother's way. When Fishburn was caught stealing and went to prison, I changed my name and moved away. When he died I sold the house. I didn't dare before that, in case he got out, or he had one of his friends come and find me." Her voice was very low and she did not once look up at Hester.

"Then I kept a lodging house, an' . . ."

"You don't need to tell me," Hester stopped her. "I know how you came to be here. I imagine that was why your brother couldn't find you."

Mary looked up. "I didn't want him to know I was here. I s'pose the few people that knew me lied to him to cover it up. They'd have known how I didn't want him even to . . . to know I'd come to this. He used to look up to me . . . when he was little. We . . ." she looked down again. "We were close then . . . close as you can be, when we scarce saw each other. But I never stopped thinking of him. I wish . . ."

Without thinking, Hester reached out and put her hand on Mary's where it lay on the rough tabletop. "I think he might have understood. He was a good man, but he knew none of us were faultless. He hated cruelty, and he wasn't above bending the law a little to stop people hurting women, or especially children. A lot of people admired him, but there were some who hated him, and a good few were scared half silly if you even said his name. Don't put him on a pedestal, Mary, or think that he put you on one."

"Too late, now," Mary replied with self-mockery.

"It's not too late to help clear his name," Hester said urgently. "I'll fight as hard as I can, and more important, so will my husband. But I can't do it without the truth. Please tell me what you know of him, his character, good and bad. It will spoil everything if I try to defend him from an accusation, and then make a fool of myself because it was true. After that no one would believe me, even if I were right."

Mary nodded. "I know." At last she met Hester's eyes, shyly, but without flinching. "He was good, in his own way, but he had things to hide. He grew up pretty rough. Had to beg and scrounge, and I shouldn't wonder if he stole a bit. The hospital had to put him out when he was eight. Had no choice. I was the lucky one. It wasn't till the Webbers lost their money that I even knew what it was like to be hungry, I mean the kind of hungry when you hurt inside, and all you can think of is food . . . any kind, just so you can eat it. He always knew."

Hester cringed. She did not have to imagine it; she had seen it in too many faces. But she did not interrupt.

"He ran with some pretty rough people," Mary went on. "I know, because he didn't hide it. But I didn't ever ostracize him. All I wanted was that he would stay alive." She took a deep breath. "But I didn't know how bad it was, or I'd have been much more scared."

Hester moved without thinking, her muscles knotted.

Mary nodded imperceptibly. "He had some bad friends up and down the river, mostly Linehouse, and the Isle of Dogs. A bank was robbed, and three of them were caught. They were sent up to the Coldbath Fields. One of them died there, poor creature. Only twenty-three, he was. The other two got broken in health, and one of them at least drunken out of his mind. When they got sent down was when Durban joined the River Police. I never asked him if he was in on the bank job, and he never told me. I didn't want him to think I even thought it of him, but I did. He was pretty wild, an' a temper on him like one of those snapping eels."

She sighed. "It was all different after that. He got a fright, and he never went back to the old ways. Reckon maybe that's what made him such a good policeman, he knew both sides of the road. You may not be able to help, or make anyone see that there was so much good in him, but I'd be grateful to you all my life if you'd try."

Hester looked at the sad woman in front of her, broken and alone, and wished she could offer her something more than words.

"Of course I'll try, every way I can. My husband liked Durban more than anyone else he knew. I liked him myself, although we didn't meet very often. But apart from that, the reputation of the River Police depends on proving that Jericho Phillips and anyone to do with him are liars."

"Jericho Phillips?" Mary said quietly, her voice tight in her throat. "Is he the one doing this?"

"Yes. Do you know anything about him?"

Mary shivered and seemed to shrink further into herself. "I know better than to cross him. Does he know . . . who I am?"

"Durban's sister? No. I don't think anybody knows that." Suddenly a great deal more was clear to Hester, the urgency with which Durban had looked for her, and yet would tell no one why, not even Orme, the fear that must have consumed him for her. If Phillips had found her before he did, it would be a threat even more vivid than to kill another of the boys. "And he won't know anything I do," Hester added aloud. "I mean to see Phillips hang, so by the time you are out of here he will be dead, and you can start a decent life without giving him a thought. You'll have a little money, because Durban would have wanted you to.

We have it safely for you. You are his only relative, so it has to be yours. And if you would like a job, and don't mind some hard work, I'd like to have your help in the clinic I run in Portpool Lane. At least think about it. There'd be a room for you, good work to do, and some decent friends to do it with."

Hope flared in Mary's tired eyes, so bright and sharp that it hurt to see it. "You be careful of Phillips," she said urgently. "He isn't alone, you know. He started that business on his boat with money, quite a lot of it. Looks like nothing on the outside, but I heard Fishburn say it was like the best bawdy house on the inside, comfortable as you like. And photograph machines don't come for nothing."

"An investor?"

Mary nodded. "Not just that, he's very well protected. There's a few people who wouldn't like anything bad to happen to him, and at least one of them is in the law, and stood up for him in court. A really top lawyer, not one of them that hangs around the courthouse hoping to pick up business, a Queen's Counsel, all silk robes, wigs, that kind of thing."

Suddenly Hester was ice-cold, imprisoned in something terrible, without escape, as if the iron door were locked forever. She could kick and scream forever, but no one could hear her. A Queen's Counsel, one who had defended Phillips in court.

"I'm sorry," Mary said apologetically. "I can see I've scared you, but you have to know. I can't sit by and let something happen to you when you've been so kind to me."

Hester found it hard to speak; her lips seemed numb, her mouth full of cotton batting. "A lawyer? Are you sure?"

Mary stared at her, struggling towards a dark understanding. She had no trouble recognizing the pain. "Phillips has power over lots of people," she said, lowering her voice as if even in prison she was afraid of being overheard. "Maybe that's why my brother never caught him. Lord knows, he tried hard enough. Be careful. You don't know who he's got in his pocket, who'd like to escape but can't."

"No," Hester whispered back without knowing why. "No, I suppose you can't."

TEN

*I*t was the middle of the afternoon and Monk was busy catching up on some of the more pedestrian cases of theft from various yards along the waterfront when one of the men came to his door and told him that Superintendent Farnham had arrived and wished to see him, immediately.

Farnham was sitting down when Monk went into the room, and he did not rise. He was clearly unhappy and in a very bad temper. He indicated curtly for Monk to take the chair opposite him.

"The Phillips case is over," he said grimly, his eyes hard and flat. "You lost. In fact, not only you, Monk, but the whole of the River Police. You don't seem to be aware of quite how much." He held up his hand to keep Monk silent, just in case he should think of defending himself. "It was bad enough when the wretched man was acquitted, through your inefficiency and your wife's emotionalism, although one expects such a thing from women, but . . ."

Monk was so furious he could barely keep still. "Sir, that . . ."

"When I have finished!" Farnham exploded. "Until then, you will hold your peace. I am disappointed in you, Monk. Durban recommended you highly, and I was fool enough to listen to him. But thanks to your meddling, your obsession with this Phillips case, not only I, but most of the senior police in general, and half the ferrymen, lightermen, dockers, and warehousemen up and down both banks of the river also know a great deal more about the late Commander Durban than we wish to. Leave it, Monk. That is an order. There is quite enough crime on the Thames that genuinely needs your attention.

Solve it, all of it, with speed and justice, and you may begin to redeem not only your own reputation but ours as well."

"Commander Durban was a good officer, sir," Monk said between his teeth, acutely conscious of everything Hester had told him the previous evening. "I have learned nothing about him to his discredit," he added bluntly.

"That only suggests that you are not a very good detective, Monk," Farnham replied. "There is a considerable amount that it seems, for all your effort, you failed to discover."

"No, sir, there is not," Monk contradicted. It was a firm lie, and he intended to stick to it. "I have traced him back to the day he was born. I just choose not to discuss it with others, when it is none of their business. He was a good man, and deserves the same dignity of keeping his family affairs private that is accorded to the rest of us."

Farnham stared at him across the table, and gradually some of the temper died out of his eyes and left only tiredness and anxiety.

"Perhaps," he conceded. "But now we have newspapermen asking more and more questions about him, why he was so obsessed with this damned Phillips case, and why you're just as bad, if not worse, and we are doing nothing to curb you. You're leaving half the regular work that should be your responsibility for Orme to do. He denies it, but others say it's true. He's a loyal man, Orme. He deserves better than to be lumbered with your job while you chase after Phillips. Phillips beat us. It happens sometimes. We can't catch every single villain on the river."

"We need to get this one, sir. He's like a malignant wound, one that if it isn't cut out will poison the whole body."

Farnham raised his eyebrows.

"Is he? Or have you just convinced yourself of that because he beat Durban, then he beat you? Can you swear to me that it isn't pride, Monk? And prove it to me?"

"Sir, Phillips murdered a young boy, Figgis, because Figgis wanted to escape the servitude Phillips had him in, which was far more than labor. He was an object of pornography for the use and entertainment of Phillips's customers . . ."

"It's filthy." Farnham shivered with disgust. "But there are brothels all over London, and every other city in Europe. In the world, for all I know. Yes, he murdered the boy, God knows why. It would surely have been much simpler to have put him on one of the ships leaving port, and much less of a risk . . ."

"It was discipline, sir," Monk interrupted. "To demonstrate to the rest of his boys what happens to those who defy him."

"Not very efficient," Farnham countered. "They wouldn't go if they didn't believe they'd be the ones who'd get away."

"Then he'd simply kill one of the others," Monk explained, watching Farnham's face. "One of the younger, more vulnerable ones, whoever the escapee was most fond of."

Farnham paled, and started to swear, then bit it off.

"It's more than that also," Monk went on. "Have you considered, sir, what kind of men his clients are?"

Farnham's lips curled; it was a subconscious expression of revulsion. "Men with obscene and uncontrolled appetites," he replied. "The use of street women may, by some stretch of the imagination, be understandable. The abuse of terrified and cowed children is not."

"No, sir, it's not," Monk agreed vehemently. "But that was not the aspect of them that I was thinking of. They are deplorable, but Phillips's clients are also rich, or they couldn't pay his prices. It's not a brothel he runs, it's entertainment, costumes, charades, photographs. They pay well for it."

"Your point, Monk? We know Phillips profits. That's why he does it. It's hardly worth making a point of."

"No, sir," Monk said urgently. "That's only part of the reason. Perhaps even more important than that is its power." He leaned forward a little, his voice becoming sharper. "They are important men, some of whom hold high office. They know their appetites are not only twisted, but because it is boys, they are also criminal." He saw a hideous understanding dawn in Farnham's eyes. "They are highly corruptible in all sorts of other ways, sir. Have you never wondered why Durban couldn't catch Phillips before? He was close many times, but Phillips always got away. Oliver Rathbone conducted his defense, but who hired him, do you know that? I don't, but I would dearly like to."

"It could be . . ." Farnham stopped, his eyes wide.

"Yes, sir," Monk finished for him. "It could be almost anyone. A man in bondage to a devil inside himself, and a monster like Phillips outside, is capable of all manner of acts. He could lie at the heart of our justice, our industry, even our government. Do you still want me to forget about Phillips, and concentrate on warehouse robberies, and the odd theft from cargoes on the water?"

"I could tell this damn journalist this," Farnham said very quietly. "God knows what he'd do with it. He's saying now that the corruption in the River Police is deep and lasting, and that the public has a right to know exactly what it is, and where it leads. He's even suggesting, so far only verbally, but print will follow, that we should cease to exist as a separate body at all but be broken up and come under the local stations. Our survival depends on this, Monk."

"Yes, sir. I've heard rumor of it already. But then he may be one of Phillips's customers, or in the pay of one."

Farnham looked as if Monk had slapped him, but he did not retaliate. It was himself he was furious with, because he had not thought of it. "He even put up the possibility that Durban was a partner in Phillips's trade," he said bitterly. "And his pursuit of Phillips was in order to take over all of it. That's what he'll write, if we don't find a way of stopping him." His shoulders hunched tightly, as if every muscle in his body were knotted. "Tell me, Monk, don't leave me defenseless when I talk to this bastard. What did you find out about Durban? We can't afford dignity now, for the living or the dead. I won't tell him, but I need to know, or I can't defend any of us."

Monk weighed his trust and his loyalties. He needed to trust Farnham, for the sake of the future. "He lied about his family, sir," he admitted. "Said his father was a schoolmaster in Essex. Actually I don't think he knew who his father was. His mother died in a foundling hospital, giving birth to him. He grew up there. He was put out in the streets to earn his own way when he was eight. That's why he had such compassion for mudlarks and other children, or women on their own, the hungry, the frightened, the abused. It was fellow feeling. He'd known it himself."

"Oh, God!" Farnham ran his hands through his sparse hair. "Any crime known against him? And tell me the truth, Monk. If I get caught in a lie just once they'll never believe me again."

"Not known, sir," Monk said reluctantly. "But friends of his robbed a bank. Bad associates. Growing up in the streets, that's unavoidable. It was just after that that he joined the River Police."

"Thank God. Now who is this Mary Webber he was hell bent on finding? Childhood sweetheart? Common-law wife? What?"

"Sister, sir. Older sister. She was adopted, but the family who took her, the woman was crippled and couldn't cope with a baby, so he was left behind. Mary used to save up pennies and send them to him. They lost touch when she married and later discovered her husband was a thief. She was too ashamed to let Durban know that. The hospital gave him the name of Durban, after one of their benefactors who happened to be from Africa. She changed her name when she married, and then again when her husband's creditors came after her."

"Where is she now?"

"I know, but it's irrelevant, sir. She's safe, for the time being."

Farnham blasphemed gently. "I apologize, Monk. You did a superb job finding out about Durban. I hope nobody but me ever has to know about it. I'll put a flea in this newspaperman's ear that will keep him busy, and far away from us for as long as possible. If he speaks to you, tell him you are under orders, on pain of losing your job, to say nothing. Do you understand?"

"Yes, sir. Thank you."

"You'll keep me informed?"

"Yes, sir."

Monk told Orme briefly what Farnham had said, and was only just outside the station walking towards the stairs down to where the police boat was waiting when a man approached him. He was ordinary, slightly shambling, impossible to describe so he would be known again. He wore an old seaman's jacket, shapeless enough to hide his build, and a cap on his head, which hid his hair. His eyes were narrowed against the bright light off the water.

"Commander Monk?" he said politely.

Monk stopped. "Yes?"

"Got a message fer yer, sir."

"From whom?"

"Din't give me no more, sir. Said as yer'd know." The man's voice was innocent, even courteous, but there was something knowing in his manner, and the creases that almost concealed his eyes suggested a sneer.

"What's the message?" Monk asked, then half wished he had refused to listen. "Never mind. If you can't tell me who it's from, maybe it doesn't matter."

"Gotta deliver it, sir," the man insisted. "Paid ter do it. Wouldn't reckon my chances if I mess wi' this gentleman. Nasty, he would be, real nasty . . . if yer get my meanin'?" He looked up at Monk and he was definitely smiling now. "Glad ter see yer listenin', sir. Save my neck maybe. Gentleman said ter tell yer ter back off the Durban case, whatever that is? D'you know?" He lifted an eyebrow. "Yeah, I can see yer do. 'E said it would be best people think like they do, 'cause Durban did wot 'e did. Otherwise, this gentleman said 'e'd make the 'ole thing public. Said 'e 'as all the evidence that yer took on this Durban's job wi' the police, wi' all 'is papers and things. An' yer took over 'is other interests an' all, the business o' getting little boys, that is. Yer got one special trained up fer yerself, an' all. Clean and bright, 'e is. Go down a treat wi' certain gentlemen wi' special tastes. Scuff, I think 'e called 'im. That sound right to yer, sir?"

Monk felt sick to his stomach, his body cold. It was obscene, as if a filthy hand had reached out and touched everything that was decent and precious, staining them with its own dirt. He wanted to lash out at the man, hit him so hard he broke that leering face and left it a bloody pulp so he would never smile again, never speak clearly enough to say words anyone could distinguish.

But that would be exactly what he wanted. And he was probably not unarmed. An attack would be the perfect excuse to knife him in the stomach. It would be self-defense. Another example of River Police brutality. He could say honestly that he had accused Monk of procuring a small boy for Phillips's use. Who could prove otherwise?

Was this what Durban had faced, threats of blackmail? Do what I want, or I'll paint every decent act of compassion as an obscenity. The accusation will stain your name. Because of their own filth, there will be those who believe it. You will be unable to do your job. I'll cripple you.

Or do what I say, turn a blind eye to the cases I tell you to, and I'll keep quiet. And when you've turned away from some, out of fear of me, I'll have another unbreakable thread to bind you with, and this one will be true. You will have denied your duty, corrupted yourself to stay safe."

"I hear you," Monk replied. "Tell your paymaster to go to hell."

"Oh, very unwise, Mr. Monk, sir. Very unwise." The man shook his head, still smiling. "I'd think again on that, if I were yer."

"You probably would," Monk agreed. "But then you are obviously for sale. I am not. Tell him to go to hell."

The man hesitated only seconds, then realized that he would gain nothing by remaining, and turned and went away at a surprisingly rapid pace.

Monk walked back into the station. What he had to do was best done immediately, before he had time to weigh his words and be afraid.

Orme looked up, surprised to see him back so soon. He must have read the concern in Monk's face. He stood up, as if to follow him into his office.

"I need to speak to everyone," Monk said distinctly. "Now."

Orme sat down again slowly and one by one the other men stopped what they were doing and faced him.

He had their attention. He must begin. "As soon as I stepped outside a few minutes ago," he said, "I was accosted by a man who delivered a message. He did not say from whom, but the implication was obvious." It was difficult to trust. He hated making himself so vulnerable. He looked at their waiting faces. This was his future. He must trust these men, or lose their respect and the one chance he had to lead them.

"This man told me to leave the Jericho Phillips case alone," he went on. "If I don't, Phillips will make sure that I am accused of procuring small boys for use on his boat, to be rented to his clients, and then photographs taken in obscene and illegal acts to be sold for entertainment." He drew in his breath and let it out slowly to try to stop the terror in his voice. It embarrassed him that he could not stifle it completely.

"He will say to the press that initially Commander Durban was not Phillips's enemy, but his partner, and that they fell out over sharing the profits. He will say also that when I took over Commander Durban's position here, I took over his business interests as well, and that the boy my wife and I have taken into our home is intended for that purpose also." He had committed himself. He had not intended to. He had also said that Scuff was remaining with them. He realized without any real surprise that he meant that, and he knew Hester had long ago stopped debating with herself. It remained only to hear what Scuff thought, once the immediate danger to him had passed—if it did.

He looked around at the men's faces, afraid of what he would see: amusement, disgust, disappointment, the struggle whether to believe him or not, fear for their own positions.

"We must stop him," he went on, avoiding meeting the eyes of anyone in particular. He would not try to demand or intimidate, and certainly not beg. "If we don't, he will do all he can to bring down the whole River Police. We are the only force standing between him and running his filthy trade unhampered." Should he tell them the rest, the even greater danger? He had trusted them this far; now was the time to win or lose them altogether. He looked at Orme and saw his steady gaze, grave and unwavering.

There was hardly a sound in the room. It was too warm for the black stove at the end to be lit. The doors to the outside were closed, muffling the noises of the river.

"It's worse than just the boys as victims," he went on, now looking at their faces one by one. "Phillips's patrons are men of wealth, or they couldn't afford his prices. Rich men have influence, and usually power, so his opportunities for blackmail are limitless. You can imagine them for yourselves: port authorities, harbormasters, revenue men, lawyers." He clenched his hands. "Us."

No one moved.

"You see the danger." He made it a statement rather than a question. "Even if we are not guilty, there is the high chance that we may be accused. And which of us would not be tempted to do as we were told, rather than have that charge made in public, no matter how innocent we were? The thought alone is enough to make you sick. What would your wives have to endure? Your parents or children?"

He saw in their faces the understanding, and the fear. He waited for the anger, but it did not come. He did not even sense it. "I'm sorry that my haste to convict Phillips allowed him to be acquitted for the murder of Figgis. I'll get him for something else." He said it calmly, but as he said it he knew the promise would bind him forever.

"Yes, sir," Orme said as soon as he was certain Monk was not going to add any more. He looked at the men, then back at Monk. "We'll get him, sir." That too was an oath.

There was a murmur of agreement, no dissenting voices, no half-heartedness. Monk felt a sudden ease, as if he had been given a blessing he did not expect or deserve. He turned away before they saw him smiling, in case anyone misunderstood the emotion of joy for something more trivial, and less profound in its gratitude.

Oliver Rathbone was increasingly unhappy about the Phillips case. It invaded his thoughts at the times when he had expected to be happiest. Margaret had asked him what it was that caused his anxiety, and he could not answer her. An evasion was undignified, and she was intelligent enough to know it for what it was. To lie was not even a possibility. It would close a door between them that might never again be opened, because guilt would bar it.

And yet in the quiet ease of his sitting room, with Margaret opposite him, wishing to talk with her, he remembered how much he had enjoyed it only a month or two ago. He recalled her smile in repose. She was happy. In his mind he could hear her laughter at some joke. She liked the subtle ones best, always catching the point. Even their long discussions when they disagreed were delicate and full of pleasure. She had an acute grasp of logic, and was surprisingly well-read, even in subjects he would not have expected a woman to know.

But he sat in silence, not daring to speak about the Phillips case, and the rift with Monk and Hester. It seemed to touch so many things. Like a drop of ink in a glass of clear water, it spread to stain everything it touched.

Still it was painful to sit in the same room, not talking to each other. He was being a coward. It must be addressed, or gradually he would lose all that he valued most. It would slip away, inch by inch, until there was nothing left to grasp. What was he afraid of, truly? That he had lost the respect of Monk and Hester? A sense of honor?

With Phillips he had won, but the victory was sour. He had been supremely clever, but he knew now that he had not been wise. Phillips was guilty, probably of having murdered Fig, but certainly of the vile abuse of many children. And, Rathbone was beginning to believe, also of the blackmail and corruption of many powerful men.

He looked across at where Margaret sat sewing, but he was careful not to meet her eyes, in case she read in him what he was thinking. He could not continue like this. The gulf was widening every day.

There was no answer other than to find out who had hired Arthur Ballinger to retain Rathbone in Phillips's defense. He had already asked, and been refused. It must be done without Ballinger's knowledge. Ballinger had said it was a client; therefore, it would be in his official books at his chambers. The money would have gone through the accounts, because it was the office that had passed it to Rathbone.

Since it was a client, and money was involved, it would have been noted by Cribb, Ballinger's meticulous clerk. It must have begun roughly the time Ballinger had first come to Rathbone and continued until the time of the trial and Phillips's acquittal. If Rathbone could find a list of Ballinger's clients between those times, it would be a matter of eliminating those whose cases had been heard in some other matter and would now be public knowledge, or of course those still pending but due to come to trial soon.

But he could hardly go to Ballinger's office and ask to see his books. The refusal would be automatic, and cause highly uncomfortable questions. It would make the relationships between Rathbone and his father-in-law virtually impossible, and obviously Margaret would be aware of it.

Yet it would be wildly dangerous to pay someone else to do it, even if he could find anyone with the requisite skills. The temptation to extort blackmail afterwards would be almost overwhelming, not to mention the chance to sell the information elsewhere, possibly to Phillips himself.

There was only one answer. Rathbone would have to devise a way to do it himself. The thought made him thoroughly miserable. A kind of sour chill settled in the pit of his stomach. After all, he had no idea who might be blackmailed by Phillips. Who were the victims of such appetites as he fed, and thus could be manipulated as Phillips wished? It could be any of the men Rathbone had previously considered his friends, honorable and skilled.

And then an even more painful thought forced itself into his understanding. If people were aware of Phillips and his trade, they might equally well think such things of Rathbone himself! Why not? He was the one who had defended him, and gained his acquittal at the price of his own previously treasured friendships.

Yes, tomorrow he must go to Ballinger's office and find the records. He really had no other endurable choice.

It was one thing to make up his mind; it was quite another to execute the plan. The following morning as his cab set him down outside Ballinger's offices, he realized exactly how far apart he and Ballinger were. He knew from past experience that Ballinger himself would not be in for at least another hour, but the excellent Cribb was always prompt. Had the offices been any other than those of his father-in-law, he would have considered trying to lure Cribb away and into his own service.

"Good morning, Sir Oliver," Cribb said with courtesy that bordered on genuine pleasure. He was a man of about forty-five, but with an ascetic air that made him seem older. He was of average height and had a lean, bony face that showed intelligence and a very carefully concealed humor.

"Good morning, Cribb," Rathbone replied. "I hope you are well?"

"Very, thank you, sir. I am afraid Mr. Ballinger is not in yet. Is there anything with which I can assist you?"

Already Rathbone loathed what he was doing. How much easier it was to be honest. The embarrassment and strain of this was awful.

"Thank you," he accepted. He must cast the die quickly or he would lose his nerve. "I believe there is." He lowered his voice. "It has come to my knowledge, and of course I cannot tell you from whom, that one of Mr. Ballinger's clients may be involved in something distinctly unethical. A matter of playing one person against another, if you understand me?"

"How very distasteful," Cribb said with some sympathy. "If you wish me to inform Mr. Ballinger, of course I shall do so. Perhaps you would prefer to leave it in writing for him? I can give you pen and paper, and an envelope with wax to seal it."

Rathbone smothered his scruples with an effort. "Thank you, but I have nothing sufficiently specific so far. I know only when the man in question was here. If I might glance at his diary for the period it would confirm any suspicions, or deny them."

Cribb looked troubled, as Rathbone had known he would. "I'm very sorry, sir, but I cannot show you Mr. Ballinger's diary. It is confidential, as I am sure your diary is." He shifted his weight very slightly from one foot to the other. "I know you would not wish anything . . . wrong . . . , sir."

Rathbone did not have to try to look confused. "No, I would not," he agreed. "I had hoped that if I explained my dilemma to you, you might have some idea how to solve it. You see, the difficulty is that the man may well be a personal friend of Mr. Ballinger's, so much so that he may refuse to believe it of him, until it is too late. Unless I can prove it."

"Oh dear," Cribb said quietly. "Yes, I perceive your difficulty, Sir Oliver. I am afraid Mr. Ballinger is more charitable in some of his judgments than perhaps the circumstances justify."

Rathbone understood exactly. That was Cribb's loyal way of admitting that Ballinger did not choose all his friends with care.

"Perhaps, sir, we might discuss this problem in my office? It might be more discreet, if you don't mind," Cribb suggested.

"Of course," Rathbone agreed. "Thank you." He followed Cribb to the tiny room, barely more than a large cupboard, where a well-polished desk was crowded in between walls covered from floor to ceiling with shelves of files. Cribb closed the door, as much for room so that they might both sit as for privacy. He looked at the wall briefly, knowing exactly where every file and folder was.

Rathbone followed his glance to the diary for the month in question.

"This is a very difficult problem indeed," Cribb said, facing Rathbone again. "I really don't know what is for the best, Sir Oliver. I have the greatest respect for you, and I am aware that you are concerned for

Mr. Ballinger's welfare, both professional and personal. I need to think on this very deeply. Perhaps I might fetch you a cup of tea so we may discuss it in some comfort?"

"Thank you," Rathbone accepted. "That would be very good of you."

Cribb hesitated an instant, looking very steadily at Rathbone, then he excused himself and left, closing the door behind him.

Rathbone felt vile, as if he were about to steal something. The diary was on the shelf. He was committed. Whether he looked at it now or not, Cribb would believe that he had.

What was Rathbone trying to do? Find the truth, whoever it saved, or lost.

He took the book down and searched the right pages. Rapidly, little more than scribbling, he took down the names. He was barely finished and had only just replaced the diary on the shelf when Cribb returned, carefully making a noise with his feet on the boards outside before he opened the door.

Cribb set the tea tray down on the desk.

"Thank you," Rathbone said, his mouth dry.

"Shall I pour, sir?" Cribb offered.

"If you please." Rathbone found that his own hands were shaking. He considered offering Cribb some kind of appreciation. What would be suitable, and not insulting? Thirty pieces of silver?

Cribb poured the tea, a cup for Rathbone, nothing for himself.

It was the most difficult thing Rathbone had ever swallowed. It tasted sour, and he was aware that it was he himself who had poisoned it.

"Thank you," he said aloud. He wanted to add something, but it was all contrived, insulting.

"You are welcome, Sir Oliver," Cribb replied calmly. He appeared to see nothing odd in Rathbone's manner, in fact to be totally unaware of his appalling discomfort. "I have given the matter a great deal of thought, and I am afraid I can think of no solution for it."

"I was wrong to have asked," Rathbone replied, and that at least he was absolutely certain about. "I must seek some other solution." He finished the tea. "Please do not trouble Mr. Ballinger with it until

I can think of some way to ease his mind at the same time as I tell him of it. If I am fortunate, it may turn out to be an error anyway."

"Let us hope so, sir," Cribb agreed. "In the meantime, as you say, it would be better not to distress Mr. Ballinger unnecessarily."

Rathbone thanked him again, and Cribb walked with him to the front door. Rathbone went down the steps into the street heavy-footed, imprisoned within himself and weighed down with a moral dilemma from which there was now no escape.

He went straight to his own office and spent the next four hours comparing notes of cases he knew, court dates, and trials past and pending against the names he had copied down from Ballinger's diary. He pursued every one to its conclusion, finding out who the people were, of what they were accused, by whom they were defended, and what had been the verdict.

Most of the cases were trivial and easy enough to dismiss as regular business. In fact, many were to do with family estates, wills, and quarrels over property. Some were trials or settlements out of court for cases of financial incompetence or malfeasance. Those that had gone to trial and were concluded he could also discount. Their course was clear, and now in the public domain, simple cases of moral decline ending in tragedy, common enough.

In the end he was left with only three who could be Phillips's benefactor, or victim! Sir Arnold Baldwin, Mr. Malcolm Cassidy, and Lord Justice Sullivan. It was that last name that caused him to freeze and his hands to clench the paper. But that was ridiculous. Lord Justice Sullivan had to have a solicitor, like any other man. He would have property, in all likelihood a house in London and a home in the country. Property always involved deeds, money, and possible disputes. And of course there were wills and inheritances and other matters of ownership and litigation.

His immediate task was to learn more about each of the men on the list, and if necessary to actually meet them. Although exactly how he would determine which of them it was, he realized he had no idea. What did a man look like who was driven by such an appetite? Was he frightened, plagued with guilt, compulsive like one who gambles or drinks to excess? Or did he look like anyone else, and that darker part of his nature emerged only when he permitted it, secretly, on the river at night?

This was forced upon him even more plainly upon meeting both Cassidy and Baldwin, the first at a luncheon, the latter at one of the gentlemen's clubs of which he was a member. He observed nothing about either of them that made him wary; indeed, it was only his own suspicions that caused him any preoccupation whatever.

Meeting Sullivan proved more difficult, and he felt a crowding sense of inevitability, as if in his mind he had already determined the man's guilt. Since he was the judge who had actually heard the case, the situation was hideously tangled, by that fact alone.

In order to meet the judge, Rathbone had to connive to obtain an invitation to a reception to which he had not originally been invited, a most unseemly act. And it was not easy to ask Margaret if she would come; to her it was even harder to offer any explanation that was not clearly an evasion.

"I'm sorry, my dear," he said, busying himself with sorting his cuff links so he did not have to meet her eyes. "I realize it is unfair to expect you to give up your evening at such little notice, but the opportunity only came today, or I should have told you in better time. There are people who will be there whom I wish very much to meet. I cannot discuss it, because it has to do with a case." Now he faced her. The words had come to him just in time, and it sounded perfectly reasonable. What was more, they were true, if taken obliquely enough.

"Of course," she replied, searching his eyes to understand his meaning.

He smiled. "I should enjoy it far more if you were able to come with me." That was untrue, but he felt he had to say it. It would be simpler if he were alone. He would not have to guard himself against being too closely observed, and possibly caught in an inconsistency.

"I should be delighted," she replied, then turned away also, not having seen the candor she was looking for. "Is it formal?"

"Yes, I'm afraid it is."

"It is not a concern. I have plenty of gowns." That at least was true. He had seen that she had more than sufficient in the latest fashion, simply for the pleasure of it. She could look superb, but always in the discreet taste of a woman of breeding. She would not know how to be vulgar. It was one of the things that most pleased him about her. He would like to have told her so, but to say so now would be forced. It would be robbed of all sincerity, and he did mean it.

They arrived at the reception at precisely the best time, neither early enough to seem too eager, nor late enough to appear as if wanting to draw attention to themselves. To be ostentatious was ill-bred, to say the least.

Margaret was dressed in cool plain colors, shading towards the blues rather than the reds, and subdued, as if in shadow. Her bodice was cut low, but she could wear it without showing more of herself than was modest, because she was slender. Her skirt was full, and she had always known how to walk with great grace.

"You look lovely," he said to her quietly as they came slowly down the stairs, her hand resting lightly on his arm. He saw the color warm her neck and cheeks, and was glad he meant it; it was no empty compliment.

They were greeted by the hostess, a thin, handsome woman of excellent family who had married money, and was a little uncertain whether she had been as wise as she thought. She smiled shyly and welcomed everyone, then fell back on polite conversation about nothing at all, leaving people wondering if they had accepted an invitation they were offered only out of courtesy.

"Poor soul," Margaret said quietly as she and Rathbone moved into the crowd, nodding to acquaintances, acknowledging briefly those whose names they could not immediately remember, or whom they wished to avoid. Some people did not know when to allow a conversation to die a natural death.

"Poor soul?" Rathbone questioned, wondering if there were something he should have known.

Margaret smiled. "Our hostess made a financially suitable marriage, and is more than a little out of her depth within 'trade,' instead of aristocracy," she explained. "But if one wishes to, one can learn."

He raised his eyebrows. "I beg your pardon?"

For the first time in several days, she laughed outright. "You look concerned, Oliver. Do you regard yourself as trade? I had not seen myself as impoverished. And I certainly did not marry you for money. I refused wealthier men than you. I thought you might be interesting."

He let out his breath slowly, feeling a certain warmth rise up his cheeks. This was the woman he had fallen in love with. "I am professional," he replied with mock tartness. "Which is nothing at all like trade. But it is still a considerable advantage to have a well-bred wife, even if she does have rather more wit and spirit than is entirely comfortable."

She gripped his arm for a moment, then eased away. "It is not good for you to be comfortable all the time," she told him. "You become complacent, and that is most unattractive. Perhaps you had better find whoever it is you wish to see."

He sighed. "Perhaps I had," he conceded, the misery swelling inside him again, making it hard to draw his breath.

It was not difficult to encounter Sullivan without it seeming forced, but Rathbone could feel his heart pounding; it was hard to get his breath, and when he spoke, to keep his voice steady. What would he do if Sullivan simply refused to see him alone? Rathbone must phrase it so that he had no suspicion. Or does a guilty man always suspect?

They were separated from the next group by a yard or two, and Sullivan had his back to an alcove full of books and objets d'art.

"Ah! Nice to see you, Rathbone," he said warmly. "Still celebrating your victory, I imagine? You achieved what I would have thought was damned near impossible."

Rathbone hid his feelings about his own part in the trial, which were growing more and more repugnant to him all the time. "Thank you," he accepted, since to do anything less would be discourteous, and he had to be civil at least until he could find a time and place to speak to Sullivan alone. He was used to seeing him in his wig and robes, and at a distance of several yards, from the floor of the court up to the judicial bench. Closer he was still a handsome man, but the features were a little less clearly defined, the skin blotchier, as if his health were compromised, perhaps by self-indulgence, and the resultant dyspepsia. "It proved less difficult than I foresaw," he added, since Sullivan seemed to be waiting for him to say something further.

"River Police dug their own graves," Sullivan replied grimly. "Both

Durban and Monk. I think their power needs curbing. Maybe the newspapers are right, and it's time they were dispersed and command given entirely to the local stations on shore. Too much a law unto themselves at the moment."

Rathbone choked back his protest. He could not afford to antagonize Sullivan yet, and he would learn nothing if he put him on the defensive.

"Do you think so?" he asked, assuming an air of interest. "It seems they have a particular knowledge, and I must say, up to this point, an excellent record."

"Up to this point," Sullivan agreed. "But by all accounts, Durban was not as clever or as honorable as we had assumed, and this new man, Monk, has followed too much in his footsteps. You have only to look at the Phillips case to see that he is not up to the job. Promoted beyond his ability, I dare say."

"I don't think so," Rathbone protested.

Sullivan raised his eyebrows. "But my dear fellow, you proved it yourself! The man involved his wife, a good woman no doubt, but sentimental, full of well-meaning but illogical ideas. And he, apparently, fell victim to the same wishful thinking. He presented inadequate evidence to poor Tremayne, and so the jury had no choice but to find Phillips not guilty. Furthermore, we know that now he cannot be tried for that crime again, even if we find incontrovertible proof of his guilt. We cannot afford many fiascos like that, Rathbone."

"No, indeed," Rathbone said with perfectly genuine gravity. "The situation is now very serious indeed, more than perhaps Monk has any comprehension."

"Then you agree that perhaps the River Police should be disbanded?" Sullivan prompted.

Rathbone looked up at him. "No, no, I was thinking of the critical problem of blackmail." He watched Sullivan's face and knew from some movement of shadow in his eyes that he had struck a nerve; how deep he had yet to find out. He smiled very slightly. "Naturally, in order to defend Phillips, I had to study the evidence with extreme care, and of course, question him closely."

"Naturally," Sullivan agreed, his face oddly stiff. "But do be careful, Rathbone. Whatever he told you as your client is still confidential, regardless of the fact that the verdict is in, and he is acquitted. I am not the judge hearing the case now, and no privilege pertains to me."

"None at all," Rathbone said drily. "I was not going to let anything slip, beyond generalities. He has never denied that he makes his living by satisfying the more pathetic and obscene tastes of men who have the money to pay to have their fantasies indulged."

Sullivan's face reflected a conflict of emotions, fear, contempt, and flickering excitement also. "With such knowledge, it must have cost you dearly to defend him," he observed.

While they might have pretended amiability, it was now gone completely, and both men knew it. What remained was mutual dislike, and a thin film of disgust.

"A lot of people I defend have practices that revolt me," Rathbone replied. "I am sure you have conducted cases where both the crime itself, and the character of the accused, offended you profoundly. It would not cause you to recuse yourself from the case, or some cases would never be heard."

Sullivan gave a slight shrug and half turned away. "I am aware of the difficulties of the law, and justice," he said without expression. "Is someone accusing blackmail? Or is all this merely theoretical?"

Rathbone steadied his breathing with difficulty. Sullivan was a judge. Rathbone had stolen the information from Ballinger, which he could not afford to have anyone know, for his own sake, for Cribb's, possibly even for Margaret's. But Rathbone had something to learn, and something to redeem. He must lie.

"Regrettably, I believe it to be fact, at least in one case, possibly more. Phillips does nothing unless there is profit for him in it. In the case of supplying boys to satisfy these appetites, there is double profit, first for the satisfaction itself, second to keep silence afterwards, because in some instances, if not all, it is illegal. It seems these men will not, or cannot, control themselves, even when it is of such fearful cost to them." He watched the blood ebb from Sullivan's skin, leaving his cheeks blotched. His expression did not change in the slightest.

"I see," he said very quietly, in little more than a whisper.

"I was certain you would," Rathbone agreed. "Since they are obviously men who can pay blackmail sufficient to keep Phillips's silence, they are wealthy men, and so likely to also be men of power, and even of far-reaching influence. We can have no idea who they are."

"You do not need to spell it out, Rathbone. I perceive where you are going. It is very grave, as you say. And if you throw around wild and rash accusations, you will place yourself in very great danger indeed. I imagine you realize that?" It was quite definitely a question, and it required an answer.

"Of course I do, my lord," Rathbone said grimly. "I have taken intense care regarding to whom I spoke about this." It might not be wise to let Sullivan think he had told no one else. "But I cannot ignore it. The potential for corruption is too great."

"Corruption?" Sullivan asked, staring at Rathbone. "Are you not exaggerating a trifle? If certain men have . . . tastes that you deplore, is their private behavior, or the company they keep, really your concern?"

"If they can be blackmailed for money, then I suppose that it is not," Rathbone replied, measuring every word. "Then they are victims, but until they complain, it is a private suffering."

A footman passed, hesitated, and moved on. A woman laughed.

"But if they are men of power," he continued. "And the price is no longer money but the abuse of that power, then it is the business of us all. Most particularly if the power concerned is high office in finance, or government, or most especially in the judiciary." His eyes met Sullivan's squarely, and it was Sullivan who flinched and looked away.

"What if this man were to pay his blackmail in blindness to bending the law?" he asked. "Or what if he used fraud, embezzlement of money to pay Phillips, after his own funds have run out? Or police authority, to allow or even abet in a crime? Port authorities might overlook smuggling, theft, even murder on the river. Lawyers, or even judges, may corrupt the law itself. Who can say who is involved, or how far it may seep into the fabric of all we believe in, all that separates us from the jungle?"

Sullivan swayed, his face gray.

"Get a grip on yourself, man!" Rathbone said between his teeth. "I'm not going to let this pass. Those boys are beaten and sodomized, and the ones who rebel are tortured and murdered. You and I have both connived to let Phillips get away with it, and you and I are going to put that right!"

"You can't," Sullivan said weakly. "No one can stop him. You've seen that. You were used just as much as I was. If you turn against him now, he'll say you were a customer, and defended him to save yourself. That your payment was blackmail." Hope flickered on his face, pasty and sheened with sweat. He took several steps backwards, but there was nowhere to escape to.

Rathbone followed him, even further away from the crowd. People assumed they were speaking confidentially and left them alone. The crowd swirled around them and away, oblivious.

"How in God's name did this happen to you?" Rathbone demanded. "Sit down, before you fall over and make a complete fool of yourself."

Sullivan's eyes widened as if the idea appealed to him. Insensibility! There was a way to get out after all.

"Don't entertain it!" Rathbone snapped. "People will think you are drunk. And it will only delay what is inevitable. If you could control yourself, if you could stop, surely to God in heaven, you would have?"

Sullivan shut his eyes to block out the sight of Rathbone's face. "Of course I would have, damn you! It all began . . . in innocence, before it became an addiction."

"Really?" Rathbone said icily.

Sullivan's eyes flew open. "I only wanted . . . excitement! You can't imagine how . . . bored I was. The same thing, night after night. No thrill, no excitement. I felt half alive. The great appetites eluded me. Passion, danger, romance was passing me by. Nothing touched me! It was all served up on a plate, empty, without . . . without meaning. I didn't have to work for anything. I ate and left as hungry as I came."

"I presume you are referring to sexual appetite?"

"I'm referring to life, you smug bastard!" Sullivan hissed. "Then one day I did something dangerous. I don't give a damn about relations with other men. That disgusts me, except that it's illegal." His eyes suddenly shone. "Have you ever had the singeing in your veins, the pounding inside you, the taste of danger, terror, and then release, and known you are totally alive at last? No, of course you haven't! Look at you! You're desiccated, fossilized before you're fifty. You'll die and be buried without ever having really been alive."

A world he had never thought of opened in front of Rathbone, a craving for danger and escape, for wilder and wilder risks.

"And do you feel alive now?" he asked softly. "Helpless to control your own appetites, even when they are on the brink of ruining you? You pay money to a creature like Jericho Phillips, and he tells you what to do, and what not to, and you think that is power? Hunger governs your body, and fear paralyzes your intellect. You have no more power than the children you abuse. You just don't have their excuses."

For an instant Sullivan saw himself as Rathbone did, and his eyes filled with terror. Rathbone could almost have been sorry for him, were it not for his complete disregard for the other victims of his obsession.

"So you went to Ballinger to find a lawyer who could get Phillips off," he concluded.

"Of course. Wouldn't you have?" Sullivan asked.

"Because he's my father-in-law, and I was Monk's friend, and knew him well enough to use the weaknesses that were the other side of his strengths."

"I'm not a fool!" Sullivan said waspishly.

"Yes, you are," Rathbone told him. "A total fool. Now you have not only Phillips blackmailing you, you have me as well. And the payment I shall require is the destruction of Phillips. That will silence me forever on this issue, and obviously it will get rid of Phillips, on the end of a rope, with luck."

Sullivan said nothing. His face was sweating, and there was no color in his skin at all.

"I won't ruin you now," Rathbone said with disgust. "I need to use you." Then he turned and walked away.

In the morning Rathbone sent a message to the Wapping Station of the River Police, asking Monk to call on him as soon as he was able to. There was no point in going to look for Monk, who could have been anywhere from London Bridge to Greenwich, or even beyond.

Monk arrived before ten. He was immaculate, as usual, freshly shaved and with a neatly pressed white shirt under his uniform jacket. Rathbone was mildly amused, but too sick inside to smile. This was the Monk he knew, dressed with the careless grace of a man who loved clothes and knew the value of self-respect. And yet there was no lift in his step, and there were shadows of exhaustion around his eyes. He stood in the middle of the office, waiting for Rathbone to speak.

Rathbone was horribly familiar with the charges against the River Police in general, and Durban and Monk in particular. He had resented it before. Since last night it woke an anger in him that he could hardly contain.

He wanted the rift between Monk and himself healed, but he avoided words; they only redefined the wound.

Monk was waiting. Rathbone had sent for him, so he must speak first.

"The situation is worse than I thought," he began. He felt foolish for not having seen it from the start. "Phillips is blackmailing his clients, and God only knows who they are."

"I imagine the devil knows too," Monk said drily. "I assume you didn't send for me to tell me that. You can't have imagined that I was unaware. I'm threatened myself, because I've taken in a mudlark, largely for his protection. Phillips is suggesting that I am his partner in procuring."

Rathbone felt the heat of guilt in his face. "I know where the money came from that paid me," he said. "I will donate it to charity, anonymously, I think. I am not proud of the way I obtained the information."

A flash of pity lit Monk's eyes, which surprised Rathbone. There was a temperance in Monk he had not seen before.

"The instructing solicitor was my father-in-law," he continued. The next was more difficult, but he would not prevaricate or attempt to excuse. "I will not tell you how I learned who his client is. There is no need for the guilt to be anyone's but mine. It is sufficient for you to know that it is Lord Justice Sullivan . . ." He saw the incredulity on Monk's face, then dawning perception and amazement. His smile was bleak. "Precisely," he said with bitter humor. "It throws a new light on the trial, does it not?"

Monk said nothing. There was no anger in his face, no blame, although it would have been justified.

"I faced him last night," Rathbone continued. "Obviously, he is one of Phillips's clients, and victims. He used the word addiction to describe his craving for the illicit thrills he gains from his pleasures. Perhaps it is. I never thought of pornography as anything but the grubby voyeurism of those who were incapable of a proper relationship. Perhaps it is more than that, a dependence of character, as with alcohol or opium. It seems with him it is the danger, the risk of being caught in an act that would unquestionably ruin him. I found him both pathetic and repellent."

Monk was beginning to think. Rathbone saw the ideas race in his mind, the keenness of his eyes.

"I imagine he may be of use to you," he suggested. "That was my purpose in unmasking him, at least to myself. But I advise you to handle him with care. He is erratic, both angry and frightened, possibly a little less than sane, as you or I would see sanity. He might very well rather put a bullet through his brain than face exposure."

"Thank you," Monk said, meeting his eyes.

Rathbone smiled. He knew in that moment that Monk understood how difficult it had been for him, in all its complexity of reasons. He said nothing, but words were far too clumsy, too inexact anyway.

ELEVEN

Claudine Burroughs arrived early at the Portpool Lane Clinic. It was not that there was a particularly large amount to do, it was more that she wanted to tidy up linens, make certain of supplies, and put things in order. She had started working there because she needed something to occupy herself that left her feeling less empty than time spent with her acquaintances. She could not call any of them friends. She felt that hardship had a warmth to it, an implicit trust in kindness, even a common purpose or dream. She found none of these things in the visits, tea parties, dinners, and balls she attended. Even church had seemed more a matter of discipline than of hope, and of obedience rather than kindness.

She had chosen this particular charity because no one else she knew would ever involve themselves in anything so vulgar, or so practical. They wished to appear virtuous; they did not wish to put on old clothes, roll up their sleeves, and actually work, as Claudine was now doing, sorting out kitchen cupboards. Of course, at home she would not have dreamed of doing such a thing, nor even would her cook. Any respectable household had scullery maids for that kind of task.

Actually she found it rather satisfying, and while her hands were in the hot, soapy water, her mind was turning over the small signs of anxiety and unhappiness she had seen in Hester lately. She appeared to be avoiding Margaret Rathbone, who was also distant and on occasion a trifle sharp.

Claudine both liked and respected Margaret, but not with the same warmth she felt for Hester. Hester was more spontaneous, more vulnerable, and less proud. Therefore when Bessie came into the kitchen to say that Hester was here, and she was going to make her a pot of tea and take it to her, Claudine told Bessie to finish restocking the cupboards, and said that she herself would take the tea.

When she put the tray down on the table in the office she could see at a glance that Hester was still just as worried as before, if not more so. She poured the tea to give herself an excuse to stay. Right at this moment she wanted, more than anything else, to help, but she was not certain what was wrong, there were so many possibilities. The first was money, either personally or for the clinic. Or it might be a serious case of injury or health that they did not know how to treat. That had happened in the past, and no doubt would again. Or it could be quarrels with the staff, differences of opinion in management, or domestic trouble or unhappiness. But what she considered most likely was something to do with the criminal trial where Hester and her husband had given evidence. But she could not ask. It would be both clumsy and intrusive to do so.

"I think Mrs. Rathbone . . . I mean, Lady Rathbone . . . will not be in today," she said carefully. She saw Hester stiffen, and then relax a little, and she went on. "But she looked at the finances yesterday, and we are really doing quite well."

"Good." Hester acknowledged it. "Thank you."

That seemed to be the end of the conversation. However, Claudine would not give up so easily. "She looked concerned to me, Mrs. Monk. Do you think she may be not quite well?"

Hester looked up, giving it her full attention now. "Margaret? I hadn't noticed. I should have. I wonder if . . ." She stopped.

"She is with child?" Claudine finished for her. "Possibly, but I don't think so. To be honest, she looks anxious rather than sickly to me. I was being less than honest when I said 'not well.' "

Hester did not bother to hide her smile. "Not like you, Claudine. Why don't you fetch another cup? There's enough tea here for two."

Claudine did as she was asked and returned a few moments later. They sat opposite each other, and Hester spoke candidly. "This case of Jericho Phillips has divided us. Naturally, Margaret sides with her husband, as I suppose she should . . ."

Claudine interrupted. She was aware that it might be unseemly, but she could not hold her peace. "I do not believe that God requires any woman to follow her husband to hell, Mrs. Monk," she said decisively. "I promised to obey, but I'm afraid that is a vow I could not keep, if it should go against my conscience. Maybe I will be damned for it, but I am not prepared to give my soul over into anyone else's keeping."

"No, I don't think I am either," Hester agreed thoughtfully. "But she is only recently married, and I think she loves Sir Oliver very much. Also, she may well believe that he is absolutely right. I have not troubled her with the investigation I have been making, or the horrors of the case that I have learned, because it would place her in a position where she might have to stand against him."

Claudine made no reply but waited for Hester to explain.

Hester told her the barest outline of Phillips's business, and what she had since learned of the extent of his power to blackmail.

Claudine was disgusted but she was not greatly surprised. She had seen behind the masks of respectability for many years. Usually it was far pettier than this, but perhaps great sins start as simple weakness, and the consistent placing of self before others.

"I see," she said quietly, pouring more tea for both of them. "What can we do about it? I refuse to accept that there is nothing."

Hester smiled. "So do I, but I confess that I don't yet know what it is. My husband knows the name of at least one of the victims, but cutting them off is not much use. We need the head of it."

"Jericho Phillips," Claudine put in.

"He is central, certainly," Hester agreed, sipping her tea. "But I have been thinking about it a lot recently, and I wonder if he is alone in his enterprise, or if perhaps he is only part of it."

Now Claudine was surprised.

Hester leaned forward. "Why would one of Phillips's victims pay to have him defended and able to continue with his blackmail?"

"Because he also provides the pornography to which this wretched creature is addicted," Claudine replied without hesitation.

"True," Hester agreed. "But when Phillips was in custody, who went to this man and told him to pay for Phillips's defense? Phillips would hardly have sent for him, or the man's secret would be out, and he would have destroyed his power over him."

"Oh!" Claudine was beginning to understand. "There is someone else with power who, for his own reasons, wishes Phillips to be safe and to continue to profit. One has to assume that if Phillips were found guilty, this man's loss would overall be greater than his gain."

Hester winced. "Very direct. You've seized the point admirably. I am not sure how much we can succeed until we know who that person is. I am afraid that he may be someone we will not easily outwit. He has managed to protect Phillips very well up until now, in spite of everything either Durban or we could do."

Claudine was chilled. "You surely don't think Sir Oliver was blackmailed, do you?" She felt guilty even for having the thought, let alone asking. She knew the heat burned her face, but it was too late to retreat.

"No," Hester said without resentment. "But I wonder if he wasn't manipulated into defending Phillips, without realizing what it really meant. The trouble is, I don't know what I can do now to reach Phillips. We're all so . . ."—she sighed—"so . . . vulnerable."

Claudine's mind was racing. Perhaps she could do something. In her time here in the clinic she had learned about sides of life she had not previously even imagined in nightmare. She understood at least something of the people who came and went through these doors. In clothes and manners they were different from the Society women she knew, and in background and hopes for the future; in health, ability, and the things that made them laugh or lose their temper. But in some ways they were also heartbreakingly the same. Those were the things that twisted inside her with a warmth of pity, and all too often of helplessness.

She finished her tea and excused herself without saying anything more about it, and went to see Squeaky Robinson, a man with whom she had a most awkward relationship. That she spoke to him at all was a circumstance that had been forced upon her, at least to begin with. Now they had a kind of restless and extremely uneasy truce.

She knocked on his door; heaven only knew what she might find him doing if she went in without that precaution. When he answered she opened it, walked through, and closed it behind her.

"Good morning, Mr. Robinson," she said a little stiffly. "When we have finished talking I will fetch you a cup of tea, if you would like it. First I need to speak with you."

He looked up warily. He was wearing the same rumpled jacket as usual, and a shirt that had probably never felt an iron, and his hair was standing up at all angles from where he had obviously run his fingers through it in some degree of frenzy.

"Good," he said immediately. "Say what yer 'ave to. I'm thirsty." He did not put his pen down but kept it poised above the inkwell. He wrote all his figures in ink. Apparently he did not make mistakes.

Her temper flared at his dismissiveness, but she kept it under control. She wanted his cooperation. A plan was beginning to take shape in her mind.

"I would like to have your attention, if you please, Mr. Robinson," she said carefully. "All of it."

He looked alarmed. "Wot's 'appened?"

"I had thought you were as aware of it as I, but perhaps you are not." She sat down uninvited. "I shall explain it to you. Jericho Phillips is a man who . . ."

"I know all about that!" he said tartly.

"Then you know what has happened," she responded. "It is necessary that we conclude the matter, so that we can all get back to our own business without the distraction of his behavior. He is causing Mrs. Monk some distress. I would like to be of assistance."

A look of total exasperation filled his face, raising his wispy eyebrows and pulling the corners of his mouth tight. "Yer got no more chance o' catching Jericho Phillips than yer 'ave o' marryin' the Prince o' Wales!" he said with barely concealed impatience. "Get back ter yer kitchen an' do wot yer good at."

"Are you going to catch him?" she said frostily.

He looked uncomfortable. He had expected her to be deeply affronted and lose her composure, and she had not. That gave him a surprising and inexplicable satisfaction. It should have infuriated him.

"Well, are you?" she snapped.

"If I could, I wouldn't be sittin' 'ere," he retorted. "Fer Gawd's sake, fetch the tea."

She sat without moving. "He takes and keeps small boys to be photographed performing obscene acts, is that so?"

He blushed, annoyed with her for embarrassing him. She should have been the one embarrassed. "Yes. Yer shouldn't even be knowin' about such things." That was a definite accusation.

"A lot of use that's going to be," she told him witheringly. "I assume he does it for money? There could be no other reason. He sells these pictures, yes?"

"O' course 'e sells them!" he shouted at her.

"Where?"

"What?"

"Don't pretend to be stupid, Mr. Robinson. Where does he sell them? How much more plainly can I put it?"

"I dunno. On 'is boat, in the post, 'ow do I know?"

"Why not in shops as well?" she asked. "Wouldn't he use every place he could? If I had something I knew I could sell, I would offer it everywhere. Why wouldn't he?"

"All right, so 'e would. Wot about it? That don't do us no good."

With difficulty she forebore from correcting his grammar. She did not want to anger him any more than she had already.

"Is there not any law against such things, if it involves children, boys?"

"Yes, o' course there is." He looked at her wearily. "An' 'oo's goin' ter force it, eh? Yer? Me? The cops? Nobody, that's 'oo."

"I am not quite certain that there is nobody," she said softly. "You might be surprised what Society can do, and will, if it feels itself in danger, either financially or more important, in comfort and self-respect."

He stared at her, surprise and the beginning of a new understanding dawning in his eyes.

She was not quite sure how much she wished to be understood. Perhaps she needed to change the subject rapidly, if she could do so and still learn from him what she needed to know. The wild idea that had begun in her mind was becoming stronger all the time.

"There is a law against it?" she repeated urgently.

"O' course there's a law!" he snapped. "It don't make no difference. Can't yer understand that?"

"Yes, I can." She wanted to crush him but could not afford to. She needed his help, or at the very least some cooperation. "So it would have to be sold where the police would not see it."

"O' course it would," he said in exasperation.

"Where?"

"Where? All over the place. In back alleys, in shops where it looks like decent books, financial books, ledgers, tracts on 'ow ter mend sails or keep accounts, or anything yer like. I seen some as yer'd take fer Bibles, till yer looked close. Tobacconists sell 'em, or bookshops, printers, all sorts."

"I see. Yes, very difficult to trace. Thank you." She stood up and turned to leave, then hesitated. "Down in the alleys by the riverside, I suppose?"

"Yeah. Or anywhere else. But only where folks go as knows wot they want. Yer won't find 'em on the 'Igh Street or any place as the likes o' yer'd be going."

She gave him a slight smile. "Good. Thank you, Mr. Robinson. Don't look so sour. I shall not forget your tea."

Claudine was not happy to return home, but sooner or later it was inevitable; it always was.

"You are late," her husband observed as soon as she entered the drawing room, having gone into the house through the kitchen rather than be seen at the front in her clinic clothes. Now she was washed and changed into the sort of late-afternoon gown she customarily wore. It was fashionable, well-cut, richly colored, and a trifle restricting because of the tightly laced corset beneath it. Her hair was also becomingly dressed, as that of a lady in her station should be.

"I'm sorry," she apologized. There was no use explaining; he was not interested in reasons.

"If you were sorry, you would not keep doing it," he said tartly. He was a large man, broad-bellied, heavy-jowled, a highly successful property developer. In spite of his years, his hair was still thick and barely touched with gray. She looked at his sneering expression and wondered how she could ever have found him physically attractive. Perhaps necessity was the mother of acceptance as well as of invention?

"You spend far too much time at that place," he went on. "This is the third time in as many weeks that I have had to mention this to you. It will not do, Claudine. I have a right to expect certain duties of you, and you are not behaving appropriately at all. As my wife, you have social obligations, of which you are not unaware. Richmond told me you were not at his wife's party last Monday." He said it as a challenge.

"It was to raise money for charity in Africa," she replied. "I was working for a charity here."

He lost his temper. "Oh, don't be absurd! You insulted a lady of considerable consequence in order to go fetching and carrying for a bunch of whores off the street. Have you lost absolutely all sense of who you are? If you have, then let me remind you who I am."

"I am perfectly aware of who you are, Wallace," she said as calmly as she could. "I have spent years . . ." She nearly said "the best years of my life," but they were not. Indeed, they had been the worst. "I have spent years of my life performing all the duties your career and your station required . . ."

"And your station, Claudine," he interrupted. "I think too often you forget that." That was definitely an accusation. His face was reddening, and he moved a step closer to her.

She did not move back. She would refuse to, no matter how close he came.

"That station, which you take so lightly," he went on, "provides the roof over your head, the food in your mouth, and the clothes on your back."

"Thank you, Wallace," she said flatly. She felt no gratitude whatever. Would it have been so bad to have worked for it herself, and owned it without obligation? No, that was a fantasy. One then had to please whoever employed you. Everyone was bound to somebody else.

He did not hear the sarcasm, or chose not to. But then he had very little sense of irony or appreciation of the absurd. "You will oblige me by writing a letter to Mrs. Monk and telling her that you are no longer able to offer your assistance in her project. Tomorrow." He took a deep, satisfied breath. "I am sure that after her unfortunate appearance in criminal court she will not be in the least surprised."

"She was a witness!" Claudine protested, and instantly knew from his face that it was a technical error.

"Of course she was a witness," he said with disgust. "The kind of life she leads, the people she associates with, she is bound to see all sorts of crimes. The only miracle is that she was for the prosecution, not for the defense. I have been extremely tolerant so far, Claudine, but you have now exceeded the limit of what is acceptable. You will do as I have instructed. That is all I have to say on the matter."

Claudine could not remember ever having been so angry, or so desperate to fight back. He was taking from her everything that had brought her the most joy in her life. She realized that with a shock of amazement. It was absurd, but working in Portpool Lane gave her friendship, purpose, and a sense of belonging, of being valued, even a sense of mattering. She could not allow him to simply remove it because he thought he could.

"I am surprised," she said, controlling her voice as well as she could, although she was aware that it trembled.

"I do not wish to discuss it further, Claudine," he said coldly. He always addressed her by name when he was displeased. "I have no idea why you should be surprised, except that I have allowed it so long. It is totally unsuitable."

"I am surprised that you find it so." She was attacking now, and it was almost too late to draw back. She plunged in. "And I admit, it frightens me."

His eyebrows rose high. "Frightens you? That is a foolish thing to say. You are becoming hysterical. I have simply said that you are no longer to associate yourself with a clinic for whores. Forgive me for using the word, but it is the correct one."

"That is immaterial." She brushed it aside with a wave of her hand. She was not a beautiful woman, but her hands were lovely. "What alarms me is that I have allied myself with people who have publicly stood up against a man who traffics in children, small boys, to be precise, for the use of men in their more revolting appetites.

Since we are using correct words," she mimicked his tone exactly, "I believe the term is sodomy. This abuse of children is practiced by all sorts of men," she continued, "of a bestial and debased nature, but this man caters to those with money, that is, largely of our own social class." She saw the blood rush to his face in a scarlet tide. "It frightens me," she continued relentlessly, her voice now quivering with real fear, although not of what she was claiming, "that you do not wish, very publicly indeed, to show yourself to be in the battle against it."

She drew in her breath and let it out slowly, trying to control the shaking of her body. "I do not suspect you of such an appetite, Wallace, but I am more than slightly worried that you forbid me to continue in my support for Mrs. Monk, and all those who fought at her side. What will people think? It is bound to become even more public than it is now. I am not sure that I can oblige you by retreating from the conflict."

He stared at her as if she had grown horns and a tail.

She found herself gulping for air. She could never go back now, as long as she lived. She knew how Caesar must have felt when he crossed the Rubicon to declare war on Rome.

"Are you sure that is what you wish me to do?" she said softly.

"I don't know what has happened to you," he said, looking at her with loathing. "You are a disgrace to your sex, and to all that your parents hoped of you. You are certainly not the woman I married."

"I understand how that pains you," she replied. She was well on the far bank of the Rubicon now. "You are the man I married, and that pains me, which perhaps now you also understand. There is little for us to do but make the best of it. I shall do what I believe to be right, which is to continue to help those in need, and fight with every ability I have to bring men like Jericho Phillips to justice before the law. I think you would find it in your best interests to pretend that you support me. You would be hard put to justify any other course to your friends, and I know you value their opinion. Whatever their private habits, they could not be seen to think differently." And before he could reply, she left the room, and told her maid that she would take supper in her boudoir.

In the morning she left for the clinic very early indeed, before six. It was light at this time of the year, and when she arrived half an hour later, she found Ruby up and working in the kitchen. She had already decided that it was Ruby whose help she would ask.

" 'Mornin', Mrs. Burroughs," Ruby said with surprise. "Summink 'appened? Yer look kind o' upset, bit feverish. Like a cup o' tea?"

"Good morning, Ruby," Claudine replied, closing the back door behind her. "Yes, I would like a cup of tea. I have not had breakfast yet, and I imagine you haven't either. I brought some butter and a pot of marmalade." She produced it and set it on the table. "And a loaf of fresh bread," she added. "I wish for your advice, in confidence."

Ruby looked at the excellent Dundee marmalade and the crusty bread, and knew that it must be serious. She was alarmed.

Claudine saw it. "There is no need to be concerned," she said, going over to the stove and opening the door, ready to make toast. "I wish to do something that I hope will help Mrs. Monk. It will be un-comfortable, and possibly a little dangerous, so I imagine she would stop me if she knew, which is why I am speaking to you in confidence. Are you willing to help me?"

Ruby stared at her in wonder. She was very aware that Hester was in trouble; everyone knew it. " 'Course I am," she said decisively. "Wot'd'yer want?"

"I want to sell matches," Claudine replied. "I thought of boot-laces—that might also work—except people do not need to buy them very often. Flowers would be no use at all, nor would any kind of food." She straightened up from the stove and began to slice the bread. The aroma of it filled the room.

Ruby pulled the kettle over onto the burner and reached for the tea caddy, her mind whirling. "Why d'yer wanter sell matches?" She was utterly lost. She knew it could not possibly be for money. Clau-dine was rich anyway.

"As an excuse for standing in the street outside the sort of shop where they would sell the photographs that Jericho Phillips takes of little boys," Claudine replied. "We know the faces of some of his boys; perhaps I can find these photographs, or at least tell Commander Monk where they may be found. Then he will have another way in which to trap Phillips. Or he may trap some of the men who buy them . . ." The further she went in trying to explain her idea, the more desperate and foolish it sounded.

"Cor!" Ruby let out her breath in a sigh of amazement and admiration. Her eyes were wide and shining. "Then 'e'd 'ave the proof! 'E could make 'em split on Phillips, eh? It wouldn't be like 'angin' 'im, but it'd make 'im mad, for certain. An' it'd make 'is customers as mad as wasps in a fire, an' all! I'll 'elp yer, an' I won't tell no one, I swear!"

"Thank you," Claudine said with profound gratitude. "Now, shall we have breakfast? I trust you like marmalade?"

"Cor! Yeah, I do. Ta." Ruby looked at the jar and she could almost taste it already. "Yer'll 'ave ter 'ave a blouse an' skirt wot's right, an' a shawl. I can get yer one. It'll smell, mind. But it should. Yer can't go lookin' like that, or they'll con yer in a second. An' yer'll 'ave ter keep yer mouth shut as much as yer can. I'll tell yer wot ter say. Or better, pretend as yer deaf, an' can't 'ear nuffin'. An' boots. I'll get yer some boots wot look like yer'd already walked ter Scotland an' back in 'em."

"Thank you," Claudine said quietly. She was beginning to wonder if she really had the courage to go through with this. It was an insane idea. She was totally incompetent to carry off such a thing. It would be humiliating. They would see through her disguise in an instant, and Wallace would have her committed as a lunatic. He would have no trouble at all. What other explanation could there be for such behavior?

Ruby shook her head. "Yer got some guts, Missus." Her eyes shone with awe. "I reckon even Miss 'Ester'd be proud o' yer. 'Course I won't tell 'er!" she added hastily. "I won't never give yer away."

That sealed the decision. There was no escape now. She could not possibly forfeit Ruby's faith in her, and that burning admiration. "Thank you," Claudine said again. "You are a loyal and excellent ally."

Ruby beamed with pleasure, but she was too thrilled to speak.

Naturally Claudine did not go until it was dusk, when she had far greater chance of being unrecognized. Even so, she walked with her head down, shuffling a little in unfamiliar and extremely uncomfortable boots. She must have looked dreadful. Her hair was greased with oil from the kitchen, the smell of which she found distasteful, like a stale pan. Her face was carefully smeared with grime, similarly her hands and as much of her neck as showed. She had an old shawl around her, and was glad to hold it tight, not for warmth, because the evening was mild, but to conceal as much of herself as she could. She carried a light tray that would be hung around her neck on a string, and a bag full of matchboxes to sell. She also had about one and sixpence worth of change, mostly in pennies and halfpennies. Ruby had told her that more would be suspicious.

She began on the dockside beyond Wapping and walked slowly until she found a corner between a good tobacconist and a public house, then stood there with the tray resting just below her bosom and felt as conspicuous as a squashed fly on a white wall, and about as useful.

She also felt afraid. As darkness settled she could see only the short stretches under the street lamps clearly, or wedges of broken pavement where light spilled out a window, or a suddenly opened door. There was noise all around. In the distance dogs were barking above the clatter of hooves from the traffic on the busy cross street seventy yards away. Closer to her people were shouting, and above it was the occasional burst of laughter.

She was ridiculously grateful when someone bought matches, and actually spoke to her. Just that they had seen her and acknowledged her as a human being broke the loneliness that had hardened around her like imprisoning glass. She smiled, and then with a shock of shame remembered that Ruby had also blackened two of her teeth. She said they were beautiful, far too even and white for the sort of woman she was pretending to be.

What was even stranger and more disconcerting was that the man did not even notice. He took her for exactly what she was pretending to be, a street woman too old and too plain to be a whore, but still needing to earn perhaps a shilling or two, standing alone in the night on a street corner selling matches, mild or freezing, wet or dry. She

was relieved, but oddly puzzled also. Was that really the only difference, clothes and a little dirt, the way she carried her head, whether she
dared meet his eyes or not?

She could stand here all night, and those who were sorry for her
might buy matches, but she would learn nothing. She needed to move
closer to the shops that sold books and periodicals, tobacco, the sort
of things a man would buy without arousing any interest or comment.
Ruby had told her where they were, and what they were like. Maybe
she should be closer to Jericho Phillips's boat? She wanted to catch his
trade in particular. Maybe it was like most other trades; people had
their own areas. One did not trespass. Certainly she was growing cold
and stiff here, and achieving nothing except a little practice.

She began to walk back towards the river and the stretch half a
mile or so to the south of Execution Dock. That was one of the places
where Phillips had been known to moor his boat. Another was further
south again, on the Limehouse Reach. There was another where the
curve of the Isle of Dogs bends back to the Blackwall Reach, opposite
the Bugsby Marshes. Too far for rich men to go for their pleasures, and
certainly a less profitable place to sell books and pictures. Was she
being intelligent? Or merely too stupid to know just how stupid she
was? Wallace would have said the latter, if he were not too apoplectic
with rage to say anything at all. She could not bear for him to be right;
that would be almost as bad as letting Ruby down.

She kept walking. It was late and completely dark now. How long
did shops stay open? Buying pornographic photographs of little boys
was surely not a daytime occupation? At this time of the year maybe
they stayed open all night? Perhaps people went to such places after
the theater? The most obvious of all would be after visiting Jericho
Phillips's boat.

That was her best chance, to go towards the river and the alleys
leading off the waterfront.

But she paced up and down fruitlessly until after midnight. Then
tired, cold, and dispirited, she went back to the clinic and Ruby let her
in. It was then that she made the wild boast that she was not beaten,
and would quite definitely return the following evening. She went into

one of the empty bedrooms kept for patients with contagious diseases, and slept until she was woken in the morning by the sound of footsteps, and one of the maids cursing under her breath.

The next evening, Claudine found herself standing on the corner of the same street again in gusting wind and a fine summer rain, carrying a tray of matches, covered with oilskin, when a couple of well-dressed men passed by, apparently not even aware of her.

She turned, as if to cross the street, or possibly even to follow after them and beg them to buy a box of matches. But instead she passed by them, and took a quick, furtive glance at the photograph one of the men was looking at. She was too disappointed that it was an adult woman to be shocked at her total nakedness. All she felt was chagrin that it was not one of Phillips's boys. To her guilt, she was also relieved. They were pictures she did not actually wish to see; it was simply that she could hardly take any proof back to Hester if she could not swear what it was.

Then she realized that of course selling one kind of pornography does not exclude selling another kind. She stopped abruptly, as if she had forgotten something, then turned and went back again to take up her place a few yards from where she had been before. This time she was on the opposite side of the street, where she could watch whoever went into the shop from either direction.

She allowed several very ordinary-appearing customers to go in and come out again, but the next time a well-dressed man went in, she crossed over and went in after him. She stood in the corner as if waiting in the shadows for her turn, well out of the sound of his voice. At a glance one might have thought she was being discreet.

When he had agreed on the cards he wished for and paid his money to the shopkeeper, she moved forward, pretended to be dizzy, and swayed to one side. As though by accident, she knocked the cards out of his hand and they fluttered to the floor. Two lay facedown, three were faceup. They showed naked and frightened little boys in attitudes only grown men should adopt, and that in the strictest privacy. One of them had bloody weals on his flesh where any clothes at all would have concealed them.

Claudine closed her eyes and sank to the floor, not entirely having to pretend a feeling of nausea. The shopkeeper came around the counter and tried to assist her to her feet, while his customer scrabbled on the floor to pick up his treasures.

The next few moments passed in a daze. She staggered to her feet, now quite genuinely dizzy, and at the shopkeeper's insistence drank a small mouthful of brandy, probably all he could afford to offer. Then she told him her husband's tobacco would have to wait, she needed some air, and without accepting any further assistance she thanked him and blundered outside onto the dark street and the beginning of more rain. It was light, only a drifting mist blowing off the river, the mournful sound of foghorns echoing up from Limehouse Reach and the long stretch beyond.

She leaned against the wall of the tenement houses, a sickness in her stomach, the taste of bile in her mouth. She shuddered with cold, her back ached, and her feet were blistered. She was alone here in the dark and dripping street, but this was victory!

Three or four more men walked past. Two bought matches. She was going to earn enough for a loaf of bread. Actually she had no idea what a loaf of bread cost. A pint of beer was three pence, she had heard someone say that. Four pints for a shilling. Nine shillings a week was a fair rent, half a laborer's weekly wage.

They were well dressed, these customers of the tobacconist. Their suits must have cost two pounds or more. That one's shirt looked like silk. How much were the photographs? Sixpence? A shilling?

Another man had stopped in front of her. She had not even noticed him approaching. It must be midnight. He was a big man, solid, holding cards facedown like the ones she'd seen in the shop.

"Yes, sir? Matches, sir?" she said through dry lips.

"I'll have a couple of boxes," he replied, holding out two pennies.

She took them and he helped himself to two boxes off the tray. He looked up at her, and she glanced at his eyes to see if he was going to ask her for something more. Then she froze. Every shred of warmth vanished from her body. She must be as white as a winter sky. It was Arthur Ballinger. She had no doubt of it. She had met him at several social functions with Wallace. She remembered him because he was Margaret Rathbone's father. Did he remember her? Was that why he was staring at her? This was even worse than in the shop! He would tell Wallace, he would be bound to. There was no conceivable explanation she could give. What reason could a lady of Society have for dressing up like a pauper and selling matches on the street outside a shop that sold pornography of the most depraved kind?

No, it was far worse than that! Ballinger would understand the reason. He would know she was spying on him, and others like him. She must speak, say something to shatter his suspicion and make him certain she was just what she looked like, a peddler, a woman of grinding poverty.

"Thank you, sir," she said hoarsely, trying to imitate the voices of the women who came to the clinic. "Gawd bless yer," she added, and choked on the gasped air and the dryness of her throat, now so rasping it nearly strangled her.

Ballinger backed away a step, looked at her again, then changed his mind and strode away. Two minutes later he was out of sight and she was alone in the street, which was now so dark she could barely see the ends. The lamps hung like straight-edged towers girded by pale wreaths that moved, dissolved, and formed again as the wind from the water gusted between the dark housefronts.

A dog trotted by soundlessly, its shape indistinct. A cat ran, low to the ground, shinned up a wall, seemingly without effort, and dropped on the other side invisibly. Somewhere out of sight a man and a woman were shouting at each other.

Then three men came around the corner, abreast, swaggering towards her. As they passed under the lamp she saw their coarse faces. Two of them were looking at her with anticipation. One of them ran his tongue over his lips.

She dropped the match tray and ran, ignoring her ill-fitting boots on the uneven cobbles, the enclosing darkness, and the stench of garbage. She did not even look which way she was going, anything to get away from the pursuing men, shouting after her, laughing and yelling obscenities.

At the end of the street she turned left, around the nearest corner that allowed her not to cross the open stretch where she would be seen.

This alley was darker, but she knew they would still hear her boots on the stones. She turned again, and again, always running. Her dread was that she would find one of the alleys blind, and they would trap her against a wall with nowhere else to go.

A dog was barking furiously. Somewhere ahead there were lights. A tavern door was open, and a yellow lantern gleam spilled out onto the cobbles. The smell of ale was strong. She was tempted to go in; it was bright and looked warm. Perhaps they would help her?

Or perhaps not. No, if someone tore at her clothes they would see the clean linen under them. She would be exposed for a fraud. They would be furious. They would feel mocked, duped. They might even kill her. She had seen the wounds of too many street women who had incurred someone's uncontrolled rage. Keep running. Trust no one.

Her breath stabbed in her aching lungs, but she dared not stop.

There was more shouting behind her. She tried to run faster. Her feet were slipping on the cobbles. Twice she nearly fell, only saving herself by swinging her arms wildly to keep her balance.

She had no idea how long she ran, or where she was when finally she fell, exhausted, huddling in the doorway of some tenement house on a narrow street, walls above her almost meeting at the roofs. She could hear scuffling, the scrape of animal claws, and breathing, but no human boots on the road's surface, no voices shouting or laughing.

There was someone near her, a woman like a pile of laundry, all ragged and tied together with twine. She crept near her, glad of the warmth. Perhaps she could even sleep a little. In the morning she would try to find out where she was. For now she was invisible in the dark, another bundle of rags, just like all the rest.

Hester arrived at the clinic in the morning to find Squeaky Robinson waiting for her. She had barely sat down at her desk to look at the figures for medicines when he knocked and came straight in without waiting for her to answer. He closed the door behind him. He looked angry and worried. He had a piece of stiff, white notepaper in his hand. He started to speak without even the barest civility of a greeting.

"Two days!" he said sharply. "Nothing at all, not a word. And now 'ere's her 'usband writing us letters demanding 'er ter come 'ome." He waved the paper in proof.

"Who?" Hester asked him. She did not question his manners; she could see that he was very obviously distressed.

" 'Er 'usband!" he snapped. He looked at the papers. "Wallace Burroughs."

Then she understood, and was instantly as concerned as he. "You mean Claudine hasn't been here for two days? And she hasn't been home either?"

He closed his eyes in exasperation. "That's wot I jus' said! She's gorn missing, taken off, the stupid..." He fumbled for a word violent enough to express his emotions, and failed to find one he could use in front of her.

"Show me." Hester held her hand out for the note, and he passed it to her. It was brief to the point of curtness, but perfectly explicit. He said he had forbidden Claudine to involve herself any more deeply in the affairs of the clinic, and she had apparently defied him, and had now been missing from her home and her duties for two whole days and nights. He required immediately that whoever was in charge of the clinic should send Claudine home, and not in future address her or importune her for further assistance, either with time or for financial offerings.

At another time Hester would have been furious with his arrogance and his patronizing and domineering manner, but she read in his tone not only injured pride but also genuine anxiety, not just for his own well-being but for Claudine's.

"This is serious, Squeaky." She looked up at him. "If she isn't at home, and she isn't here, then it may be that she is in some trouble."

"I know that!" he said sharply, his voice unusually loud. "Why d'yer think I came ter yer? She's gorn an' done summink stupid."

"What sort of thing? What do you know, Squeaky?"

"I dunno nothin' or I'd be tellin' yer," he said. His exasperation had reached the point where he could not keep still. He moved his weight from one foot to the other in agitation. "Nobody's gonna listen ter me. Yer'll 'ave ter ask Bessie an' Ruby an' anyone else, or put the word out. Tell Mr. Monk, if yer 'ave ter. We gotta find 'er, or she'll come ter some 'arm. Gawd knows, she's daft enough."

Hester drew breath to give a string of alternatives as to where Claudine could be, all of them safe, but of course she knew that Claudine would not have gone on any kind of social trip without telling them, and at the moment her mind was worried and angry over Jericho Phillips, just as they all were.

"I'll speak to Ruby and Bessie." She stood up. "Then if they have nothing, I'll start with the women we have in at the moment."

"Good," he said firmly. He hesitated over whether to thank her or not, and decided not to. She was doing it for herself, not for him. "I'll wait 'ere," he finished.

She left him and went to find Bessie, who knew nothing at all, except that she thought Ruby was looking busy and self-important these last couple of days, and now she was a bit preoccupied this morning.

"Thank you," Hester said fervently.

Ruby was alone in the scullery looking over what vegetables they had left.

Hester decided to preempt any denial by assuming guilt, not a practice she normally approved, but this was not normal. Claudine was lost, and they must find her, and ease any damage to any hurt feelings later.

"Good morning, Ruby," she began. "Please forget the carrots and listen to me. Mrs. Burroughs is missing and may be in trouble, or even danger. Her husband does not know where she is. She has not been home for two nights, and she has not been here either. If you know something, you must tell me, immediately."

"She were 'ere night afore last," Ruby said intently, dropping a bunch of carrots on to the bench.

"No one saw her here. Are you sure you have the correct night?" Hester asked her.

"Yes, Miss. She came in tired and pretty rough. Din't want no one ter see 'er. Slept in the fever room. Went out early. I saw 'er."

"Did you, indeed? Where did she go?"

Ruby looked straight at her. "I can't tell you, Miss. I gave 'er me word." Her eyes were shining, and her face was a little flushed.

Hester was assailed by a terrible thought. It was adventure in Ruby's eyes. Claudine had gone to do something Ruby held in supremely high regard, something wonderful. She found herself almost choking on her own breath. "Ruby, you have to tell me. She may be in terrible danger! Jericho Phillips tortures people and murders them!" She saw Ruby's face go white. "Tell me!" She lifted her hands as if to take Ruby by the shoulders and shake her, and only just restrained herself in time.

"I promised!" Ruby said in a whisper. "I gave 'er me word!"

"You are released from it," Hester said urgently. "Honorably released. Where did she go?"

"Ter find out where they sell 'em pictures wot Phillips takes," she answered huskily.

"What?" Hester was appalled. "How? Where did she go to? You can't just walk into a shop and ask if they sell pornography! Has she lost her wits?"

Ruby sighed impatiently. " 'Course not. She went dressed like a match seller, all scuffed up an' dirty, like. She dressed proper, old boots an' all. I got 'er an old skirt and shawl from one o' the women wot comes in 'ere, an' greased 'er 'air an' blackened 'er face, an' 'er teeth. Yer'd never 'ave known 'er from the real, I promise yer."

Hester let her breath out slowly, her mind filled with horror. "Oh, God help us!" she said. There was no point in blaming Ruby. "Thank you for telling me the truth. Count the rest of the carrots."

"She goin' ter be all right, Miss 'Ester?" Ruby asked nervously.

Hester looked at her. Her face was twisted with fear, her eyes dark.

"Yes, of course," Hester said quickly. "We'll just have to go and find her, that's all." She turned again and left, going rapidly back to her office, her heels clicking on the wooden floor with a sharp, hasty sound.

She was almost at the end of explaining to Squeaky what she had learned when Margaret Rathbone came in. It was obvious from her expression that she had overheard a good deal of the conversation.

"Good morning, Margaret," Hester said with surprise. "I didn't know you were there."

"So I gathered," Margaret replied coolly. She was wearing a flattering green muslin dress and looked as if she had come to do no more than deliver messages. Her clothing contrasted strongly with Hester's blouse and blue-gray skirt, which was obviously made for working in. Margaret came further into the room, nodding to Squeaky but not speaking to him. "Were you going to tell me that Claudine is missing?"

Squeaky looked at her, then turned back to Hester, eyes wide.

Hester was caught off guard. "I hadn't thought about you at all," she replied honestly. "I was wondering what best to do to find Claudine. Have you some suggestion?"

"My suggestion would have been not to take Claudine into your confidence about your obsession with Jericho Phillips," she replied. "She admires you so much she would do anything to earn your friendship. She is a Society lady, bred to be charming, entertaining, obedient, and a good wife and hostess. She has no idea about your world of poverty and crime, except the bits she overhears from the street women who come here. She didn't come to the trial, she was too busy keeping the clinic working, and she certainly wouldn't read about it in the newspapers. Decent women don't read such things, and most street women can't read anyway. She is naive about your world, and if you'd taken any proper responsibility you would know that."

Hester could think of no defense for herself. To argue whether the streets were "her world" was to evade the point. Claudine was naive, and Hester knew it, or she would have, had she bothered to take any thought. She was just as guilty as Margaret had accused her of being.

"Let us hope to hear that it does not end in tragedy," Margaret added.

There was a movement at the door and they all swiveled 'round to see Rathbone come in. Presumably he had accompanied Margaret. Perhaps they had come from some function together, or were intending to leave for one.

He looked at each of them in turn, his face grave. His eyes rested on Hester for a moment, then he spoke to Squeaky. "Mr. Robinson, would you be good enough to leave us for a few moments? Thank you." The last was an acknowledgment as Squeaky glanced at Hester, and at her nod went out of the room, closing the door behind him.

Hester waited for Rathbone to endorse Margaret's accusation. Instead, he turned to Margaret. "Your criticism is unhelpful, Margaret," he said quietly. "And I think it is also unfair. Mrs. Burroughs took whatever action she did from her own belief, and from her desire to help. If it turns out to have been foolish, that is tragic. All we can usefully do now is set out to look for her in the hope that she may be rescued from whatever discomfort or distress she is in. Of course Hester is determined to do whatever is possible within the law to stop Jericho Phillips. It is her fault that he is free from the noose for having killed the boy Figgis. I understand her compulsion to put right that error. We would all do better if we acknowledged our mistakes, instead of making excuses for them, and did everything within our power to put them right. Occasionally we need help in that, which Claudine Burroughs realized. The fact that her assistance may be of more harm than use is regrettable, but it is not stupid, nor is it evil."

The color drained from Margaret's face, and she stared at him in astonishment.

His expression did not alter. "It takes courage," he went on. "I think those who have never made any grand mistakes do not realize how much that costs. It is to be admired, not criticized."

Margaret slowly turned from him towards Hester. Her eyes filled with tears. She swung around and walked out, her head high, her back stiff. She did not speak to either of them.

Rathbone did not go after her. "I know that, because I have made a few myself," he said with a slightly twisted smile, his voice gentler than before. "Phillips was one of them, and I don't know how to put it right."

Hester blinked, confused, her mind racing. What he had said was true, but she was astounded that he had expressed it aloud.

She looked at his face, remembering all the battles they had fought together in the past, before ever knowing Margaret. It had been more than friendship; there had been understanding, loyalty, and a belief and a cause shared. It was a bond too deep to break easily. He had made a mistake over Phillips; the thing that mattered was that he had owned up to it. Forgiveness was instant and complete.

She smiled at him, and saw the answering warmth in his face, and a flare of intense gratitude, bright and sweet.

"We must find Claudine," she said aloud. "Before we think of anything else. Squeaky should be the best person for that."

Rathbone cleared his throat. "Can I help?"

She looked away. "Not yet, but if you can, I'll ask you."

"Hester . . ."

"I will! I promise." Before he could say anything more, and she was suddenly afraid of what that might be, she brushed past him and went to look for Squeaky.

TWELVE

When Squeaky Robinson left Hester's office he went straight to his own office, intending to wait for her. The discussion between her and Rathbone sounded as if it might become personal, and rather heated. Squeaky had not thought about it much before, but it seemed to him now as if there was a bit more to that friendship than he had supposed. He hoped Hester was not going to get hurt by it. She had already been hurt more than enough by her meddling in the Jericho Phillips affair. Women would be a lot better off, and a lot less trouble, if they had smaller hearts, and bigger brains.

And that certainly went for Claudine Burroughs too. Stupid mare! Now he would have to go and look for her, wherever she had gotten to. And the sooner that was done the better. Dress up as a match seller! Hadn't the wits she was born with! No wonder her husband was as cross as a wet hen. Not that Squeaky knew anything about hens, wet or dry. It was just something he'd heard someone say, and it seemed to fit the kind of pointless and ineffectual temper he imagined of Wallace Burroughs.

It was up to Squeaky to do something sensible. He would do it right now, before Hester could come and tell him differently. He wrote a short note to her and left it on the very top of the ledgers on his desk. "Dear Miss Hester, I know where Mrs. Burroughs might be. Gone to look for her. S. Robinson."

He went to his bedroom and changed into some far scruffier and more disrespectable clothes than the ones he had taken to wearing in his office recently, and set out from the back door. He picked up a cab in Farringdon Road and asked to be taken to Execution Dock. That was as good a place to start as he could think of.

On the way he tried to let his mind follow what Claudine would have thought. According to what Hester had from Ruby, Claudine was going to look for shops that sold pornographic photographs of little boys. He let out a howl of anguish at the idiocy of such a thing, but fortunately the driver did not hear him, or took no notice. A man could die in here, and no one would care, he thought aggrievedly. And yet if the driver had stopped and come to inquire if he was all right, he would have been even angrier.

On arriving he alighted, paid the cabby the fare, and gave him a tuppence tip, then started walking along the dockside to the nearest alley leading inland. The alleys were narrow, stifling in the heat as the sun rose towards midday. He had not been here in some time, and he had forgotten how disgusting they smelled.

He knew where the brothels were, and the shops that sold pornography of all sorts. He began asking, casually at first. He wanted to know if anyone had seen a match seller answering Claudine's description. It was tedious. Many people were disinclined to reply with any degree of honesty.

He had been working at it for two or three hours before he was mimicked, very disrespectfully, by a couple of urchins, and he realized with a shiver of horror how polite he had become. It was appalling. He had changed beyond all recognition from the man he used to be. He sounded like some daft old stranger.

He lunged after one of the boys and caught him by the scruff of the neck. He lifted him right off the ground, feet dangling, and held him in the air.

"Treat yer elders wi' respect, yer piece o' vermin," he hissed at the child. "Or I'll teach yer the 'ard way, an' yer'll wish yer 'adn't been born. Now I'll ask yer nice, one more time, because I don' like twistin' children's 'eads off. Makes me tired, most especial it does on a summer day. Where did the match woman go as was 'ere two days ago? Tell me no lies, 'cause if yer do, I'll come lookin' fer yer, in the middle o' the night, when no one'll see wot I do ter yer. Got it?"

The boy squealed, his eyes bulging with the savagery of the grip around his collar.

Squeaky dropped him on the ground, and he howled.

"Answer me, or yer'll be sorry," Squeaky whispered, bending down till his face was close to the boy's. "She's a friend o' mine, an' I don't want nothin' bad to 'appen to 'er, got it?"

The boy whispered out a reply. Squeaky thanked him and walked away, leaving him to scramble to his feet and make for the nearest alley.

Squeaky set out in the direction suggested, feeling guilty and a little self-conscious. What on earth was happening to him? He used to behave like that all the time. He had not actually hurt the child at all. In the past he might well have cuffed him 'round the ear until his head had buzzed. Was this what working for Hester Monk had done for him, made him soft? He would not be able to go back to the streets even if he wanted to. He was ruined!

That wasn't the worst of it. He loped along the narrow footpath at alarming speed, always deeper into the warren of alleys, dead ends, and tunnels bending back on themselves towards the river again. But worse than actually becoming respectable was the secret knowledge he would admit to no one: he rather liked it.

He asked more people: peddlers, shopkeepers, pawnbrokers, beggars. Some he threatened, some he bribed—which was really very painful indeed, because it was his own money.

He traced her as far as the tobacconist and bookseller, where she had apparently collapsed and knocked into a man buying postcards, sending them all on to the floor. What on earth was the stupid woman playing at? But through his anger, which was really fear, he knew exactly what she was doing.

With a little more threat, bribing, and invention he heard about her sudden hysterical flight, but no one knew where she had gone after two or three twists. Mad woman, they said. Who could explain anything she did? Drunk, most like. He wanted to knock them over for that. Claudine would never be drunk! Might be happier if she were, now and then.

It was getting dark, and the clammy air of the day was cooling off. Where the devil in hell was the woman? Anything could have happened to her in these miserable alleys. At the very least she would be frightened, possibly worse than that. Another night was coming on. He began to lose his temper with people more genuinely. Perhaps the old Squeaky wasn't so completely lost, just a little submerged under layers of newfound habits in politeness. That thought did not make him as happy as he had expected it to.

It took him another hour of questions, tracking down strangers, and several false hopes and misidentifications before finally, close to eleven o'clock, he found her sitting in a heap on the steps of a tenement off the Shadwell High Street. What on earth was she doing here? She looked utterly wretched. Had he not been looking for her specifically he would never have recognized her.

He stopped squarely in front of her, blocking her chance to get up and run away. He saw the fear in her face, but she was too tired to move, and she simply stared at him, defeated, not even knowing who he was.

The words of anger died on his lips. He was horrified at himself at how relieved he was to see her—if not well, at least alive and uninjured. He swallowed and drew in his breath.

"Well," he said to her. Then he lost his temper. "Wot the bleedin' 'ell are yer doin' 'ere, yer daft cow?" he shouted. "Scared the bleedin' daylights out of us, yer did! 'Ere!" He thrust out his hand to help her up. "Well, come on then! Wot's the matter with yer? Broken yer bleedin' legs?" He waved his hand, almost jabbing it at her. Now he was afraid that she really was hurt in some way. What on earth was he going to do if she was? He couldn't carry her; she was a substantial woman, built the way women were supposed to be.

Very cautiously she grasped his hand. He heaved to pull her up, overcome with relief when she stood. He was about to shout at her again when he saw the tears in her eyes, and the gratitude.

He sniffed and turned away, to avoid embarrassing her. "Well, come on then," he said gruffly. "We better be gettin' 'ome. If we're lucky we might find some sort of a cab in the 'Igh Street. Can yer walk in them great ugly boots?"

"Of course I can," she said stiffly, and promptly stumbled. He had to catch hold of her and support her weight to stop her from falling.

He made no remark about it, and tried hard to think of some other subject to talk about.

"Why din't yer go 'ome then?" he demanded.

"Because I was lost," she replied, not looking at him.

They walked in silence for another fifty yards.

"Find any pictures?" he asked. He was not sure if that was a good thing to say or not, but perhaps it was worse to take her failure for granted.

"Yes, I did," she said immediately. She named the shop and the exact address. "I have no idea which boys they were." She shuddered violently. "But it was the sort of thing that Phillips does, I imagine. I would prefer not to know any more about it."

"Really?" Squeaky was surprised. He had not expected her to succeed at all. That must have been when she knocked the cards out of the man's hand. "So you din't really faint then?"

She stopped abruptly. "How do you know about that?"

"Well, 'ow d'yer think I found yer?" he demanded. "I been askin'! D'yer think I just 'appened ter be wanderin' along 'ere, fer summink ter do, then?"

She started to walk again, hobbling a bit because her feet were so sore. She said nothing for quite a long time. Eventually all the words she could find were "Thank you. I am grateful to you."

He shrugged. "It's nothin'," he replied. He did not mean that it was of no importance to him, he meant that she did not owe him any debt. He wondered if she understood that, but it was far too awkward to explain, and he did not know where it might lead.

"Mr. Robinson," she said about a hundred yards later. They were in the Shadwell High Street, but there were no cabs in sight, only the usual traffic of carts and drays.

He looked at her to indicate his attention.

"I saw some customers go in and out of that shop," she said a little hesitantly. "I recognized one of them," she went on. "That was why I ran away."

"Oh yeah? 'Oo was it?" He was not sure if it would matter, and who could possibly recognize her, looking like this?

"Mr. Arthur Ballinger," she replied.

He stopped abruptly, catching her arm and swinging her to a halt as well. "Wot? Ballinger, as Lady Rathbone were?" he said incredulously.

"Yes." Her eyes did not waver. "He is her father."

"Buyin' pictures o' little boys?" His disbelief sent his voice up almost an octave.

"Don't look at me like that, Mr. Robinson," she said sharply, her voice catching in her throat. "I am acquainted with Mr. Ballinger. I ran because he looked at me very closely indeed, and I was afraid that he had also recognized me."

"Where d'yer know 'im from?" he asked, still dubious.

She shut her eyes, as if her patience were exhausted. Her voice was flat and tight when she answered. "It is part of my duty, and I suppose my privilege, as Mr. Burroughs's wife, to attend a great many social functions. I met him at several of those, along with Mrs. Ballinger, of course. Much of this time the ladies are separate from the gentlemen, but at dinner we will all sit where we are directed, according to rank, and I have had occasion to sit opposite Mr. Ballinger, and listen to him speak."

It was an unknown world to him. "Listen ter 'im speak?" he asked.

"It is not appropriate for ladies to speak too much at table," she explained. "They should listen, respond appropriately, and ask after interests, welfare, and so on. If a gentleman wishes to talk, and usually they do, you listen as if fascinated, and never ask questions to which you suspect he does not know the answer. He will almost certainly not listen to you, but he will certainly look at you closely, if you are young and pretty."

He caught a sadness in her voice, possibly even a shadow of real pain, and felt an upsurge of anger that startled him.

"Ask opinions or advice," she continued, lost in memory. "That is flattering. But it is unbecoming to offer either. One is not supposed to have them. But I am quite sure it was Ballinger. I have listened to him on several occasions. One has to listen, or one cannot ask appropriate questions. Sometimes it is even moderately interesting." She stopped suddenly.

For a moment he was not sure if it was because she was still remembering something of the past that alarmed her, or if it was simply that her feet pained her too much to continue. Then he realized that they had reached an intersection of two fairly busy streets, and she was hoping at last to find a cab.

When he had hailed one and they were at last sitting side by side, necessarily rather close together, she spoke again.

"If Mr. Ballinger is involved in this business," she said, looking towards him in the dark, her voice anxious, "it is going to be . . . very distressing."

That was an understatement, he thought. It would be monumental. Lady Rathbone's father!

"It may even reflect upon Sir Oliver," she added. "Since he was the one to defend Phillips. There will be many people who will not accept that he had no idea of the connection. He may be accused of participating in the profit, being . . . tainted by it. Mrs. Monk will be very unhappy."

He said nothing. He was thinking of just how awful it would be. The few moments of conflict in Hester's office would be a summer's day compared with what might be to come.

"So I would be very grateful, Mr. Robinson, if you would say nothing about my seeing Mr. Ballinger, at least not yet. Please?"

It would be the honorable thing to do, the right thing. "No," he agreed without hesitation. "No, I won't tell 'er. Yer say when yer ready."

"Thank you."

They rode in silence for quite a while. He was not sure, but he thought she might even have gone to sleep. Poor creature, she must be so tired she would have slept on her feet, now that she knew she was safe. Guaranteed she was hungry too, and would like a clean, hot cup of tea more than anything in the world, except maybe a bath. Funny how women liked a bath.

When they arrived at Portpool Lane it was after midnight but Hester was still there. She had fallen asleep in one of the chairs in the big entrance hall where they first saw people as they arrived. She was curled up with her feet half underneath her, her boots on the floor.

She woke as soon as she heard their footsteps, jerking her head up, blinking. She recognized Squeaky before she realized that it was Claudine with him. She scrambled to her feet and ran across to throw her arms around Claudine, then with flushed face and eyes shining with relief, she thanked Squeaky profoundly.

"That's all right," he said a bit self-consciously. "Weren't nothin'. She were lost, that's all." He made a casual gesture as if to dismiss it.

Hester decided to allow it to pass. Just at the moment she was dizzy with relief that Claudine was safe. She realized only now how deeply afraid she had been that some harm had come to her. If she had gone around asking about Phillips, he was quite capable of killing her, and they would probably never even know. She would appear to be just one more beggar woman dead of cold or hunger, or some unspecified disease. Even a knife attack or a strangling would not occasion a great deal of remark.

She thanked Squeaky again, told Ruby that Claudine was safe, and decided to allow Wallace Burroughs the privilege of having a good night's sleep, or not. She would send him a letter in the morning, unless Claudine wished to go home and tell him herself. If she did not, then that was up to her.

Another message she would definitely send would be to Rathbone, to tell him that Claudine was safe. It would be polite to address it to Margaret as well.

Over breakfast in the large kitchen she asked Squeaky what Claudine had discovered, if anything, but he told her he had no idea. He looked slightly surprised when he said it, and it was several moments before she realized that it was not Claudine's lack of discovery that startled him, but his own reply to Hester. That must be because it was a lie, to defend Claudine.

She looked at him more closely, and he returned her look with a straight, slightly belligerent gaze. She found herself smiling. Squeaky was definitely defending Claudine.

When she had eaten her toast and drunk her own tea, she made more, set it on a tray, and took it up to the bedroom Claudine was using. She found her just beginning to wake up, ravenously hungry and longing for a cup of tea.

Hester sat on the bed while Claudine ate and drank. She addressed the subject.

"What did you discover?" she asked.

Claudine stared at her over the top of her cup.

"I asked Squeaky, but he won't tell me," Hester explained. "He said he doesn't know, but he's lying. So that makes me think it's important."

Claudine finished her tea slowly, giving herself time to think. Finally she put the cup down on the bedside table and took a deep breath. "I found a shop selling pornographic photographs of young boys. I saw a couple. They were terrible. I don't want to talk about them. I wish I didn't have them in my mind. I didn't realize how hard it is to get something out of your memory once you've seen it. It's like a stain no amount of soap or water can remove."

"It dulls with time," Hester said gently. "As you get more and more things in there, there's less room for the horrors. Push it out every time it comes back, and eventually the details will fade."

"Have you seen them?"

"Not those. But I've seen other things, on the battlefield, and heard them. Sometimes when we have someone in here with a knife wound, the smell of blood brings it all back."

Claudine's face was gentle, full of pity.

"Why wouldn't Squeaky tell me that?" Hester asked her. "That doesn't make sense."

"That wasn't what he wouldn't tell you," Claudine replied. "It was who I saw on the pavement just outside the shop, with cards in his hand. He bought some matches from me and stared at me very closely. I was scared he'd recognized me."

Hester frowned, her imagination struggling. "Who did you see?"

Claudine bit her lip. "Mr. Ballinger, Lady Rathbone's father."

Hester was stunned. It seemed preposterous. And yet if it was true, it explained Rathbone's predicament exactly. "Are you certain?" she said aloud.

"Yes. I've met him several times, at dinners and balls. My husband is acquainted with him. He stood no more than two feet from me."

Hester nodded. It was hideous. How on earth could Margaret bear that, if she believed it? If it became known? Had Rathbone had any idea? How would he see it: disgust, pity, loyalty, protection for Margaret and her mother? She could not believe that he knew already. And yet he would have to one day. Perhaps he could in some way prepare?

"Your husband was worried about you," she said to Claudine. "Would you like me to send a letter? I could say you were kept in some kind of emergency, but we had better offer the same explanation."

A shadow crossed Claudine's face. "I don't think he is going to forgive me, whatever it is," she replied. "I am not quite sure what I am going to do. I shall have to give it a great deal of thought. If . . . if he puts me out, may I live here?" She looked frightened, and embarrassed.

"Of course," Hester said instantly. "If you wish to, for whatever reason." She nearly added that Rathbone would give her legal help, then she thought that was a little premature. Surely Wallace Burroughs would calm himself and behave a little more reasonably. Although his behaving reasonably was a very long way indeed from giving Claudine any kind of happiness. "I shall write to him that you were helping someone in an accident." There was a note of gentleness in her voice. "He will never know differently," she went on. "You had better say the same. You know enough details to give them to him if he should ask you."

"He won't. He is never interested in such things," Claudine told her. "But thank you."

Hester very briefly told Squeaky that she was going to the Wapping police station to find Monk, then she left immediately, dreading the chance of running into Margaret on the way out.

She caught a cab on Farringdon Road, and half an hour later was in Wapping. She had a further hour to wait before Monk returned from the water, but she was prepared to wait far longer, had it been necessary.

He closed the door of his office and stood waiting for her to speak.

Briefly, leaving out everything that was irrelevant to the issue, she told him of Claudine's adventure, and that she was certain beyond any doubt that it had been Arthur Ballinger she had seen.

"She must be wrong," he said. "She was tired, frightened, upset after seeing the cards . . ."

"No she wasn't, William," Hester said levelly. "She knows Ballinger."

"How would she know him? He's not her solicitor, surely?"

"No. They move in the same circles in Society," she explained. "Claudine may scrub kitchens and cook for the sick in Portpool Lane, but in her own home she's a lady. She probably knows most people in Society, more or less. Now she is terrified because he looked so closely at her she was afraid he had recognized her too."

He did not fight any longer; the grief in his eyes showed his acceptance.

"We have to be prepared," she continued more gently. "I don't imagine Oliver knows, but perhaps he does. It may even be the reason he took Phillips's case in the first place. But I'll wager Margaret doesn't. Or her mother." She winced. "I can't imagine what that will be like for them, if they are forced to know."

Monk breathed out slowly. "God! What a mess!"

There was a sharp rap on the door and before Monk could answer, it opened and Orme stood there, ashen-faced, eyes hollow. Hester saw him before Monk did.

"What is it?" she demanded, fear gripping her like a tightening noose.

Monk swung around to Orme.

Orme handed him a sheet of paper, folded over once.

Monk took it and read, his hand shaking, the color draining from his cheeks.

"What is it?" Hester demanded more urgently, her voice high-pitched, her heart pounding.

"Jericho Phillips has Scuff," Monk replied. "He says that if we don't stop pursuing him, all of us, the River Police, then he will use Scuff in his trade. And when he's finished with him, he'll either sell him on to someone, or if he's a nuisance and causes trouble, then he'll kill him."

"Then we will stop." Hester nearly choked on the words, but she could not even imagine letting Scuff endure that. The possibility did not exist to consider.

"That's not all," Monk went on, his voice shaking now. "I must publicly condemn Durban and say everything bad about him that I can, including his early involvement with the men who robbed the bank. Then I must retract all the charges I've made against Phillips, and say that they were motivated by my desire to vindicate Durban's name, and pay my debt to him. His price is Scuff's life. If I don't, his death will be slow, and very unpleasant."

She stared at him for interminable seconds, unable to grasp what he had said, then slowly it became clear, indelible, impossible to bear. "We must do it." She felt as if she were a betrayer even as the words were on her lips, and yet any other answer was unthinkable. What happiness or honor could there ever be again if they let Phillips keep Scuff, and one day torture him to death? The power of terror and extortion was sickeningly clear, and without escape.

She saw something else in Monk's face, intelligence, understanding, and deeper horror.

"What is it?" she demanded, leaning forward as if to grasp him, and at the last moment stopping. "What do you know?"

"I was thinking that I should go to Rathbone and tell him about Ballinger," he replied, almost in a whisper. "He needs to know, for his own sake, hideous as it will be for him. And he might be able to help; I don't know how."

"Poor Oliver," she said quietly. "But I would tell everybody any truth, if I had to, to get Scuff back."

"Claudine thought Ballinger might have recognized her," Monk said quietly, his voice rasping. "It seems he did, and told Phillips. That's why Phillips has taken Scuff now. They know the net is tightening." His face was very pale, eyes hollow. "We have to get Scuff back, or get some hostage of our own that will force Phillips to let him go. I'll go to Rathbone . . ."

"I'm coming too," she said instantly.

"No. I won't shut you out, I promise . . ."

"I'm coming! If you go after Scuff, and anyone is hurt, I can do more for them than any of the rest of you." For the first time her glance took in Orme, pleading. "You know that!"

Monk turned back and faced her. "Yes, I do know it. I also know that you would not forgive me if anything went wrong and you might have prevented it, and I couldn't live with that. I give you my word that I will not go without you. Or Orme, if you'll come?" he added, looking at the other man.

"I'll come," Orme said simply. "I'll get a boat ready, and some pistols."

Monk nodded his thanks, and touched Hester's hand in passing. It was just a momentary warmth, skin to skin, and then it was gone.

Monk went straight to Rathbone's office and asked to see Oliver.

His clerk, Dobie, was apologetic. "I'm sorry, Mr. Monk, but Sir Oliver is with a client at the moment. I expect him to be free in half an hour, if it is urgent," he said courteously.

"It is extremely urgent," Monk replied. "Unless his client is coming up for trial tomorrow, it cannot wait. Jericho Phillips has kidnapped another child. Please interrupt Sir Oliver and tell him so. Tell him it is Scuff."

"Oh, dear," Dobie said with extreme distaste. "Did you say Scuff, sir?"

"Yes."

"Very well, sir. Would you please wait here?" He did not bother to ask Monk to be seated. He could see very well that he was too distressed to sit down.

Monk paced back and forth. The seconds seemed drawn out, even the minutest sound ringing in his ears.

Finally Dobie returned, solemn-faced. "Sir Oliver will see you immediately," he said. "I shall ask all other clients to wait, until you inform me otherwise."

"Thank you." Monk strode past him and opened Rathbone's office door.

Rathbone turned, face pale, eyes wide. "Are you sure?" He did not elaborate; there was no need.

"Yes," Monk replied, closing the door behind him. "He sent a message to say that if I didn't stop pursuing him, and blacken Durban's name in public, he'd use Scuff in his trade, and then kill him." It was difficult to even say the words, as if they gave it a more intense reality. "I'm going to get him back, and I need your help."

Rathbone started to say that it was not a legal matter, then realized that of course Monk knew that. He had not yet come to the worst.

Monk told him quickly, sparing nothing. "Claudine Burroughs dressed as a match woman and went to try to find where they were selling Phillips's photographs. She succeeded in finding at least one shop. The photographs were appalling, but what matters is that she recognized one of the purchasers, because she knew him socially. She is afraid that he also recognized her, and that is why Phillips has attacked."

Rathbone frowned. "I don't follow your logic. Why would Phillips do that? He won't care about individual customers, even if Mrs. Burroughs was right."

Monk hesitated for the first time. He loathed doing this. "It was Arthur Ballinger," he said quietly. "I think he warned Phillips that we are closing in on him, and this is Phillips's retaliation. I'm sorry."

Rathbone stared at him, the blood draining from his face. He looked as if he had been struck such a blow as to rob him momentarily of thought, or the power to respond.

Monk wanted to apologize again, but he knew it was futile.

"It is the only thing that has changed," he said aloud. "Before that, Phillips was winning, and he knew it. He had no need to do anything but wait us out. Now we have seen Ballinger, and that must matter to him."

Rathbone moved to the chair and sat down slowly. "I'll do what I can." His voice was hoarse.

"I'll do what I can to help you rescue Scuff," he said, his voice strained. He stood up and swayed very slightly. "Sullivan is the weak link. He will know where Phillips's boat is, and I can force him to take us. He'll know the times and places because he goes there. I don't think we have time to waste." He moved to the door.

Monk followed him. He wanted to ask about Ballinger's involvement, but the wound was too raw, and too deep to probe yet. He could barely imagine how it must hurt Rathbone, not for Ballinger, but for Margaret. He thought of Hester, whose father had taken his own life after a financial scandal that had ruined him. He had believed it to be the only decent way out, and he had had no fault but faith in a man who was beneath honor of any kind.

They took a cab and rode in silence to Sullivan's chambers. The hot air was sharp with the smells of horse dung, the leather inside the cab, and stale sweat.

Monk's imagination was crowded with fear for Scuff. How had he managed to get caught? How terrified he must have been when he recognized Phillips, knowing what lay ahead of him. Was he already burned, bleeding? Where would Phillips begin, slowly, delicately, or straight into the maximum pain? The sweat broke out and ran cold on his own skin as he tried to force the images out of his mind.

They reached Sullivan's chambers still without speaking again. It was understood that Rathbone would address the subject for both of them.

As expected, they were told to wait, and possibly Lord Justice Sullivan would see them. Rathbone replied that it was a police emergency, concerning a matter of the utmost personal importance to Sullivan, and that the man would rue the day he did so if he attempted to block their way.

Within half an hour they stood in Sullivan's rooms, facing a man who was both angry and frightened. His big body was clenched and shivering, sweat shining on his skin in the heat as the sun shone in through the long windows.

"What is it you want?" He ignored Monk and looked only at Rathbone, as if expecting the details from him.

He was not disappointed. Rathbone came immediately to the point.

"We wish you to take us to Jericho Phillips's boat tonight, secretly. If you do not, innocent people will die, so there is no bargain to be made, no equivocation or denial possible."

"I have no idea where his boat is!" Sullivan protested, even before Rathbone had finished speaking. "If the police wish to board it, that is up to them. I am sure they have informants whom they can ask."

"There are all sorts of people we could speak to," Rathbone replied icily. "With all sorts of information to give or to trade. I am sure you already understand that, in all its shades of meaning. We must do it tonight, and without Phillips receiving any warning so he could move the child he has kidnapped."

"I can't!" Sullivan protested, his hands white-knuckled, the sweat running down his face.

"For a man who thrives on the thrill of danger, you seem to singularly lack courage," Rathbone said with disgust. "You told me you loved the danger of risking being caught. Well, you are about to have the greatest excitement of your life."

Monk stepped forward, not out of pity for Sullivan—who appeared to be about to choke—but because he was afraid they would lose his usefulness if he had a stroke. "You can leave once we are there," he said raspingly. "If we find the boy alive. If not, believe me, I will expose you to the whole of London—more important, to the judiciary who presently admire you so much. You may well have friends there, but they will not be able to help you, and unless they are suicidal, they will not try to. Ballinger will not get Sir Oliver to help you, and I will not make the mistakes I made with Phillips."

"Monk!" Rathbone said urgently, his voice sharp, like a lash.

Monk swung around and stared at him, ready to accuse him of cowardice, or even complicity.

"He is no use to us a gibbering wreck," Rathbone said gently. "Don't frighten him witless." He looked at Sullivan. "Nevertheless, what Monk says is true. Are you with us? You wanted danger—this should be full of it. Weigh the risks. Phillips might get you, and he might not. We certainly will, no shadow of a doubt. I personally will ruin you, I swear it."

Sullivan was almost beyond speech. He nodded and mumbled something, but the words were unintelligible.

Monk wondered if the excitement for which he had risked so much had only ever been an idea to him, and being caught, exposed, and torn apart never a reality. There must be a streak of sadism in him as well. There had never been chance, or excitement, or a hope of escape for the boys. Disgust welling up inside him, cold and sour, he turned away. "Rathbone will tell you what to do," he said. "Perhaps he'd better bring you."

"Of course I'll bring him," Rathbone retorted with a sting in his voice. "Do you think I'm not coming?"

Monk was startled. He swung back, eyes wide, warmth inside him again.

Rathbone saw it. He smiled very slightly, but his eyes were bright and clear. "You'll need all the help you can get," he pointed out. "And possibly a witness whose word may stand up in court." His mouth twisted with irony. "I hope. Apart from that, do you think I could miss it?"

"Good," Monk responded. "Then we will meet at the Wapping Stairs at dusk. Hester will join us."

Rathbone was stunned for a moment, then denial swept in. "You can't possibly let her come!" he protested. "Apart from the danger, it'll be something no woman should see! Haven't you listened to your own evidence, man? We're not going to find just poverty, or even fear or pain. It'll be . . ." he stumbled to a halt.

"I gave her my word," Monk told him. "It's Scuff." He found it hard to say. "And apart from that, she is the only one with any real medical ability, if someone is hurt."

"But it will be men at their most . . ." Rathbone started again.

"Raw?" Monk suggested. "Naked?"

"No woman should . . ." Rathbone tried again.

"Do you think you'll manage?" Monk said with an edge of pain in his voice that surprised him.

Rathbone's eyes widened.

"Have you ever seen a battlefield?" Monk asked him. "I have, once. I've never known such horror in my life, but Hester knew what to do. Forget your preconceptions, Rathbone; this will be reality."

Rathbone closed his eyes and nodded, speechless.

Monk waited on the dockside just beyond Wapping Stairs at dusk, Hester beside him. She was dressed in trousers that Orme had borrowed from the locker of a young River policeman. It would be dangerously impractical for her to go on an expedition like this either hampered by a skirt or recognizably vulnerable as a woman.

Darkness was shrouding the water, and the farther side was visible only by the lights along the bank. Warehouses and cranes stood up hard and black against the southern sky, and after the warmth of the day, a few threads of mist dragged faint veils across the water, catching the last of the light.

There was a bump of wood against stone as Orme drew up with one of the police boats. The second boat loomed out of the shadows with Sutton already in it, Snoot crouched beside him on the rear seat.

Footsteps sounded along the quay. Rathbone crossed the shaft of light from the police station lamp, Sullivan reluctantly behind him, his shoulders high and tight, his eyes sunken like holes in his skull.

No one spoke more than a word, a gesture of recognition. Sutton nodded at Rathbone, possibly remembering many of their narrow escapes.

Rathbone nodded back, a bleak smile brief in his face before turning to the business of climbing down the wet, slimy steps into the two boats. They had four River Police to row, and, as soon as they were seated, they slid out into the still water, which was slack at the turn of the tide. They moved out noiselessly except for the bump of metal against wood as the oars rattled in their locks.

No one spoke. Everything had already been said, all the plans argued over and decided. Sullivan knew the price of refusal, and worse, of betrayal. Even so, Hester sat beside Monk in the stern of the second boat and watched the judge with coldness creeping up inside her, cramping her stomach and tightening her chest until she found it hard to breathe. There was a desperation in him that she could smell in the air, sharp and sour, above the detritus drifting on the oily water. He was cornered, and she was waiting for him to attack. Something, long ago, had separated him from the compassion he should have had, and left him erratic and ultimately unreachable.

At another time she could have pitied him as a man incomplete. Now all she could think of was Scuff alone and terrified, intelligent enough to know exactly what Phillips would do to him. He would know that Monk would try everything he knew or could invent to rescue him; he also knew that they had all failed before. Phillips had beaten them, and mocked them, and escaped to continue unhampered. He had won every time. All the love in the world did not blind Scuff to the reality that they could fail again. He was a child with hope, optimism, and a lifetime's knowledge of failure behind him. The difference between surviving and not was wafer-thin.

She did not even think what Scuff's death would do to Monk. She could feel his weight beside her. He was too muffled by his clothes to warm her, but the feeling was there in her memory and imagination. The darkness inside was colder and denser than anything on the water around her. They could not afford mistakes of judgment, hesitation, even mercy.

They made good speed in the strange stillness of the turn of the tide. In only a few minutes the tide would begin to run again, gathering speed upriver, rising, slapping against the steps, lifting the ships at anchor, pulling everything upstream, carrying in the hungry sea, bringing back the rubbish and the flotsam of life, and death, and trade.

They were almost at Sufferance Wharf on the south bank. The low line of a moored boat was just discernible, perhaps twenty yards from the stone embankment. It was riding at anchor, only its lanterns visible at bow and stern. All was silent except for a footfall now and then on the deck. A faint scuffle as someone briefly opened a hatch and the inside light and noise escaped: voices, a stifled laugh, and then gone again. It was in one of those movements that Hester saw the motionless figures of watchmen on deck, prepared to repel boarders. They might have guns, but it was far more likely to be knives, or sharpened grappling hooks. A quick stab, a lunge, and there would be another corpse carried up with the returning tide.

She knew Monk and Orme were armed. She could not imagine that Rathbone was, since he usually forswore using weapons; but then she had discovered that she did not know him nearly as well as she had supposed.

They were almost to the boat. Monk stood up and hailed them. She saw with slight surprise how easily he balanced now, in spite of the slight rocking as he moved his weight. He had learned quickly.

The watchman answered. He demanded to know who Monk was, but his voice was quiet, controlled. He was only twenty feet away.

"Got a gentleman to see you," Monk said. "Gave him a lift."

The boat rocked a little. The seconds ticked by.

Hester's breath choked in her throat. What could they do if Sullivan's courage failed him and he would not board? What if his terror of Jericho Phillips was greater than his terror of Monk, or even of Society's ruin of him?

"Get up!" Rathbone whispered to him harshly. "Or I will let Monk give you to the brothel owners you've put away in the past. That death will be very slow, and very intimate, I promise you."

Hester gasped. She saw Monk stiffen.

Sullivan staggered to his feet and swayed as his clumsiness rocked the boat and nearly plunged him over the side. Monk caught hold of him just in time.

Sullivan spoke his name, and repeated the password that identified him.

The watchman relaxed. He turned and spoke to his companion, who had come to reinforce him, just in case Monk should try to board as well. He offered his hand to Sullivan. The boat pulled close enough for Sullivan to scramble up and heave himself on to the deck just as Hester saw the shadow move behind him. A moment later first one watchman fell, and then the other. Orme, Sutton, and more River Police crowded over the deck.

Sullivan stood frozen.

Monk, Rathbone, and Sutton clambered over the gunwale. Hester picked Snoot up and passed him into Sutton's hands, then gripped Monk's outstretched arm. The next moment she was on the deck herself, leaving only one man to keep the boat.

Silently they moved over to the hatch. She saw the faint gleam of light on the barrel of a gun in Orme's hand, and realized from the way Monk held his right arm that he had one also. This could end in blood and death.

Orme bent and opened the hatch. Light flooded up, and the noise of jerky, nervous laughter with a slight edge of hysteria sharp and veering out of control, prickly with excitement. There was an odor of whisky, cigar smoke, and sweat. Hester gulped. Fear shot through her, like pain, not for herself but for Monk as he went inside and down.

He was followed immediately by Orme, then Sullivan, Rathbone, and two of the police. Two more remained on deck to impersonate the unconscious men who were now bound and gagged. Hester followed through the hatch and into a surprisingly clean and comfortable cabin. It was small, only a couple of yards across, clearly an anteroom to the main saloon, and whatever rooms were beyond that for more private entertainment. She was familiar with the geographic layout of brothels, although few were as extensive as the property at Portpool Lane.

The salon was filled with half a dozen guests, well-dressed men of varying ages. At a glance they had little in common but a fever in the eyes and a sheen of sweat on the skin. Jericho Phillips stood at the far end, next to a small rise in the floor, like a stage, on which were two boys, both naked, One was about six or seven years old, bending over on his hands and knees like an animal; the other was older, just entering puberty. The act they were performing was obvious, as was the coercion of a lit cigar smoldering in Phillips's hand, and unhealed burn marks on the older boy's back and thighs.

"Come ter join us at last, 'ave yer, Mr. Monk?" Phillips asked with a curl of his lip that showed his teeth. "Knew yer would, one day. Must say though, I thought it'd take yer longer." His eyes flickered to Sullivan, and then to Rathbone, and he wet his lips with his tongue. His voice was brittle and half an octave too high.

Fear was acrid in the air, like stale sweat. Some men shifted from one foot to the other, tense, on the edge of some kind of violence. They were robbed of the release for which they had come, uncertain what was happening, or who the enemy was, like animals on the edge of a stampede.

Hester was rigid, heart pounding. Did Monk know how close they were to mindless violence? This was nothing like the army in the moments before battle: tight with discipline, ready to charge into what could be death, or worse—hideous mutilation. This was guilty and tainted men afraid of exposure and its shame. This was animals unexpectedly and at the last moment robbed of their prey, the feeding of their primal hungers.

She glanced at the other police, at Phillips's guards in the room, then caught Rathbone's eye. She saw the desperate revulsion in him and something more: a deep and tearing pain. Beside him Sullivan was shaking, his eyes darting one way, then the other. His hands clenched, then unclenched as if his fingers sought something to grip.

It was Sutton who sensed the danger. "Get on with it!" he hissed at Monk.

"I don't want to join you exactly," Monk answered Phillips. "I'd like some of your guests to join us, just to clear the way a bit."

Phillips shook his head slowly, the smile still fixed on his lips, his eyes dead as stone. "I don't think any of 'em would care to go with yer. An' as yer can see, they're gentlemen as yer can't push around like they was nob'dy." He was motionless, not moving his hands, or his gaze from Monk's face, but several of the men seemed to be waiting for some signal from him. Did his men have knives? Easier to use in this enclosed space, less likely to injure your own.

"Yer already made a fool o' yerself once," Phillips continued. "Yer can't do that again an' 'ope ter keep yer job, Mr. Monk. Not as I minds if yer don't! Ye're too stupid ter be a real bother ter me, but I wouldn't care if yer went. 'Oo'ever comes after yer won't be no better neither, just like Durban wasn't." His voice was softer, and still he did not move his hands. "The river'll go on, an' men wi' 'ungers they can't feed wi'out me, or someone like me. We're like the tide, Mr. Monk; only a fool stands in our way. Get yerself drownded." He relished the word on his tongue. The tension was slipping out of him now. The years of self-discipline were winning. He was in control again; the moment of fear had passed.

Monk had to balance Phillips's likely impulses either to panic and bolt for freedom, or to marshal his returning confidence and attack the police. Neither would help find Scuff. The one advantage he had was that Phillips did not want violence either; it would be bad for business. His clients wanted imaginary danger, not the reality. They sought sexual release, bloodshed, but not their own.

He made his decision. "Jericho Phillips, I am arresting you for the murder of the boy known as Scuff." He held the gun so that it was clearly visible now, pointed at Phillips's chest. "And Mr. Orme is going to arrest Sir John Wilberforce there." He named the only other guest whose face he recognized.

Wilberforce burst into protest, his cheeks scarlet, streaming with sweat. Orme, his back to the bulkhead, raised his gun. The light gleamed on the barrel, and Wilberforce abruptly fell silent.

It was Phillips who spoke, shaking his head slowly from side to side. "Makin' a fool o' yerself again, Mr. Monk. I dunno where your boy is, an' I din't kill no one. We been through all o' that, as 'is Lordship Sullivan'll 'ere tell yer, an' Sir Oliver an' all. Yer jus' don't learn, do yer!" He turned to Wilberforce, the sneer broadening on his face, his contempt naked. "No need to get inter a sweat, sir. 'E can't do nothin' to yer. Think o' 'oo you are, an' 'oo 'e is, an' get an 'old o' yerself. Yer got all the cards, if yer play 'em right."

There was a snigger of laughter from one of the other men. They began to relax. They were the hunters again, no longer the victims.

Orme had taken off his jacket and given it to the older boy to cover his nakedness and his humiliation. Sutton did the same for the younger one.

The movement caught Hester's eye and suddenly she realized that they were all frozen here, arguing, and any torture could be happening to Scuff. There was no purpose in pleading with Phillips to tell them where he was. She slipped between two of the customers and touched Orme. "We have to look for Scuff," she whispered. "There may be other guards, so keep your gun ready."

"Right, ma'am." He yielded immediately. He nodded to Sutton, who was almost beside him, Snoot now on the floor at his heels. The three of them inched towards the doorway as the quarrel between Monk and Phillips grew uglier. Monk's men were posturing themselves to take over with violence, moving to get the physical advantage, disarm those most likely to have weapons, or to be able to seize one of the children to use as a hostage. Wilberforce was drawn in. Sullivan swayed from one side to the other, his face dark, congested with a desperate hatred like a trapped creature between its tormentors.

Monk would strike soon, and then the fighting would be swift and hard.

Hester was afraid for him, and for Rathbone as well. She had seen a horror in his eyes far beyond the cruelty or coarseness of the scene. He was struggling with some decision of his own that she did not yet recognize. She imagined that it could be a kind of guilt. Now at last he was seeing the reality of what he had defended, not the theory, the high words of the law. Perhaps some time she would even apologize to him for the harsher things she had said. This was not his world; he might really not have understood.

Now all that mattered was to find Scuff. She dared not let her mind even touch on the chance that he was not here, but held captive locked in some room on shore, or even dead already. That would be almost like being dead herself.

She followed Sutton through the doorway and found herself instantly in a passage so narrow the slightest loss of balance bumped her shoulders into the wooden walls. Sutton had already turned left towards the bow of the boat. Snoot was almost under his feet, but as always not making the slightest sound except for the faint scrape of his claws on the damp wood of the floor. The smell of bilges and the mustiness of wet rot were stronger as they went forward. Sutton turned abruptly left again and scrambled down a steep flight of steps. He reached for the dog, but Snoot slithered down, fell the last short way, and was on his feet again in an instant.

Here the ceiling was low, and Hester had to bend to avoid cracking her skull on the crossbeams. Sutton half-crouched as well. The smell was stronger here, and the dog's hackles were raised, his small body shivering and bristling in awareness of something deeply wrong.

Hester could feel her breath tight in her chest and the sweat running down her back inside her clothes.

There was a row of doors.

Sutton tried the first one. It was locked. He lifted his leg and kicked it hard with the flat of his foot. It cracked but did not give. Snoot was growling high and softly in the back of his throat. His sensitive nose picked up the odor of fear.

Sutton kicked again, and this time it gave way. It crashed open to reveal a small room, little more than a cupboard, in which cowered three small boys dressed in rags, their eyes wide with terror. They were comparatively clean, but the arms and legs poking out of their clothes were thin and as pale as splintered matchwood.

Hester almost choked with hope, and then despair.

"We'll come back for you," Sutton told them.

Hester was not sure whether that was a promise or a threat to them. Perhaps their choice lay between Phillips and starvation. But she must find Scuff; everything else would have to wait.

Sutton forced open another door to a room with more boys. He found a third, and then a fourth that was right at the very stern, empty. Scuff was nowhere.

Hester could feel her throat tighten and the tears sting her eyes. She was furious with herself. There was no time for this. He had to be somewhere. She must think! What would Phillips do? He was clever and cunning, and he knew Monk, as it was his business to know his enemies. He found, stole, or created the right weapon against each of them.

Snoot was quivering. He darted forward and started to run round in tight little circles, nose to the floor.

"C'mon, boy," Sutton said gently. "Don't matter about rats now. Leave 'em alone."

Snoot ignored him, scratching at the floor near the joints in the boards.

"Don't matter about rats," Sutton repeated, his voice tight with grief.

Snoot started to dig, scraping his claws along the joints.

"Snoot!" Sutton reached for the dog's collar.

There was a faint scratching sound beneath.

Snoot barked.

Sutton grasped his collar but the dog was excited, and he squirmed out of Sutton's grasp, yelping.

Sutton bent forward and Hester was right behind him. Looking more closely at the floor, she saw that the lines of the boards were not quite even.

"It's a trapdoor!" she said, hardly daring to believe it.

"To the bilges. Mind your hands, there'll be rats. Always is," Sutton warned her, his voice breaking with tension. He reached for the knife at his belt, flicked open the blade, and used it as a handle to ease the trap open and pull it up.

Below them Scuff's ashen face looked up, eyes wide with terror, skin bruised and smeared with blood and filth.

Hester forgot all the decorum she had promised herself and reached down to pull him up and hold him so tightly in her arms she might easily have hurt him. She pressed her face into his neck, ignoring the stench of rot on his skin and hair and clothes, thinking only that she had him at last, and he was alive.

He clung to her, shuddering uncontrollably, sobs racking his thin chest.

It was Sutton's voice that brought her back to the present, and the danger she had momentarily forgotten.

"There's rats down 'ere all right," he said quietly. "It's straight to the bilges, an' there's been another boy down 'ere, poor little thing, but there in't much left of 'im now, just bones an' a bit o' flesh. Don't look, Miss 'Ester. Take the boy out of 'ere. Enough to drive 'im out of 'is 'ead, stuffed in 'ere with rats and the 'alf-rotted corpse of another child. I'll tell you this, if Mr. Monk don't get that son of the devil 'anged this time, I'll do it with me own 'ands . . ." His voice trailed off, suffocated by emotion.

Reluctantly Hester let go of Scuff, but he couldn't let go of her. He whispered softly, just a little cry, and fastened on to her more tightly. She would have had to break his fingers to loosen his hold. She staggered to the door, arms around him, keeping her head low beneath the boarded ceiling, and met Orme at the top of the steps, his face shining with relief.

"I'll tell Mr. Monk," he said simply, swiveling to go back up again. "I'll . . . I'll tell 'im." He stood still for a moment, as if imprinting the scene on his eyes, then grinning even more widely he swung around and made his way rapidly back to the main saloon.

Hester lost count of how long she sat on the floor cradling Scuff in her arms before Monk came down, just to look at the boy for himself. The other boys explained that the corpse below the trapdoor was that of Reilly, the other missing boy who had tried to rebel. He had been almost old enough to sell to one of the ships leaving London, but he had tried to rescue some of the younger boys and had been locked in the bilges for his rebellion, as an example. He could be identified by the small charm around what was left of his neck.

"We can hang Phillips for that," Rathbone said hoarsely, his eyes dark with horror and that terrible grief she had seen in him before.

"Are you sure?" she asked. "Really sure, Oliver? Please don't promise something you only believe. I don't want comforting. I need the truth."

"It's the truth," he replied.

At last she let go of Scuff and reached out to touch Rathbone's arm, very gently. Even though her hand was cold and filthy, warmth shot between them like the force of life, and passion, and gentleness.

"Then what is the truth?" she asked.

He did not evade her. "You asked me before who it was that paid me to defend Phillips," he replied. "I thought I could not tell you, but now I know it was also he who set Phillips up in business in the beginning, knowing the weakness of men like Sullivan, and feeding it until it became consuming."

She waited, understanding something of his horror, imagining his guilt.

"Yes, I know." His voice was so low she could barely hear it.

Margaret's father! No, she was wrong, she had barely touched the magnitude of the horror he felt. This drowned anything else she had conceived of. It touched the very core of his own life. She struggled for words, but what could she say? She tightened her hand on his and lifted it very slowly to her cheek, then let it go. She rose and carried Scuff past him up into the light of the passage outside the saloon, leaving Rathbone by himself.

The big room was nearly empty. Monk was standing in the center with Orme. The rest of the police were gone, as were the other clients. Monk looked pale and unhappy. There was a bruise already darkening on his cheek.

"What's happened?" Hester demanded, surprised. But there was no fear in her. She had Scuff by the hand; he was standing up now, but pressed hard against her side.

"Most of them are under arrest," he answered.

She felt a chill. "Most?"

"I'm sorry." His voice was tight with pain, and guilt. "In the dark and the fighting, the men we left upstairs got drawn in. Sullivan betrayed us and got Phillips away. I should have watched him and seen it coming. We'll get him back, and when we do no one will help him escape the rope this time."

She nodded, not wanting to blame him, and too near tears to speak. She felt as if some enormous weight had all but crushed her. The injustice of it was monstrous. They had tried so hard. Even as she fought for breath she knew her disappointment was childish. No one had ever promised justice, not quickly, or that she would see it happen. They had Scuff back, alive. He might have nightmares for years, but they would look after him. She was never going to let him be alone or cold or hungry again.

She shook her head, blinking hard. "In time," she said a little stumblingly. "We've got Scuff, and you've proved what Phillips is. No one will doubt you, or Durban, or the River Police now."

He tried to smile, then turned away. No one mentioned Sullivan, or what might happen to him, what he might testify to, beyond tonight. What was there that they could prove against him, if he accused them, as Phillips had suggested?

It was well past midnight now, and all Phillips's men were either under arrest or waiting under guard for more boats to come and collect them. There were boys frightened, humiliated, and in need of care. They were all half-starved; many had bruises on their bodies, and some had bleeding and suppurating burns.

The police were busy with the arrests.

Rathbone questioned the boys gently, drawing out detail after hideous detail. He persisted, writing everything down in a little notebook from his pocket.

Meanwhile, Sutton rummaged for all the food he could find. Most of it was delicacies meant for the jaded palates of gentlemen, not the empty stomachs of children, but he made something better of it than Hester could have.

She did the best she could to treat the boys' hurts with cold water, salt, and good shirts and underwear torn up to make bandages. For once it was a disadvantage not to have been wearing petticoats. As soon as there were boats available she would get them to the clinic in Portpool Lane and do all this better. For now just care and gentleness helped, and the knowledge that they were on the brink of freedom. She did not stop to think how much better it would be if she could tell them that Phillips was on his way to prison, and would soon be dead.

Monk climbed the steps on to the deck as the pale, cold fingers of light crept across the water. The high tide was past and beginning to drop again. The outlines of the warehouses and cranes were sharp black against the sky. Even as he watched, the darkness receded and he saw the stakes of Execution Dock tracking the shining surface of the river. It was not until he looked more closely that he realized there were bodies there, just tipping above the tide.

A string of lighters went by, their passage creating a wash, which uncovered Sullivan's dead body. His throat gaped open where he had slashed it himself in a last act of despair. Possibly it was some kind of reparation, because trapped inside the pirate gallows, eyes wide open, mouth in an eternal shriek as the water he dreaded closed over his living face, was what was left of Jericho Phillips.

There were footsteps on the wood behind him and Monk turned to see Hester. "Don't . . ." he began, but it was too late.

She looked across the retreating wash, her mouth pulled tight, her eyes filled with great pity. "I've seen dead men before," she told him, slipping her hand into his. "I would sooner that God had to deal with that one than we did. We'll just try to heal some of the pain."

He put his arms around her and held her, feeling the strength in her, and the gentleness. It was all he needed to face any battle, now or ever.

About the Type

This book was set in Centaur, a typeface designed by
the American typographer Bruce Rogers in 1929.
Rogers adapted Centaur from the fifteenth-century
type of Nicholas Jenson and modified it
in 1948 for a cutting by the
Monotype Corporation.